ZANE PRESENTS

ONE SAFE
Place

Dear Reader:

We welcomed Alvin L.A. Horn to our Strebor Books family with *Perfect Circle*, a novel featuring characters all in search of love in the Emerald City.

Alvin returns to the cloudy skies of Seattle with *One Safe Place*, the follow-up, and he blends and captures the complexities of relationships with some of the original characters. Psalms Black, a former Secret Service agent, flexes his power whether he's on a mission to exact revenge or protect his lover, Gabrielle Brandywine, once the Secretary of State of the United States.

The novel is complete with love and lust while action-packed with kidnapping and crime scenes. All in all, everyone seeks one safe place where survival is key.

Alvin is known for his spoken word talent and showcases his creativity with verse throughout the tale. The noted artist was a winner of a 2012 *Billboard* spoken word award. For more flavor, cocktail recipes are interspersed, adding another touch.

As always, thanks for supporting myself and the Strebor Books family. We strive to bring you cutting-edge literature that cannot be found anyplace else. My personal web site is Eroticanoir.com and my Facebook page is Facebook.com/AuthorZane.

Blessings,

Zane

Publisher
Strebor Books
www.simonandschuster.com

ALSO BY ALVIN L.A. HORN
Perfect Circle

ZANE PRESENTS

ONE SAFE Place

ALVIN L.A. HORN

SBI

STREBOR BOOKS

NEW YORK LONDON TORONTO SYDNEY

Strebor Books
P.O. Box 6505
Largo, MD 20792
http://www.streborbooks.com

ISBN 978-1-59309-550-5
ISBN 978-1-4767-5170-2 (ebook)
LCCN 2013950690

First Strebor Books trade paperback edition April 2014

Cover design: www.mariondesigns.com
Cover photograph: © Keith Saunders/Marion Designs

10 9 8 7 6 5 4 3 2 1

Manufactured in the United States of America

For information regarding special discounts for bulk purchases, please contact Simon & Schuster Special Sales at 1-866-506-1949 or business@simonandschuster.com

The Simon & Schuster Speakers Bureau can bring authors to your live event. For more information or to book an event, contact the Simon & Schuster Speakers Bureau at 1-866-248-3049 or visit our website at www.simonspeakers.com.

ACKNOWLEDGMENTS

God, I want to thank you for your grace to bless others to have blessed me with their patience to help and understanding. I've had some tough days, weeks, months and a couple years, but still had an opportunity to write. While nominations and awards and wonderful reviews have come, they can never replace the people who have cared for me. Many have helped me navigate a maze of obstacles such as economics and health, and dysgraphia—my learning disability—and learning to live life after you have lost loved ones. Now despite it all, people are reading me and that is the greatest reward. My readers see something in the way I write and appreciate my narratives from my God-given creativity.

The blues and joys of life have been the fertilizer that has enriched my flourishing on paper. The blues and joys of life have prompted me to writing characters in situations with engaging contemplations, meditations, theories and accepted wisdoms and enjoining philosophies and judgments drenched with emotions, but never watered down. The songs says, "Nobody wants you when you're down and out," and I have felt that burning spear thrown from afar and close to home, but I have been blessed more with great and faithful friends who accepted my struggle and often stepped in and done for me without me asking, and often never letting me return the favor. I want to say I love you all for just being who you are.

Thank you Minty, Elissa, Tracy, William, Charmaine, Diedra, Candy, Ron, Kari, Lady Flava and Omar W, Beverly, and Wyneice, Robert and Hazel and all others on a long list. Area codes will help to keep the list shorter much love to the 206, 425, 253, 415, 210, 405, 248, 317, 702, 862, 559, 843, 301, 513, 704, 214, 646, 212, 231, 713, thank you all.

Go RB Vikings, Quakers, and Bulldogs, and Seahawks and Huskies and Seattle Supersonics forever.

I give thanks to all the women elders who have taught me the value of the love of a woman all in their own way. I write about women like you—the textured fabric of life I have been wrapped in. Every woman handles the weight of mankind differently and that creates narratives, and I love writing them.

To the women near my age and younger, I see you, I feel you in my soul, and watch your journeys. I observe your smiles and hear your cries. I admire your heart and soul in being mothers, and lovers, and all that comes with being in a world full of trials and tribulation, but your smiles are to live for. Every woman who smiles is pretty, beautiful and sexy. I hope to always be a heart that beats in a way that brings you smiles.

To the men who helped to mold me with your rights and wrongs, thank you. I can walk into any room and represent myself well knowing my world is not narrow, but wide open. Because of you I am a gentleman and enjoying being one. Because of you I love the old soul in me, in how I dress, talk, and enjoy the music I listen to, and make. Because of my male elders, I am the renaissance man that I am, so I pen you in layers of storylines.

To the correction and fixers of my spilled ink that flows out of bounds or never made sense... Thank you Omar Willey, Charmaine Parker, and Stefanie Manns.

Thank you Charmaine Parker, the lady who knows how to put twenty-eight hours into twenty-four, plus always another ten-minute call. I'm also very thankful for the people around you who support you.

Zane, thank you for letting your family of authors express creative minds to open the hearts and minds of readers. There is no shame in what goes on in the mind, as there is nothing new under the sun; it really comes down to whether people want to look or…read. Thank you for allowing the ink to flow into stores and doors.

CHAPTER 1

Prison Blues

"You stole my wife; you took my daughter. So, ol' friend, I need for you to get my other kids. I don't care about their mother; I simply need you to get my other kids." The tone of the voice had the resonance of a public bathroom toilet flushing and sucking the waste away. "You stole my daughter, and raised her as your own, but it's cool. Go take more of what's mine, and keep it. I can assume you'll keep them safe? Until—"

"Take more of yours? Keep it?" Tylowe said. His eyes glanced over at his friend, Psalms Black, who sat looking relaxed, but coiled like a snake ready to strike. Tylowe's expression seemingly asked, "Did you hear this fool's belligerence?" Tylowe didn't expect a response, amazed that his ex-friend, Elliot, was still an arrogant ass despite his circumstances.

Elliot Piste, with the toilet-flushing voice, was an inmate at a correctional facility in British Columbia, Canada. Tylowe Dandridge had married his ex-friend's wife after he had gone to prison, but first Tylowe had become the principal contributor in putting his former friend in prison. Elliot, the once ultra-handsome black Frenchman originally from Senegal, was Tylowe's old college classmate. He had a history of treating people whom he should care about ugly, and karma made a bitch out of him from his own ugly ways. Now, years later, Tylowe and Psalms Black, a distant friend of Elliot's, sat in a visitor's room across from him.

Tylowe and Psalms had made the trip to Vancouver from Seattle on their motorcycles. Tylowe had a history of crossing the border and having his life changed. It appeared to be no different this time as he sat across from the man he had helped to put in prison.

Elliot and Tylowe were buddy-buddy until Elliot crossed one too many lines. Twice a woman had come between them. The first time, Tylowe had his heart ripped apart after trusting the malicious Elliot. The second time, Tylowe had his heart healed when Elliot ripped a woman's heart apart. Tylowe saved her, and now she was his wife.

They sat in uncomfortable metal chairs. Elliot sat as if he were sitting in an easy lounger, looking relaxed. He looked at home. He sat sixty-plus pounds heavier than when he had first entered prison. An inactive gut hung low, and man boobs were starting to take over for once-rippling pecs.

In the past, most men were intimidated by his tall, handsome looks. At one time, he looked as though he were wrapped in dark, African silk hide, but now he was cracking like an old alligator shoe. A once-upon-a-time pretty boy now looked pretty ugly.

Tylowe stared at Elliot and thought about Denzel Washington in the movie *The Hurricane*, the story about an innocent boxer kept in prison for a crime he didn't commit and being unable to fight as the boxer he was. But, prison never defeated Hurricane's soul. Elliot had let prison beat him down, and he was unremorseful and polluted with unrepentant bile.

High above any normal ladder height in the visiting room, the windows had rusted. Metal screens crisscrossed, causing filtered dull light to cast dreary sadness. Psalms laughed to himself, and thought, *Long prison sentences must equate to slow death of the brain, body, and soul, creeping in like cancer.*

When Tylowe and Psalms had first arrived, the sun was shining, but the clang of metal doors and buzzers must have controlled the weather outside once they were inside. The two men sat across from a cancer and storm.

Elliot tried to hide that Psalms intimidated him as he always had, even in their legendary days of youth. They were always cordial, yet never friends. Psalms reminded him in a voice lower than the lowest piano key.

"So Elliot, Tylowe comes here at your behest, and you mentally masturbate your ego to spew your arrogance in his face? How can you expect this man to do anything for you?"

The tension was so damn thick; a Killer whale would have passed it by even if it tasted like a thousand salmon in one bite. Elliot's eyes avoided Psalms, keeping Psalms from staring down through his irises and looking for his soul.

Nasty blood had spilled between Psalms and Elliot, and they had kept the story of what happened between the two of them. Tylowe understood something was amiss, but what it was he didn't know. Elliot was a nasty asshole with no remorse or retention of civility. Tylowe found out that Elliot had slept with one of Tylowe's girlfriends back in college, and he and Elliot worked it out. Years later though, Elliot crossed the line again and it caused Tylowe a lifetime of hurt.

Elliot had two men sitting in front of him who despised him. He tried to keep a relaxed expression on his face, and spoke directly to Tylowe.

"Look, dude." Prison vernacular had overtaken his French-American dialect. "You know you're gonna do it. I can't blame you for stealing my wife, but you also took my daughter, and she won't even write me. So go do what you do and play Mr. Hero, and find my other kids."

Tylowe and Psalms listened to Elliot give the details of the situation and basic knowledge of the kids he claimed, and about the mother of these kids. The story distressed Tylowe. The thought of his wife and the fact she would find out more about the repulsive life of her ex-husband instigated an internal struggle.

Elliot, the ex-husband! Tylowe felt insecure with the fact he faced for the first time, physically sitting across from Elliot—the man who used to put his manhood between the thighs of Tylowe's wife. Tylowe twisted in manly pride, and time had not changed the past anxiety when looking at a man who had caused such pain in Tylowe's life.

Married life. Tylowe was approaching the mid-century age with enough money and plenty of free time and material pleasures. The kids were grown and living their life, no longer in need of his parenting. Did he need this challenge to make him feel manlier? Had a cushy life made him less manly? Most men his age started putting feelers in the water, too often turning to younger women for a sense of danger, hoping a young thang might satisfy a desire. That fulfilled desire kept divorce lawyers in business, as desires make men and women bad liars. Did he need to climb dangerous mountains and risk falling? Tylowe played with the questions of his mind and heart, and it created soul acid burn.

He was an ex-college football and track all-American, but had he gone soft? Looking at the wasteland of a man sitting across from him caused anxiety to bubble under his skin. Why did he bring Psalms, a warrior, along instead of coming alone? Tylowe's mind skied downhill from Mt. Rainier and right into Lake Washington. He found himself sinking and going nowhere.

Tower of Power's horn section led the charge to "You're Still a Young Man" in his motorcycle helmet's stereo as he traveled to the prison that day. About a year or so ago, he started to question his life as it had become.

His body was fuller, but still toned. He'd lost the six-pack, but he had no hanging belly fat. Salt-and-pepper hairs graced his goatee, but the salt hadn't taken over yet. Women still made eye contact and pushed an aggressive agenda his way even though most knew he was married.

Meeah, his wife, acted like she loved to love him, but he questioned her true feelings. Why didn't she look at him like she used to? His mind wavered. He didn't think he heard sweet, little nothings of endearment anymore. Deep inside he knew she loved him, but to what extent—or was he being simple-minded and self-deluding? Time was messing with his mind.

With the kids grown and gone, were they the perfect married couple, getting up and doing what they did daily out of sheer habit? He sat in his chair with incomplete thoughts, sinking in to mental quicks and concerned about his worth. Elliot had caused disruption and death to Tylowe's heart before, and now Tylowe wanted to run back across the border.

Now, he sat at odds with why he would want to find Elliot's kids, the half-brother and half-sister of the stepdaughter he loved as his own, Mia. The two men sat and listened to Elliot talking of saving his kids with a coldness of disconnect mixed with logic and sheer smugness.

Elliot stood and nodded his head toward the exit door. He gave a dismissive motion to leave, and finally looked in Psalms' direction with a defying stare, as if he felt nothing could happen. Tylowe and Psalms stood.

"Report back to me when you have my kids." Elliot's sewer voice flushed more arrogance in Tylowe's face.

Across the room, a chair leg must have slid on the cement floor with a fair amount of weight in the chair because it made a loud, high-pitched squeal. All heads in the room turned except for

Tylowe's. Standing directly in front of Elliot, Tylowe punched him in the mouth with such quickness it would resemble Floyd Mayweather knocking out Manny Pacquiao. Elliot started falling in slow motion sideways in Psalms' direction. Before hitting the ground, Psalms hit him with a left hook in his liver and kidney area. The punch swung like a sword. Elliot crumpled to the floor in a fetal position.

His foot twitched. Vomit drooled from between his bloody lips. He looked dead, but he made snoring sounds. People looked away quickly. The other prisoners told the visiting civilians to mind their own business. The guards came to attention.

"He'll wake up with a broken jaw, and will piss blood for a while, but he'll be okay," Psalms said coolly.

Tylowe slowly slithered a word out of his mouth as if he were writing his name in snow with a long pee. He said a word that no one who'd ever known him would have thought he'd say, "Son-of-a-B-i-t-c-h!"

A female guard walked over. A tough, manly look characterized her face and body. Her body language signaled a fake confidence of being something to behold. Psalms assumed someone had told her that.

Her voice filtered through her nose with some anger. "He must have made an aggressive move, eh, and you two fellows defended yourselves? Eh?" Her questions met with deadpan faces. "Gentlemen, it looks as if your visit is over. Have a lovely day. We'll make sure your friend here gets back to his cell, after a stop at the infirmary. I understand one of you has a high-ranking U.S. governmental ID. The women prison guards will send you a thank-you card. How about that, eh?"

The guard looked at the two men. She rolled her lips, then pursed them in an overt attempt to come across as sexy. She failed. She winked. Tylowe and Psalms pierced an analyzing stare at her stupidity. They both turned away and walked toward the exit.

"Popping him in his mouth, that was eight years too late, but still on time," Tylowe said.

"Whatever the timing, it's going to be a bitch sitting in prison with his jaw wired shut. Any street cred he had in this place will be challenged, unless he has protection. Oh—and uh—you might wanna brush those pieces of teeth out of your knuckles," Psalms said, and nodded toward Tylowe's hand.

Tylowe raised his hand, and saw imbedded teeth in his knuckles. Almost the coolest dude around had lost his suave demeanor by slugging Elliot. His rare burst of anger took over for any pain he should have felt.

"Let's go get you a tetanus shot," Psalms said.

After some medical attention to Tylowe's hand, the two caught the train back across the border, leaving their motorcycles in the basement of a building that used to belong to Elliot, but was now owned by Tylowe.

The headphones over Tylowe's ears kept the noise of the train out, and song after song played from his favorite band, Incognito. Their groove helped to ease deep thoughts as they glided along the train rails. Near the Canadian-American border, the train crossed over a bridge near an ocean view. It sparkled with sunset reds, causing a trance.

"Deep waters, I'm drowning…deep waters, slowly drowning."

The song had nothing to do directly with his life, or his current obstacles, but maybe it did. His love, his wife, Meeah, was waiting to pick him up at the train station. She and Tylowe were drifting. He smiled at the blue water with red highlights of sunset and thought, *When love is good it may seem like you're floating, but when love is struggling, it can be compared to drifting—drifting apart.*

He turned the music down on his tablet and used it to write what he still had hope in.

As One
She is not perfect enough in her own mind
She is she, and she is all I want, as she is
But I'm a man with faults and sins
I'm not perfect
Why?
Because of what's inside me, and outside of me and plus things outside my control
I'm too short with this, and I'm too tall with that
I'm too narrow, but on any given day I'm too wide
But when she looks to me, talks to me, and touches me
She makes me all right
Yet I want to give her more
Reason being, she gives understanding that we are in this together to learn and overcome
Her softness is a high that leads me to be better and to do better
To recognize what is in my power and what is not
She holds me up high
Would never tear me down
For that kind of love
I seek ways for her to stay in love, and want to give her reasons to forgive my short comings
Confused at times she may be
Only because at times I can become lost in direction
Her response is soft and guiding, non-judgmental

She is essential to my existence
My soul is in emotional poverty without her
Her faith is challenged at times
Man is always trying to play God
I need her and God to save me
She tells me, I'm all she needs and wants
We are in this world together as one

The train rolled back into Seattle. Tylowe and Psalms agreed to meet in a day or two to devise a plan.

Meeah, Tylowe's wife—the ex-wife of Elliot Piste—picked them up at the train station. They dropped Psalms off at his property. Tylowe had another issue. She asked about the small bandage on his hand, and he blew it off as nothing, no big deal. He had other problems, yet their marriage—was it in trouble? Problems and their priority was a problem in itself.

CHAPTER 2

Damaged Goods

Psalms Black

It's morning, and her nipple has been between my lips since first light. I suckle as I tread back and forth from dreams to waking with sweeping thoughts moving in angles of time. I often solve problems in my dreams—letting dilemmas drift like beach wood floating out at high tide and then settling on the shore at low tide. Like each wave, volumes of thoughts flood my mind and the washout leaves me with objectives and schemes.

I am safe with her. I don't know if it's manly or not to suck on her breasts as if I'm four months old and not have a sexual thought, but I feel safe. Nothing else matters when I'm this close to her, even though she gives me worry. The world could explode, but this room would survive with her firm, gumdrop nipple between my tongue and the top of my mouth. I drink her skin ever so gently, but as if I'm sucking survival.

I dream, hoping the world won't shatter around me. A fractured humanity surrounds us. A man walked into a Seattle restaurant, and for no reason, gunned down ordinary folks who were enjoying a meal. A mother taught her mentally troubled son to shoot guns of mass destruction, and then he turned the guns on her and twenty-six other people. For every one of us, it wouldn't take much more than a grain of sand from the universe to send any one of us to an end. A negative, reactive, evil heart can seemingly end the world in a heartbeat.

What does all that mean? I don't know. I dabbled in music and played sports in college against the best to get a higher degree of education in the ABCs. The ABCs can never teach us to stop the evil of the XYZs. Mainly what I can do and what I do is fix people's problems. By nature I'm a soldier—a bodyguard—who at one time signed my life over to my country to die for someone I was to protect for my daily bread—bread as in my money. I am an ex-Secret Service agent.

For sure, I'm not one to analyze myself for what I do. I let others question the sanity of my reality; although, how someone might go about probing into me, they should tread lightly.

I've been in a semi-fetal position most of the night, glued to her sweet potato-colored skin, feeling safe. She is my soul mate, without being my lover.

My lips stay connected to the solace of her breasts as I peer over at her slightly cleft chin. When she smiles, her cleft goes deeper; when she's sad, it can grow wider. Her full bottom lip hangs ever so slightly enticing me to suck on her nipple harder.

The window is open a bit, and the smell of the Puget Sound's ocean water floats in. The bottom edge of the curtain rumples in the breeze. The filtered brightness is making me squint, but I still see dust particles floating in the air. I hear a loud motorcycle; it's most likely a youngster. The revs are too high for early morning, at least before it's time to show off while cruising around Alki Beach. A moment later, another motorcycle goes the other way; whoever that is, they are proud of their Harley—the low rumble is smooth. Listening is survival.

A ferry horn blows in the distance. She pulls her nipple out of my mouth abruptly, and sits up and swings her feet out of bed.

"PB, you want some grits? I have some turkey sausage."

I grunt. She understands my stares, grunts, and sighs although our times together have always been limited. It's been months since I last lay down next to her. A troubled woman since she was birthed in to a family of dysfunction, it seems she loves trouble in an illogical sense. It seemed that she'd been self-serving most of her life, for her own survival. Now it seems she is helping to serve others who have troubles. I always worry about Evita. She is never too far from trouble. I have worried about her since we were kids. I've been her savior—many times. When those times occur, I wonder if she lives close to the edge just so I can save her. Then again, that's what my psychological evaluation from the United States Armed Forces said. I have a rescuer syndrome to a certain degree—and that's good, if you are paid to fight, kill, or protect.

My friend Mintfurd has said, in street terms, I have a Captain-Save-A-Hoe compulsion. He would be one of the few men living to say such a thing, because I trust him, and know what he really means.

I have saved Evita more times than I can remember. She is not the only one I have saved or rescued, but for her to live, I would give my life. It's a love thing that I have no words to explain. It's not that she has ever done one damn thing for me. That brings into question, is love about what someone has done, or is it just birthed into our emotions like a flicked-on light switch? Or maybe a light with dimmer control?

Evita is strangely beautiful. Her brown skin turns copper when she tans. She is not pretty, but strangely beautiful. Most men won't turn their head on a first look, but if she stares at you, you see it. You almost don't want her to smile, not because her teeth are bad, but because her lips are spread wide and full; you get lost in them. Her eyes are narrowly close but are opal dark, and round. She is the reflection of a black woman, showing a mix of Native American complexion on her skin. Her hair—au naturel black. I can comb my thick fingers through it and not get tangled. It goes down to her middle back. When it's wet, her hair takes on a curly perm appearance. It looks like nothing could go through her hair, not even a bullet. Like me, a blended mix of bloodlines highlights her features.

Her family, like my black grandfather and many Northwest long-timers, came back to the States after World War II, or the Korean War, and stayed in the Northwest. They thought, why in the hell enlist in the Army to get away from the Jim Crow South, then taste freedom, and then go back down South? No. Hell no!

Servicemen returned to the States by planes and big ships after surviving on foreign soil and finished serving their enlisted time on military bases near the Seattle-Tacoma area. Those men heard, "Hey, boy!" less often, and found work for decent wages instead of in cotton fields. They found jobs in steel mills and shipyards, railroad yards, and maintenance-type jobs at the Boeing Airplane Company, instead of the back-breaking, disrespectful, share-cropping jobs of the South.

Before the 1960s, in the rural South, many household still had wood stoves, well water, the life-threatening, overtly corrupt police, and bigoted justice systems. Former soldiers took their G.I. Bill money and bought nice houses in neighborhoods that had indoor plumbing for the first time in their lives. They could sit on a toilet inside their own home, and then take a hot bath in that same room: no more outhouses. Some houses in the Northwest had two inside toilets.

Coming home after World War II and later, the Korean War, to big cities like Seattle and Tacoma and their surrounding areas, black men and women could cook on gas or electric stoves and had heat coming through vents or hot water radiators. Former soldiers could bring their families up from the South. The migration of brothers and sisters, mothers and fathers, cousins, and girlfriends to Seattle and Tacoma is how many blacks came to live in the Northwest.

In the Northwest, Negro children went to schools with other kids who did not look like them. They sat next to them; they played sports and music with other races and religions, and learned more in the schools. Some went to local colleges or trade schools. The police are corrupt anywhere, but were at least in the Northwest, they were not hunting you down with white hoods.

Most thought, "Why should I go back down South and deal white-hooded white men, threats of lynching, and having to cross the street when a white woman walked on the same side of the street?" Black men found that they could stay on the same side of the street; they could even party, date, or marry any woman, whether Asian, Native American or even white…for the most part. Racism had, and has, its cancerous veins. Southern blacks still found themselves not equal, but the whites in the Northwest had better hearts or less violent attitudes than what people of color had dealt with down South.

My grandfather's vintage stereo with a high-end tube amplifier and turntable, and all of its speakers encased in beautiful walnut is in the living room. I hear pops and clicks from the record playing along with bongos, and a mesmerizing organ driving thick bass, horns, and strings. Curtis Mayfield's voice enters and sings of a runaway child.

Evita, who had taken her dark nipple away from my lips, peeks in the room. "Is that too loud for you?"

"Turn it up," I tell her, as my first word of the day. She knows that's one of my favorite LPs, *Superfly* by Curtis Mayfield.

She sways to the music as her always covered, very African American ass comes to the nightstand and removes an empty bottle of Bootlegger's Black Beer. I watch her upside-down question-mark ass walk out of the room. Her hips slam dust particles with each step she takes.

I've known Evita for thirty-plus years. We have slept in the same bed. I have smelled her scent. I have held her close. I have never seen between her thighs. I have not tried. She said no, and that's the way it's been.

As a teenager, she was my first sexual experience. Evita let me watch her fingers move under her panties, but she didn't remove them. It made me go crazy, and I stroked myself so hard I thought I might yank my skin off. At some point her voice wheezed as her body jerked. She turned over onto her stomach and pulled her panties down just far enough to expose her bubble butt. Seeing the long crease between her ass cheeks made me animalistic. I straddled her ass, and humped her and stroked my hardness. She knew how to seductively move her ass as if she was experienced. She was. She made it clear; I could not put my hardness in her pussy. She kept her hand cupped over her pussy.

She did offer her asshole. Evita took her other hand and spread her ass for me to see, and I thought about it, but my lack of experience had me confused about what to do. All I knew to do for sure was to masturbate, and so I did, and came for my first time. I groaned to the depths of one of the volcanic mountains nearby while my cum ran down the crease of her ass, and disappeared under her cupped hand covering her pussy.

That happened after a time I had rescued her. I guess she was rewarding me.

Every once in a while we crawl in the same bed, like now, and act like an old couple whose sex life is over. But we hold each other as if we had the best orgasms a man and woman have ever experienced.

I have never tasted her sweetness. She says it will ruin what we have. I have never understood that, but you don't pressure someone you love…right? After so many years, I never even think about sex with her.

We don't have a sad affair concerning us never having had sex; as a matter of fact, she has recited the rap part of Prince's "Lady Cab Driver" many times:

"This is for the women, so beautifully complex
This one's for love without sex."

I always laugh, and think of how I've had sex with many other women, and have sex right now with only one, but Evita and I make love in a way that will always be reserved for her, a safe place. She is the one for love with no sex, and I have another for love and sex.

Damaged goods. In her early twenties, she had a boyfriend, a man much older than her. She wanted out of the relationship; he beat her and cut her from her skin on down to her soul. He broke a wine bottle, sliced her all the way through, and inserted lifelong wickedness into her womanly parts. With the boyfriend passed out in a drunken stupor, and her life slipping away with each pulse of blood pumping out her body, she found the strength to call me. I just happened to be home on a summer college break.

I arrived to find a dying Evita, brave in spirit, but with an almost lifeless body. Before I arrived, all she could do was wrap her lower body in sheets. The sheets were so bloody, I wanted to remove them and put other clean towels and sheets around her, but she begged me not to. Her boyfriend had mutilated her to the point that she'd rather die than for me to see what he had done.

I got her to the hospital, and now many years later she is here, living in one of my houses. He sliced one of her breasts, but she made the best of the disfigurement. She had vines tattooed over the long scar, with hearts hanging as the fruit, and blossoming flowers and multicolored flower buds waiting to bloom attached to the vines. One wilting, unopened black rose, with teardrops falling, is tattooed over a scar near her navel. As far as I can tell, the teardrops keep flowing past her waistline; no telling how far the teardrops fall. She lives, but a lot of her heart died years ago.

Wilted. The ex-boyfriend, God rest his soul. I'm sure I sent him to go live with Satan. His ass is burning now and forever more for killing a part of Evita's soul. One may ask, "Doesn't that make you judge and jury?" I believe in justice, but not a justice system set forth in laws put in place by so-called impartial men. Judges, lawyers, and the police have motives different from mine. The money they make from the jobs they create from crime is not my motivation. Real justice—my justice—is pure from any form of monetary gain. Call me an executioner, and I know what that is.

I'm a former bullet catcher who's fortunate that I never had to catch one. Nowadays, I catch pain for others and fix troubles for the intended targets. Sometimes trouble remains, but the bull's-eye is eliminated. Sometimes my justice is purely avenging, and sometimes it's to prevent me from avenging on a level that only God and the devil understand.

I stare at the light coming through the curtain. I can't see anything clearly, but I know what's out there. I smell the ocean, and hear waves and seagoing vessels on Puget Sound. From the front of the house here on Alki Beach, the islands are to the west and downtown Seattle is to the east. I know what is out there. People making the world go around; some wanting to spin in the wrong direction.

I know a beautiful woman who is partly dead inside. I know she is spinning like a warped record, and sometimes the needle has to be moved manually. Then she sings:

"This is for the women, so beautifully complex
This one's for love without sex"

And for me, I love her no matter what.

Evita calls me by my nickname, PB, for Purple Black. I'm a light-brown-skinned man, the shade of honey spread thin over white bread. Under my right eye, I have a small birth mark. It resembles a grape stain, and it's a dark purple, wine color. As a teenager, a few started calling me Purple Black, aka PB. My birth name is Psalms Black.

I'm watching Evita as she comes back and forth into the room while she makes my breakfast.

"PB, I may go to Atlanta next week, to hang out with Esperanza," she says to me. Her expression is asking me to not ask or say anything. I didn't plan on saying anything—she is free to do what she wants to do. That look was really more about her wanting me to say something.

Evita's slippers *swish-swish* away, and my eyes stay glued to her ass as Curtis Mayfield sings, "Give Me Your Love." Being close to her is confusing at times to my sense of responsibility, but at least with her somewhere near me, I know she's in one safe place.

CHAPTER 3

Drifting in Place

Along Lake Washington, bits of sunrise crept around the edges of the curtains into the Dandridge house. Meeah and Tylowe lived on Lake Washington, a body of water that was twenty-two miles long in the middle of urban Seattle and surrounded several other smaller, suburban cities.

Meeah reached for a remote control. Holding a button down, the grand master bedroom's motorized curtains lifted by rolling up. Floor-to-ceiling windows with a 170-degree view of the lake entered with the eastern sunrise. The brightness reflected off the serene lake and the hardwood floors.

Tylowe opened his eyes to the view of him and Meeah. A mirror above the bed reflected him covered up, but his wife's beautifully naked body lay on top of the covers. For the beauty he viewed, he put another man in prison and gained the legal and moral rights to love her. She was as beautiful as the day he first crossed paths with her ten years ago, on the end of an open-air pier in Vancouver, B.C. Now her brown, leaf-colored skin had gained some freckles—angel kisses on the bridge of her nose and under her eyes. The freckles highlighted Meeah's natural beauty, and Tylowe loved kissing her face.

A few added pounds had spread throughout her body, but that also increased her sexiness in his eyes. Ten years ago, she had long, straight hair, but now she had gone natural. If one looked, a few strands of white hair could be found in her mane, but not many. On most nights, Tylowe buried his face into her hair as the two spooned and slept. The softness and scent of the Jamaican oils acted as a sleeping agent to sweet dreams.

The mirror reflected her naked body stirring. Her fingers roamed her husband's chest, moved up to his face, and traced his handsome features. His eyes stayed pinned to the mirrored reflection above, enamored with her curves and how her body movements easily persuaded his heart to push blood faster throughout his body. Her ass teasingly swayed and rose, then slowly humped the air. One hand reached back and squeezed her ass for him to see in the mirror above. Her fingernails dug in, then she provocatively released and moved her hand underneath herself. She arched her back even more, and slapped her pussy lips. She angled herself knowing he could see. Her finger slid inside her wetness, and played for him to see that it felt good. She gasped and lowered her ass. Meeah moved closer to her husband and placed her head on his chest, and placed that wet finger under his nose. He kept staring at her body in the mirror, and he took in her scent. Blood moved throughout his body faster.

She moved her body up so she could place her lips near his ear. "It seems your ride to Vancouver tired you, honey, but Mama wants Daddy this morning." She whispered in Tylowe's ear, then flicked her tongue on the side of his face. He had avoided talking much and interacting with his wife since last night after she'd picked up him and Psalms from the train station.

In the morning, they usually woke up each other's bodies with kissing, touching, and more. Tylowe and Meeah could be the world's model of dedicated lovers, bringing joy to each other with no limits.

Tylowe made no effort two days before, and he didn't touch her yesterday. Something didn't register. This was happening more often. Meeah excused this time to the fact that he'd left so early to go riding with Psalms to Vancouver, and had come back so late. But, this morning, Meeah wanted some loving to get her day off to a good start. She wanted to feel his warm, soft skin creating friction between her thighs. Years of being together had not diminished their desires for hardcore sex.

She worked to remove the covers from his lower body and placed her leg over his. He felt her wet heat on his thigh as she mock humped his leg. Lifting her breasts, her fingers squeezed her nipple for him to see the firm darkness; she signaled for him to suck on her.

Her voice teased. "Baby, I want you. It's been a couple days." She pursed her lips, and leaned in close to his ear and repeated her desires again with more explicit verbiage. She wanted it hard and forceful. She wanted to submit to the weight of his body, and the push and pull of his strength.

As she wanted, she got it. He tossed her onto her back, and straddled her near her breasts with his ass barely touching her stomach. His legs bridged his weight from becoming too much. Leaning over, he slipped his tongue deep into her mouth. The kiss she wanted rushed blood to her lips, and her eyes squeezed tightly. She felt his hardness increase in weight as it grew longer and wider between her breasts.

He lifted up and smiled. "So you want me, huh?"

She nodded her head while craning her eyes to stare at his hardness between her breasts. Meeah opened her mouth and teased his eyes with her tongue licking the air. Tylowe slid his hard and wide dick head between Meeah's lips, and he felt the wet warmth of her mouth. She felt him grow even thicker. She cupped his balls gently, and the warmth of her mouth and palm of her hand made him go faster and more forcefully.

The two lovers had taught each other the rites of passage to their bodies over the years. The two satisfied souls knew how much, how fast, how slow, how long, and how much pain and pleasure each wanted, and could take; they trusted each other.

Tylowe drove his hardness to the brink of going too deep to the back of her throat, but didn't. She stayed relaxed knowing he knew the limit. This drove her hips to squirm; he reached back and slid two fingers into her slippery, morning tight pussy. She felt his finger go about an inch to the soft ridges of the top of her opening. She groaned and her body vibrated. He held still, absorbing the feeling of her hot, wet mouth.

Tylowe pulled his hardness out of her mouth, and she mockingly complained. "Ooooh, baby, let me suck it…please, come on, baby."

He shook his head no, and backed away, but she didn't let him go far. She reached for his hardness and placed it between her breasts. She cupped her breasts tightly around to make his hardness a home. Meeah enjoyed the sight of his wide, mushroomed head peeking in and out between her breasts as he humped.

The sun had risen high enough to make the room glow and put heat on his back. The residences a mile across to the other side of Lake Washington had a view for anyone who had a telescope in his condo window. Tylowe's muscled ass and firm back could be seen sliding back and forth. He now had his thumb on her clit, circling as his fingers went in and out of her wetness.

"Come on, baby, ride my titties…ride 'em…I want to see the dick shoot, come on, baby… come on." Tylowe smiled, and almost laughed as his wife had lost a lot of her Canadian-British accent, especially during sex. When handling business, her Sade looks and her distinctive Canadian-British accent seemed connected, but not now in the heat of passion.

Tylowe removed his fingers and slid off of her. "Turn that ass over now," he demanded.

She smiled and flipped quickly, raising her ass high and spread. The view made his hardness jerk and seep. He stroked his hardness a few times and grunted with each stroke.

Meeah buried the side of her face in a pillow, and gave Tylowe reason to stroke his dick a few more times; she reached back and dug her finger into her ass and pulled her cheeks apart. He got off on seeing all her wet nastiness. He stroked hard and almost released all he had in him all over her ass, but he stopped. He moved in closer and spanked her ass with his hardness. She felt his pre-cum on her ass and put her fingers in it. She painted her ass with it.

"Give me that dick, please, give it to me now. I need you inside." The intensive feelings Meeah felt had her starting to drool on the pillow. As if she had a string pulling his hard-on directly in, Tylowe slid in and right down to the bottom. It hurt like she wanted it to. She wheezed as her fingers released her ass, and she grabbed and squeezed the pillow turning her face into it, and she cursed. He held his penetration, and she began to relax, taking in shallow breaths. She encouraged him to give it to her with full force by grinding her ass against his pelvis, and said, "Come on, baby… come on, daddy…ride my ass hard."

Humping as if James Brown and D'Angelo played live in their bedroom, Tylowe started a hard-driving, funky, nasty rhythm, varying fast, slow and deep within the middle of her groove. She spread her legs wide, lowering her center of gravity, but her ass remained angled for his animalistic humping. It turned into a long, repetitive military cadence. His hardness hit the same exact spot in her over and over. The intensity made her talk nasty and it inspired him to pound his hips against her ass.

His arm reached around and under her. His middle finger made it to her clit; she loved it as his finger and his driving hips worked at the same pace. Meeah started to get loud, and to scream, cuss, and breathe out of control.

"Oh damn, oooh damn, I'm ah, I'mmmm-ahhhhhhh, yeah." Meeah's eyes rolled under her eyelids, her lips pressed tight, and she tried to breathe through her nose, but her mouth had to open to get enough air.

Across the lake, people might have been hard, or wet, or having orgasms while they watched.

Tylowe held his finger still on her sensitive clit. Pulsation came through her little round marble of sensation. Her heartbeat pounded hard through her back as he held his ear to her back. He felt her juices slowly dribbling along the thick vein under his dick and down to his balls.

He slowly pulled out of her, and his hardness pointed to the mirror above the bed. Meeah turned over. She was flush in the face and breathing deep, but slow. He had a look on his face that she could not understand. Normally she could read him well after all these years.

"Hey, baby, you felt so good." She blew him a kiss. "Baby, lie on your back and let me ride you and get you off."

"Meeah, just let me slide back into your pussy and let it hold my dick. I want to lie on top of you, and let you hold me, okay?"

She spread her legs and Tylowe slid back into her, and lay on top of her. She wrapped her arms around him, and she looked up in the mirror at the body of her husband. She was physically satisfied, but pondered things.

His hard-on slowly eased its tension and he rolled onto his side. He helped her to move onto her side, and spooned in behind her. A half hour passed before they both exited the bed and went about their day.

Meeah's mind raced to dead-end assumptions. Her husband's body made love to her that morning as she wanted, but his spirit might as well have been sinking in the middle of the lake. Were they changing winds? Unlike all couples known to her, or ones she'd read about, Meeah and Tylowe had that fairytale love. They never fought; they might disagree, but anger never determined what they did or didn't do.

The first three years of marriage were full of wonderfulness. *Is this real?* The fifth year was anniversary bliss and the kids they were raising from previous relationships were almost done with high school. The seven-year itch was simply a movie as the kids were doing college life, and Tylowe and Meeah's relationship set examples for their friends. After ten years, the kids were out of college and gone from home. Twelve years later—swells of uncertain emotions were causing rough waves.

A few times Meeah noticed Tylowe going into himself and not as open as he used to be. Her mind wondered and played with her good senses, and she hoped her mind wasn't creating regretful logic. She replayed the morning, and it felt like what plants in need of watering looked like. The two of them, far from dead, but maybe wilting, called for some soul searching to fertilize a normally regenerating love.

Tylowe's mind drifted in place all day like a wine bottle in a lake with no current or breeze.

CHAPTER 4

Sometimes Humanity Floats and Sometimes It...

Psalms Black

"PB, you have four things you need to know how to handle, three for you and one for me."

I'm listening to my administrative assistant, Velvet, as I'm walking in the sand along Alki Beach. I just finished working out, jogging, stretching, and shadow boxing against the Seattle skyline. At this moment, it may look as if I'm talking to the slow swells washing ashore. My Bluetooth cancels out most background noises except the wind blowing off Puget Sound, but I still talk low even though no one is near me. It's an old habit from my previous profession. I maintain a sense of where and what is near me...always. Everything is a tool or a weapon. Everyone is a potential person that can cause harm.

Velvet's voice comes through clear. "I did my research on Sasha Ivanov, and all who seem to be connected to her," Velvet says. Some of Velvet's friends call her Skillet—an old nickname from something she did to a friend, she says. When she talks, her voice is pure sex kitten; it pours out of her mouth like low-lying fog, but her voice is hot steam. Velvet is professional, and she doesn't put it on: it's just her normal voice.

"Velvet, tell me about that after the other things, including what is it that you want me to do for you." I turn and look at my property, both my little bungalow and the condo office building next to it.

Seattle's Alki Beach is a watered-down, smaller version of Venice Beach in L.A. Strollers and privileged-acting yuppies with cups filled with expensive coffee topped off with sweet-slick marketing compete for sidewalk space. Others drive by with their cup holders carrying swindle-priced, fancy-named brews.

Velvet is on the first-floor office; I know she sees me across the street. I live on the top floor of the condo, but I woke up in my little house next to Evita this morning. I let Evita live there; it is her choice. I have tried to give her a condo loft in my main building, but she wants to live in the old house. I feel as long as I know where she is, I can protect her from the world and maybe herself.

I originally bought the little bungalow along with the two next door, and two others a mile down the road. I built condos in each spot to replace the old bungalows. A neighborhood planning group originally challenged my plans. A part of me had to wonder if it was the color of my skin. I planted some folks inside who shared the same skin color of my detractors. They sipped their wine, listened in, and heard what I suspected.

"How dare he come in here with a lot of money, acting uppity? Where did he get his money? Is he a drug dealer?" I understood their code…Black man.

I look at my properties, the old house and a modern, state-of-the-art high-rise condo, and I know I have invested my money well.

I got my money the old-fashioned way. I was in the right place at the right time. All money comes when it is meant to be. I didn't threaten anyone. No gun was held to anyone's head. Money I never asked for, $50 million, became mine, and all I had to do for it was to go away. They have no fear of me ever coming back and wanting anything more, even though they have a net worth of billions.

"Are you coming into the office?"

"I'm headed to my condo."

"Well, that is one of the things you need to know. Your honey is up there waiting for you."

"Yep. I know."

"Okay, the other thing, PB. You and Suzy Q need to sit down and set up security for the Mint Condition private concert video shoot at the Paramount. You two have gone past the green on my calendar and in to the yellow on that project. And, oh—don't forget I want twenty seats for that."

"Next."

"Sasha Ivanov, her father died a year ago. From what I can tell he married a woman from the island of Martinique by the name you gave me: Queen. I called the embassy and a Martinique library. It's a marvelous thing I speak French." Velvet has stunning beauty and impressive confidence, despite being far from a small woman. Full-figured, full of life, and full of inner strength most of time, she was always dedicated to me, and what I'm about. I trust her to be behind and in front of my business. "Queen is the daughter of former President Jean-Pierre Frêche," Velvet relays.

As my right-hand lady, Velvet has never surprised me with her intellect and capabilities. French, Spanish, and Japanese are the languages I know that she speaks. Velvet is a single mom who home-schools her son. I kind of do the uncle thing. Even though I don't think I'm good with kids, the little dude is so damn smart he makes it easy.

"So a Russian mob boss married a black woman from the Caribbean. Do we have any idea where this Queen is now?"

"PB, people all through the Caribbean can appear to be white, so maybe this Queen looks white. A mixture of indigenous people, Africans and Europeans, means some people have different complexions. No different from you with your golden eyes and golden skin.

"People have a hard time making out what I am or what I'm not. I'm tall, big-boned, with a darker Caucasian complexion, but many say I have black features." Velvet identifies herself as Brazilian and German. "Anyway, PB, I sent everything that I found to your tablet. I think you'll find some of it informative."

"Now what is this thing I need to do for you?" I asked.

"PB, let me put you on hold, for ten seconds."

"All right."

While she has me on hold, I see a man who sleeps outside on the wooded hill behind my place, and spends his day on the beach reading books. He always has books by Aristotle, Socrates, Langston Hughes, Richard Wright, Ralph Wiley, Malcolm X, Zora Neale Hurston, and Iceberg Slim. He often recites passages from books by Gandhi, Bruce Lee, Bill Russell, Hannibal, and Shakespeare.

I walk over to him and hand him my business card. I do this almost daily or have Evita feed him. He knows to take my card down to the neighborhood store, and he can get free food—no beer or wine. He can eat free at Salty's Fish and Chips or any food or coffee joint along Alki. I pick up the tab. Food should be free to the hungry, no matter how they became that way.

I'm not a Bible thumper, but I am God-fearing, and His Son fed thousands with a fish and some bread. So the least I can do is to help a man who wants to eat.

I start to cross the street and I see Evita looking out the window. She knows I'm going next door to my condo. She knows and has always known about my other lover. I'm in love with two beautiful women. One has my soul, and the other one has my body and mind. Evita has made it clear that she loves me in a way that makes no sense. She pushed me in the direction that I'm going now. This morning happened to be a rare morning that we spent together.

Velvet breaks my concentration. "Okay, I'm back. I have a friend— I believe you may have met her at Sterlin and Lois Mae's wedding, Darcelle. She has been the victim of poor choices in men. She may have been watching me all these years of slipping, tripping, and falling down with the wrong man."

"Velvet, what are you asking me, and why are you telling me about a woman's misfortune with men? Is she in danger?" I look up and down the block, and back across the street. I've had my eye on three different SUVs: blue, black, and brown, all with tinted windows.

"PB, please listen. Darcelle was married to a pro-baseball player. He played for the forever-losing Mariners."

"Who?"

"Clarence Thomas."

"Oh yeah, an irrelevant man he is, like the Supreme Court Justice Clarence Thomas. But he hasn't played for the Mariners for at least fifteen years. I know he bounced around from team to team before baseball sat his washed-out ass down."

"Well, asshole Clarence, while married to Darcelle, had ass waiting for him in every ballpark. Babies started popping up. The babies all had white or Asian or European mamas. Strange he wouldn't have a child with his black wife. Mr. Swinging Nuts avoided having sex with her, and when they had sex he wore condoms and put his pinky-finger-size penis in her ass, and only in her ass. How sweet of him to protect her from disease, and wimp out on impregnating her."

Velvet can be long-winded and sometimes I have to help her to the point. "Okay, Velvet. Sounds like a reality show, but what do you want?"

"PB, please listen. Mr. Swinging Nuts threw his back out, so with his career about over, he turned physically abusive when he couldn't swing a bat anymore. Lois Mae, Sterling Baylor's wife, helped Darcelle many years ago to get the courage to leave. That was long before Lois Mae met Shelton.

"Darcelle remarried a white guy from England. She has never said it, but I believe the white dude on her dance card might have been to save her from the so-called evils of the Black Man."

"Interesting. Have you heard other black women thinking like that?"

"No, but Darcelle is different. She wasn't raised around black people. Adopted as a baby, she grew up north of Lake Washington and she dated and did the prom thing with white guys. When Darcelle met her first black boyfriend, Clarence, she latched on hoping to gain some Blackness. That she did say. Girlfriend was at the top of her class in everything including law school, yet she was naïve, and had no game. She didn't understand game.

"She's a darker-skinned sister and everyone automatically thinks it's an issue when they see her with her mixed child. You know how that goes. But this is the great Northwest. You see white people with black children frequently, mixed and adopted. You're mixed, PB, but you were raised by a black man with a parentage of white; me, many think I'm at least part black, but I'm not. I'm socially mixed with all kinds but with more black people in my life. Darcelle being dark-skinned, well—"

"Okay, I know what time it is when it comes to the color line. Tell me what do I have to do with this? What do you want from me?" I can lose my patience when people don't get to the point.

"Will you let me tell you what I want to tell you? Thank you. Like I said, she married a white guy from England, and that was a fiasco of nasty. The foul piece of a man wore diapers and had Darcelle change the damn diaper while giving him head. Thank goodness he never took a dump, at least so she said."

None of this shocked me. I have traveled the world and met many people with oddities, but I had to ask. "Ah, Velvet, two things, did your friend know any of this before she married this English noble fool?"

"She's a good woman, PB, and she was trying to please her man, okay? Don't be judging anybody. Before they married, it was pretty vanilla sex. After they married, the circus-freak sex show came to town with the quickness. She admits to liking freakish sex, but then he had a huge baby bed built for adults, and wanted her to dress like a little girl. So, a year later she divorced the English punk. That was ten years ago.

"Now a year ago, just as Darcelle is about to run for city office, she received a call telling her that her ex-husband is in an incestuous relationship with his mother, and always has been." Velvet went silent, but I heard air deflate from her lungs. I let the sound of cars passing by soften the foulness that entered into my ear. "And, it was true, the woman who called, it was Mommy Dearest herself. Darcelle confronted homeboy, and he owned up to it. The dude even admitted he had a relationship with his older sibling at one time. Sickos!"

"Hold on, Velvet."

"Okay."

"Hold on for a minute now, I'm coming into the building." I enter through a private entrance in the rear of my high-rise condo building. It's where I keep my boy toys and workshop. I had to ask

Velvet to stop with the ugly, messy information for a minute. People have called me sophisticated and hard assed, but my soul can feel the bombing of what people can do, and it affects me. I have silent tears when I hear about or see an ugly life on display.

"Velvet, go on, finish."

"Well, Darcelle being a lawyer making a lot of money, and in the public eye, she had to give up a lot to get this dude to give her a clean-cut divorce ten years ago. Now she is preparing to run for a city office, and after all this time, this foulness comes back to haunt her. The ex-husband...PB," her voice loses any hint of sexiness, "I am not asking you to do anything, but she needs help. The dude, he is the father of her daughter who is almost ten years old. The dude, he wants a lot of money, and he's threatening to go to court to get visitation. He got a sweet, more than amicable divorce settlement, but now he wants more. On top of all this he has never wanted a relationship with his daughter and I doubt he wants one now. His daughter is just a pawn to his nasty, fucking twerp of an ass.

"Darcelle is living in fear of this monster touching her daughter or any of his twisted family coming close to her. He mockingly threatened Darcelle, telling her, 'You know things can happen.'"

"You know all this to be fact?"

"PB, I know not to put you in the middle. God only knows what may happen by me telling you what I am telling you. I did my homework. I had her call him using the phone tapping equipment you showed me how to use. I have it digitally recorded. He is a monster and his mother is twisted."

"Send me the info."

"PB—"

"Say no more. Just send me the info."

I look down at my arm; I see a vein pulsating and hairs standing up. My sense of justice has awakened. When it comes to abuse, it is akin to life and death as far as I'm concerned. One must live, and the other must die. I like living, so abuse within my reach must take an exit and disappear.

Sometimes the ocean has a foul smell. It could be for many reasons—things wash up, but mostly it's pollution from the foulness of people. Sometimes something has died out there. Like humanity can float and thrive; sometimes it dies and rots.

For now though, I need to clear my head. My lover is upstairs waiting for me.

CHAPTER FIVE

Papillon Hot Butterfly

Gabrielle (Gabby) Brandywine

I'm having a morning eye-opener: three strawberries, one ounce of lemon juice, one ounce simple syrup, one ounce vodka, Club soda, and crushed ice while staring at the Northwest winter morning sunshine. Up ten stories, I stare downward, avoiding the blinding sun and enjoying the water, watching the ferries go from Seattle over to the local islands and coming back.

On the beachfront down below, I'm watching my ex-Secret Service agent, my lover man, who is sparring with the ocean air with quickness and hardly any effort in his fluent movements. He possesses the kind of power men fear. Psalms is on Alki Beach, shadow boxing in the sand.

With downtown Seattle in one corner of his world, and the Puget Sound in the other, he works out with the street behind him as if his back is against the ropes in a boxing ring. He beats the air until I'm sure the air is heated to one-hundred degrees in twenty feet in each direction surrounding him.

Since I've known him, I've had the opportunity to see him do what he is doing now, many times, and I never grow weary of watching him. I have watched him shadow box and heat up the air with his rapid-firing fists along an iced-over river in Moscow. I watched his body move along the Panama Canal with the icy quickness of a Doberman as he seemingly cooled the hot air with the speed of his kicks. Along the Great Wall of China, I watched him attack the breathed air of past warriors, and it evoked a vision of him fighting and defeating Genghis Khan. Psalms Black has the build of Mike Tyson, yet he moves like a jaguar in the Amazon jungle.

I have felt that same power in his lovemaking, taking me and making me feel that he wants me. The responsiveness of his proficiencies in lovemaking takes the form of a ballet dancer's grace performing between my thighs. My ex-Secret Service agent, my lover, has picked me up and floated me down on his manhood in a way a man cannot be trained. He is all-natural in all he does. Psalms touches every square centimeter of my body with his strong hands, and I sweat between my inner thighs from the softness of his caress.

He gives me hot flashes and my body's clock is not there yet. When he touches me, it feels like whispers to the pores of my body that he has opened up with the heat of his touch. He licks and sucks on my skin as if he's licking the middle of an oyster, and he is trying to go as slow as an hour clock drains sand as he eats the middle. He sniffs all my pores and openings, and he makes sounds that have no names. It's undeniably him. When those golden eyes scan my body, I watch his hardness become his weapon of choice. He slays all my fears, and imprisons the stipulations I thought I needed to maintain some control. He replaces my wants with total fulfillment in my desires so I can lose all control. When I'm in his control, I'm truly free.

As my Secret Service agent, my feelings grew more intense each time he was assigned to protect me. I wanted him. I wanted any part of the man who would take a bullet for me. Black Knight Syndrome, maybe? I am no different from any other woman who wants what they want in a man, no matter whether if it's good or bad for them. I have surrendered to my fearless man.

Psalms has many dimensions. One night in Paris, Agent Psalms Black was off for the night. My security detail worked in teams, and my other agents, EL'vis, Dean, and Phil Armstrong, were on duty. If there were times for a single agent, Psalms was one of the few agents allowed to do so. I eavesdropped on the on-duty agents speaking to Psalms as he needed to inform them of his whereabouts. I'm sure they knew I was listening, and he would be at a small jazz club later that night sitting in with a band, I overheard. I had no idea what that meant since I knew so little of him at the time. He, unlike the other agents, hardly ever talked to anyone.

I instructed my agents that we were going out that night. They found it odd, but I was the boss. I was the most powerful woman in the world, and if I wanted to go out on the town in Paris, it was their duty to serve. Hell, I had told the Prime Minister of France earlier in the day that he needed to grow a pair when dealing with Israel.

It was imperative that whenever I was in public, whether in interviews or meeting heads of state, I had to look professional and elegant. A woman in my position was judged quickly and critically. My personal stylist always traveled with me, and, yes, that was on the taxpayers' dime. She always had my wardrobe prepared, my makeup flawless, and my hair never open to criticism.

Always on the stage front as the Secretary of State, I'm confident in my skills and presentation. That night I walked in the club dressed in a red after-five dress that any woman in Paris would envy. Normally, sexy is not the look I'm after, but I felt desirable from head to toe. I'm known as the sling-back-heel woman. I had on red suede sling-backs with black leather toes. My agents had me sit at a table along a wall near the rear exit for security logistics.

On the stage, Psalms played a huge stand-up bass with the same precision he could shoot his service revolver with. He played the bass without missing a beat as if it were his heartbeat. The band played jazz and blues, and Psalms played as if he had been with the band all his life. He is a man who one may never truly find out all he is capable of, what he has done, and what he will do.

His thick, long fingers strummed and pulled strings. His fingers, his fingers, his fingers, oh my goodness. I sat there squeezing my thighs, and my thick lips—I was squeezing them thin. I had to remember to breathe.

My serotonin levels always elevated with him standing near, even if I gave a press conference on climate change. With his body nearby and ready to serve and protect, I would give an elegant and relevant presentation and just happen to look over at him and the climate changed between my thighs. I'd smile out to the audience, and my mind would send a movie in to my vision replacing the people in front of me. I would see his head between my thighs and hear the soundtrack of his tongue licking and eating and sniffing me, and the volume would be on ten. I would think that in front of hundreds, just from a glance his way.

He was always in my head holding my attention in ways other men had not. I'm sure most women see a certain man and develop some kind of crush, but in time, they mentally move on. But, this man—I felt my soul stalking him, even in his sleep.

I had daydreamed after seeing him play that stand-up bass, wanting his hands to treat me as an instrument. I wanted him to master me. I wanted to experience a rainforest of his sweat dropping on my back. I wanted him climbing in and out of me, feeling his power stroke my insides until I couldn't take anymore. I wanted his hands to cup my ass and squeeze hard while his lips locked onto my collarbone and worked down to my breasts. I wanted that man.

I stood in the window watching Psalms give a homeless-looking man money or something. He is a giver, rarely a taker. He crosses the street and his walk is powerful. Cars seem to slow down, knowing the damage he could cause to their vehicles. He walks and it makes me relive classified fantasies of every time he was in my presence before we became lovers. I can hear Minnie Riperton singing:

Every time he comes around I feel like I'm on fire
When he looks into my eyes and sees down to my soul.

I write my memoirs in a journal in the form of short stories and poems. I laugh at my closet poet's mind, knowing I'm the person who can't share my off-color thoughts and dreams. Not this public figure! But I write them, wishing one day I can share them and maybe leave them with someone who would want them because they want to know me and not exploit me.

A year passed before I opened a door to Psalms entering a danger zone with me. I was putting two careers in serious peril. When I finally crossed the line, and asked him to cross over with me, it happened while in another country. I'd had enough of being with plastic people that day and needed some realness. I love representing and serving my country to the point I endured rejection by many of my own people for what I represent to them. I endure all of that and not have any love at the end of the day waiting for me? Enough. I made my move.

Agent Psalms Black made one last inspection of my hotel suite at the end of a conference while we were in Bahrain. He was a man of detail. His eyes move like graph paper lines when he scans.

He removed his sunglasses and his golden eyes...his golden eyes.

Under his eye—his birthmark is noticeable. Although he's not ashamed of it, he felt it drew the wrong attention while doing his job to protect whomever. He said his birthmark was a bull's-eye target to the right killer. That night in my room I spoke to him like no other time. He was my target. I needed for him to live and to give me some life.

"This might seem extraordinarily peculiar to speak to you but, Mr. Black, I seriously need to have some conversation that's not based on 'How is the weather?' and 'How was your day?' and to give back more than a nondescript response. I would love to drop all the pretentious verbiage. I would like to have a drink...share a drink with you, and talk with you about anything other than world affairs," I said to the agent assigned to protect my body.

Without looking at him, I poured a double shot of G'Vine Gin on the rocks. My eyes played shy when any other time, I kept my eyes pinned on Psalms. I was sure of my words, but unsure of what I was doing, yet understanding the risk. I chose to break the ice, supplant protocol, and get to know the man protecting me.

That was seven years ago when we chanced embarrassment and careers. We became lovers. Awareness of our surroundings was something we both kept conscious of as we became lovers and best friends. I look at Psalms walking through his condo door. The extra-wide designed doors in his condo make the average man look like a minor, but Psalms looks manly, wide, and powerful coming through them. He is wide and powerful both physically and intellectually. Damn, he makes me sear with lust and serious cerebral thoughts.

Psalms stares at me with his golden eyes. It feels like he sees me without any clothes on with his graph-paper-line scan. I want his naked, firm body to lift me up and lay me down on the hardwood floor and make my naked body squeak with wet, sweating fiction. I want to role play with him and have Psalms drag me as I submit. I want to feel myself sliding and reaching and touching his calves and on up to his muscled thighs and ass. As he is dragging me, I can see his hardness pointing, ragging, dripping, and my body slips and slides. Once we're in his bedroom, I'd crawl on all fours, and I'd grab his hardness, hold it, and suck it as hard as he often sucks my breasts. I imagine he is torturing me with pleasure.

I come back to my current existence, and Psalms is still staring at me and doesn't speak. Psalms offers no greeting or engagement—remnants of my relationship with men assigned to protect me. Speak when spoken to—a power trip request or demand by the lonely or self-absorbed.

I sat down with almost every world leader. I, Gabrielle (Gabby) Papillon Brandywine, an African-American woman born and raised in Galveston, Texas, rose to be distinguished and disliked, but respected for the most part.

There's a price to pay for being a powerful woman before, during, and after serving in office. The media intrusion in to a public figure's life remains and, as for me being a woman, privacy is still an issue. Everything I do and say is a matter of public interest and record. A love life is almost impossible for a woman in high governmental office. A romantic dinner out in public and the media frenzy could easily overshadow a peace treaty signing.

I don't have the option of retiring from office, and becoming an exhibition and behaving like a-booty-shaking-washed-up-ex-baller's-whore-or-wife and I do not want to do either. It is a shame for any woman to become a spectacle on a reality show that too many women look to for training in class.

Powerful men can drop their drawers and get caught with women who make money on their backs. Mostly powerful white men in Congress abuse their power and have mistresses, and abandon their wives, while those wives have been at home and raising the children, or may even be on their deathbeds. These politically corrupt men will dump a devoted wife for a newer piece of ass as fast as a fat conservative radio shock jock needs to swallow a Viagra pill to get it up. Those same nasty-ass men will run for the presidency years later, and the press will only hint about their low-life deeds. A double standard, yes! A woman in high governmental office can expect to be burned at the social stake and seen as a cold-blooded whore if she goes from man to man.

Unlike most men, standards of a professional woman in her public life apply to her private life as well. If I ever step out of bounds, the ramifications can be devastating to a life that is already hard enough. The fact is even when a woman is in bounds, the media still wants to know who is she screwing, and when. If you're not screwing someone, it may be assumed you're a lesbian.

Some of the most talented women who have worked for me live alternative lifestyles. They don't come out because of how they'll be treated, and it is wrong! So, I'm doing what many women have to do, keeping my private life behind a curtain. Whether a single mom or a woman in a public position, we have to keep our private lives hidden all too often. Being entitled to do as you please as a woman, and be respected, is a pipe dream, unfortunately. To conduct yourself as you please, with "it's nobody's business" attitude that is reserved for a reality show ex-housewife or a side piece waiting to become a scandal.

The man moving toward me is smiling; he hardly ever smiles at anyone or anything else. When he smiles at me, he melts me. He is what I like and love. I feel respected by Psalms as if I'm his woman, but…in public because he used to be my government-issued protector, so we act like associates. Many will assume he was my lover on the taxpayers' dime in furnished offices and hotels abroad. Well, he was my lover, and we did do the do. But, I'm here in his place now, after both of us have left high-profile positions.

I often have to initiate conversations with Psalms, and it is one of the few things I don't care for. But, as long as I'm close to him, I'm happy. "Psalms, you look good down on the beach working out. Are you sore? How about we take a shower, and I'll rub you down?"

He is leaning over into my breathing space. His lips brush against my cheek. His deep timbre hums in my ear like a hummingbird removing nectar. "I thought you were coming to town next weekend." Before I can respond, he kisses my thick upper lip, and then slips his tongue across my teeth as he removes my empty glass from my hands. It could be the vodka or maybe his kiss, but I'm feeling a bit woozy.

I bite his tongue and hold it for a count, but not hard enough that he can't pull it back. "I was," I say. He slides his tongue in deep and I bite lightly again. I used to have a rather large gap until I was a teenager. I showed him pictures of me from back then, and ever since Psalms has had a fetish about what used to my gap. Every once in a while, he calls me Gabby if he wants to hush me up because I'm running off at the mouth over an intense subject.

Sometimes he calls me Butterfly, when I make him cum so hard, and he's about to drift off to sleep tucked against my skin. My middle name is Papillon: French for butterfly. His tongue plays nasty in my mouth like when he's going down on me, and it sends showers to my pussy. Then he comes back, licks my lips all around and I hold still for him to do that. It almost has the same effect on me when he licks on my plump pussy lips. Psalms tells me I'm a hot butterfly.

The media glorifies and ridicules the thickness and visual of my lips. Tabloids have mocked me as being Meagan Good's real mother. We do share the same lip contour and likewise visual lip size, and a slight resemblance facially. The big difference is, she might be a size four and I'm a size—well, it's in the teens and varies from end to end, depending on my stress level. I'm in the tabloids all the time and my build is parodied on late-night TV. I'm built with curves, lots of breast, and a full, well-rounded ass. A few heads of state were careless, and cameras have caught them gawking. I've been glorified for my breasts and ass in a rap song.

One song remarked:

"Her hair is fly girl whip appeal
Her rump is running humpty-dumpty wild and wide
Her breasts could feed the poor
If only her conservative mind was fine like her Hollywood face
The girl looks like a freak
But that can't be when she talks like she better than you and me."

All I can do is laugh, because little do they know about the real me. I am open-minded. Psalms and I do things others have to go watch pornos to get a clue. Psalms pulls back his tongue, and I act as if I'm going to bite his tongue if he tries to insert again... knowing I won't. I'll just melt as I always do.

"Psalms, I hope it's all right that I'm here. Henry Kissinger had to cancel a dinner lecture at East Seattle City University. The chancellor thought a former Secretary of State would fill the bill. So, I'm here for four days, if that's okay with you. I canceled my own classes."

"Gabrielle, you know you don't have to ask, even though you

weren't asking. It must be nice to cancel your classes whenever you want to. All that money they charge those kids to get into UC Berkeley and you, Professor Brandywine, pull a disappearing act, like 'Oh well.'"

"I have a suite at the Westin if you want to stay there instead."

"Gabrielle, I spotted your security detail down on the street." As always, he doesn't respond to statements or questions that don't really need to be answered or responded to.

"I know they're not the best security, but the college provided them. I'm okay, babe, nothing will happen to me."

"You may not be on the world stage anymore, but people still want to cause you harm. If you are coming here, I want to know so I can put my people on you to protect you, okay?"

I'm a woman who runs shit, and one of the beauties of being with Psalms is I can hand control to him and completely trust him and his love. I can be a black woman first and foremost and drop all the public image of how I'm an American patriot only.

I nod my head and let Psalms know I understand he wants to protect me, and I should have informed him I was coming. He's not trying to keep me away from an unexpected visit. Psalms Black is almost too honest. He will hurt my feelings with his brutal honesty, so he will tell me to go if that's what he wants.

I know about his other woman, the one for love with no sex. I know he has protected her from herself for most of her life. She's no threat to me, but I don't like it. I could do something about it. I do think about doing something. Maybe I should, but I know who I am. I understand my worth in his world. I know no other woman can do for him what I can. If someone were to think less of me for how I feel—oh well. I love that man: he will be all mine one day, and one day soon. But for now, we lead an almost secret life.

I worked my ass off to be the most powerful woman in the world, often thought of as much as the president I served under and by some, liked more. At my service and assistance, I had the Secret Service, the FBI, the CIA and Homeland Security for certain situations. I've met and made connections; I've made friends to help me in my endeavors, all for Psalms and I have to have a life together.

Psalms removes his shirt and is headed to his room. I make myself another morning eye-opener and wait until I hear the shower running. I always anticipate him taking me hard and forceful with very little foreplay. The thought alone makes me almost too wet. I love him sliding in his hardness when I haven't kissed it or touched it yet it, and taking it and giving it to me hard.

Some Sunday mornings, I've been on different national TV talk shows: *Face the Nation*, *Meet the Press*, *This Week*, and yes, even the Fox Network's *Fox News Sunday*. Most people watch and see me as classy, graceful, educated, and skillful in how I answer questions that could cause political wars, or wars period.

Most never think I have another side that just wants my man to hold and pin me down, and pound his hardness into me as if he is trying to hurt me. I raise my ass to that in a toast. If most knew of the places our tongues go, they would write laws to put me in prison. Bill Clinton slid a cigar into his mistress' ass. Many think a lady should never do certain things, but this lady does it all and can't wait until the next time.

The queen farts with her royal elitist facade, and I love rough, hard-pounding sex, despite what my public wants to think of my persona of gracefulness.

Right now, I'm stripping down and joining my ex-Secret Service agent in the shower to go help him relax, and for me to get off.

CHAPTER 6

Someone Could Get Hurt

The stereo was loud, but not enough to keep people from holding conversations. Ledisi caressed her sexy voice in to her version of D'Angelo's "Brown Sugar" through the speakers. Seattle's morning sunshine ended up fighting with the clouds and lost. Grayness now was the color of the day on the Seattle skyline.

Holding court at mid-day at Uncle's BBQ, Psalms sat at a table with Suzie Q and Tylowe. The two guys had sides of red beans and rice, greens, and yams with a beef hot link for lunch. Suzie Q, wiry but strong, and capable of delivering as much pain as any man, devoured her food like a hungry lioness after a kill. On her plate was a half-pound of beef brisket, and sides of mashed potatoes and gravy, baked beans, greens, yams, mac 'n' cheese, mixed veggies, green salad, and a cornbread muffin.

"Where does it all go, Q? A doctor may be in order to see if you don't have something inside of you eating you alive. It's a wonder you don't have the biggest ass anyone could have." Tylowe shook his head.

"You black guys like women with large bottom ends, eh? Well, if that is the case, my little skinny, white bottom has a long way to go, eh?" After many years in the states, Suzie Q had not lost any of her Scottish-Canadian intonation. The former Royal Canadian

Mountie turned private investigator/security agent, had joined forces with Psalms Black. The two offered much sought-after services. Suzie Q had been a part of the ordeal that had put Elliot in prison.

A few years ago some friends of Tylowe utilized Suzie Q's services when she hunted down a man who had tried to kill them. Suzie Q shot the man, badly wounded, and somewhat tortured him. She needed the man to confess to some crimes, and when she was done with him, he did. She then helped that man take his own life after he realized what would happen to him in prison. Her girl-next-door, Drew-Barrymore-face hid her rough character.

Tylowe chewed on a hot link while staring at Suzie Q. "Q," he said, "Black men love women with a sizable ass. Hell, white men love some ass, too, but many are scared, not knowing if they can handle it all. But lack of ass ain't your problem."

Before he finished, the three of them were already laughing.

"Let's count the ways. You carry a gun bigger than most porn stars' erections. I think your boxing skills might make a few men run. And you're faster and stronger than the average fellow. Now your accent might be a turn-on to some men, so that is a plus." Tylowe laughed at his own joke.

Psalms chimed in. "But that thing about you don't have sex with men, only with women, I'm sure that might keep a lot of black men from wanting your skinny, little, white ass."

"Oh, I guess that might be a problem for me bottom, eh? Not offering any bun for the beef hot link, eh?" Suzie Q winked, pursed her thin lips, and then sucked on her hot link. Both men put the hot links down and gave her a look of, *"Not while we're eating, silly woman."*

She tore off a piece of meat with her teeth and chased it with dark beer. For some reason, she spoke louder. "I guess some of the brothers don't care who I do because they be asking for a chance to bend my skinny, little ass over. They hit me up in public and on my Facebook page, when I clearly state in public and on my page that I have women who love me. So, I send their wife or the women posted on their page a song by my favorite artist, Meshell Ndegeocello, 'If That's Your Boyfriend (He Wasn't Last Night).'"

A man sitting behind Suzie Q spit up his soda. The brother had hit on Suzie Q when she had first walked in ahead of her table-mates. He wore a wedding ring. He regretted handing her his business card.

Tylowe smiled, but joking around didn't go too far with him as of late. Psalms changed the subject as he leaned in, and the others did, too. "I have gathered info on our Russian problem. The person running the show for the Russians is the daughter of a so-called mob-boss. Her name is Sasha Ivanov. She has been taking over for her dead father, the man who was married to Elliot's baby mama. Sasha's father, when he was living, apparently believed or acted as if the kids were his.

"These kids are in trouble because they each have bank accounts in the Cayman Islands worth millions, and they can draw them out when they turn twenty-one. The only people who can touch the money before they age out is their mother, who seems to have disappeared, and Sasha Ivanov, if the mother dies and the kids die before they turn twenty-one.

"Queen, the mother of the kids, could be in hiding or dead. But she has an aunt living in Vegas. This aunt was the sister of the former president of Martinique. The aunt had a different father, so her last name is not Frêche as the President's was. This may play in our favor if Sasha Ivanov is hunting down the kids as Elliot thinks she may be.

"I have a man at Homeland Security. Queen's passport shows

she went to Vegas often. Also, known ties to Sasha Ivanov have been tracked to Vegas as of late." Psalms looked over to Suzie Q.

She took a swig of her brew.

Tylowe was amazed at the knowledge that could be had and known, and that he had friends with this kind of know-how.

Psalms pressed his lips tight before he spoke. "If Sasha Ivanov got to the kids' mother, all I can say is the Russians I've come across know how to torture like Q is ripping meat off that bone."

Suzie Q, at that moment, put the bare rib bone down and took her time to suck each one of her fingers with full sound effects, removing the sticky sauce.

"So you can see the problem we have. I was able to call in some favs to trace some of this info and Gabby used some State Department intel available to her, yet all the information is suspected to be wrong. We need to assume so and plan accordingly. This is not going to be easy. Someone could get hurt. I'm gonna be honest, Tylowe, this kind of situation may not be for you. I don't doubt you can be a warrior, but getting in to a fray with these people can be pure violent.

"When we add the fact that this involves Elliot, and what is real or not real, there is no way we can trust his intent and information. Let's not be simple-minded when dealing with him. You know that. Something didn't sit right with me when we had our little visit with him. It is my nature to be distrusting, and it could be just that…but that MF."

Psalms looked over to Tylowe. "You don't know, but I had a problem with him back in college and he doesn't know I know what he did. I wanted to get even, but he was your friend back then, and I was conflicted on a few things I had already done. But that MF is not to be trusted…ever."

Tylowe nodded, and kept nodding to the beat of the Anthony Hamilton song that played, "The Truth." There was anger in Psalms' voice that seemed displaced, but Tylowe kept his mind on everything he had heard.

The little bell over the entrance door dinged. In came two well-built, white men, ex-military—Psalms knew right away. The two men wore heavy material suit coats, tailored for extra room. Their dress jeans had wide legs. Psalms knew that guns and extra clips were tucked in the coats, and another gun in an ankle holster was hidden beneath the wide-leg jean. Suzie Q's hands moved smoothly to her weapon as her eyes pierced behind her dark sunglasses. The style of sunglasses she wore was reminiscent of the 1960s Black Panther militant shades.

The two men scanned the room. Both men locked eyes with Psalms. It was more like Psalms had chains on their eyes and he slowly twisted the chains tight with his golden eyes. Then as if he released them because he was done, they turned away. The two men turned to someone outside and both nodded. Psalms blinked his eyes toward Suzie Q, signaling her to stand down. She relaxed, but kept a hand on one gun in her coat. The two men separated and made a human corridor with their huge bodies like parting the Red Sea for royalty, and the former Secretary of State Gabrielle Papillon Brandywine walked in. A city official and a state official muckety-muck walked in with her.

Tylowe released a long exhale. He knew right at the moment what Psalms meant. He was not that kind of warrior anymore, if he ever was. Without knowing that those guys were bodyguards, he saw the alertness of a Doberman in Suzie Q, and Psalms turned in to a tuned precision machine like a heat-seeking missile, and sensed the potential violence that could erupt.

Those two were ready for action. To avoid trouble is to be aware of trouble before you're deep in it; act first instead of reacting. Tylowe's eyebrows moved inward, and wrinkles formed on his forehead. Reflecting on how people could find often on the daily news the aftermath of a bloodbath, not knowing they might be surrounded by men and women with guns anywhere, anytime, he laughed aloud.

"Something funny?" Psalms asked Tylowe with a smile.

Tylowe had a smirk on his face. "You knew damn well your girl was coming in here. You could have said so."

"Would it have changed whatever you're feeling?"

"What makes you think I'm feeling any certain way?"

"Your comment says so. You're no different than we were in kindergarten at Van Asselt Elementary: always overanalyzing everything. Do you need to go write a poem or something?" Psalms smirked and tilted his back as if he was looking down on Tylowe, when in fact Tylowe had at least a good three-inch height advantage.

"Dude, I'm glad I went to Leschi Elementary so you didn't bully me the whole year."

"Yet here you sit next to me wanting my help." This time they both laughed.

"Can you two stop reliving playing Cowboys and Indians, and seeing who can swing higher on the swing while looking under each other's dress, comparing dick size?" Once Suzie Q's aggression radar went up, it was up. She was a bit pissed at Psalms for knowing other guns were going to be coming in the room, and he knew it.

"Q, we good?" he asked.

"For now." She glanced over her shades at Psalms, and then the bodyguards, before she gave Gabrielle Brandywine a stiff smile that resembled someone injected with an overload of Botox.

Psalms and Suzie Q had forged a lucrative and successful security company. Complete trust in each other's abilities and laying down all their personal demons and what they'd done in the past made them closer than conjoined twins in some ways. They hid nothing from each other, helping them to recognize one would cover for the other no matter what. They knew about each other's dead bodies and where they were buried. Understanding everything was for the greater good, till death do they part, even taking all you know to the grave.

Suzie Q and Tylowe knew Psalms Black's lover. Psalms' trusted friends, including Tylowe and his wife, Sterlin, Lois Mae, Ayman, Vanessa, Velvet, and a few select others, socialized with him and Gabrielle at his condo or at their homes.

Right now they all acted like casual patrons. Psalms and Gabrielle made knowing eye contact as she ordered her food. Her bodyguards each took a table on each side of the door, but close to her. Two other bodyguards sat in the SUVs, observing the comings and goings. Other patrons smiled at her, but let her be. The bodyguards knew to cut off anyone who wanted to talk to her—as if she would want to talk about world affairs with strangers. She wanted to eat good barbecue, and talk with her hosts, and watch her man from a distance.

An oldie came on, The Jackson 5's "Lookin' Through the Windows." Gabrielle smiled at Psalms.

Tylowe, Suzie Q, and Psalms finished their meals while debating about and finally agreeing on how to find and rescue the kids. Tylowe explained he could not let his stepdaughter have siblings living unprotected in a harsh world. He had saved Mia from Elliot, her biological father's evil, and he had to do the same for her brother and sister.

Tylowe said his goodbyes and started to leave, but stopped by Gabrielle's table and they spoke briefly. Psalms and Suzie Q put plans together for the security of the Paramount Theater's private concert video shoot. They also covered how to protect Tylowe. The family man was not a warrior like them. The job ahead: to protect Tylowe the best they could from what could be a high dose of potent ugliness—the bloodshed brought on by the forces of good and evil.

CHAPTER 7

Happy Hour

Evita waited impatiently to make a left turn. The after-work traffic made her turn up the volume of her music with the hopes of it having a calming effect. She wanted to be inside Friday's happy hour at Jay's Lounge, a live and jumping place for good drinks and to mix cologne and perfume with the so-called known, hip folks. It was her every Friday, after-work pit stop.

She revved her engine as if that would signal to the oncoming traffic to let her through—no such luck. "Sweeeeeeeeeet, sweet sticky thing," the Ohio Players sang crystal glass-breaking, high-pitched harmonies through the car stereo. Evita bopped her head as traffic kept her stuck in the turn lane. Sitting behind the wheel of a nice car like the Audi R8, a rare expensive sports car, the common people—normally with less—will act as if they don't see you. When you're unusually noticeable and possibly made so by high income, some will admire what you have, but most simply want out of the Northwest gridlock. A rare vehicle can be despised by the have-nots without any consideration given to how one might have achieved his or her gains. Cars may have full gas tanks, but the people were most likely running on empty, in need of a coffee refill.

If anyone knew the life and times of Evita Quinn Rivers, they would run and jump in the cold water off a Seattle pier, as if trying to wake from a bad dream. Finally, a break in traffic allowed Evita to wheel her two-toned black and red car into the parking lot and stop at the valet. She revved the motor, loving the manly feeling of power it gave her.

The car was a gift from Psalms. She lived in his house. She had made her own money, but even that came with Psalms' help. Evita arose from the cold, cold world of a hard life some ten years ago, and Psalms always took care of her. Since their days as teenagers he had protected or saved her.

Evita wanted to give instead of taking, and chose to work with kids. While she lived the fast life on the streets, she encountered many troubled youth. They lived troubled lives after they had become emancipated from their parents or guardians and struggled. Evita wanted to help that segment of society.

With Psalms' money and her direction, they started a foundation: True Essence Humanity, helping kids get on the right path and stay the course of independence. Gabrielle Brandywine was the foundation's spokesperson. The two women each had troubles of their own—a good man they shared, but in different ways, and a good cause. They didn't deal with each other, but each knew of the other.

With a high-profile person, such as the former Secretary of State, at the forefront, the foundation brought in major sponsorships. Even nationally known coffee and software corporations joined in. Many of the children who transition through the program lived alternative lifestyles and dealt with sexuality issues as they tried to figure out how they fit into society.

The valet, a masculine-looking girl, sported short-spiked, dark-burgundy hair and wore a parking valet tux. The valet's back was turned to the entering cars, as she texted and stuffed her face with a huge hamburger. She had a fast-food bag around the burger, but sloppily bent forward to avoid the extras in the burger from falling on the uniform. Evita revved the motor and got the attention of a former, almost graduate of her program. The girl ran over and opened Evita's door while licking her greasy fingers. Evita immediately thought a car detail would be needed soon.

"Ms. Evita, I could put your car under the cover in the parking garage. If not, I have a spot right over there in the first outdoor slot; you won't have to wait when you come out."

"Thank you, Phoenix, and as always, please put my car under the cover. Keep it under a hundred if you take it out." They laughed and came close to hugging, but shook hands instead. She remembered Phoenix could be inappropriate and Evita didn't play. Phoenix, a naturalized citizen from Canada, had been a runaway at an early age and became prey to pimps and drugs. At first, Phoenix thrived in the program, but it became a revolving door of problems. Other kids became targets for Phoenix's sexual conquests and preying on the weak-minded, until Evita evicted Phoenix from the program. It took a few short prison stays, but Phoenix finally broke free from the streets, and Evita helped out by finding her this job.

With each step leading to the entrance, Evita felt her behind moving under her tight skirt. It couldn't be helped. Her large behind and swayback put on a show under her clothes. Evita wished she could wear heels and expose her shapely calves, but scars distracted from the toned features. If she wore heels, she'd wear pantsuits. The only time her legs were bare was in the house, or when she and Psalms visited a foreign land. All her clothes looked classy and sexy, but were also designed to hide cuts, burns, and scars. She had pretty, perfect feet with no scars, but could only expose them when she wore pants.

A few times in public, she wore sheer dark stockings with a thick line up the back. The tattoo work on her legs had colors to distract away from the scars. All her life, someone else had dictated her clothing, her sexuality, and her impression of her own beauty. Evita had bits and pieces of her ideas of outward beauty ripped off her mental bones.

Young Evita dressed like a Catholic schoolgirl to the point that even Catholic nuns would have forced her to release a little sex appeal. Growing up, her abusive father made her dress extremely conservative. Even on Saturdays, she dressed as if she were a nurse in a 1950s mental asylum.

She owned three skirts: tan, blue, and plaid. Nowadays, it was rare if she wore blues or tans, and for her, plaid had the same effect as someone swallowing sour milk. The sad child had three blouses: white with a frilly collar, white with short sleeves, and white with ruffles. Even old ladies shook their heads in disapproval at a teen-age girl wearing patent-leather shoes. She always wore black or white patent-leather shoes, or brown or blue oxfords that were two-toned with white uppers and looked to be polished with dull nurse's shoe polish. She had one Sunday dress and she wore it every Sunday.

Evita's mother was a timid little lady with African-American and Native-American blood, and hair so long she could sit on it. Most thought she was Filipino. Her father, a black man, was a dock worker who drank and stayed high on painkillers. When he couldn't get enough painkillers for an old work injury, he would become like a hungry wolf—crazed—and he would whoop his wife with switches from a tree that he forced Evita to go pull off. Evita would offer herself as a sacrifice to protect her mother, but that sometimes resulted in mother and daughter both receiving a whooping and other abuse. As with all the families living on 38th Avenue South, life seemed subdued and uneventful, but, behind many closed doors, monsters lived.

Evita's homely clothes caused her to be bullied, and she became cautiously shy, and awkward. Ugly-souled children, and some adults, verbally tortured Evita with many unpleasant incidents. Psalms beat down males who mocked her, and gave thug girls sinister stares that said, *"I dare you to bother Evita."*

From birth, life for Evita was different levels of hell. Hell One was her bipolar daddy who dictated her life with hellish deeds which led to Hell Two, Daddy pushing Evita too close to the ledge, 'til someone pushed Daddy over for good. Hell Three was the drunken rage of another evil man who left her with physical and mental scars—mutilations that ended with Psalms Black sending the evil man to hell. These hells, the ones she lived, and the ones men died because of her, haunted her soul. Another part of her soul seemed to sleep well, knowing she had power to create demise.

Evita walked through the glass doors into an instant social scene. Glasses clinked, and laughter rose to the mirrored ceiling. TVs replayed old Supersonics game highlights in honor of the NBA team that would hopefully come back to Seattle. Suits and skirts played themselves sexy and the "Hey what's up, girl?" game was in effect. It was the weekend, and folks were here for the potential hook-up.

Ex-pros fronted like they were still relevant with a few current bench-sitting players. Skirts batted their eyes and pursed their lips at men built to destroy other men in games. Everyone else came to have a good time after work, and to watch the expensive sleaze and tease. Hip folks!

Evita checked her coat and walked past the bar. She recognized a few faces in the crowd, some welcomed and a few best to ignore. She spotted her coworker at a bay window booth overlooking the Lake Union moored yachts. Time to unwind, have some laughs, and sip on a Chocolate Cream martini: 1 oz. Vodka or Vanilla Vodka, 1 oz. Chocolate Liqueur and 1 oz. Irish Cream.

As she got to the table, a man patted her ass. Her streetwise peripheral vision triggered action. Evita didn't turn around. Instead, she lifted her boot high off the ground and angled backward and downward. The thin heel ripped down the leg of the man, and in quick succession Evita grabbed a table napkin, then turned and stuffed it in the man's wide open mouth. Before a wounded dog sound left him, she beat back his howl by almost choking him with the table napkin. Almost in that same move, Evita slipped her hand behind the man and acted as if she were hugging him to fool those who might have looked up, but it was actually the point of her nails he felt, like a knife about to push through his skin. The man had double trouble. Evita was getting high on the torture she was putting on him.

The man and Evita had exchanged long glances when she walked in, but apparently in his head he thought he had hooked her. The sound that squeaked through his stuffed mouth sounded like a weak seal wanting fish to eat. Evita released her fake hug and the man turned quickly, and headed outside to hide his embarrassment. Evita's co-worker wasn't sure what had happened, yet knew well enough that Evita was dangerous if provoked. Living the street life and growing up in foulness, you learn to live and survive by being ugly when needed. The problem is, sometimes you go over the thin line.

"Let's drink. Whoever he was, he had to leave and look for another party. Some people shouldn't drink and be around others." Evita sounded calm, but she wasn't. Her coworker, Jamie Bubble

Booty, walked her out to the patio. Despite a few others being out there, Jamie fired a joint up, and Evita took a long, burning drag. She held her mouth open in a circle as she ran her tongue around her lips while holding the smoke in her lungs. She exhaled after the charge of bud altered her cerebral stream; she pursed her lips and whistled the smoke out. Shortly thereafter her drink came to the table. She relaxed for real then, and told Jamie what happened.

"You're so hard and sweet, like rock candy," Jamie teased. "I always have to deal with men putting their hands on my butt. It protrudes into two rooms when I come through the door, so men see my ass as a playground for their ignorant shit. They think I'm okay with them putting their hands on it. I wish I was a bad-ass, but I'm not, so I give them the best 'That's fucked-up' stare I can give."

"Bubble, I wish I was more ladylike, but after living that hard life, being a lady is something I always have to work at. It's not my first nature, or maybe even my second. My mom was so docile that I despised her dainty, gracious ways. I somewhat regret that now, but then again I don't. My father beat her like a heavy bag, and he slapped me around like a speed bag. It's one of the reasons I have PB teach basic self-defense to every child who has ever come through the program."

"I suppose he taught you to defend yourself?"

"Yes, he did, but trust me, I learned a lot on my own. But if I get high or drunk with the wrong person, it might not make a difference. I could have beaten the shit out of the man who cut me up, if only I had thought better of myself."

Jamie smiled, and reached for Evita's hand, observing her unflawed, long fingers. Evita's hands were the rare place on her body that had no tattoos covering scars. Her nails were painted a frosted neutral with black, knife-like, pointed French tips.

"Evita Rivers," Jamie took a deep breath, "I've been in love, but it always ends up hurting in the end…so far. I wish…I dream, of having what you have with PB. He gives you your freedom to do as you please. That makes me want to join a church just to shout, 'Hallelujah.' He supports your causes, and you actually never have or have had sex. You have sex with whomever you choose, and he never raises his hand to you…Hallelujah! It makes me want to plot your death so I can see if he'll like me a tenth of how he loves you. There is only one man I have ever loved…still love. We love defiantly against what others wanted for us. But…but, time and space got in the way, and we let a few people add distractions," Jamie's voice trailed off.

"Until your last breath you have time. And Bubble Butt, please don't kill me anytime soon, I have some shopping to do first, okay? Let's talk about something good."

"Evita, you don't shop all that much, but I'll let you live. You're my friend, and if I need to see any woman happy and live through her, it might as well be you."

The conversation switched to topics easier on the soul for a while, until a news report flashed on the TV. The police in Seattle had killed an innocent Native American man. The man had carved small totem poles with a pocket knife, and the police had shot him for not putting it away fast enough. The man was hard of hearing. It had happened some time ago, but Jamie had Native American blood running through her, and it ran with boiling, busting heat seeing the news. She went outside and smoked another joint.

At the corner of the bar, a man sat staring at Evita. She didn't know him, but maybe their lives had crossed. She gave him a nickname, Pretty Boy, and chuckled. He saw her laughing alone and looking back at him. She was thinking of leaving when Jamie came back, but knew Pretty Boy would approach her table, and he did.

Pretty Boy, a man most women would call fine, stood at her table and they role played. Evita savored the last of her drink with her face pointed downward, but her pupils lifted high and scanned. She smiled at him, but only because she knew she wouldn't be stomping her boot on this man. Well, maybe—possibly. She let her mind go into freak zone. Pretty Boy, a man manicured five times more than Prince, was deep in to his metrosexual appearance. He slipped his body into the seat across from Evita.

"So, Pretty Boy, did you pay to sit across from me?" Evita made sure she beat him to the punch and spoke before he had a chance to roll out some bullshit. "You must buy every woman in the bar a drink first in order to sit across from me. That's an order."

Pretty Boy, a white man with a slight olive skin tone, had a hairline from front to back that was perfectly trimmed. His facial hair was impeccably groomed, even his brows. His nails shined, polished like the diamonds in his ears and on his pinky finger rings. Pretty Boy's suit was tailored, a slim Brioni, as worn by James Bond in the *007* movies, and for sure not off the rack. He held up his arm and rotated his fist in the air several times—signaling.

The server made her way over quickly. "Are you buying a round for a select group, sir?"

"No! A drink for everyone in the bar and restaurant." His accent was not from any region in America that Evita recognized.

"Ah sir, we'll, ah, have to run your card in advance, if that is okay with you?"

With two fingers from his inside breast pocket, he pulled out his phone, swiped his finger to unlock it and scrolled and pressed a few times. He handed his phone to the server. "Run your scanner across the barcode showing on the screen and it will transfer all you'll need."

The server's eyes widened and left with Pretty Boy's phone. Evita pressed her lips flat, as flat as she could press her thick lips. She did that instead of shake her head at the man's game. Men with money did nothing for her. She had slept with rich men and done all the nasty, freaky, and weird things that money could buy.

"Not impressed," she said to him. What did impress her, were the good looks of a pretty man. The only reason she had not kicked his butt was he was pretty. The toeing of the line of femininity in a man Evita liked, because in her own senses, she wasn't feminine.

Her attraction to Psalms had nothing to do with his manly body, capable of destruction. Psalms was pure visual machismo, and many women looked upon his powerful, sexual body and it overwhelmed their senses. Evita's attraction to Psalms was wholly internal to the soul of the man he was. Psalms and the word *handsome* could be found in her dictionary, but a pretty man—she could eat and drink. In her world, pretty men often were submissive in and out of bed so that she could make them do anything she wanted for her own freaky nature.

The server returned Pretty Boy's phone. "Sir, do you want our patrons to know who bought their drink?"

"No!" He put the phone back in his inside breast pocket and came out with two one hundred-dollar bills. "That is for you and the barkeeps."

Evita tried hard to make out the geographical location of his accent, but she was not going to ask and tip him off to her interest in him, yet. He even thought she might have recognized his voice and face from her past, but she gave up thinking about it. The man was gorgeously fine and that was all that mattered. Jamie went by the table and nodded—nothing needed to be said.

"I am going to say goodbye to someone and visit the ladies' room.

If you're here when I get back, you're here." Her eyebrow arched high.

He nodded.

She walked away, but looked back and the man had his eyes on her ass—glued.

When she came back from walking Jamie to her car and each smoking a separate joint, she found Pretty Boy waiting for her with a fresh drink. She drank her sweet drink and stared at the man awhile before they began to have a decent conversation. His earlier pretentious actions didn't come through in his conversation, but… pretty quickly, Evita started to feel uneasy in her head. She might need some food in her stomach, she thought.

She felt some numbness. Her mind went cloudy, and she lost her ability to speak clearly. Her eyes were open, but her body and mind were escaping somewhere outside of her control. With what little sense she had left, Evita knew she had been drugged. A silly grin graced her face, thinking, *I was going to fuck him, but it looks like I'm fucked. Whatever this shit is, it won't let me respond like I want to…Damn! How do I let PB know…he might not come by the house or call for a week or more. I'm not ready for this…it can't be… help, I…I'm not ready for this…I need to call…* Her mind went blank.

Evita left the happy hour.

Two impeccably dressed gentlemen helping a lady out of the door and to a car is what it looked like. It wasn't.

CHAPTER 8

Aware Of Your Life

Psalms Black

Blue and red lights flash reflections in windows. Police position themselves in "I'm here on official business" stances near their vehicles in tactical locations to keep the uninvited public at a distance.

I'm standing inside by the front doors of the East Seattle City University Performance Hall. Gabrielle is at the podium speaking about world affairs, tangling the truth for those who want things to sound a certain way when the reality is something else.

I'm waiting for Velvet's friend, Darcelle. Ms. Darcelle Day. She is a prominent Seattle lawyer who made poor choices in the court of love. Yeah, I said something made for a movie, but her choices in men have helped endanger her daughter and her career. Careers can be reconstructed or rearranged, but a child's life—I have to step up.

My phone vibrates and buzzes like the buzzer sound on *Lockup Raw* when a door is opening and an inmate is coming or going, always into potential death. I answer it.

"Yeah, Q. No, leave tonight. Tylowe will fly out in the morning and join you by tomorrow afternoon. This will give you time to check the lay of the land. Yeah. He'll meet you with the paperwork, and it looks good. Just keep in mind we don't know if the mother is living, hiding, or what. We don't know the whole story.

We have no way of knowing if the Russian, Sasha Ivanov, has a bead on all this, but for sure, she cannot be too far behind.

"I don't have to ask, but you will have your federal gun carry permit with you? I know you're not a virgin to any of this. I really wasn't telling you what to do, crazy ass—you know where I'm coming from. Now don't let Tylowe get hurt…right." Suzie Q hangs up the phone, but not before telling me to kiss her little Canadian Rocky J Squirrel ass, as she always does.

People mingle outside of the hall auditorium. Security. They see me, and want to call other security. I have on glasses that most believe are to hide my eyes, and they are, but they're not tinted as much on my viewing side as someone might think. The glasses are multipurpose. An imbedded high-powered directional microphone is on each side. From thirty meters away, I can hear someone's private conversation, and dial in by turning my head at angles. One of the tools of the Secret Service, FBI, and for sure the CIA— and one I use in my civilian work.

I'm in a dark blue blazer, blue jeans, and blue suede shoes. My fashionable shoes, if I have to move fast, have rubber gripping pads on the ball of the foot area. The heels look hard, but they are rubber, and the tips are steel toe in case I have to kick some ass.

It's tux heaven in here. I don't fit in, and I'm not trying to. Standing out is a way to see almost everything of significance around me. People not wanting to been seen by anyone will avoid looking at me, when all others look in my direction.

The description I have of Ms. Darcelle Day lets me know that's her walking up the stairs. She is short, maybe five feet tall and petite in a sense, but she has breasts clearly coming and an ass trailing. She has fine facial features, except for her lips. Even from a distance, I can see her thick lips infused in to a permanent puckering position. She walks as if she is self-assured—at least, that's what her walk says.

Ms. Day is one sexy lady. Small women, generally, don't get a second look from me. Pretty and petite is cool, but I feel as if I might break a small woman just by the wind I make walking by. Ms. Darcelle Day walks as if she can handle herself. I block out the mental image of her changing a diaper on a man, and then having sex with the mental mutant MF.

People we come in contact with daily, weekly, or once in a life-time—we never know what goes on in their world behind closed doors. A serial killer can be the coworker you worked with for ten years or more. A sweet, giving female elementary teacher can be a molester of young boys. The little old lady at church could be an embezzler or money launderer. A soccer mom with the minivan might be a high-priced whore on the weekend to help pay for an overpriced-sub-division-cracker-jack-fake-looking-like-I-have-money-mini-mansion. A saintly acting man leading his church congregation to heaven might have ten married women in that church he is sexing up. Take a look at the next person you come in contact with, and ask yourself what lies beneath their skin.

I open the door for Darcelle, and nod my head in the direction of the lounge area. We take seats at the end of the bar. "Thank you, Ms. Day, for meeting me here. I kind of needed to be over this way."

"I'm a little underdressed with most of the women here wearing sequined cocktail dresses. I see most the men here own more than one tux. Looks like I should have stopped over at Neiman Marcus and picked up a little black dress."

Her voice. She might give Velvet a run for the sultry award. Why did she have to say little dress? I'm smiling when I don't want to.

She smiles, and I listen to her voice do tricks to make her bigger than her outward persona. "Money is floating down from the Issaquah hills tonight, I see, and into the Bellevue city limits by way of Benzes and BMWs on Interstate 405."

I nod.

"All this...Microsoft and other Seattle-based companies playing Northwest Wall Street games. Six and seven-figure salaries spawning like salmon, and dumped like thrown-out coffee grounds."

She shakes her head, and I nod again. The waiter brings us water, and she keeps talking.

"Most of the folks sitting in the Performance Hall don't know the poor they push into corners, away from their world and their gated communities. To soothe their souls, they make donations to other countries in hopes of curing ills, but ignore their own backyard garbage."

Darcelle is nervous. She wants to avoid the subject we must discuss. Her nervous tic is drinking water as if the water in Seattle will run out. I hear handclaps and hear Gabrielle over the outside hall speakers. She had said, "We must take care of home in order to help the world."

Ms. Day piggybacks on Gabrielle's statement. "Yeah, to most that means more tax breaks and tax shelters, and more police protection for their neighborhoods. They want to give less money to inner-city schools while they have high school campuses that resemble a mini Penn State university; a place to hide their elitist crimes and 'I-don't-care-about-anyone-else-but-my-babies' attitudes.'"

I have to ask, "Do you have fixes or merely ethical political rants for votes? I've spent my life around elected officials; I've heard it all. All you said is true, but do you have fixes?"

Darcelle lifts her head high and angled while her lips spread wide, smiling but not parting. "Velvet told me you weren't to be messed with on any level. You cut that fat in one slice."

She gulps another glass of water. I know she wants to avoid why she is here to meet with me, but I lay it out. "This place will be lively after the former Secretary of State, Ms. Brandywine, finishes with her speech. The few in here with us drinking now will change soon. The elbow rubbers who couldn't afford the hundreds of dollars to buy tickets to be inside the hall for dinner and speeches bought tickets to the after-party. Let's talk about why you are here."

"Okay, Mr. Black…Velvet saw the trouble I'm in and told me she knew someone who might help me. So, I ask. Please help my daughter and me. Conventional means—police and courts—will leave us in more trouble, costing more money, which will do nothing in the long run. I value my career and where it can go, but my daughter is the only thing that matters when the dust settles."

I nod.

"My repulsive ex-husband and his foul mother…I don't know how or what you do, and I may lose some sleep over it if I did know, but knowing my daughter is in a safe place, I'll happily cry myself to sleep."

"Ms. Day, we will never discuss what I can do or what can happen unless I have something for you to do. Your little girl is all that matters. I'll need to get more information. Mostly, where are these people, meaning where do they lay their heads and where do they go, and who do they know? I can find out on my own, but it will be quicker if you help."

Darcelle is looking at me with fear as she most likely is dreading what her mind is concluding.

"Ms. Day…Ms. Day, focus on your daughter and do me one favor."

She takes a long draw of water, and swallows twice before her eyes seem to clear, and I have her attention again. "Mr. Black, could you call me Darcelle? It might feel less like I'm in something so deep."

"Okay, Darcelle."

"The favor you ask, sir?"

"If you do become an elected official, do some good for the people and not yourself. Don't talk to the public using semantics to confuse those of lesser understanding, even if it means you won't be elected. If you're elected to office, don't do as other city officials have. Please stand up and do not allow the police to terrorize the common citizen. Do not represent the deep pockets who tear down necessary public housing and build new condos, and then make only ten percent available to the poor."

"Mr. Black, if I do become an elected official, I will be for the people. It does seem you have your own rants of moral righteousness."

"Not a campaign slogan to me, Ms. Day...Darcelle." I want to smile but don't. However, she does.

"Sir, please right a wrong for me, and I'll do what is right, no matter what the cost."

I nod, and she lets me know she is going to the restroom. In the time we've been talking, the waitperson has filled her water glass four times. Stress does unpleasant things to the body and kills brain cells the same as alcohol. She comes back, and I have other questions on another subject.

"Darcelle, many have woke up and found the wrong person next to them, and tried to turn the nightmare in to a romantic dream come true. We'll call it love trying to force it to work when it sure in the hell didn't fit in all our squares and triangles."

"Squares and triangles, huh? I've been called an L7."

"Whatever you want to call it, love has not fit into your grooves."

"No," she agrees. Her lips roll, smoothing lip gloss. Weak men would fall and worship Darcelle's facial expressions, but she has little concept of her allure, or her concept has been destroyed.

"Darcelle, I don't know you, but you do whatever you think is best for you. Cool, but when I step in to do anything for anyone, I have something to say to that person about how they got to the point that they needed me. I don't work for money or Atta-boy awards. I work for what is right.

"I feel I have the right to play devil's advocate in the hopes of helping you see the devil next time he tries to put a triangle in your square. I don't know either of the men you have been married to, but it reads like each time, you were reaching for something to complete you or fill a void. Enlighten me, please."

"You have an answer for everything. They're just not good ones when it comes to me. I didn't think I would get judged, but it's like this. As I see it, Mr. Black Man with those golden eyes and thick-cream-in-your-coffee skin, your appearance tells me you've had struggles at some point with someone. Your short hair doesn't hide the mixed curls that would stand out if your hair was longer.

"No matter how black you live, another black person, or white person, has insulted your mind and soul. I'm one hundred percent black—hell, I even had a DNA test to see what's in me. No Native American as many blacks claim and no European blood flows in my blood. Do I understand what it means to be black? Hell no! I see mentally confused black people who were raised in all-black families, churches, and had the total black experience of an environment. I was raised in a totally white American world. My black skin and black hair, black ass, and black lips were loved by a white couple who loved me with all their heart, yet that seemed to make me dysfunctional.

"When I say dysfunction, it's not to mean I hate or hated my dark, black skin just because I never ate black-eyed peas and greens or did any other stereotypical black things. My dysfunction means there have been times when I've been confused on where I should be and where to go. On many levels and situations, love for a man has been confusing."

Darcelle's voice has hurt and some anger. She drinks another full glass of water. We sit in silence for a long moment.

I do know that my questions and statements, at times, can be harsh. I can tell she is a good woman, and I have made her feel guilty about her choices when she's already hurting. I let my I-wanna-fix-the-world attitude cross the line.

She is accurate to the personal attacks I'd dealt with as a mixed-race child. I don't experience it as an adult, but light skin versus dark skin and all the in-between effects on black people are here to stay.

How we as black people got to this internal conflict doesn't matter. I know some people think if we all study how we got here, we'll have some kind of Kumbaya awakening. Bullshit. Yet, I have no answers. I try to clean up the hurt I put on her.

"Darcelle." She takes five seconds to look at me. "Darcelle, love is all about confusion. We can meet a good person, but they could be ten years older or younger, and to them that could mean you're not perfect enough for what they seek in life. We can meet a person who is attractive and loving, but their size is wrong for the activities or lifestyle we live. Maybe we meet someone with children, and we don't want children, or shit, some people have families that are just too damn crazy to deal with. A person cannot trade their family like a used car.

"How I worded what I said—I apologize. I know anyone can find themselves in a situation they had not intended." The blue and red police lights reflect in the window. My heart and mind go back in time and visualize a dying, bleeding woman in my arms.

I must have been lost in thought for a moment; Darcelle taps me on the arm. "Can I call you PB like Velvet tells me you go by?"

"Yeah."

"PB, I make good money, and for some men that's a problem. Maybe some women don't make it easy for a man in that department. You know, just because a person doesn't say something is a problem—harboring resentment is a death sentence to be handed out in any relationship. Being a lawyer, I have handled a few divorces. I had to stop handling them. The worst of ugliness can walk through the door seeking representation. I have represented men and women, and detested what they wanted to do to the other side. Men and women can be some fucked-up people, and I've had my moments.

"PB, you're puzzled about how I could have married a man who wore diapers, peed on me, and who fucks his mother. Everything you can think of…well, let the nastiest imaginable thoughts come to mind and it happened. I let him do it in the name of love, and to fit that old-school train of thought that what goes on behind closed doors is behind closed doors. If you wonder if I liked it, it doesn't matter. I did it, and I'm paying for it now, for loving unconditionally, although utterly foolishly.

"So, Mr. Black, I need you! Help me, please. Yes, I have issues; yes, I do! Maybe, with that critical mental stick you carry around, you may be helping me see the devil next time, and I'll keep the triangles and circles out of my square ass.

"Maybe you should look at your own life, though. Not everyone can liberate themselves. Here is a thought, PB—while you're saving or protecting everyone, think of the ones you don't or cannot save. That should tell you that you're not the answer. You're a fix after the fact."

"Good point. I pray over that often, and all I can do is continue to pray. But Darcelle, you didn't give me an answer to the one thing I needed to know despite your situation."

"And that is?"

"Backbone. I needed to know, do you have a backbone? I needed to hear are you aware of your life, and life itself. If not, when I fix your problem, you'll make the same mistakes again, and as you said, I cannot save everyone, especially if I have to save the same people over and over.

"No matter how I put it to you or anyone else, they have to face their own hell and become stronger, not weaker. All shall rise to joy when after laying aside insecure emotions in thoughts and actions and by gaining faith in yourself, and first and foremost, in God. Neither man, nor woman, can steal one's joy if we are leaping to new heights, or rewriting a failed history by staring into the face of the enemy. The enemy is the old self, which lacked faith in its own soul and relied on someone else's. Excuse me if I seem to be preaching my point, but my grandfather had a Bible in his hand morning and noon, and a woman many nights, as he was studying. He shared his observations and analyses with me and I have found many to be true."

Darcelle stares at me and finishes another glass of water. Her eyes are watery. She slowly shifts the scope of her vision to the windows. The outside lights, in reds, blues, yellows, and greens, reflects in her watery eyes. They reflect arresting of the old. Dinner jazz volume goes up as conversation filters out of the Performance Hall. I don't hear Gabrielle's voice or any other speaker's anymore. Darcelle Day and I finish our conversation with her giving me information I need.

Does she have a man in her life now? I don't need another person trying to do something counterproductive to what I will have to do, even though I don't know what that is yet. She says her life is lonely and has been for years because she doesn't know whom she can trust to come in to her life. I feel sad for her.

I invite her to an event later. She says she will come. We shake hands, and she leaves.

CHAPTER 9

Totally Naked

"I know somebody is in the room. I can hear you breathing. Are you getting off looking at me sitting here tied up and naked? You like what you see?"

Evita perceived evil close to her; she thought it was one person, but not the same person all the time. She'd been awake, clear-headed and bound since morning. She figured she must have been out through the night. She sensed it was mid to late afternoon. She was warm. A hood over her head made her skin itch from the heat inside.

Evita, hearing how her muffled voice resonated in the room, thought she was in a medium-sized room, with other furniture. She turned her body and placed her bound feet to the side of the mattress so they could touch what was under her. Carpet. The person in the room with her moved to a standing position. Evita could hear their breathing change, but not to any level of panic. Yet, the pace of the inhale and exhale changed.

It was not the first time Evita had been bound. Her life on the wild side of the streets had taught her about forced and unforced captivity. Evita didn't consider screaming; she knew no one was going to hear her. Pros had taken her. With her hands and ankles tied and no gag in her mouth, her captor or captors apparently weren't worried about her screams being heard. She had an inner chuckle about watching a crummy movie where a woman screamed and begged to be let go, and she'd never tell anyone. She placed her feet back on the mattress and placed her tied hands between her legs and closed her thighs.

"Are you going to kill me?" She repeated the same question two more times. Evita was gauging distance and windows. She knew her back was near a wall. To her left, her voice reverberated, dead in a way, alerting her it was possibly wood there: furniture or a door. To her right, her voice sounded thinner, like a glass window was nearby. Evita calculated that most likely she was not in a basement or a warehouse.

"I need to use the bathroom. Now! Or you deal with the smell."

Her hood was dark with a tight thread count; light was almost nonexistent. Evita needed to walk, to know if she could, or if whatever drug had taken her down was still having an impact. She needed to know the texture of her surroundings, and hopeful she would pass close by light to signal for help. Lastly, she wanted her kidnapper to come close to analyze. Psalms' survival lessons. His training, first as a Navy SEAL and then as a Secret Service agent, taught her to dissect situations, and think of possible counter measures.

"Now, asshole...now!" Evita feared to speak aggressively, but she needed her captor to get pissed, even if it caused her harm. Evita was in the survival mode of deduction.

A forceful grab of the hood near the back of her neck almost lifted Evita off the bed and off her feet. The captor stood her erect and led her like a dog on a choker chain and spun her around many times. Evita let out a wounded cry, but she did that each time so she knew she'd turned 360 degrees as a marker. She kept her eyes open and peered straight ahead knowing it would keep her from getting dizzy, although she was in the dark. Evita started to get a sense of her captor; at least the person holding her was not a pro.

The person now leading her in a few turns was about her same height because the pull on the rope was not a downward force. The person behind her was trying to use a straight arm to keep distance, but the distance was short. Evita's bound ankles had enough slack to allow her to take baby steps, and she kept count, just in case she needed to know.

Evita walked into a small room with a tile floor, and six feet from the entrance, she felt a cold toilet hit her leg. The toilet seat was down. It smelled clean. She knew she was in a nicer place: most likely a house.

Evita did her business, number one and two, and found a tissue roll next to her. Because her hands were bound loosely, she managed to clean herself, and water was turned on for her to wash her hands. Evita played ignorant of being able to follow the sound of where the water was coming from, and she was led to the sink.

Led back to the room, her eyes detected light—outdoor light, a window. The captor did not spin her around on the return. She was pushed from the back of her neck. Evita fell onto the bed. The hand that pushed her was small.

Time to listen for planes, trains, cars, dogs, human or mechanical noise.

Evita now knew all she could. She was by water. She could tell by a distant sound.

In the darkness, under the hood and in her mind's eye, she saw Psalms carrying her away to a safe place like times before. This time was so different: she understood she would be dead if Psalms didn't save her. A desire made her heart beat irregularly. If Psalms didn't save her in time, she still wanted him to carry her away, even if totally naked. Then her heart lost several beats. *What if he sees what is wrong with my body after all these years? Maybe he won't even touch me or bury me.*

CHAPTER 10

The Most Powerful Man I Know

Gabrielle

Deniece Williams' "Cause You Love Me Baby" smoothly enters my ears, and I'm sure my head looks like a bobblehead with rhythm to the cars we are passing. I reach to turn the volume up, but PB beats me to it with the volume control on the steering wheel. The back of his hand touches my cheek as softly as the music.

Night lights on the Eastside of Seattle sparkle and seem to bounce with the music. Microsoft's neon signs are affixed on high-rise buildings, overlooking high-rent office space and high-end retail stores. I feel a slight G-force as PB powers the car on a wide, circled ramp onto the freeway.

I'm free from security restrictions tonight. I'm never away from a security detail unless I'm with PB. People want me dead. I would be a crest for their cause in and out of my great country. People hate—to the point of taking a life—as if it might bring some form of satisfaction, or avenge their cause. The ugly get only uglier. They kill Americans and will kill even more of them, and paint it pretty.

Most worry about death in terms of one day their time will come. Some worry about death in the form of an accident or sickness they hope to avoid. Fortunately, not many have to think death can come at them from the hands of a killer dreaming, plotting, hunting, and executing their mission. The killer who pulls a trigger, or pushes a button, maybe sets a timer, and *boom*...they smile and revel in the same fulfillment of an orgasm that never stops…I live with that daily.

I wake up and wish I could plan my day with all I want to do. I go about my life, eating, drinking, laughing and possibly dancing the night away, and from there, I'll make love to my lover. In the middle of any joyous or ordinary moment, my killer or killers can rise up, and remove my smile, my breath, and take my last heartbeat. Tonight could be that night, but hopefully after I make love to the man next to me.

Why kill me?

Men starve women and children for land, or just to say they are in control. Many times, in my capacity of leadership in the administration I was in, I had to take a stance to support a cause I did not believe was right. America's best interest is always the last deciding factor. I cannot say I'm proud of everything I supported or took a stand for, but there is the greater good. I understand to some I'm an awful person for the decisions I have been a part of. Some are right; decisions can be awful and we often find out after the smoke has cleared. With everything any and all have done in their lives, turning back the hands of time is just a song when it's all said and done.

I'll be judged in history for my effectiveness or failures. Ultimately, the president I served under will receive the praise or blame, and ten or maybe twenty years later, I'll be forgotten or a side note.

I just left from the dinner where I told bits of truths and left out the whole reality of decisions made. People listened to me and acted as if they cared for forty minutes. People paid two hundred dollars for a steak that most likely came from another country. Some paid one-thousand dollars or more for a table to bring their friends to impress. Unknowingly, they ate farm-raised fish imported from a poor country where people will starve. But tonight, because it was all cooked to picture-perfect presentation, we say it's all for a good cause.

How ironic life is. I helped drive contracts and treaties on countries to become trade partners with our great country. While the ink was still wet, I took lots of pictures with heads of state, helping foreign countries to keep oppressing their own people, while people here lost their jobs. One might wonder, why did I do it? I have to ask myself that very question at times. But I sleep fine knowing good does occur in the long run...I hope. To others, in order for them to sleep, I'm better off dead, or they want to die as a martyr in a gas chamber or at the end of a smart bomb.

Right now, I'm getting away with my man to escape from politics. PB hasn't said much, and that happens often, but he has told me we are headed down to a boat landing on Mercer Island. We will board a private ferry boat, known as the Washington Loch Ness Monster, because it is so old. It is a restored, 120-foot ferry from the 1920s. It's been converted into a yacht with state rooms and a large performance ball room. The ferry belongs to PB and Tylowe, and a youth foundation that PB and his other woman administer. I'm a spokesperson for that foundation.

The other woman—she is not his woman in the sense that I am. She's a troubled child whom he watches over. Psalms Black does not lie. I'm not sure he knows how, but he's not a liar. He says he and the other woman—Evita—don't have sexual intercourse, and I trust him.

Why should I share any part of him? I'm the former Secretary of State of the United States, and a beautiful black woman at that. Black and white and foreign millionaires want my hand in marriage, and don't even know me. Hollywood male sex symbols flirt intensely, wanting a prize like me. CEOs invite me to their chateaus for dinner and to parties wanting to court me—so why PB?

The man holds the steering wheel, and his thumb and forefinger look like they could crush any man's collarbone to tiny pieces. But when he touches me...his hands, his hands, his hands...when he caresses my clit with that same thumb and he slides his middle finger inside me, it feels like every nerve ending in my body explodes in a joy that no other man has ever come close to making me feel. Dammit, I just squirted a little bit...shit.

Why PB?

Power. Men I know and meet are full of some kind of power, but not enough of what it takes to make me happy. I could have a husband, a head of state, or a senator, or CEO of a Fortune 500 company. Money makes men powerful in a sense, but it's not for me. I'm not amused or intrigued. The men I know can give me every material thing there is to have, and almost all of these men don't give a damn if I'm black. If anything, to a white man or a foreigner, I'm a prized black queen to make him even more powerful due to the perception of social consciousness.

I look over at PB who is driving us to the ferry. For the last fifteen years or more, I have ridden in expensive vehicles. Many of them were Mercedes. Now, I'm riding in a SLS AMG Gullwing coupe. I don't get to go fast in cars, passing other cars, unless I'm with PB. We pass cars quickly, but the way he drives it feels like he's not speeding. I chuckle, knowing he takes advantage of his special government security permits if he's pulled over. His license plate has a code for local police to give him clearance to come and go as he pleases. Retired Secret Service agents are always on call in a national emergency.

On the stereo, the playlist is a mix of his and mine. From Deniece

Williams to Miki Howard's "Love Under New Management," I feel a rush, like my heart is racing. I keep my body moving happily as I'm with my lover. I'm singing background, loud and clear. PB smiles as he keeps his eyes on the road.

When he looks over at me, I'm reminded I can't go without his looking in to my eyes. My lover, my man, is the most powerful man on earth. That's how I feel about him.

When he talks, he talks with me, and not at me. PB speaks as if he has the same amount of knowledge I have, maybe more, but he shares of himself in a way that I want to know all he knows. That's a power that turns me on. At one point, when I was still in office, I could rely on his opinion concerning world affairs.

We became a team. We made world-influencing decisions, yet he knew how to keep me from feeling I was not the one leading. He has never reminded me of his help or how he led me to a decision.

For sure his body is sculpted of God's best for the human eye to see. He is physically fierce, but he can make love to me with the gentleness of baby's caress, and he can take me to the mountain top with his visceral passion. Damn, I'm damp.

PB knows what he wants and does what he wants, and most of the time, it's for someone else. He would take a bullet for me, not because it's his business, but because he loves the ground I walk on. That's how he treats me and looks at me. He's a man's man, larger than life, without any put-on of a Hollywood big-screen ego. I have the most powerful man on earth. I'm sure many women feel that way about their man, but my man fits my soul. He apologizes with sincerity, and I want to say I'm sorry back to him for no reason.

He's not bought, he's not kept. He was rich before he was rich. He has no fear of me and won't hurt me, which is the most powerful feeling of all. Trust. That is why I have little concern about his other woman. I'm in a safe place with him. Although I want her gone!

We pull into a gated driveway and head toward the ferry. Cars are parking, and people are getting out and walking down the road. We pull into a reserve spot near the boat. Tylowe and Meeah are standing by their car waiting for us. I love them. They are the perfect couple. Do I wish I was a wife, perhaps a mother? The power game for women in my position is problematic. If you give in to your career, some feel you'd be letting down a husband, and possibly children. I had incomplete thoughts on the subject for years, and now age has made the decision for me.

The women are dressed attractively, but warmly, to keep the chill off their legs, wearing pantsuits, or dress jeans. Most of the men are wearing jeans and nice sweaters. Music is flowing from the ferry.

I've been anticipating this all day: good people, great food, music, and spoken word as we cruise Lake Washington. I can't wait to change out of this dress and into something warmer to be on the water. Later, I want to peel my off my clothes, and even my skin, for PB.

CHAPTER 11

What Are You Doing For the Rest of Your Life?

The ferry barely moved through the dark water of Lake Washington. Lights from houses along the shore reflected like floating glass globes. Oldies played loud. Several rolling mini-bars wheeled through the crowd while bartenders made drinks.

At a table on the upper deck overlooking everything, Tylowe and Psalms had dark beers in hand. Meeah and Gabrielle sipped Gin Mojitos: 2 oz. of Farmer's Gin, a few sprigs of fresh mint, light green spearmint, 2 Tbsp. of fresh lemon juice, 2 Tbsp. of fresh lime juice, a splash of Sprite. Mix and muddle in the mint. Add the juices and ice. Pour in the gin last.

Rufus and Chaka Khan's "Everlasting Love" played. The music reached in to the mature gathering of souls as the ferry headed past Seward Park and into the Renton Bay area. Some of Seattle's coolest, most chill folks danced and socialized in the cool air, but the party groove made it a hot night.

The people on board were a full range of friends of both Tylowe and Psalms. Some they knew from business. Some were city officials. Others were just friends, from average wage earners to the affluent nouveau riche. Most were African American, but there was also a distinct segment of whites, and people of Asian and Hispanic descent, too—a blend as diverse as Seattle itself. A few LGBT people were also there, right at home partying with everyone on the boat while the ignorant were ashore.

The policy on the ferry for everyone was: no cell phone cameras or personal cameras allowed. Hired photographers took down everyone's email addresses, and would send them all the pictures they wanted of the evening, free of charge. Of course there was censorship of any kind of compromising pictures; Psalms and Suzy Q prided themselves on security and well thought-out plans to cover all circumstances. Their business was in demand on the West Coast as well as in some foreign countries.

From East Seattle City University, Coach Ayman Sparks with his wife, Vanessa, and Coach Sterlin Baylor with his wife, Lois Mae, joined Tylowe and Psalms' table after dancing to the Ohio Players' "Love Rollercoaster."

The men had all known each other since their college days at the University of New Mexico. Psalms and Tylowe, originally from Seattle, had been close since grade school. Ayman and Sterlin coached the local, nationally ranked college basketball team together. Tonight, all the old classmates and their mates enjoyed one another's company. The only one missing from the group from back in the day was Elliot, who was sitting in prison.

Since Tylowe and Psalms had their plan in place, they would have to think of Elliot at some point that night, however strange it might feel.

Tylowe made an effort to distract his mind. "Sterlin, who would have thought your ass could dance?" Tylowe teased.

"You call that dancing? I thought he was in pain." Ayman sounded as though he wasn't joking, but he was.

Lois Mae came to her husband's defense. "Leave my baby alone; he can dance just fine. I love the way he moves."

"Lois Mae, don't talk about his moves around here. This is a PG boat ride until the poetry starts." Everyone laughed.

"Tylowe, you got nerve. How many times is Meeah going to squeeze your butt as if she were checking a flotation device to see if it will float?" Lois Mae and Tylowe always had regular, playful banter.

Gabrielle whispered in Psalms' ear that she wanted to dance. It was rare for her to be in public relaxing with everyday people. Most of what she said or did publicly was carefully measured to protect her from being misquoted in off-the-cuff remarks. In her mind, the opportunity to dance with her man freely was almost as good as sex.

"Babe," Psalms whispered back to Gabrielle, "I'm not shaking my ass down to the ground, except maybe later tonight when we're alone."

She smiled as her skin heated from the thought.

Mintfurd Elongate walked by, along with Velvet. Some called Mintfurd "Big Boy" instead of his given name. He and Velvet were announcing that the spoken word and jazz show would be starting soon in the performance ballroom, and they wanted people to head inside.

Mintfurd and Psalms were college foes in wrestling. Mintfurd went on to the Olympics, and Psalms went into the service. Relocating to Seattle on an invite from Psalms, Mintfurd now used his brain and his brawn for security work. Together, he and Psalms designed and installed custom surveillance equipment.

Mintfurd wasn't an ugly, fat dude, nothing like a thuggish-looking Rick Ross. Despite his size—more than six feet six inches, and 400 hundred-plus pounds—Mintfurd had the prettiest face a man could have. At least that is what women thought and said. He had a noticeable, alluring mole near his bottom lip and attractive, kissable lips. It wasn't that he looked obese. His facial features weren't stretched and his stomach didn't hang. Even men much taller looked small compared to him with his wide bodily girth. He was just a mountain of a man: a good-looking, handsome, and huge man. When he smiled, it looked as though he were blushing and made him look younger.

Sadly, his size kept women from thinking about any kind of relationship with him. The average-sized woman looked like a child near him. Even a woman like Lois Mae, at six feet tall and not exactly slender, still disappeared behind him.

Women whispered ignorantly about whether he had a small penis, as many believed to be true of men his size. Some thought he might not be able to get it up—another rumored problem. Then there was the visual thought of what sex would be like with a man his size. One thing women did love about him was his voice—a mink-fur soft baritone. Yet, women avoided him as partner, but befriended him as big brother. The same women who couldn't imagine themselves sleeping with him, would close their eyes, and listen to his voice to vibrate their clit.

Because his size intimidated most women, prostitutes had been his only sexual outlet. Unknown to women, Mintfurd had no problems in the bed. All the prostitutes could attest to his penis size, and his hardness being worthy of feeling. Many were amazed that his body size had remarkably little effect on how he could move smoothly, quickly, and powerfully. Psalms treated Mintfurd as a little brother, feeling in some ways sorry that the man had never felt love.

People started moving to the warmth inside with drinks in hand, leaving the tranquil Northwest fresh air. A camera couldn't do justice to the night sights of the boat from the shore. The ladies, Gabrielle, Meeah, Velvet, Lois Mae, and Vanessa, all hung back as the guys moved inside to secure their seats.

Darcelle made it on board just in time, and approached Velvet and Lois Mae, her good friends. She was in better spirits realizing that no matter how tough her conversation had been with PB, he was going to help her out of a sticky situation.

Darcelle was introduced to Gabrielle, and the girls sipped their drinks while the men finished setting up inside for the show.

"Gabby, I know it must feel good for you to be around, quote, unquote, regular folks," Lois Mae said. The others chimed in with nods and short vocal affirmations.

"Ladies, to be honest, it has been since before I was anywhere near politics that I could let my hair down, so to speak."

The music coming out of the speakers almost every twenty feet sounded like a concert. Maysa Leak's jazzy voice asked, "What Are You Doing the Rest of Your Life?"

Normally, Gabrielle spoke with confidence. But that was all a façade. Speaking abstractly with and to associates, political cronies, and Sunday morning talk shows had poisoned a lot of her heart. It was difficult for her to be totally honest in her communications. She wanted to let words flow from her soul, but it was a challenge. She had to work hard at trusting her heart to be out on her sleeve. Psalms made it easy for her in their one-on-one relationship, but with other men and women, she had to ease in to being open as she spoke.

"I want to thank you all for accepting me despite my political stances. Every time I come to Seattle, you guys take time to go out shopping with me, or to hang out. Most of us love the comfort and safety that a man can bring us and give us, but I need my sisters just as much and often more, than anything in the world. This is much better than having power over men and nations, being out here on this ferry moving to nowhere fast, just going, without people making a fuss because I'm here...I'm happy."

"Honey, normal is what you make it. With all you have heard and seen in your line of public service, we will never see or understand. You get no judgments from any of us. Besides, we can't believe you're that conservative, anyway." Gabrielle led the laughter charge after hearing that.

"Shhh...I can't let that get out." Her smile lifted her cheeks to the deck lights that reflected off of them. "Look at it like this, maybe I was keeping it from being worse than it could have been. When you're playing with the big dogs, you have to lead them like blind mice to what they think they want to do. Picking my battles and winning is a great feeling in the political arena, no matter what side controls the lies. Yet...I had to fight so hard. When a woman is assertive in a man's world, they will call her a mad bitch in heels to her face. On one hand, I wanted to be reasonable, humble, and thoughtful of those who deserve respect, but on the other hand, I did not want to be thought of as weak."

Gabrielle lifted her third cocktail and finished it when most were starting or receiving their second. Liquid courage filtered through her heart to help her speak about her life.

"What has been said in print, and the news, and by people in general, hurt my father badly. I can only assume it shortened his life to see his baby girl spoken about in such horrible ways. I buried him at sixty-five years old. Now my mother is in full Alzheimer's, and I can't help but wonder if there is a connection to her not wanting to remember the things she has heard said about me? Now it's just my little sister and me, and I'm protective of her. I don't want her to be near any spotlight or have to care for my mother alone. I want her to live out of the spectacle of my life. I want her to live her life free and clear. I help as much as I can, but I worry. She makes poor choices in men."

A police boat cruised by, causing a slow roll of the ferry from side to side.

"Lord, don't let me get seasick," Velvet said. "I hope this ginger ale helps."

"You'll be fine. If my big Texas ass can withstand it, you can, too," Lois Mae said, as the women laughed a bit.

"Nah, girl, I'm not talking about the waves; I'm talking about poor choices in men," Velvet explained. "You look up women who make poor choices in men on Google, and my picture pops up in record time. Even the slowest computer becomes fast, scrolling for pages with only my face and big ass showing."

All the women laughed so loud, people all turned their heads as they were heading in.

Meeah went and stood by Gabrielle, but spoke to the wind blowing in her face. "Each one of us has seen hurt, pain, and the depth of depression from things that took us down. So today— days like this—are special, and not to be taken lightly by any of us." Meeah reached down and touched cheeks with Gabrielle. "Life is never what it seems. I think, to a certain degree, we all have false faces to help us get through life. Not that we are living a lie, but… you know. At times, we smile and put on our best face saying life is good. If your heart is hurting, or if you're tired and confused over the way things are, these are times like now, when you let it all go and feel this breeze lift trouble away for as long as it blows."

"Girl, you over here preaching to the choir," Vanessa said. "Somebody say amen."

Velvet had actually lifted her finger to signal she had something to say. "I shouldn't speak for everyone, but all of us know death and birth, love and other struggles, and the good life. Girl, you better make life the best it can be. Gabrielle, your sister will be all right. She's got you to look up to. And I know it took me a minute to get it right. I see myself in the mirror physically and spiritually, and think sometimes, life has passed me by. I'm not hot and sexy as I was at twenty-five. My butt is still round, but now it's around the bend. And, ah, ah, I'm only forty-two and—"

Lois Mae cut Velvet off. "Skillet, you're going to hell for lying, your around-the-bend-ass is forty-eight, the same as I am. There are no men near us; you can tell the truth."

Velvet almost spit her soda on her coat. "Okay, you don't have to tell the fish in the water. There might be one of them bald eagles flying by who might squawk to a potential man."

The ladies were laughing as Lois Mae teased her best friend. They had a long history, even at one time sharing the same man. They had worked through tough friendship times. "Convoluted, silly girl...please. There is a big difference between a bald eagle pooping on your head and a Seahawks football player pooping on your life. I'm talking about men who are most likely twenty-plus years younger than you are. Those boys are not getting down with your cougar attack when a herd of young, cheerleading kitty kat and potential baby mamas are lined up. You can look, but keep your old long-in-the-tooth cougar butt out of the fresh, kitty kat litter box."

The laughter might have made it to land from the middle of the lake. The long version of Isaac Hayes' "Joy" had Gabrielle and the other ladies' heads bobbing and feet tapping. She stood straight as a photographer came by. The ladies lined the rail and took many photos before they headed inside to enjoy the performances.

CHAPTER 12

Some Rivers Can't Be Damned

"**S**tepping to the microphone, Seattle's Queen of Spoken Word, Empress Oasis." Tylowe, the MC for the show, walked away from the stage. A tall woman with regal, old style afro puffs walked in front of the microphone and nodded to the bass player to start his groove. She captured all eyes because her breasts were at least a bra size H, and fully supported under a red, full-length evening grown.

The lights lowered, and candlelight on the tables reflected off of the glass and silver. Everyone in the room felt sexy. A large platter of seafood was on each table, filled with clams, shrimp, cod, and oysters settled over rice pilaf and hummus. It was all-you-could-eat at each table.

"Thank you for having me as your verbal aphrodisiac oasis as you enjoy your meal. Here is something to go with those oysters."

Come to Me
Let us prepare a blazing, scorching, hardening, liquefying meal of each other
Pre-heating…melting in grooves
Mr. Maestro, Ms. Virtuoso…arrangement in the front and rear
Cymbal ride my ass in rhythm
I come to hear and taste you 33 and 1/3 red vinyl perfect-circled-black-velvet-textured
fusion

Mixing me

Pound my soul and I whisper…my favorite things…in your ear

Slow cooking…defrosting dreams of body and soul in 4/4 time while
I'm on all fours

Dou making love around the center-island stage

A taste of gospel runs, I chant…stirred Afro-Blues, I moan…whispered
baritone

mood, I hear you groan and grunt

Smoky finish…flugelhorn ballad…boiling…simmering curving this
diva in the

positions you crave

Sweet cream…sweat drop flavoring…balladeer kisses the cook

I'm stirring and spooning

Keys of 88 ingredients turn our sheets in to erotic music of direction

You add a pinch of this and that, and slap my ass

I consume the mix and the remix

You lick my bowl

I turn the heat up

Make you watch the late show

I sniff and suck my finger that was in my bowl

You squeeze your utensil

Damn it's time to clean up before we go for any more sweets

But suck on this…to inspire me to turn my broiler on High and I cook
your meat to well

done and firm, but it feels so tender going in my mouth…

Empress Oasis ran her fingers over her nipples teasingly and
blew a kiss. Then she reached between her breasts and pulled out
a large strawberry. Her tongue reached out and licked it in a long
stroke before she bit deeply. Juice dripped off her lips and fell

between her breasts. The audience went wild with a roar. The evening went on with various jazz vocalists and spoken word with erotic themes.

Dancing took place during the show intermission. Tylowe and Meeah went outside, and they both leaned on the rail. They didn't face each other. Many words needed to be said, all of which seemed to be anchored to the bottom of the lake. There was trouble in paradise. In their life, trouble was like, what is that smell, when you can't identify what, where, and how. They kept staring into the dark water, but a song temporarily purified and clarified their hearts, through their ears. "Make It Like It Was" by Regina Belle, sung in to their problems.

They turned toward each other with almost smiles. Eyes met.

"Baby." Tylowe leaned in and kissed Meeah's cheek.

"Baby," she said back to him, and leaned in and kissed his bottom lip. "Please tell me your thoughts.

"A relationship like ours—all these years, I couldn't have had God do any better. I'm blessed, but…but there is something different between us, and it is almost impossible to know what it is."

"Almost?"

"Tylowe, I want you to know I acknowledge whatever we are experiencing. It's no fun for either of us." Tears rolled slowly down her cheeks and dried by the time they reached her chin from the wind blowing. She felt her facial skin tighten in the tracks of her tears. "It can't be just one thing, so tell me one thing at least before we go back inside soon."

The couple stared again into the dark water. Tylowe and Meeah might as well have been wandering at sea in a raft with no wind or oars. Thoughts might be tied to an anchor dragging on the bottom of the lake and dredging mud with no substance.

"Are you still in love with me?"

"Yes, Meeah, I am still in love with you, but I'm not your shining black knight anymore."

"Why would you say that?"

"For the very reason you would ask me why. Meeah, you poured praise of me as the man who made your life worth living. You stopped telling me things that made me feel I was that man, some time ago."

"I stopped?"

"Yeah, you did."

"Damn."

"Damn, what?"

She closed her eyes and bowed her head. "Tylowe, nothing has changed in how I feel about you. But…could it be we are taking each other for granted? I, too, feel I'm not the queen you worshipped. What is happening to us? We don't fight; we make love almost all the time. You still look as good as the day I first set eyes on you."

"Hey, baby, you are more beautiful now that you're not so skinny." He lifted her chin and smiles met their sightline.

"I was never skinny. I see we can still joke and laugh with and at each other, so what's wrong?"

"I don't have the answer, but I want it to be like it was."

"Tylowe, you are my prince, and I look at us after all these years and how happy we used to be. And we have been happy up until… I don't know. All I can do is live in the memory of when I used to make you happy."

"Meeah, I do the same, I wake up with how we used to get up and live, and go back to bed as one. We are not those same lovers we used to be. But, we have to go inside now."

"Are we fading away…away from each other?"

Tylowe tilted his head to the side and pressed his lips tight, wishing she had not asked that question. Their eyes met, but had no focus. He put his hand in the middle of her back and guided her back inside for the second half of the show.

Once inside the doors, they kissed—an automatic reflex, with not one ounce of passion. Meeah's body seemed to deflate. She wanted to go back outside and crawl over the rail and hope a lifeboat was waiting. She went to the ladies' room, and he went to the stage.

Another detached moment of incompleteness swooped down like a Bald Eagle feeding on something no human wanted. Snow melted on mountains many miles away, flooding rivers into empty coldness in Lake Washington. Tylowe's soul walked back into a warm room, but with frozen thoughts attached, and they weighed down his soul as if a snow-packed mountain had avalanched on him.

Lost in their direction, it felt like cold-water contractions in their relationship. Of course, many times words spoken are often reflexes of not knowing what to say, leading to what you actually meant to say and how you honestly feel. Once words enter into someone's ears, they can't be pulled back. When the "send" button is hit, the email is then read and received. For sure, the text will hardly cover what the heart wants someone to know. Meeah and Tylowe had been trying to reach each other, and nothing seemed to find its way home. They tried to use memories of better days, and let them transcend in to feelings that would save their connection.

Manipulating the past in to feelings of "We are okay" had fallen overboard. Their marriage—the spark—was still desired, but could they renew or rekindle it? Images alone of what used to be could not fill their consciousness without knowing what the problems were. Where is the love?

The show continued with more hot soul music. The Seattle Phenomenal Queens, Lady A, Madam Howell, and crème de la crème Bascom, brought the house down with down-home R&B, and they did a set of music before a comedian took the stage for a short while. After he had people laughing and enjoying their drinks and refills, the co-host, Permanency, reminded the audience that the affair was for a worthy cause to help local youth and, to please help in any way they could with either time or donations.

Then, she introduced a few VIPs in the audience. Several others were introduced before Gabrielle Brandywine. To her surprise, she received a welcoming response, and she stood and waved. Despite her politics, women seemed to understand she was an achieved black woman first, and her job couldn't have been un-problematic, whatever her political affiliation was. It did help that she was widely known for her fashion sense in clothing and hair. Gabrielle had been on the front cover of many magazines.

Gabrielle attended a black church while in Washington, D.C. and whenever asked in non-political interviews, she spoke of black music, books, culture, and other arts and entertainment. Her life, to many African Americans, was a paradox.

She'd had one rumored romance with a retired Black Hall of Fame NBA player prior to meeting Psalms, but that was all every-one ever knew of her intimate, personal life.

After the long ovation for Gabrielle, the co-host invited Psalms Black to the stage to play stand-up bass, and Mintfurd Big Boy to the microphone.

Both men looked to be able to knock Roman temple columns down like Hercules. Mintfurd seemed to make the stage shrink. Psalms played a few bass runs to get the groove going. Gabrielle smiled knowing those were the same expressions he made when he was in the throes of making love to her. When he was about to get off, he would make intense, almost painful, expressions that were so sexy to her. Then as she always did, her eyes went to his fingers, and she became wet again.

Mintfurd opened his lips, and despite his massive size, his handsome face expelled words in a rich tone. Women in the crowd sighed and lost breaths. His hands moved while he recited his spoken word as if he were dancing, or holding, a woman.

Ode to Your Sweet Ass
Can't mask that scent
Please baby gurl, don't powder it, don't perfume it
Like a gold miner, I dig down into your cave and come out dirty, but satisfied
Both you and me
Can't dam your river
But I fill every hole that's open and it's still seeping wetness out of control
Smellin' it
Filthy but clean
Pheromone city
Erotic country
Slippin' into your darkness
Open to freak interpretation
Your hips speaking volumes
Slammin'
On my face
Dance baby dance
Spanking and snapping to the beat
Curlin' your toes

My tongue is putting it down in your groove
My tongue is polishing your crown jewel
Breasts sweating
Beast-like movements
Grunts
Uncontrolled
On time
Release the hounds
My tongue wallows in it
Side to side, and then, back to in and out
Tongue strokin'
Tight in between
Slide in where I fit in
I sit you down on mountain
Bootsy sings, "Stretchin' Out"
Damn...do you smell it?
It's funky in here
Play that funky music on my face
Do me, with your funky ass
Backing it up
Pounding forward
Breaking glass
You shout, "$#!+"
I say, "Take it, with all your sweet pretty little @$$"
I grab hair, pulling in the reins
Not slowing down, just controlling the action
Love your funky stuff
Love the feeling building up
I keep filling you up
You stay bent over taking it all

You feel me cummin' all the way through you
And it smells funky sweet in here
I go to sleep with my nose resting in that scent that can't be masked

Mintfurd stepped back from the microphone and bowed his head. Psalms changed the groove on the bass to a slow-jam pace as the crowd clapped and snapped fingers.

The single ladies, Velvet and Darcelle, sat at a table next to their married or coupled friends. The tables were almost connected, so Gabrielle and Darcelle were next to each other. The two had quickly connected, both being lawyers and with political backgrounds. Velvet and Gabrielle noticed Darcelle sat stone faced, like she was transfixed by a magic potion.

Little Darcelle, all five feet and stout, 130 pounds of her, got lost in Mintfurd's voice. His poem and how intensely erotic it was, and the power she felt from the visual of a man ten times her size seized her complete consciousness.

Maybe her own physical size had kept her from looking at men who tipped the scales at 200-pounds plus. Mintfurd clearly tipped the scales at well over, but something about him and his persona turned her insides into a whirlpool.

Gabrielle looked behind Darcelle's head as did Velvet, and they connected in thought, smiling at each other and nodding. Velvet knew Darcelle needed some mental separation from what had been happening in her life, yet had doubts those two could have a meeting of the minds.

Mintfurd and Velvet were close enough for her to know Mintfurd had a freakish nature, and was most likely the last thing Darcelle needed to encounter.

Mintfurd didn't know what a relationship was; he had no experience in love. If he'd had any, it had been once upon a time before he'd become such a big boy, and that was a long time ago. His life was sex with prostitutes; he had shared that with Velvet. The thought of Darcelle moving from bad to bad made Velvet shake her head at the thought.

Lights on the stage and candles on the tables slowly moved side to side as if a wave must have hit the ferry. The room became quiet, and Mintfurd moved close to the microphone again. He recited another poem after Psalms had finished a bass solo and started walking his bass notes up and down.

Survived
Deep cuts
Burns of all degrees
Don't care
I need love
All of the past…made me come to my knees
I lay spread out in pain
Don't care
I give my faith to love again
I kneel in grace
Giving another chance
To love again
I will
I'll give my all
I'll climb up yesterday's ladder
From which I fell
To be loved again
Only thing I die for is love
Tears have left traces like growth rings of an old tree toppled over, but
I spring anew with the scent of tenderness again

I have drowned in pools of hurt feelings, I couldn't make it to shore
But with love I can synchronize swim up from darkness
My heart will walk on water if love is on banks of reality
Before foolishness pushed my heart in front of train wrecks waiting to
happen
Why would it be any different again?
You, you, you, my love
I give in to you for hope and faith
Pain from emotional bullets and mean-spirited knifes, and modes of
failed operations
I know the pain
But I live to stand before you
Even though my heart flatlined before
But then you, you, you, my love
Like an injection of love serum
I'm love ever ready
Again, I'm released from room A to Z
I walk out into the sunshine
On the curb in front of Loveland Infirmary of Hope
I wait for a ride to go give my love again
To you, you, you, my love
I survived...for you.

The recital was so emotionally performed, some women had tears on their faces, and almost all stood and applauded. His voice remained and echoed in Darcelle. She had not clapped or said one word. Frozen in place, she looked, but she'd heard it all.

Even at his massive size, Mintford moved with the grace of a man about to tango across the room. Many women had crushes on his voice and pretty-handsome face by the time he exited the stage, but Mintfurd's size was still too much for all, except for Darcelle.

With the entertainment over, dancing took place, and a Gerald Alston song played, "Take Me Where You Want To." It went along nicely with the romantic piece Mintfurd had done.

Velvet had a big smile on her face while playing an inner porno movie in her head. She was watching Darcelle and Mintfurd having sex in her mind with Darcelle squatting down. She could see Darcelle riding Mintfurd's tongue, and it going into the small woman. She could imagine what else the two could do. Velvet's lips pursed tight in a sinister smile with the thought, *Some rivers can't be damned.*

The evening ended with more dancing as the ferry returned to the dock.

CHAPTER 13

Voyage to Atlantis

Psalms made one more inspection of the boat, making sure everyone had vacated. The sound system was still on and Jimi Hendrix's "All Along the Watchtower" had Psalms walking to the beat. He double-checked from the engine room and helm. For what he planned, Psalms needed the boat to be secured, and no intrusions potentially causing an interruption. The security system guarded the boat against anyone coming aboard after docking, but maybe lovers had hidden away seeking adventure. It had happened before. Sometimes people had too much to drink, and passed out or hid away to have some private fun.

There was an incident on the ferry during the event. A husband and his wife on the lower deck got in a shouting match. The man grabbed his wife's face and cupped her cheeks tightly, trying to hush her. The security team broke it up and brought the husband and wife to a room away from spectators. Psalms came to the room along with Mintfurd.

Psalms stared at the man, but his eyes scanned the woman differently because of tell-tale signs of something more. He rolled his lips and spoke. "You were invited to be with classy people and enjoy all that we have, the food, drink, and music, and you act a fool?"

The husband tried to sound hard. "Hey, fuck you, man! And let me and my woman out of this room and off your fucking boat!"

Psalms moved quickly in the direction of the man, and every-body stepped back in fear, except for Mintfurd Big Boy, and Zelda. Zelda was a tough girl, training to watch how Psalms and Mint-furd operated. Psalms didn't touch the man, but instead he slowly reached for the wife's arm, and slid up the long sleeve of her sweater. She held her breath out of fear. Her light, tea-colored arms had black-coffee and plum-colored bruises. "Don't move," he said. "I'm going to look—"

"Hey, get your hands off my woman! Who in the fuck do you think you are?" The husband stood maybe an inch taller than Psalms, but seemed smaller in stature. His voice was crumbling bravado as Psalms' face grew tight and his eyes narrowed.

Psalms ignored the man, more pissed that someone had vouched for him to be on the boat. He would check that person later. Psalms spoke to the wife again. "Don't move. I'm going to look at your neck."

Her eyes blinked as he pulled her turtleneck sweater down to her collarbone. The same colored bruises were on her lower neck. A melting iceberg of tears was dissolving her makeup. One could see, at one time and not that long ago, she had a black eye. An extremely pretty woman in her forties was aging fast from stress and abuse.

Psalms nodded to Mintfurd, and he ushered the woman out of the room, and the other security officer and woman left Psalms alone with the husband.

The former Navy SEAL and ex-Secret Service agent went to work on the wife-beating husband. Unlike the husband's crudeness in inflicting pain on his wife, Psalms left no marks, and the man wasn't allowed to make any sounds.

When done, Psalms opened the door, and Mintfurd went to the

wife sitting across the way with the female security officer, and they brought her back into the room. The woman saw her husband crying like a child who had received a whooping. He was in immense pain as he whimpered.

"Ma'am." Psalms waited for the woman to look up at him and connect eye to eye. "Listen to me; it's for your own good. This lady here is going to ask you some questions. Please answer all of them. Do you have children with this man?"

The woman shook her head, then said, "I have children, but he is their stepfather. My children, a boy and girl, are ten and eleven. We've been married for eight years…the beatings are getting worse." She moaned as if she had a sour stomach and needed to have a bowel movement.

"You're getting a divorce, and he is going to pay you a reasonable amount of child support, and you, ma'am, will not see this man for any reason whatsoever. It's over. He's not coming home with you. He understands. Do you understand?"

She nodded her head.

"I'll have a lawyer contact you on Monday." Psalms thought this would be one way for Darcelle to return a favor since he was going to help her with her ex-husband problem.

"You will not see this man ever! You will get counseling for you and your children; the lawyer will help you with that, too."

Two hours later, Psalms walked through the empty ferry and either dimmed or turned off all the lights above the water line. He turned on the underwater lights on the open water side of the ferry. Streaks of red, yellow, and bright blue beamed through the water twenty meters away from the boat. With everything secure, he walked into the stateroom. Designed to look like a luxurious hotel's open-floor planning room, it had every amenity.

Music filled the room; the group Cameo's jam "Candy" blasted through the stereo. Gabrielle danced out of the bathroom; she had on a diving wetsuit, and was fixing her hair to go under a swim cap. She swung her rather big behind in a sexy, funky motion. Her curvaceous body drew Psalms' eye, and he bopped his head to the music and her grooving. She danced for him, inciting his blood to flow. He wanted to tear the wetsuit off her body—quickly.

Under the wetsuit, her nipples protruded. He walked over to her, and squatted just far enough as she unzipped the suit, giving him access to her breasts. He placed his lips on her nipples and sucked hard. She combed her fingers through his cropped, wavy hair. He stepped back and licked his lips. She ran her fingers over his thick, wide lips, and leaned in and kissed, in slow motion, the wine-stain birthmark under his left eye. They both stepped back, and their stares ventured into imagining their bodies pounding each other. She loved the way he looked at her as if he were about to take her down to the floor and sex her up. Gabrielle wanted no foreplay, just the forced hardness of his thickness slowly, ever so slowly, inside her wetness. His eyes mesmerized her as he gazed. She wanted his hardness to pin her down and send slight aching pain with pleasure between her thick thighs. He wouldn't hurt her unless she wanted him to, but the ardent look he gave her made her wet. The diving wetsuit was to keep water out, but it also kept moisture in. Her wetness made a sweet mess inside the suit.

Psalms slowly dropped his pants, and teased her eyes by turning to the side and ripping off his boxers.

He laughed softly. "It's just underwear."

"Hey, baby, coming off your ass, they're not just underwear, honey.

How about curtains to doors number one, two, and three?" She sucked her bottom lip and smiled.

Psalms changed in to a wetsuit. They were going for a midnight swim at 2 a.m. The Lake Washington water was cool, but not unbearable if wearing a wetsuit.

Nighttime swimming was something the two of them had done even before they had left the government. Psalms and Gabrielle had swum in parts of the Rhine River in Switzerland and France, and in the waters off the shores of Tahiti, and the clear, blue waters of the southern Caribbean near St. Lucia. Both were avid swimmers. He grew up swimming in Northwest waters, and she swimming off the shores of Galveston, Texas, and sometimes in the dangerous bayous. She had no fear of the water.

The two of them had swum together in the Red Sea, the Nile River, and the Panama Canal. While backpacking in the Grand Canyon, they had swum against the current. They had often made love in the water, on top and under, and mostly at night.

It was going to be one of those nights. Psalms had waited to make sure that Gabrielle didn't have too much to drink. She had a tendency to drink too much even though she never appeared drunk; she simply sipped all day, on most days.

From her days of climbing the political ladder, and as the Secretary of State, she often had to drink with the good ol' boys. It was not something that she had done prior to her college days, but it had become a habit. She enjoyed taking the edge off after making decisions.

She and Psalms had a few talks about it, but he never forced her to quit or told her he wanted her to. He wanted her to question herself about her behavior. He knew people didn't quit for others. People stopped a certain behavior when they were ready or when a certain event in their life forced them to. He also thought it was her way of dealing with the stress of the decisions that she had made and the outcomes of her past work.

"Assessments and conclusions, leading to declarations to do what had to be done and then awaiting the results of the end game, only the game never ends," she'd said on the Sunday talk show circuit, along with, "I understand my dealings with issues and the decisions of any administration, is people lose and have lost their lives. But, their sacrifice is, was, and will always be, for the greater good of our country."

Psalms imagined how Gabrielle grappled with the thought of whether or not she did the right thing. For the most part, he had left her alone when it came to her drinking. The woman had been the youngest Secretary of State of the United States and a woman— a black woman. How she chose to release tension, he felt, wasn't his call.

The two of them made it to the deep water side of the docked ferry. With large swim fins on, they made it down the ladder into the water. Their wetsuits help to insulate them from the chilled lake water, and they had headlight bands on their heads, water goggles, and snorkels to assist their night swim.

They swam about twenty meters from the boat and dove under the water. Underneath, their bodies met and they held tight, squeezing to the point the wetsuits squeaked even under the water. While under, they kissed with the last of their breath while tussling like spawning fish swimming upstream. Their hands roamed as their tongues invaded each other's mouths while holding their breath in the dark. It was a sensation that made them boil in the cool water.

Surrounded by wetness and darkness, heads popped out of the water, gasping for breath. They panted as their large swim fins made it easy to stay afloat. Psalms reached for the waistband of Gabrielle's wetsuit and found the area that had a custom-made opening. He could open the crotch area of her wetsuit. The cold water concentrated blood in her already thick pussy lips, making them swell.

Hovering and kissing passionately in the middle of the dark water, twenty meters from the boat at 2 a.m., the lovers played underwater in the darkness. Lights from the shore and stars above put them on a stage that no one could see, but they were making love for everything underneath them.

His thick fingers found her inner wetness; it was hot in the middle of the cold water. His finger pushed past her full pussy lips. He felt her contract as if sucking on his finger. He started sliding his finger in and out of her. She dipped her head underneath the water, but he could hear her humming, groaning. Bubbles floated up as his finger firmly pushed inside her. Psalms' finger stroked in and out of her hot wetness. He dragged his finger up to her clit; she liked it when his finger flicked back and forth.

Her head popped out of the water as she gasped for air. She liked that feeling of running out of air and knowing she was safe with Psalms, and feeling the comfort of his body pressed against hers. They drifted closer to the boat and the underwater lights started to highlight them. Their shiny wetsuits, leather-smooth, reflected the changing colors of the boat's underwater lights. Their swim fins, flipping smoothly under the water, made the water around them pretty and kept them afloat.

As they kissed above the water, he took his other hand and slid his finger down her backside and down between the crease of her ass. Psalms stopped over the opening of her ass. The tip of his finger pushed inside, and while his middle finger slid inside her pussy, his thumb played with her clit. He began to work her into a frenzy underneath the water. Gabrielle made loud, senseless sounds. She sank back beneath the water. As he had many times before, Psalms held her body so she could not come up for air unless he let her. His fingers worked and worked in and out of her ass, her pussy, and on her clit all in rhythm, massaging, caressing around and around until bubbles floated up, and her body trembled and jerked. Psalms pulled her up, and she sucked in a massive gulp of air. She laid her head on his shoulder, trembling from the lasting aftershock from coming so hard, having an orgasm while not being able to breathe. She loved that erotic-asphyxiation feeling of running out of air while having an orgasm. Often she begged for his hands to hold her throat closed, not to the point of hurting, but just so the carotid arteries of her neck would aid in her pleasure. With strangulation or the sudden loss of oxygen to the brain, the buildup of carbon dioxide increased the feelings of overexcitement, lightheadedness, and erotic pleasure, heightening orgasmic sensations. She trusted him, knowing Psalms understood the limit, and he could revive her; it helped to get her off into intense spasms.

Still floating, he flipped his swimming fins a little harder and held her as she recovered. As she started to move, using her own fins to stay afloat, he opened the crotch area of his wetsuit. His dick was hard and straight up like a pointed periscope.

Gabrielle went back under the water and sucked his hardness. He lay his head back and felt her sucking him good, and the fact he couldn't see her added to the pleasure. She couldn't do it for long, but she wanted to give him pleasure and not leave her man hanging. They swam back to the boat. Alongside the boat, she held on to the ladder as he moved behind and over the top of her ass. Waving their swim fins slowly, they stayed near the surface. He slid his hard dick into her pussy from behind. If anybody was to see, one might have thought it was how porpoises had sex. Humping hard with the water messing up his cadence, his hardness pulled out of her pussy. The cold water surrounded his balls, and made them gather tightly. He slid back inside her heat, stroking her and causing a considerable amount of splashing as he thrust his hips. Gabrielle pushed her ass up and out of the water to help a deeper penetration.

They stopped for a moment as if they had many times, and they knew what to do. She climbed partly up the ladder attached to the boat, and he did, too, so he could keep humping her ass as his dick found her slippery hotness again. He gripped the ladder, held and yanked it to help him hump on her ass so hard she could have pulled the bolts out. He groaned and groaned as he humped her hard and fast. He threw his head back and thrust into her, and a hard release of his hot, inner fluid shot into her. She felt his thick warmness, and clamped her thighs tight, and held still while her pussy muscles manipulated him to give all he had to the last drop. He groaned as his hardness dissipated, and he purposely fell back into the water separating from her body. Gabrielle climbed aboard, and Psalms took a couple of backstrokes before joining her.

Back in the stateroom, a hot shower caressed them with warmth. They washed each other from head to toe and all in between; they steamed their way into bed and began to drift asleep.

The last thing they heard on the stereo was The Isley Brothers singing "Voyage to Atlantis."

CHAPTER 14

Intrusive Torment

"Stop, get your hands off me! Get your hands off me!" Evita felt two sets of hands manhandling her. First her feet were untied, then each ankle retied to the bed posts. Then, her hands were tied wide apart. A warm and wet towel was wiped over her body. The scent smelled like lilac soap. From her fingers, underarms and breasts, and from her torso on down to her private parts, her legs and feet, she felt someone was bird bathing her whole body.

Whomever had bathed her had taken a considerable amount of time washing around and in her vagina and anus. It had turned in to foreplay with someone using something oily, massaging into those same areas.

"Stop touching me. Get your hands off of me." Evita's plea went unanswered, and someone kept touching her. With the fact Evita had both male and female genitalia, the person or people enjoyed their intrusive assault on her. She heard the breathing become heavier on one side of her; on the other side, she heard a wet sound. She knew a woman was playing with her own pussy, and also knew a man was masturbating. Which one was touching her, she couldn't tell. She was fighting for her genitals not to react.

Evita began to assume that, after so much time had gone by and she had not heard any speaking voices, whomever it was, worried they might be identified. Such a thing gave her hope of surviving. She relaxed her body, and forbade her mind and soul to be tormented by the molesting violators assaulting her body. Maybe she was going to live to fight another day.

CHAPTER 15
Choices

Tylowe walked out of the airport and into the Vegas sun. It was warmer than Seattle's spring weather, but it wasn't the summer heat warming his bald head. Suzy Q pulled up to the curb in a classic convertible 1965 Jaguar. She had rented it from an exotic car company.

Her thin lips separated just enough for Tylowe to see her chewing a large wad of gum. She wore sunglasses, the same multifunctional kind as Psalms used, but Suzy Q's were extremely dark.

She adjusted her black-and-white polka-dot scarf. In her red, thin, cowboy-style blouse, she looked the part of a movie star from the 1930s. She didn't smile at Tylowe, but instead turned her head toward him and blew a big bubble with her gum until it popped. She was pretending to be a Hollywood starlet, picking up her co-star. He threw his bags in the backseat and eased into the old but preserved leather seat.

No music was playing, so immediately Tylowe reached for the updated radio controls. He scanned radio stations, but couldn't find his taste in music. So, he reached into one of his bags and pulled out his iPod and headphones.

They hit the highway with Suzy Q racing against the Vegas hotels in the backdrop. Tylowe enjoyed the view for a while before he tilted his head back against the headrest. From the moment the plane had landed, he had been on edge. He closed his eyes and let the sun paint red behind his eyelids in an attempt to calm his nerves.

Their destination was, hopefully, where the children might be staying. He and Suzy Q would broach that situation in the morning. With time on his hands, Tylowe planned to meet up with a few old college classmates who lived in Vegas.

Booked into The Flamingo for the night, Suzy Q had other plans; she was hitting the night scene to hang with people who rolled like her. She was looking forward to partying with the above-ground Vegas underground that played freely, with no opposition from anal attitudes. Suzy Q was about to get her party on with cross-dressers, gays, lesbians, transvestites, and even some straight folk who just wanted a wild party. She had already tapped her connections for the places to be.

In his hotel room, Tylowe reviewed all the information that Psalms had gathered again. He needed to get out of his room before he went over the plan, yet again, to rescue the kids and contemplate all the things that might go wrong.

The idea of things going wrong revolved in his heart and mind. As he dressed, he found himself staring in the mirror of his four-cornered room. He went to the window and eyed people walking, trying to get lost in the moment. *What if I get hurt or even die? Me trying to save Elliot's other children...The trauma Meeah and my daughters would experience... Life for them would change forever in ways that could tear their lives in to shredded emotions and beliefs. All we have built to become family could be destroyed.* It saddened his mood.

He went down to the sports bar and placed a bet on Floyd Mayweather's upcoming fight, and decided to walk the strip. It felt nice to have on a thin, knit short-sleeve shirt without needing a coat at night. The Vegas night lights and nightlife had taken over the strip.

Entertaining his visual senses, Tylowe smiled at how women loved to come to Vegas to sport attire they would never wear in their hometown. Stilettoes pinched toes and strained body parts, but they strolled the strip. It's sexy to see, but damn how does a woman walk from hotel to hotel? Tylowe laughed as women openly flirted with their lips pursing, smiling and eyes latching on to way-too-long stares. Most of them knew damn well it was only flirting, with no end game other than going home and claiming to have met a hot guy.

Tylowe recounted how hundreds of times, he had heard men claiming they had come to Vegas and other vacation spots and met the finest and the hottest women they had ever seen. In truth, most of these men were stuck in a fantasy land. If ever a man had come to Vegas and scored, it would be rare. If anything, men had paid for a piece of ass at a dude ranch, kissing women who had condom breath. Maybe a few men had paid a woman to come to their hotel room. Paying for it was not the same as saying you got a hook-up because you were such a hot guy with exceptional skills and good looks. Most men and women walking down the strip and hanging out in Vegas hotels, bars, and lounges had a ball because they spent a lot of money, and that qualified as a good time.

Tylowe viewed the women walking down the strip. Most were letting their hair down, relaxing from the constrictions of their daily life. He walked over to the nightclub where his old college mates told him they'd met at a Neo-Soul night going on with a live band.

The previous night, he had been on a ferry cruising Lake Washington with his beautiful wife, the two of them struggling to flow as one. He told her he was going to Vegas with Suzy Q for business. That had never been a problem, and it wasn't this time, either. Suzy Q protected Tylowe and Meeah as if they were her blood family.

On board the ferry in Seattle, the women had been pretty, friendly, and beautiful. Tylowe turned the corner into the lounge area of the Vegas nightclub and saw a packed house of women that most men would label as not just pretty, friendly, and beautiful, but fine.

These women had perfect makeup, perfect nails, perfect lip gloss and perfectly batting eyelashes. The women all fit in to perfectly stylish dresses covering varying body types, and were all wearing tall heels.

Tylowe smiled as if someone had told him a good joke, and reflected on a saying, "What happens in Vegas…" Of the women in the club, most were near his daughter's age, in their mid-twenties, and some were his friends' daughter's age, in their thirties. The other women in the club were forty-ish, and were trying to look as young as someone's daughter in how they dressed and flirted with the men in the lounge. Some pulled it off well, he had to admit.

Some of the men were in suits, and some wore XXXL shirts and pressed, creased oversized jeans. Tylowe felt a bit out of place wearing a knit shirt with a collar that fit his body and jeans that hugged his physique nicely.

Tylowe arrived a half hour earlier than his old classmates had scheduled to meet. He headed to an empty spot at the bar and ordered a beer. The band was playing an oldie, Grover Washington, Jr.'s "Mister Magic," with added funk to the groove.

A tap on his shoulder distracted him out of his musical moment. "Hello, Mr. Dandridge. Is that you, with that sprinter's behind still staring at me after all these years?"

At first he wasn't sure that someone was talking to him. The band was playing, people were talking, and drink glasses were clinking. The noise slowed his response. When he did turn around, he saw a face he had not seen since college. Erika Corwin had been a hurdler on the girls' track team and a former lover—or what people today refer to as a booty call. She and Tylowe were the same age, nearing fifty. True to the saying that black don't crack, Erika had not aged since maybe she had turned thirty. Tall and still looking athletic, the only thing different about Erika from back in the day was that where she once had a huge afro, now was a short, curly hairdo.

"Erika, how are you? It's been a long time."

"It's been way too long, and how have you been? 'It's Been A Long Time'—that's a song you and I used to listen to."

"Yeah, you're right. New Birth. We wore that record out—and a few other things."

"I know that's right." They both laughed.

Tylowe and Erika hesitated for a long second, not sure how to react to each other. When they did reach to hug, it almost felt like going back in time. Tylowe ingested her scent. Strangely, he remembered it from thirty-plus years ago. She kissed his cheek: it wasn't an aggressive kiss, but a soft, slightly seductive, long peck on the cheek.

"Oh boy, you still smell good, hmm."

They slept together on and off all through college, and old feelings elapsed as the two revisited moments in their memories. They shared a silence in a noisy lounge while their eyes connected, reminiscing on the sex they once had: under the bleachers behind the track, in their dorm rooms, everywhere.

The first time it had happened, they hardly knew each other. Flirting as freshmen do, they teased each other as they worked out each day, signifying to each other, "I'm too much for you, you don't want this." One day, Erika followed Tylowe behind the bleachers as he went to relieve himself. She watched from a distance, but he knew she was watching. He made little effort to hide as he was bold then, and full of ego. He tempted her by leaving his sweats down long after he had finished taking a leak. He swung his dick back and forth and his ass followed.

Erika approached him. She could see the tight jockstrap's bands curving around his firm sprinter's behind. Thirty years ago, she tapped him on his shoulder almost the same way as she had done moments ago.

That tap on his shoulder back then had led to kissing, and then to the both of them getting on the ground naked. It was the first time Tylowe had seen a woman with a huge bush of pubic hair. It was so thick that he couldn't see her vagina. It freaked him out at first until he felt his dick slide in and out. The added friction from her thick pubic hair almost made him cum too quickly. He had to control how crazy he went so that he didn't cum too fast.

The behind-the-bleacher adventure was a nice recollection. Tylowe's other memories were of the times he was in Erika's dorm room having sex. Slightly over six feet tall, Erika had long, firm legs. With her long legs spread wide over her bed, her toes could touch the floor on each side of the bed.

Tylowe visualized eating her pussy from behind. It was easy access because she could tilt her ass just so and expose her thick, full pussy lips through the thick pubic hair with her asshole in full view. His tongue would part her pussy and her lips would close around his tongue or dick. The jock and jockette would get in to athletic, nasty sex, often with Erika using her extreme flexibility. Tylowe remembered her taste, and the nastiness and feel. His dick thickened and his balls stirred while remembering. He spread his legs a little wider while he sat at the bar next to Erika. She noticed.

The memory intensified: going back in time, riding and pounding Erika's round, hard ass into the bed as her roommate would sit on her own bed naked, with legs spread, fingering herself as she watched the live porn show. Her roommate was a girl on the volleyball team whose sexuality was clouded, and wasn't having sex with guys regularly, if ever, but for sure she was horny.

Erika's roommate loved to watch and masturbated every time Tylowe's dick was in Erika's mouth or pussy. She loved to watch Erika on her knees while Tylowe stood above her letting his dick slide back and forth between Erika's lips.

The two lovers often acted as if the roommate wasn't there as Tylowe did the Standing 69. Tylowe made sure the roommate could watch his tongue extend and pump into Erika's pussy.

It had Tylowe cumming hard, watching the roommate slide her fingers inside her pussy and taking her other finger to rub her clit while panting, groaning, and body stirring.

A few times the roommate had sat on the headboard above Erika and Tylowe, so he could lick her pussy at the same time he was grinding away in Erika's thick bush from behind. He would pull his dick out just as he was cumming and shoot his thick creamy load on Erika's ass, and the roommate would cum and squirt simultaneously.

Tylowe had humped Erika's ass often because of the freaky options. He remembered those, as well as a few other athletic sexual conquests back in the day. He reflected on those moments and felt a thickness stirring in his pants. He needed a drink.

He ordered Erika a drink as she took a seat next to him. She spotted his wedding band.

"Married, huh? It's been a long time for you. The woman—I think her name was Sharon? I remember you were engaged when you wrote me a letter telling me I couldn't visit you in Seattle any-more." Erika laughed. "I always wondered was that a form letter that you sent out and you just changed the name of the recipient. Wow, when I think of it, that was maybe twenty-five years ago. You two have kids?"

Tylowe was wowed how people with no reason to retain certain information often would, even if it was old news.

People would catalog info such as a name or an event, and then recall it when a chance came around.

He looked at her ring finger; she wasn't wearing one. "Ah, she—Sharon and I didn't get married. It's one of those long, strange stories. You remember a dude—Elliot—that I hung out with?"

"Yes, I do remember him, a real piece of work he was. I remember the guys you hung out with. Ayman, the basketball player—any-one who's in sports knows him, after he won a national title. I remember Sterlin, and his girlfriend, the soon-to-be superstar singer who was screwing everybody, and he was pussy-whipped behind her ass. Oh, then there's Psalms. So fine, and so danger-ous-looking that both men and woman would stay out of his way. And oh yes, Elliot. He was always trying to get me to give him some even though he knew you and I were doing the do. I heard he's in prison. I remember your friends well."

"Nice play-by-play. And yes, Elliot was, and is, trouble. He came between me and my dream girl back then, and things went south." Tylowe didn't think of that past often, but it still stung at times and his voice showed it. He was almost mumbling.

"But, you do have another dream girl now?" Erika pursed her lip just a bit with a little gleam sparkling in her eyes.

"I have a wife. I did have a daughter by Sharon. My daughter is a grown woman now. My wife has a daughter I raised as my own, so that makes two kids."

"And this wife is your dream girl?" Erika's smile was dangerous to a man's eye. Tylowe looked away in the direction of the mirror behind the liquor shelves.

"Erika, it's been a long time. What's going on in your life, and what's going on that I would run in to you? 'Of all the gin joints in all the towns in all the world, she walks into mine.'"

"*Casablanca!* Humphrey Bogart and Ingrid Bergman. I have not forgotten when we dated, we watched late-night TV together after we were too damn sore to move after making love most of the night."

It was not Tylowe's intent to remind her of what were tender moments to her. She loved viewing old black-and-white movies with him after they'd had sex and made each other sore from the physicality.

"Erika, we didn't date or make love. We fucked!'

"Well, I guess you can put it that way." She laughed and put her hand gently on his forearm, and he turned to face the club action to help remove her hand.

"So, Erika, tell me what's going on in your life?"

"Well, I'm retired from the police department here in Vegas, and currently I'm a security analyst for Homeland Security. I'm divorced and have been for almost ten years. Tell every woman you know they should never marry a cop. I married one and know so painfully well. He was an ass who would put his pecker in a rattlesnake hole if he thought it might feel good. He was getting and taking pussy from almost every woman he pulled over. If not, he was screwing every woman who came to Vegas wanting to make it big here and soon found themselves lost and turned out."

Tylowe moved his tongue around his mouth wishing to be someplace else. He didn't want to hear a man or woman who was hurting or bitter about old affairs. He did not want to hear a woman scorned.

He had no interest in Erika, other than memories of freaky times. If he'd had some interest in her before, she'd turned him off with her verbal blast of his friends and recounting her ex-husband, for sure.

The one thing Tylowe understood about his present situation with Meeah was she couldn't be the total blame, and he was sure his wife thought the same of him.

"You know what I have found, Erika? Two people can both have high-ass shit piles of drama, but even if one's pile is smaller, any amount of shit is a contributing factor to the flushing down of a relationship."

Tylowe knew if he didn't cut her off quickly, she would soon be telling him how she did everything for her man, as in she cooked, cleaned, and gave him crazy sex whenever he wanted. The famous line was soon to come: "He wanted for nothing." He knew that the next man in Erika's life—and maybe there was one now—would be paying for the sins of another man.

"Tylowe, good men like you are too few and far between. Not like my ex. I did everything for him, took care of the house, and fucked him in every way he wanted and whenever. I was a good woman."

Tylowe gave her an "I'm sorry to hear that" smile. He did understand that she might have been a great woman. But years later, people have to move on, or continue to live hurting themselves and others.

"Erika, I'm sorry to hear the outcome of your marriage. But hey, how did you happen to come in here tonight? Is this the place to be?"

"You're meeting Jon Jon and Rufus, from back in the day, right? I talk to Jon Jon's wife often. She caught him playing around as you know you guys do, so he pays dearly to go anywhere. She doesn't let him go to the backyard if he doesn't ask or have a chaperone. So, anyway, she said that he was meeting a Tylowe here.

"'Tylowe?' I said. I could not pass up an opportunity to see my old beau. And here you are. I hope that don't trip you out. I'll move on out when your boys come, and let you guys have some male bonding time."

"Cool, it's good to see you, but I need to go outside and make a call to the wife. She is my dream girl, and I want to check in with her."

"Oh, if she got you locked up, she must be a dream come true."

"We make the best of what comes our way in life. Hey, Erika, it's nice to see you after all these years. You're still looking good. A retired cop, and now working for Homeland Security. That lets me know you are an achiever.

"Seeing old friends is a reminder of our yesteryears. Today, yesterday, and tomorrow come with questions that can only be answered when we pass in the night or when the sun comes up. We all have questions of when, where, and who. Sometimes even history cannot answer questions. There are factors, issues, and events that will always remain unknown. Time erodes some history, and we may never have a chance to cross paths before our time has come and gone, but here we are. It's been nice, and I know I don't have to assume about whatever happens."

"Well, Tylowe, that is something I also remember about you: you and your poetic mind. You were always stimulating with insightful stuff."

"We find along the way that when faced with our history, it can make our lives complete, or make us keep on keeping on."

Erika smiled, realizing she may have pushed Tylowe's button with her tirade about her ex-husband. Maybe it was speaking of

Jon Jon's personal business or her generic and stereotypical opinion of him. Maybe Tylowe had just had his fill. Maybe she didn't realize anything specific.

"Tylowe, it has been really nice seeing you. You do Facebook? Hit me up."

"My dealership has a Facebook page, All World Motorcycle. Look us up." Tylowe stood up, too, as she did. He gave her a long hug, as he knew she wanted one. As he passed by her, she brushed her finger over the curve of his ass. He ignored her and kept walking.

"Tylowe, Tylowe...wait." Exasperation permeated Erika's voice. She hustled up behind him and tapped him on his shoulder. He turned and faced her, knowing he had heard her calling out to him, but thought he could keep his back turned. His facial expression couldn't hide his displeasure.

"Tylowe, I know this may sound a bit too forward, but if I don't put it out there, I'll regret it. I have a beautiful home in the hills with a private outdoor hot tub. I can cook you anything you want. No strings attached. Tylowe, you can fly in and out of here all you want, and we have some good ol'-fashioned, nasty-ass sex the way we used to. I'm clean, and I can save all this just for you." Erika ran her hands down from her breasts on down to her hips, and slapped her ass lightly. "If you can get here and take care of this like maybe once a month...this can be all yours."

Tylowe smiled, enjoying Erika's comedy show. For many men this was the dream hook-up. Maybe, if he were single, he might entertain the proposition presented to him. Tylowe smiled even wider knowing it would never be with her, not after all she had said. Nobody needs a hook-up booty call filled with drama. Tylowe looked at her with his smile disappearing. *No man needs some pussy from a woman who thinks she is so good, it will make up for the drama that comes along with it. I'm sure no woman wants that from a man*

*swinging his dick as a badge, using that as the reason she'll put up with
his ignorant shit, either.*

"Erika, I'm flattered and insulted all in one. Look...I have a
huge, moral condom over my mind and heart. Although I'm far
from perfect, my mind does toe the line and remember the good
times, but—nah, I can't go there with you. Have a nice life, and I
mean that in the best way possible."

Tylowe turned and walked away. This time no finger brush against
his ass, and he heard no call of his name, and no tap on the shoulder.

Outside in the parking lot, Tylowe could see the corner where
Tupac Shakur was shot in 1996. *Life goes on if people choose for it to
move forward.* Tylowe thought on that while looking at the corner.
Tupac had been shot dead, and life still didn't stop.

A sprawling gas station had been built, and the bright lights of
hotels, cars, and traffic lights blinked and flashed like heartbeats
and life flashing before your eyes. The type of guns that killed a
young poet had killed thousands, maybe even tens of thousands of
young men and women since then, and life had kept on moving.

Tylowe went back to an earlier thought he'd had before leaving
his hotel. *What if I get hurt, or even die? The trauma Meeah and my
daughters would experience...Life for them would change forever in
ways...*

He pulled his phone out and scrolled to his wife's number; her
face appeared on the screen, and he looked at her for a while
before he pushed the "call" button. It went to voicemail, so he left
a message. "Hey, baby, I wanted to say goodnight, sleep tight. I'm
looking forward to seeing you in a day or two, and we'll talk until
there are no more heartbeats to sustain us."

Tylowe turned his phone to vibrate after he left his message for

Meeah. He stood in the night Vegas air. He looked to the corner where Tupac once lived and died, and thought of the choices in women he could have made. He moved away from the traffic noise and turned his Android phone's voice recorder on:

I read you, and you make me aware like no other
I see others, and they turn my head, but
I feel you, and don't even have to open my eyes to know where you are
In my crawlspace you keep the nightmares away
My care taker of dreams
You're always that dream
I feel your squeeze
Don't ever let go
You're always that kiss
Don't stop kissing me in to the high I live
You're my hip-bone connection
A love maker supreme
Your breast to my tongue
I am well nourished
You're in my sleep
Always my peace
I awake: you put me on a platform
I'm your pride
You show it beyond words
I beam because of your wanting my success
Your embrace, says it all.

Tylowe had just turned the recorder off and put his phone in his pocket when he heard, "Hey, Tylowe, what's going on, man? Sorry we're a bit late."

Rufus, his old college buddy, walked up and bear-hugged Tylowe. Then Jon Jon grabbed Tylowe as if he were going to wrestle him down to the ground.

"Yeah, man, sorry, man, we're late. My wife is a bit of a pain in the ass, over some mess from years ago. Hey, we're here now. Let's go have some beers and talk about old times. Oh, by the way, did that crazy-ass Erika Corwin try to corner you like a wild animal, and eat your leg off? For some reason, she goes through men like a slot machine eats money at the airport."

"Fellows, it's about the choices we make in life. Going to have that beer would be a great choice right now. It's great to see you guys."

Later on, while Jon Jon went to the men's room, Rufus revealed Jon Jon's one-night stand with Erika years ago, and he had brought home the crabs. He'd never told his wife whom he had slept with, so she didn't trust who he's out with. Erika Corwin had acted like a best friend to Jon Jon's wife before, and still did, long after she had stabbed her in the back.

Tylowe smiled in Jon Jon's direction when they made eye contact, thinking, *The choices we make can change our life forever; I made a good choice tonight.*

CHAPTER 16

In the Kitchen

His eyes couldn't focus on the clock's red LCD numbers. Sunlight, too much air-conditioning, and a full bladder tortured him.

A knock on the door disturbed Tylowe even more. To open the door or to pee first was not the choice his mind wanted to handle right out of his sleep.

"Hold on; I'll be there in a moment." Tylowe sat up, stood, and made his way to the bathroom. After he finished, he exited the bathroom with a hot towel on his face and sat on his bed, next to Suzie Q.

He didn't even think to ask how she'd gotten in. Between Psalms and Suzie, he knew not to waste his breath asking how this or how that.

In a major change from her eccentric outfit from yesterday, Suzie Q wore tan painter pants and a coat. She looked like the maintenance man with a carpenter's belt attached.

"Let's get going, mate."

"Q, it is five a.m.—what the hell?"

"We must eat, go over details, and make the drive."

"Q, I know your ass was out all night. Now you come dancing your ass in here like you on go-go juice."

"Strong coffee, mate. You were in by twelve-thirty, so you should be ready to go. Come on, mate: hit the shower and let's make a move."

"How do you know what time I came in? Never mind. Give me a half-hour; I'll meet you in the lobby."

When Tylowe walked out of the shower, he was dabbing his face with a towel. He saw protection, a gun on the bed. He felt his lungs expand, but his heart slowed instead of raced.

After breakfast at a buffet, Tylowe and Suzie Q both wondered how king crab and shrimp sold cheaper at a Las Vegas buffet than they could buy by the pound in Seattle, the capital of fresh seafood.

Instead of the classic Jag, Suzie Q's valet drove up from the parking garage with an Infiniti JX. The SUV seated seven, and the windows were fully blacked out. The license plates—federal-issued plates courtesy of the former Secretary of State. The plan was if they found the kids, they would drive back to Seattle: an eighteen-hour drive, covering 1,166 miles.

The location of the kids, hopefully, was in West Las Vegas. The historic neighborhood where black people once lived is where they were headed. It was the only place blacks could live during segregation, when they cleaned rooms, cooked in the kitchens, and dumped the ashtrays.

Suzie Q spoke to the GPS, and the screen displayed where they were and where they were going, northwest of the "Spaghetti Bowl" interchange of I-15 and U.S. 95, the Westside.

Tylowe had read up on the neighborhood, and found the area had its own version of the Las Vegas Strip, called the Black Strip. It was the home of the Moulin Rouge Casino and Hotel, the first integrated hotel casino in Las Vegas. Now the area had fallen into disrepair and turned into a deserted, ghost town ghetto.

They drove past the ruins of Moulin Rouge. Tylowe pictured Dorothy Dandridge and her perfect beauty stepping out of a pink Cadillac and walking under the marquee with her name above.

Dorothy Dandridge was his great-aunt whom he had never met. Tylowe imagined Harry Belafonte walking alongside the black starlet—the same starlet who couldn't stay in most hotels along the main strip. He remembered reading that a hotel had drained their swimming pool after the negro Dorothy had swum in their pool.

They found the address they had for the sister of former President Jean-Pierre Frêche of Martinique. They drove past the house. Although it was newer than most of the other houses, it was not out of place. Some yards had sparse grass, and others had well-kept rock gardens. Dogs on chains acted as doorbells. Cars with chrome wheels the size of marching drums sat parked on dirt driveways with the doors two feet off the ground, or higher.

Suzie Q and Tylowe both knew where guns were in the homes of hoods, but that none should be aimed at them. Bad boys and girls would flush or run with any drugs they might have, rather than want to shoot it out with a black-on-black SUV with tinted windows and federal government license plates. If one of those vehicles was around, many more couldn't be far away—that would be the train of thought running through this neighborhood. Twice they drove around the block, coming back through a different way twenty minutes later. They wanted to make it look as if they were leaving from wherever they might have been in the neighborhood. No way to know if danger was near. The purpose for being there was to save kids who might be in danger.

Seven o' clock in the morning, and no cars in the driveway at the address. They pulled in, exited the car quickly, and made it to the door, but not like they were criminals approaching. The door opened as Tylowe was about to knock.

Two young children, who appeared to be twelve years old or so, stood with backpacks. Their eyes showed shock as if they were about to leave for school. Their skin color reminded Tylowe of his stepdaughter's.

"Can we speak to your parent or parents?" Tylowe asked.

The kids looked at Suzie Q awkwardly; an unknown white woman standing on their porch made them step back in awe. A few whites lived around, but they didn't come to your door. As a matter of fact, no one came to your house unannounced.

An older woman with light-tannish skin came to the door, and stepped in front of the kids. "Who are you, and why are you at my door?" Her voice was tinged with a French accent. She sent the kids to the kitchen.

Tylowe spoke to her in a soft, caring voice giving a short and informative, but truthful story. They had no intention of coming in and misleading anyone as to why they were there. This extraction was not about taking the kids against their will or forcing anything on anyone. The factual information the woman knew to be true, and it disarmed her. She invited Tylowe and Suzie Q into her home.

"Do you mind if I have a glass of water, eh?" Suzie Q asked.

Suzie Q made a beeline for the kitchen and didn't wait for an answer.

"Please give the lady a glass of water," the woman told the kids who followed her into the kitchen.

The lady's name was Princess Rose, and she had no idea where her niece, Queen, had disappeared to. She had left the kids a year ago. When Queen had brought the kids, it was clear her niece was in some trouble. As far she understood, people wanted Queen and the kids dead. Princess Rose understood the kids were with her because so few knew their bloodline connection.

Suzie Q sat quietly with her head moving slowly from side to side, listening to the kids in the kitchen with her directional-listening sunglasses that she had left in the kitchen. Their conversation transmitted from the sunglasses to the Bluetooth in her ear. "Bring the kids in here," she said abruptly.

"Are you here to kill us?" Princess Rose asked.

"We don't kill kids or someone who could be my mother." A relaxed expression almost seemed to erase away years from Princess Rose's face. She lived under stress from taking care of the kids and all the uncertainty that might be affecting her health.

Tylowe was a bit amused at Princess Rose's French accent and Suzie Q's British-Canadian enunciation.

Princess Rose called the children into the room.

Suzie asked them to repeat what they were talking about in the kitchen. The kids looked amazed, trying to understand how she'd heard them talking from such a far distance.

"You said you were different from the other people. What do you mean?" Suzie asked.

The kids looked scared. Princess Rose said both kids were in the ninth grade. The boy, Cleophus, a handsome young man who looked nothing like Elliot, was the younger one, and had advanced to the same grade as his sister. In Celia, the young lady, Tylowe could see the same beauty as in his stepdaughter, Mia. There was no doubt of the biological relationship.

"Cleophus and Celia, I'm like an uncle; I'm like family. I'm not here to cause you any harm. I'm here to protect you."

Cleophus spoke assertively. "Do you know the whereabouts of our mother?"

"Son, I do not know, but I will try to find her for you and your sister." Tylowe nodded his head to the boy and girl. The children fidgeted nervously, and he felt for their young hearts.

"Tell us what you were talking about in the kitchen...please,"

Suzie Q asked, but then suddenly held up her finger to her lips. A few seconds went by. Suzie Q whispered with harsh direction, "Get on the floor and keep quiet—not one sound."

Sitting next to Princess Rose, Tylowe reached to help and to reassure her as she went down to the floor. The kids followed, seeing their great-aunt do as she was told.

"Be quiet; don't make a sound if you wanna live. Don't scream or shout, no matter what you think you hear, mates." Suzie was all about protection and she meant business.

Tylowe's worst fear didn't come true. He wasn't fearful; he was only about the business of being a warrior. He hoped that he and Suzie being there hadn't put the kids and the old lady in danger, but right now it was about doing what he had to do. Not one bead of sweat rolled down his head or back. He checked his leg holster to release the safety on a .38 snub-nose revolver. The gun was the protection Suzie Q had left for him on his bed, along with a bullet-proof vest.

Suzie Q ducked into the kitchen while Tylowe guarded the kids and Princess Rose. They moved, first behind a wall, then into the bathroom. He closed the door behind them, but first put his finger to his lips to remind them to be silent.

Following Suzie Q's lead, Tylowe crawled on all fours with no clue as to how deep of a situation he was in. He went to the curtains, but didn't move them: that would be a mistake, and signal of his whereabouts to anyone outside. He moved to the end of the curtain and peeked down the line of sight of the wall. He saw nothing with his limited view.

Pop-swoosh-pop-swoosh sounds, as if someone had stepped on bubble wrap, plus the sound of glass breaking, jarred Tylowe's heartbeat rhythm. Silence. Two minutes passed. Tylowe had his gun out and pointed up, but not aimed.

"Clear. But, wait five minutes. I'll be back," Tylowe heard Suzie Q say.

Four minutes later, she walked back into the living room with a gun with a long silencer attached to her carpenter's belt. A little blood dripped down her cheek.

"What's going on, Q?"

"Come in the kitchen so the kids and the old lady can't hear us."

Tylowe went to the bathroom door. "Everything is okay, just stay put a little longer. Don't come out yet. You're safe."

Tylowe met Suzie Q in the kitchen.

She was putting her sunglasses back on a sweaty face as she spoke about what had happened. "Earlier, when I asked the kids what they were talking about in the kitchen, I overheard the boy saying someone was watching them, and a man with a funny-sounding accent had approached them." Suzie Q stopped talking and took several deep breaths, and reached for a glass of water and gulped quickly.

"You okay?" Tylowe asked.

"Yeah, just a little winded. That man had asked them if their mother's name was Queen. He said no, as they'd been instructed by their great-aunt. The boy also spoke to the man in Spanish, which he had learned quickly in the time they had been here, and had many Spanish-speaking friends.

"Good thing I left my sunglasses in the kitchen, mate. First, for hearing the kids, and then for the footsteps I heard on the terrace after they came in the room with us." She took another deep breath, and reached for a paper towel and wiped her damp face before she continued to talk with shallow breathing. "We have a man down, a Russian, but he's not dead. The pain in his ass from two hollow points and me twisting off his nut sac probably makes him wish he was though. His wish is coming true with a few more heartbeats."

"You're bleeding on the other cheek. Don't let the kids see that."

She quickly searched the cabinets and found some honey. She rubbed it on her cut. "Yeah, I shot through the glass here at the door. A bit blew back. Eh, I'll be okay. I twisted a little info out of his nuts, but let's get the kids and the old lady out of here."

"What about the man you shot?"

"He had a gun drawn, and if you have a gun out, you know the rule. Shoot it, or don't have it out. He wasn't here as a Jehovah's Witness to give away pamphlets. Now put your gun back in your holster."

"We cannot have him die here on this property, Q."

"He won't. I'm trying to catch my breath from carrying him down the alley and putting him in a recycling bin, no blood trail, no tracks leading back here. We're all right, mate. I carry extra-large garbage bags for the trash." It dawned on Tylowe why Suzie Q wore workman's attire. She had added extra-large for the tools of her trade.

Suzie Q got the kids out to the SUV, and Tylowe helped Princess Rose gather clothes, important papers, and a few pictures. He told her he would have a moving company come clean out her house, and store her things safely until her home was secure to return to. They hit the highway.

CHAPTER 17

Raining Drawbacks and Complications

Psalms Black

The Sirius Satellite Radio DJ has a voice like Sammy Davis, Jr., talking in the hip-tones of the sixties. I'm tuned in to *The All Sade and Maxwell Monday Show*. The DJ recites poems or passages from movies, books, and famous quotes between songs.

"This is DJ Soul Space, and to all those within range of my soul satellite, let me get a little closer to your ear and tell you about a woman I think about hearing from the moment I wake. I have a poem for you, titled 'Sade.'"

SADE…I MISS YOU…IS IT A CRIME
From the Diamond Life *of your acoustical sensual aura*
You sing to me "Your Love Is King"
You have touched every part me of me as you are the queen of smooth groove,
You "Flow" like no other
I'm a slave to what you say, and how you say it, and how good it feels
Call it foolish maybe even a schoolboy crush…yet I am not ashamed of the jones in my bones for the waterfall of your velvet lips that sing to my heart
You and I, no Ordinary Love, I've missed you
All I do is play you while waiting for you
What is old is new
Ageless

I'm tireless of the need for you to whisper in my ear

I'm lost, alongside the road of hit repeat, hitchhiking the airwave of every smooth jazz station I can stop at and request you

The first note, the first song, the first look, and I became a lost boy looking for you

I've become a grown man…with a Sade fetish

"Stronger Than Pride," I have no pride, when it comes to the soul of the 30-plus years of our love affair

I'll never "Turn My Back On You"

I still love you

"I Cherish The Day"

I ran to buy you

I had to own you

I wanted to know you

In blue hues, an album cover said "Promise" I wore the grooves out

Pinned you to my wall

I don't recall ever seeing your kind of beauty…ever

You became my video queen

I stalked any image of you

Your long lines curved your body in mental visual frames

Lips wide enough engulf the Blue Nile

Ethiopian eyes

Egyptian stride

Nefertiti backside

Even the turn of your head held my attention

"Nothing Can Come Between Us"

With your sensual allure

Nigerian painted vocal chords

English words steeped deep in passionate soul

"Never As Good As The First Time"

I remember the first time

"Love Deluxe"—it was happy times

Making love to your sultry deliverance heightens the romance of "Hang On To Your Love"

I caught a plane to Toronto

I had to see you Sade

I wanted to be "By Your Side"

Stood in line in the rain for hours, imagining raindrops were kisses from you

The hell with upper deck, I paid three times the face value to be close to you

Three rows away from your femininity

I never closed my eyes

I'm sure our hearts kept the same beat

In a trance, I could hardly breathe as I lay "By Your Side" after we…yeah

You gave me the "Kiss Of Life" in a glance

Our eyes met…

I think…and that's all that matters

Smooth Operator *you were and I know you still are*

You stripped me clean of any thought of any others

I wanted to Lovers Rock *with you*

I had an innocent as deep as a "Cherry Pie" cooling and waiting for my finger to taste your sweetness

You danced, like no other had ever moved me before

Ahhhh, huh…you stepped down and out of your shoes

I wanted to eat the polish from your toes as you pranced

My fixation has never gone away

The times I have stepped through my door to an empty room, I had to play "Somebody Already Broke My Heart"

You make sad songs seem fine

I'm happy hearing you…period
I hear you sing
"It feels fine, so fine, I'm yours, you're mine, I want to share my life
with you"
Thoughts of you are pure "Paradise"
But baby don't go away
I've been waiting, as a "Soldier Of Love"
You give me the "Sweetest Taboo" I want you any way I can have you
I'll stand in line…underwater
Sade, I miss you
"Is It A Crime"

"As you heard, many Sade song titles as a part of the poem, and we'll be playing those songs in the coming hours, along with many Maxwell songs. It is said that Maxwell's music is the male version of Sade's. However their music touches you, sit back in your car or home on East Coast lunchtime, mid-morning in the middle lands, or West Coast rush hour and feel the groove from DJ Soul Space."

Between shifting gears on the freeway in what has to be one of the worst rush-hour cities in the U.S., I get word that the kids and their great-aunt, are safe. All five are on their way back here to Seattle. Q called and told me about some complications, but all is well…at least for now. Troubling news, though, the info she got out of the Russian. If they are so willing to come into a neighborhood where they can stand out… This is not over—far from it.

I get Gabrielle out of here on my plane back to Cali. I don't own a plane, but the economy of the last few years has rich folks leasing out their toys. Gabrielle will be back in a couple of days, and we are going to spend some time in nature, as we love to do. She loves being outdoors, but that is typically problematic for her when so many people recognize her and won't give her space, even in open spaces.

I have a fire to put out involving the old man who sleeps in the woods behind my condo and bungalow where Evita stays. He knows to go down to the corner store if he needs me. He is the watch-man for my watchdog that is kenneled in the back yard of the bungalow house. My dog knows him and accepts the old man living out back in the woods behind my place. The old man went to the corner store and had them contact me that there was a problem.

I call Evita, and she does not return my calls. It's not unusual. She does her own thing, and I just let that be. I'm not her husband or her man in the true sense. She is just someone I love dearly.

I keep tabs on her to a certain degree without trying to run her life. She can be troubled. Evita tried to commit...she tried to take her own life once. That was ten years ago, so I do worry about her to a point.

Her office phone message says she is out of the office for the week. Usually that means she's in Atlanta with her lover. Evita and I cleared the air about her choices. I know Evita swings both ways, and I don't care. I love the person she is to me, and all she means to me. I met her female lover, Esperanza. She's from Argentina, but lives in the heart of the Dirty South, in the Inman Park area of Atlanta. She's an actress who also produces B and independent movies.

Evita, Esperanza, and I have hung out, but Esperanza is possessive of Evita. All I can do is stand back if that's what Evita wants. There is something that excites her about being in those types of situa-tions. I have to wonder if I acted more possessive toward Evita, would we be complete lovers? Then I realize, I'm where I am, to be in her life as her protector when I need to be.

Something I don't understand is why Evita and Suzie Q act like a cat and dog that have to live under the same roof. They never fight or act rude to each other. They can sit in the same room or even sit close, but clearly they don't like each other.

I can advise Gabrielle on world affairs and spot an enemy out to do harm in most cases. I can do many things that the average person cannot, but I don't understand those two who are seemingly ready to bite, scratch, and claw. Q won't even talk to me about Evita. Evita says I'm tripping over nothing.

I assume Evita is in Atlanta, but she should have let me know she was going out of town. My dog is in her care because she wants it there at the bungalow.

I'm driving across the West Seattle Bridge, and it's raining as if I'm in a carwash. It hasn't rained this hard in a while. Cars and trucks leak oil and over time it dries, but let it rain like this and it brings the oil up on the road. These fools on the road are weaving and changing lanes with no regard. All of a sudden they are tailgating on slippery, oily roads. I'm glad to get off the bridge and just as I do, Velvet calls.

"What do you want?" I talk crazy to her all the time and she pays me no attention.

"Darcelle has a thing for Big Boy."

"You're talking about your friend who I'm helping out of her freaky circus sideshow, and the man, who if one of his arms waves in the air, it would knock her out?"

"You're talking loud and saying nothing. For a man as smart as you are, I respect you, but your jokes are ill-timed."

I hate being told off by a woman when I could have kept my mouth closed. Velvet, for all of her impressiveness and importance to my company, can be like a shark in a tank of bloody water. She wouldn't hold her tongue even if she put her own foot in her mouth and bit it off. Her mouth can chew anyone a new asshole. I let her rant and rave for the most part and stay calm until she calms down.

"Psalms, I'mma let you off the hook today, so be nice. Big Boy, he's a nice guy, and she needs a likeable guy. Even if it's not a love connection, Darcelle needs a gentleman to go out on a few dates with to help her see there are sweet guys in this world. And hey, maybe they'll hit it off."

"Are you expecting me to play matchmaker? Oh, hell no, and—hold on. I'm pulling into a coffee stand."

"Not that nasty one with the anorexic women serving coffee while wearing thongs with flat booty cheeks and bras with size-zero breasts?"

"Sounds as if you like their coffee to know all that. Now look who's not being nice. And I'm not at that place, so hold on."

"Are you at Espresso Africa?"

"Yeah, I am, and there is a line, so hey, let's finish this convo when I get to the office."

"Okay, but bring me a Café Bombón in a grande clear glass. I'll pay for the glass, and tell them I'll stir it—and don't spill it in your fancy sports car."

"Damn, what else can I do for you?"

"Darcelle and Mintfurd Big Boy."

"I'm not going to stop you from getting in the middle of some boy-girl shit, but asking me to be a part of that—oh, hell no."

"Hurry up with my Café Bombón, so we can talk about this."

"You got selective hearing. I pay your medical. Go to the doctor about that problem."

"Velvet? Velvet—"

She hung up on me.

I step into the office and give Velvet her extraordinarily expensive coffee. Hell, it doesn't even have a shot of 80 proof or anything. I let her know I'll be right back.

In the back yard of the bungalow, my dog is in lousy shape. She doesn't have water or food, and it looks like it's been days. I'm pissed! My sweet Doberman—I take her to the vet right away, and drop her off. I want her kenneled and watched for a day or two. I call Evita again. No answer.

Even though I have some expensive, classic stereo equipment and furniture in the house, it is her place to live and come and go as she pleases. I don't go in the house unless she invites me or I ask. I don't run her life, but I'm pissed. She is normal in her behavior almost every day, but then, she'll suddenly step off a cliff. She has definitely stepped off.

CHAPTER 18

Vulnerabilities

"Y ou think you want to live. There may not be an option."
The Voice chuckled. "A nasty little piece you are. A little
dick and a pussy…what kind of circus freak are you? You
have nice-sized chi-chis."

Evita felt a hand roam her breasts, and then a forceful hand
grabbed the back of her neck. In her defiance, she didn't flinch.
The hand forced her onto her stomach. The hand slapped her
behind hard, twice, then twice more with more stinging vigor.

"Ah yes, that feels good to really lay in to a piece of chocolate
ass. That excites me; I need to go fuck a little now, but not you,
my little, sweet, nasty girl. It's too bad I cannot do you, but then
again, I would never want your little dick to touch mine. Oh but,
your ass is perrr-fect." He spanked her again with what felt like a
belt.

She groaned but refused to scream. A few seconds later, the
sound of a belt buckle being refastened relieved her ears.

"Don't try to escape or you'll feel a lot more of that."

Evita recognized the voice from the night she was drugged and
kidnapped. This was the first time someone had spoken to her,
days after she'd been tied to a bed.

She still wasn't sure about his accent. She wasn't sure that first
night, either. She was guessing—guessing someone cared enough
to have not killed her yet.

"Has she been drinking fluids and eating?"

No one verbally responded to the voice.

"Good. Get her in the shower. She's starting to smell, and her pussy or dick—whatever that is—it looks unwashed after sex."

Because Evita had both male and female genitals, she had to wash often. She was the type of woman who seemed to stay wet, with or without any sexual arousal. Adding to the current problem, she had been sexually played with; her body had responded, although her mind did not appreciate the molestation.

Evita had been there before. Her father had a good old time playing with his little girl from early on in her life until the day she ran out of the rear of the house, naked and bleeding.

At sixteen, Daddy had been touching her for at least ten years. Some days he touched her as if she were a boy. Sometimes he fondled her as the girl she really was, but then came the day he entered inside her as a man, an ugly man. Her father thought she'd lie there after he finished his business with her. The moment he got up, he pulled up his pants and went to untie her mother. Father forced Mother to watch. When he stooped down to untie her mother's ankles, Evita jumped up and ran.

She ran out of her house buck naked and through the back door of her teenage friend, Psalms Black. Evita's father ran behind her, more worried he would be found out than wanting her to come back.

Once inside the basement of Psalms' house, all hell broke loose. Twenty seconds later, *Boom! Boom!* A gun ended the possibility of Evita's father molesting her ever again. Justice had been served; the judge and jury sentenced a man to die for his sins.

Psalms was not home at the time, but his grandfather and his twelve-gauge shotgun were. Grandfather dressed Evita and told her what to say when the police came. Psalms' grandfather was not fazed by Evita's nakedness, and of whatever he had seen in her genitals, he never said a word.

This was in the days before women were always examined by a doctor in a hospital. Psalms' grandfather's midnight lover at the time was a female doctor. He called her to his home, and everything was taken care of with the police and Evita's privacy long before Psalms came home from a school track meet.

Psalms wrestled with the fact that his grandfather had to kill a man because he had been protecting a friend who knew to run to Psalms for help. His grandfather helped him to understand that, as his grandfather, he would sleep just fine for doing what had to be done. He encouraged Psalms to be there for Evita all her life if he could; she would need him. Grandfather knew Evita was going to need someone she could rely on with what he knew about her sexual situation physically and emotionally. Grandfather decided he was not the one to tell Psalms that Evita was a hermaphrodite.

Evita's body shivered, not from being cold, but the cold feeling of knowing people had died when she had been in trouble.

"Keep her feet tied and neither one of you touch her. Make sure her hood cannot come off."

Evita smirked under the hood knowing now she could cause some form of a rift between her captors. She could blurt out now that she had already been touched, but she had to think. She had to figure out the best move, and when to make it.

There were two people who had been watching her and the voice belonged to their boss. A bit of inner relief made Evita take a deep breath. She would get a shower. Evita felt nasty having used the toilet several times, and her genitals had been played with, twice.

"Is something funny?" The Voice wanted to know why it appeared Evita was laughing under her hood. She coughed several times trying to change the Voice's train of thought.

Evita noticed the other two never spoke: a man and a woman. She heard the man's grunts and groans while he jacked off when he touched her. The woman's pussy scent gave her away. Her scent sprayed the air with female aroma whenever she played in her own pussy while touching Evita. She smelled of a woman with a bad diet who ate fast-foods and not much else.

The two had some apprehension about what they were doing. They had fear of being caught. The Voice had no fear. He was in control and with the tone of his speech, he verbalized that control. The other two were disposable. Evita assumed those two would flee rather than fight if put in a conflict.

The smell of fast-foods permeated the air. Evita heard a few steps and then the door closed. The Voice left, and she was alone with her thoughts and the knowledge that the two left behind to watch her were vulnerable.

Tied and hooded, Evita felt less vulnerable herself after hearing the Voice, yet a twinge of fear still weighed on her heavier than hope. She'd had a nervous tic ever since childhood, either to bite her nails to sharp points or grind them against each other to sharpen them. Evita was nervous.

CHAPTER 19

Mojo Melodies

P salms shifted gears, speeding up and passing other vehicles in the rain. Seattle's bipolar weather, with sunshine and rain at the same time, confused whatever season it's supposed to be. He was driving his classic 1962 Pontiac station wagon, a much different ride than his Mercedes Gullwing Coupe. Psalms had inherited his grandfather's classic. From the days when people ordered options such as a stick shift for any car they wanted, it also had a big, powerful engine. Psalms had it restored to look as if it had just come off of the showroom floor, and added some modern updates: nice wheels and tires on the slightly lowered body, tinted windows, cruise-control, air conditioning, and a high-end stereo.

Driving the classic 1962 Pontiac station wagon lightened stress, taking his mind back to childhood days of riding along with the man who'd raised him, his grandfather. He could drive the station wagon and feel as if he was riding along in the countryside of the Puget Sound inland and islands.

His grandfather, Leo, was a landscape engineer and surveyor. Highly sought after for his expertise during a time when a black man could be, and usually was, harassed for being in the outlying area where blacks didn't live and so few Negroes ever ventured, he was contracted by rich whites to design and tend to outdoor living spaces and golf courses in the 1950s and 1960s. His station wagon carried tools, a portable drafting-drawing table and surveying equipment, and always a dog.

As his grandfather had access to the best hunting and fishing in the state of Washington, Psalms learned to shoot firearms as a young child. As a young child, he was the only black entrant in marksman competitions and archery tournaments, and always the winner. The place Psalms loved the most was a sprawling piece of property on Orcas Island. There was a small replica of a castle there, with rolling hills and small ponds.

Psalms and his grandfather would stay in a small house adjacent to the castle. Almost every weekend, his grandfather tended to the many gardens and other parts of the land.

There was one thing Psalms never understood until much later in life—his grandfather seemed to have a love-and-hate relationship with the castle. After school on Fridays, Psalms and his grandfather would joyously drive an hour north of Seattle and ride across on a ferry to Orcas Island. Once there, they'd settle into the small house adjacent to the castle. They'd build a fire in the cobblestone fireplace and cook dinner over the warming blaze. In the morning, they'd go shooting, hunting, or fishing, and in the afternoon, Grandfather went to work on the property. On Sunday morning, Grandfather and Psalms would have a two-man church service, playing old-time gospel music, listening to Sam Cooke and The Soul Stirrers and Psalms' favorite, "Touch The Hem of His Garment." Even now, along with his old school soul music playlists, he listened to a playlist of Sam Cooke's gospel music.

The two would have a prayer service and Bible readings. After the two-man church, Grandfather worked until an hour before sunset, when they would catch the ferry back to the mainland and head home.

The people who lived in the house kept their distance, but there was the teenage girl who sometimes stared in the window. She tried to hide herself, but Psalms often looked out of the corner of his eye and she was there. Grandfather said she wanted to see what a black child looked like.

The classic station wagon had a 45-record player, the kind they installed in cars in 1962. Psalms did not want to remove it. He'd had Mintfurd use his computer-tech skills to redesign it in to a modern car sound system. Psalms switched the music to Marvin Gaye's *What's Going On* CD.

Psalms drove the station wagon now as if he was going to run every other vehicle off the road. The normally calming ride of the classic with good memories had little effect today. His dog was sick from eating things out of its normal diet in order to survive. The old man who slept on the hill had given the dog a sandwich to help her. A good deed, but the Miracle Whip on the bread was not good for the animal's stomach.

Psalms was in warrior mode. He could be mean. As a former Navy SEAL, he had to do things on foreign grounds that the government would never declassify. But he never did them out of anger. As a private security company, Psalms and Suzie Q had done things to a few people while representing clients. Again, never out of anger, but necessity.

Psalms had a steely control of his emotions when working. Today, the fact that Evita had left his dog unfed, and with no water for three or four days, had him burning rubber on wet roads. He understood he had to harness these emotions when they showed their ugly heads. He was right to be angry as he was now. Evita had neglected a responsibility she had chosen. Her actions had hurt his feelings and his dog.

Born in an angry situation...

Grandfather was a gentle, quiet man who had chosen to tell Psalms only few things about his birth father, and why he had never been in his life. As a young child, Psalms understood the subject was taboo. Grandfather had decided he wanted Psalms to only know so much.

He'd heard more than a few times that Psalms' dad was an angry man, who used his anger to hurt, seek revenge, and to cause destruction.

He knew his young, teenaged father had impregnated a girl, and that Grandfather and Grandmother had ended up with custody as his father was too young. Grandmother died while Psalms was still in diapers, so he had no memory of her, but Grandfather would tell Psalms he looked like her and he still had a part of her. Pictures showed that she had the same wine stain birthmark under her eye as Psalms. When Grandmother died, Psalms' young father, DaDa Q Black, had run away angry because he could not be with the girl, and his mother had died. DaDa Q became a rebel with a cause, using criminality as a tool that later got him killed.

Years later, Gabrielle used her connections in the government to find out the whole truth after Psalms' grandfather took the complete story to his grave. The information led Psalms to his birth mother and family and they paid Psalms to keep the truth hidden. They paid millions.

The music changed somewhat oddly in nature. An old Muddy Waters song, played by Jimi Hendrix, began to haunt the speakers.
"I got a black cat bone
I got a mojo too."
Psalms wanted to hear the song, but another car broke his concentration. The car next to him slightly veered into his lane. The driver's head was down—most likely texting. The asshole driver

also had a Starbucks coffee cup in hand on the top of the steering wheel—with a cigarette hanging out his mouth.

Psalms honked his horn. He had a setting that sounded like a police siren. The asshole driver was in the curb exit lane and drove his car onto the gravel at seventy miles per hour. Psalms was sure a tow-truck was the next call or text for the asshole driver. He did feel bad that maybe the man had spilled his hot coffee.

Psalms focused back on the song.

"On the seventh hour
On the seventh day
On the seventh month..."

Psalms looked to his left. He gazed at the location where the old Kingdome, the multipurpose domed stadium, used to be. All Seattle pro sports teams had played there at one time, but now the Kingdome was gone. They had blown it up in a Northwest Mardi Gras-type celebration. That was the day his grandfather died: March 26, 2003. A rainbow shone over the Puget Sound today where the Kingdome used to house sports battles.

The separate stadiums sat near the old site now. The Mariners baseball stadium and the Seahawks football stadium now sat in a place that stayed in Psalms' heart.

Some landmarks and some events in history mark a person's memorable moments, whether they're happy or sad, and they visualize or relive those moments.

It wasn't so much that it was the day of his grandfather's death that made him recall the date of the Kingdome explosion. It was other deaths that marked Psalms' soul. Grandfather had taken the life of a bad man, Evita's molesting daddy, on March 26, 1983.

When Psalms learned the complete story of his criminal father, whose real name was Cinque Black, he learned the man was killed along with several other people in a bank robbery on March 26, 1973.

When Psalms killed the man that had mutilated Evita's body, it was on March 26, 1993.

"I got a Black cat bone
I got a mojo too."

Psalms hit "replay" as he made it back and parked his station wagon. He went across the street to the beach and worked out an extra twenty minutes. He kicked sand in the sea and punched the air until it seemed the air asked for a break, and started pouring rain. He sweated more than the rain that touched him. His work-out clothes appeared to have just come out of the washing machine, thoroughly wet. When he walked in to the office, Velvet raised her voice, "Hell no, get your stinky, wet ass out of here."

"Why is it a woman wants a man to work up a sweat all over her if he's putting in work, but if a man comes around already sweaty you have a problem?"

"You of all people don't like people to ask questions when you know they already have the answer. So, don't be asking a stupid question. But if you don't know, Mr. Know-It-All-Any-Other-Time, a woman wants sexual sweat from alluring pheromones, but not that pure, salty smell you have in here reeking up my office.

"Now get out of here and take a shower so we can talk."

Psalms stared hard at Velvet, and she called his bluff.

"I'm not your problem. Your other woman is out of pocket, and hurt your dog. I hate that she left your dog unattended, but I don't care that you're mad at her, so don't be looking at me all crazy. Did you ever think it might be time to downgrade her to a business partner?"

Velvet was the only woman ever that spoke to Psalms as she did, and he loved that she did—but she could get away with it.

"Psalms, I know you care about her. You have explained from A to Z the history and all that has happened between you two. But as a woman in a man's world, I have seen the danger. I have been assaulted in many different ways, and I have acted out to get my fair share of attention for deflection or emotional support in all the wrong ways. I have grown through it all. She has not!"

"I'm going to take a shower."

"Hurry up, you stink."

CHAPTER 20

Humble Opinions

Psalms showered and made his way back to the office. The glass front office on the first floor had an enclosed glass office to the left of Velvet's work area. She could look over to her son, Squire, who was doing school work. Often Psalms took her son out for a jog along Alki Beach for exercise in the middle of the day. Sometimes Mintfurd Big Boy brought her son to the weight room in the building and it showed. The eight-year-old looked ready to play high school football.

When her son looked up from his book, he waved to Psalms who spoke in American Sign Language, "I'll be over in a while."

Squire signed back, "I want to box today."

Squire was not hearing-impaired, but it was an early tool of learning that Psalms shared with the young man. Psalms' grandmother was hearing-impaired and so his grandfather taught Psalms to sign, although he never really knew his grandmother.

Velvet broke up the conversation with her own sign language by pointing her finger and staring at her son who understood he had school work to do first. He signed, "Yes, Mother."

"Don't get my son hurt with all that macho stuff. I admire the warrior that you are, but I don't want my son thinking with his hands first and brains last."

"Is that what you think I do? I think you forget I have enough brains to sign your paycheck, and as Q would say, eh?"

"I sign my own paycheck and run this office; you just were simply smart enough to hire me." Velvet laughed.

"I was smart enough to hire Big Boy back there who teaches your son math and science. I was smart enough to have him design that soundproof glass office to do his school work, so he don't have to listen to his mother's smart ass talk all that mess…and I still sign your paycheck, you're just not smart enough to know, yet."

"PB, speaking of Mintfurd, we were going to—"

Psalms cut her off, hoping to escape the conversation. "I think your friend is nowhere near being able to handle another man right now, much less Big Boy."

Velvet had a power over Psalms; she could draw him in to a conversation beyond his control. She had been the only woman who could do that. He added her manipulating potency to one of the lines in a Prince song about some women were for certain things, and not all for sex.

"And you're a relationship expert how? Look who's calling the fish smelly, when you're a shark. You were over there on the beach less than an hour ago beating the hell out of the anger Evita made you feel. I love Gabrielle, as she is a good person. I see she makes you happy, but the girl can drink…she can put the booze away, and you know it, but you ignore it. You got issues too. Your choice in women is a tattle-tale on your choices in life." Velvet spoke while she multitasked—sending and returning emails and sending out billings.

From time to time, she scanned the Internet for news and hit up her Facebook page. Her eyes avoided Psalms as he sat across the room, staring at the back of her head. She only looked up to see the water and Seattle skyline and when a ferry crossed. Her voice, a cross of Marilyn Monroe and Alicia Keys, melted men, but with Psalms, it allowed her to be sarcastically forthright about how she thought and felt.

Psalms avoided the conversation about the women in his life. Evita, although better with age, still ran over him occasionally with her lifestyle, and although Gabrielle would walk on water for Psalms, he never asked her to slow down or quit her drinking. The woman had damn near ruled the world, and did it good. She was a woman with emotion and in need of love from a man. She made love to him as if she was paid millions to do so, with every possible sexual act, and loved it intensely. Maybe Psalms was oblivious, but the woman never embarrassed him, and her behavior toward him was loving, so what was he to do? He loved the woman.

"No one is ever ready for a relationship—they may say that shit—but the truth is in my humble opinion—"

"You, with a humble opinion?" Psalms laughed and almost spit up his coffee.

"Yeah, in my humble opinion, a relationship develops between two people if it's meant to be. There is no 'I'm ready' or someone having to get ready. If love walks in, and you play the stupid card and say you're not ready, you're just dumb ass. And all that has nothing to do with forcing a relationship to work, but if the right person comes around, you're ready. It's about the right people crossing in front of you." Velvet kept on multitasking, scanning the Internet.

"I'm sorry, Velvet. I don't think your friend is ready for a man. Besides, Big Boy ain't no joke, and really, can you see them together? One of his arms is bigger than her whole body. If he went to go down on her, his big head would stretch her legs so far apart she'd think she was giving birth."

"Yeah, I do admit he might hurt me, and I'm not a small woman, but if that's what she wants, who are we to stand in the way?"

Psalms laughed for the first time since he'd dropped off his dog at the vet.

The visual of Mintfurd and Darcelle had both Psalms and Velvet tripping in imagery.

"We both know Mintfurd Big Boy has his own freakish behavior. He spends a lot of money on escorts because finding a woman on his own just has not happened. He has more women loving him as a friend than there are jellyfish out there in that water."

"PB, I'm someone that Mintfurd has trusted as he comes to me to get a woman's perspective...just like you." Velvet mockingly cleared her throat. "Big Boy has told me his life story. I'll have you know it's been over eight months now, I talked him in to not getting his rocks off with prostitutes. Yes, the man has his wants in the freak zone, but who don't? Your ass should be outlawed with you and Gabrielle out the in the water at two a.m., snorkeling in diving suits. I mean damn, PB, you made a flap in the crotch of your suit so you can pull your dick out, and you put a flap in the back of hers...I wonder which opening you slipped into? Was it deep?" Velvet's eyebrows rounded and meshed with her smirking round face. "Now that's some shit I want to watch with an under-water camera. Didn't you get scared out there in that dark water? Oh, what if something had touched you while you was humping, and you couldn't see what it was?...Ooh-wee. Tell me, just how good could sex be in dark, cold water, with fish swimming around. Don't they have sharks out there?"

"Velvet, there are no man-eating sharks in Lake Washington, and the diving suit keeps you warm. Both Gabrielle and I are good swimmers. I didn't know Mintfurd had changed up his groove with having sex with escorts. He had been tight-lipped for some time."

"He's making an effort. He tells me he's horny almost daily, but he's trying to maintain."

"Well, if you and Mintfurd are that deep in to his situation about his lifestyle, why are you talking to me about hooking up your friend Darcelle with him?"

"I can set the wheels in motion for her, but you need to help him."

"Help him do what?"

"Come on, PB! You know he don't know how to...you know he don't know to make a move on a woman. He is so used to every woman being a play date, so to speak."

"Play date?" Psalms started laughing and stood to go out to the workshop area where Mintfurd was working on either something mechanical or electronic. During the whole conversation, Velvet was scanning the news and came upon something.

"PB, PB, PB, a black woman working as a maid was found dead just outside of Vegas city limits. It appears she was brutally tortured. She's identified as a forty-year-old woman with a green card from Martinique.

"You know that's too much of a coincidence."

"Yes, it is. That had to be the kids' mother. She had to be in Vegas the whole time, just not staying where the kids were."

Psalms pulled out his phone and texted both Suzie Q and Tylowe:

Alert: the great-aunt may know more than she has let on. Can't confirm. Proceed with caution.

Suzie Q, in her dramatic fashion, responded:

10-4 Smokey.

CHAPTER 21

I Belong to Me

Gabrielle

"This is your Oakland North Bay Oldies Soul radio station. We're stepping back in time and bringing you a twin spin of Otis Redding. First, the classic '(Sittin' On) The Dock of the Bay.' Then I suggest you hug up, or at least think about loving arms around you when we play 'Try a Little Tenderness.' Only here on your Oakland North Bay Oldies Soul radio station."

I've been enjoying my morning—relaxing and catching up on some reading. I'm being a little lazy, with my legs still sore from my recent late-night swim. I mean early morning. I can smile as I look out at the sun shining over the Bay Area. I'm reliving how my legs and insides became sore, from having a thick dick sliding in and out of me, while the cold lake water tangled with my own natural juices. It felt good and painful. I can't wipe this smile off my face.

The Bat phone is ringing—my private line that Psalms has set up to electronically scrub the signal to keep anyone from recording my phone conversations.

Damn, it's my former boss, the ex-president of the United States. I'm listening to him talk about something that is touching my nerves. He knows how I feel about domestic issues. I support the common man and not big business. I don't think like his good ole boys, but yet he is asking me for my support. He's about to get an earful of attitude. I am my own woman now, and I'm not bowing down to my former boss on any subject I do not agree with.

"Look GB—Mr. President, they want federal assistance for a state problem created by a private sector company that was not required to have adequate bonding insurance.

"I need my name removed from anything that ties me to them. I'm not their lap dog! I'm not a roll of toilet paper to wipe their shit up. I know as your former Secretary of State you expect me to be loyal though all endeavors, but I'm sorry I can't support you on this. I will not!

"I'm in the private sector now, and I pick and choose who in the hell I want to support. No disrespect to you as the former President, Mr. President, but I'm not sorry about how I feel. I don't support them blowing up a little town in Texas. And then, they want me to represent them by using my good name to solicit federal funds?

"Think about this; many Texas politicians in Texas voted against giving the Northern states funding when a natural disaster, Hurricane Sandy, hit hard. That was purely immoral. Now, in the face of this non-natural disaster created by a company that thrived under a pro-corporate tax structure and deregulation, they want rescue funds? No. I will not be a part of that ..."

"Mr. President, I don't give a damn about how much money they gave us in the past. The administration gave them a pass on too many things. As I said, deregulation led to this problem. In my estimation, we gave them all they should have, and more. What did they give us in return? As of now, fourteen dead and hundreds of injured. I feel sorry for a devastated town that we let down with another failed domestic policy. The sad part, blame and real answers will be spun like sewage down a flushing toilet ..."

"I understand that for you as a former president, it's not kosher for you to ask or represent them in such affairs, but I'm not in office anymore, either. I handled your foreign affairs. The other part of your administration made the domestic decisions about who to get in bed with. Your administration dropped governmental oversight and inspections on workplaces that can be as dangerous as we see. I was never in agreement with any part of the administration on many of the domestic decisions such as this. Mr. President, I'm sorry, but I must go. We must pray over all this, shouldn't we?"

I need another glass of wine. I cannot believe GB would even ask me to be a part of domestic situations. He knows I have never believed in supporting certain deregulation when American lives are in the balance. I'm glad that asshole, The Duck, didn't call me. I severely dislike his manipulative ass. He and I never did get along. He ran things as if he was the president.

Yes, I'm a conservative, but I'm a realist more than anything. Because I'm aligned with certain people, it's assumed that I share the same views of people who were about using the American people for pure profit. NO! Of course I could never speak out when I was in the mix of all the things that were going on, but now I am a private citizen. I belong to me!

I'm pissed right now. I'm glad I have my wine to help me deal with the craziness, but I need some Psalms loving to help me through...hmph.

I love this Cabernet Sauvignon wine. It's from Black Coyote Wines in Napa Valley, an African-American winery. I have invested in several cases of wines from black-owned wineries. Despite what many may think of me, it has always been my personal policy to support black businesses. I support my people. I knew, and know, where my heart lies at the end of the day.

That is the reason I spoke loudly in support of the black United

Nations ambassador when the Republicans ganged up on my sister-friend. They knew she was doing her job. Some of them good ol' boys in the House and the Senate attacked her because they thought it would light a fire under their base. Truth be told, their base is a dying breed of old, tired white men.

I was their shining, token black woman. I knew that. They really didn't understand me, or the psychology of the spook who sat behind the door. The idea is that when I am in the mud with you, you cannot see the real me. I may be dark, even if you think my mind is white. You may think you know what I'm thinking and doing, but you know nothing. Meanwhile, I see everything that you're doing.

So few know the real me, and that's fine. I enjoy who I am. I'm not trying to fit into a box that someone else tries to fit me into. My ass is well rounded. I desire to stand alone to help bring about a positive, lasting culture. People have become consumed by pop culture instead of creating a positive culture that lasts.

Looking out over the Oakland Bay makes me want to get out of my condo for the day, but I have so much work to do. I guess I can go down to that café on the wharf and work on my computer. Let me see if I can get a security detail.

So many times I wish I could walk around like most people, but I know better. I have pulled off the big hat and sunglasses, looking like the eccentric out-of-place woman in public, but Psalms does not like me to do that. He once set it up to have me followed without my knowledge for two hours, and I never made out who was following me. That taught me I'm never safe in public.

I have a speech to give in Washington, D.C. tomorrow night. It's about how limited we are in our ability to make significant changes due to our limited mindsets. We're so focused on stopping other people from achieving their goals, when our real goals should be to make the world a better place, and not waste so much time and resources channeling negativity. My conservative base dislikes such talk as they construct change through so much negativity.

Most people want momentous changes for the world, country, city or town that benefit them personally. My speech will be about changing our relationships with neighbors, family members, and changes within one's own life. How can we change the world when we harbor resentments, and lack forgiveness for those closest to us?

Sadly, all the tuxes and evening dresses will pay to hear me with their generous tax break money. They will clap and smile plastic smiles, and never hear a word I'll say. Even sadder, those people are acting no different from most people whether they are rich or poor. Many people believe that genuine relationships are like friends on social networks—click "delete," and it's over; click "block," and find somebody else to accept as a friend.

I'm flying back to Seattle for the weekend. I was going mid-week, but I need to prepare some work for my students at Berkeley.

Psalms is preoccupied with something profoundly troubling. Not sure what it is. He takes on some security tasks that are full of risks around the world. In many ways, I think it makes him feel whole—saving and protecting. He asked me to secure a few things for him from some sources and connections I only use sparingly. I never ask why. He never asks me for anything that I would question.

I decided long ago that if I found a man I wanted to be with, I would trust that man. I could pay a dreadful price if I'm wrong about the man I love, but I stand to reap the glory of love that a woman seeks.

Lois Mae, who was on the boat the other night, is an incredible poet. From what I understand, she and Velvet are best friends. At one time they shared a man whom Lois Mae was married to. I think my situation with Psalms, and his strange relationship with Evita, is near a collision course. I'm thinking of how I can change it, but I can't force him to do anything different. Lois Mae and Velvet are friends, and I have to hand it to them. Lois Mae and I are both from Texas and grew up only about forty miles apart, so we get along well. She is an African American literary professor at East Seattle City University and has written a book of poetry about the love of a good man. One of her poems feels as if she had read my mind about how I feel about Psalms. I asked her could she write some personal lines for me within that poem and send me a copy to print. I wanted to put a picture of Psalms and me on my wall, and the poem next to the picture.

My life can be so impersonal. At my condo here in Oakland, so few ever walk through my door, but I try to make it a home. When Lois Mae sent me the personalized version of her poem, I wanted to die, and I wanted it to be buried in Psalms' grave when he dies.

There Is Something About His Love
His smile is the grace of a beautiful day
His eyes are the golden lights in the night
His wine-stain birthmark is like a piece of my heart resting near his eyes so he can see inside my heart day or night
I strive to be the most beautiful woman I can be for my shining Black Knight
I want to protect him with my mind, offering knowledge for his choosing to use me as he pleases...knowing he won't abuse me
I'm content feeling he is the one safe place
His soulful ways, I ride throughout the day

And love every part of him through any and all darkness

There is something about his love

His love lifts me to the heavens, and he makes hells for those who would oppose our love

He is a slow dance, skin-to-skin, mind-to-mind, soul-to-soul

He is a slow kiss deep kiss

He is a slow but raging powerful beat in my heart

He fits me high and tight, and universally deep

He is not science

He is logic to my soul

He is the prescription my soul survives on

He makes me weak to submit

He feeds me strength to be secure

He is the scent of arousal

He is my urban groove

The man is jazzy in many time signatures at the same time he is perpetual arrangements

He is a country love ballad of finding the perfect love

He is velvet to my rough edges

The man is the grace of a beautiful day

He knocks me off my feet when he whispers in my ear that I am his queen

There is something about his love

The touch of his hand makes me rise to the highest heights others will never reach

I rise with him to see the sunrise and to love him as the sun slides past the end of the ocean

His calm makes me float like a bottle in the ocean carrying a fraternal letter of sweet emotion

The thought of him makes my blood hotter than the desert heat

He is a desert flower of beauty that only I can touch

The view of his sensual physique is a treasure that I'd dig the abyss of his soul to keep
Throughout my day or days away from him
I live off the moments I want to spend with him
Like nourishment to my soul, I feel full just from knowing this man
His golden eyes are the light that shines his way into my heart
There is something about his love.

I realize I'm blessed to be his woman, but I've read too often if a woman gives that much trust to a man, a broken heart is going to happen. I do have my deal breakers. If I must, I will walk away and live with what has been good, and fight away the hurt of whatever made me leave. I am certain Psalms would never make love or have sex with another woman...I'm undeniably certain of that.

I'll fight for women's rights around the world, to help women receive equal treatment, and equal pay. I'll stand up for girls to receive equal education. Being one of the few women to break through the glass ceiling at the age that have, I know the struggles and hurts.

All of that is essential for us as women. Yet, I want us to be able to find men whom we don't feel the need to tell how to be a man. I want us to find men to trust enough to let them fail, while trying to do their best for us and them. While I fight for women, I want women to fight for black men. I have heard and know the world mocks them, and beats them down. I want a man whom I can believe in, and I can have faith in. I'm devoting my heart to the man that I curl my body in to, and fall asleep feeling like I'm in that one safe place.

CHAPTER 22

Another Woman

Psalms Black

Faelynn stands at my kitchen sink like no other woman could, and looks good washing dishes. I have a dishwasher. I have a house cleaner. I normally clean my own kitchen after I cook. But, since Faelynn is here, she's cleaning the kitchen after breakfast, as she always does. Her Southern roots have stayed intact. Those old-school ways are to be admired in today's less than happy times of relationships. It seems men and women do for each other out of obligation, instead of love or the pride and the joy of making someone happy.

Faelynn saunters my way and pours me another cup of coffee. She smiles at me, and walks back in the kitchen to continue giving my kitchen her Midas touch.

Maybe I've just been lucky that the women in my life, past and present, enjoy bringing me the consistency of an old-school woman. I know I enjoy bringing joy to them. I hear often that men and women have failed to maintain a respect for what they know is right. Whether a man or woman has been disappointed by the lack of being treated well with old-school loving and doing for each other without keeping score, each person in any type of relationship must still maintain a classic sense of style, of knowing how we should act and do for each other.

I watched my grandfather and his male friends, and how they

treated women. I don't see a lot of that nowadays. Those men used to wash and wax a woman's car, polish her boots, hang her pictures up on the wall, come up behind her and kiss her on the neck and then go back to cutting her grass...all with the pride of taking care of a woman. I know some of those things sound outdated, but a man should do some of the simplest things for a woman without being asked, no matter if she's doing her part or not.

This morning, I cooked Faelynn a four-cheese omelet with smoked salmon, scallops, fresh oysters, and king crab, along with red potatoes and sourdough and onion toast. I got up early before she did, and drove to Pike Place Market just as the first fish was being tossed off the boats. I love doing that for her no matter what she does for me.

I hear from men longing for yesteryear, yet I do understand many women are in the work force nowadays. That can change the dynamics of women doing or not doing...hell, she's tired. If she's tired, well, a woman might not cook and clean with pride and only out of pure necessity. Men joke about remembering when a woman would show up with a bag of groceries and clean your crib from top to bottom, and tell you to stay out of her way while she rearranged your sock drawer. She was snooping...in every nook and cranny, but if you had nothing to hide, she was hooking your crib up with pride.

Whatever people are doing nowadays, it seems like they have lost their way for too many reasons and need to come back to the middle.

Growing up, I spent a lot of time at Tylowe's house. I witnessed the days of Tylowe's mom and dad and how they loved each other.

She would never let her husband leave the house with a wrinkled shirt or pair of pants. I have to laugh…His work clothes were so stiff with starch, I'm not sure how the man walked in them. I remember her voice, "Wait a minute, take that off and give it to me for a minute, and let me iron that."

I watched Tylowe's dad come home from work and go out and weed and tend to Tylowe's mother's garden, even though he could have Tylowe and me do it. He wanted to be the one who did for his woman.

Everything in the fridge and cabinets today is prepared instant or microwave ready. It's rare that men can open the hood of a car, and offer to change the oil in a woman's car. As much as Gabrielle has a life of people serving her, she can still do for herself, and when the chance comes, she will do for herself without huff or puff. When she's here, she cooks most of the time. When she's here, she stops the house cleaner from coming and she takes over. I watch her sing and move her hips as if she is happy to hook me up with her womanly touch. Yeah, the same woman who has sat across from world leaders changes the sheets on my bed, and I can't stop her from doing what she wants to do when she's here.

Much like the pretty woman in my kitchen now; how can I not appreciate Faelynn despite any flaws she may have? She is mopping my kitchen floor as a part of washing the dishes…damn. I hear men and woman are shocked when someone does something for them just one time. Life is so strange nowadays.

I believe we have gotten caught up on analytical profiles in searching for mates and lost the passion to please each other. Now it's about, "Look, if you want me, you need to have this to come at me." Doesn't sound too passionate to me!

What about our future relationships? Babies making babies. The youngsters—I don't believe they can be saved when the old men are gone, like the ones who taught me. Nowadays, girls wanna be like reality-show women. An attitude of ignorance, of easy access to the material world of others, with a dream some man will give them the world—it has stolen hearts and minds. Shame is, though, the material world's popularity contest changes faster than the seasons and sometimes faster than a download on a smartphone.

The morning sun is reflecting off Faelynn's red silk kimono. Bobby Womack's "Woman's Gotta Have It" is flowing through my sound system, and she's swaying to the song. I turn it up. I can't help but smile at her getting her groove on early in the morning. I'm glad she is here. She is a secret to most, but Faelynn is important to me.

Her wild hair is so thick I doubt a metal, garden rake could pass through it, but in a way it looks in place. She's tall and in her kimono, she appears to be a womanly bonfire.

When she walks out of the bedroom, and into my living room, she becomes art walking across my black wood floors. Pretty she is—simply pretty to the point that all those who see her think and say she is stunning and flawless.

Gabrielle is beautiful and alluring, while still looking professional. Faelynn is pretty and head-snapping cute. Professional men act inappropriate because of her visual temptation.

Faelynn recently turned thirty-six years old and is a weekend mother who has her daughter and son every other weekend. Fae-lynn was married to their father, a world tennis star, whose tennis circuit schedule helped him dip into his choice of tennis whores. She dealt with his extracurricular games until he retired and became a tennis coach, and coached his dick into a young tennis star. He tripped over his arrogance and got caught by the media in compromising photos; he claimed that he and Faelynn had been separated for years. It was the farthest from the truth to her. Faelynn was the last to know. She should have recognized it when the man never came home for days and weeks, or when he always took the kids and left her at home alone.

Now she's a part of the new family structure in America. Courts declare men have equal rights to be the custodial parent, especially if they have money and celebrity. Faelynn has freedom and half of his money now.

She loves to travel, but woefully she went searching for love in all the wrong places after that, and I had to step in and help a wretched asshole languish in a little human hell.

Another man filmed her having sex and threatened to put it out for all to see if she didn't come up with a million dollars. Disappointingly, her sister, Gabrielle, asked me to handle the situation. Faelynn has become like my little sister. She's not my lover and not close to anything like that. She comes here to chill out and enjoy the Northwest every other week. It's the one safe place where she can let the troubles of the world mentally float out into the ocean outside my windows.

There is a considerable age difference between Gabrielle and Faelynn. Their faces are twins, but Gabrielle is chocolate and Faelynn is caramel. Both are tall, with Gabrielle being thicker and curvier and Faelynn looking like a beach volleyball player. Born twelve years apart, they are as close as sisters would be as if they had been born only days apart.

It is so funny when Faelynn is here, and if I let her hang out with me, I guess it's clear to most she is not my woman, and might be a sister, or cousin, and possibly my daughter. People—well, mostly men—want to know all about her. Some men see her, and their hearts stop and they cannot breathe when Faelynn walks by. Her attractiveness seizes men's minds, and causes them to have eye strokes.

I told Faelynn she cannot hang out with me today. I have too many things going on that don't add up, and too many things not connecting. I have to lone wolf it today. As Faelynn walks away, the Prince song "Lady Cab Driver" floats in my head…again. Even if Gabrielle was not in my life, Faelynn still could not be my woman. Meaning, she's a woman to love, but not for sex, and for sure, as for me, she is not wifely material as I am not husband material for her. She is that innocent, naïve woman who we need to protect from the world.

CHAPTER 23

Save Me...

Evita

Psalms, I hope you're looking for me. I know I disappear at times and you're used to me doing that, but I'm in trouble. I'm sorry I've made bad choices, but I don't want to die. I don't want to die. They are starting to hurt me.

I was looking forward to the shower that was coming my way. When I got in the shower, the Pretty Boy hit me with a belt, and it stung...it stung...it hurt. Pretty Boy has told me I have to do whatever people tell me to do or I'll feel more than pain than I can stand.

Psalms, I hope you're looking for me. Save me...

S uzy Q and Tylowe took an extra day to get back to Seattle. Psalms' text put them in prevent and defense mode. The thought that maybe the great-aunt of the kids could be untruthful changed the driving route from Vegas to Seattle.

At a truck stop, Tylowe took the kids and the great-aunt inside to eat. Meanwhile, Suzy had them leave their phones to charge in the vehicle. Once the kids and great-aunt were inside, Suzy Q went through their phones with an electronic device, a password code breaker that Mintfurd supplied. She downloaded and sent the info to Mintfurd for analysis.

They changed course several times along the way up to Seattle while waiting for feedback. The kids enjoyed the ride as they had never been on a road trip. They stopped at the Pacific Ocean, and touched and smelled the water. It was an experience that made them smile amidst the confusion in their young lives. Tylowe heard the kids talk as if they were at the end of the world, and there were no more places to go.

The kids had been in private schools with only a few other students for most of their lives. Both the boy and the girl had a gentle spirit and didn't seem to be troubled, but they were naïve about the world around them. It troubled Tylowe's mind that these kids may be the children of his nemesis Elliot, yet their soft hearts helped ease any ill will. Tylowe attributed the children's kindness and pureness of heart to their mother. Knowing what he knew of Elliot, the ugly side of him was nothing he would wish on his worst enemy. He hoped that Elliott's DNA would not weigh the children down. Whether the mother was a respectable woman or not was quite a mystery. The woman had been married to a Russian mob boss and had an affair with Elliot.

Tylowe looked over at the Pacific Ocean. His mind was sinking deep in the middle of murky waters of confusion. The vagueness of information of potential lies and truth lead to more difficulty than one could imagine. Tylowe smelled the salty air, and it re-minded him he had to think unobstructed by emotions. He had to protect.

He was putting his family, and all he knew to be true, in danger. A day ago, he had held a gun, and Suzy Q used her gun, and…she disposed of a man who wanted to cause harm to the kids and may-be worse. Tylowe looked back at the great-aunt.

A bit of joy rode along on the trip back to Seattle with the kids and all their questions they had about anything and everything.

The kids wanted to listen to Michael Jackson, and they did for too many hours. Tylowe introduced them to Jackie Wilson, and told them some soul music history of where Michael Jackson got his dancing and singing style. It amazed Tylowe that they listened and enjoyed the older recording. Soon both the kids were singing "Lonely Teardrops" and "Baby Let's Workout."

Tylowe had raised two girls from their pre-teen age. His step-daughter wanted nothing to do with her biological father. Clearly she was Tylowe's daughter in spiritual DNA. Both his girls were now in their mid-twenties. The ride with the two kids made him realize how much he missed being around his daughters in their younger years.

Psalms had set up an apartment in one of his condos, and Suzy

Q and Tylowe pulled into the basement parking garage near late afternoon. The kids were road weary when they met Psalms. Some people see the rock of a man, and look at him with awe. His physical presence impressed both kids. After the kids met and spoke with him, they went to separate rooms. The great-aunt settled into her room for a long bath and went to bed early. Of course, all the phones and computers had information traps as a precaution. Tomorrow, the kids would have a schedule of activities and a tutor would show up, until something more permanent could be set up. Zelda, the female security trainee, stayed in the condo with them.

Psalms, Suzy Q, and Tylowe convened at Psalms' condo.

"Glad you guys made it back safely. I think the mother is dead. Can't get good intel out of Vegas, but what we do know is strange," Psalms said.

"I may be able to get some info." Tylowe picked his cell phone off the table. He had already texted his wife to let her know he was back. He wanted Meeah to know he wanted to see her. It was beyond simply missing her for a couple of days. His encounter with an old lover and old classmates made him grateful that he'd avoided the drama-filled lives that others lived. The old lover gave him a new perspective on what kind of woman he had at home.

Tylowe felt righteous about himself. He passed up temptation, the chance to have sex with an old freak he had done nasty things with at one time. Erika offered him an all-expenses-paid booty-fling if he came to town on the regular. He didn't even think twice about getting in to that strange stuff. That was a red light he stopped at long before it turned yellow. Leading the charge in his soul was that he loved his wife, despite the uncertainty in their relationship.

If their time was up, and their marriage was over, he knew mourning the loss of Meeah in his life and the touch of another woman would simply be torture and remind him of what he'd had. The last time he had lost someone, he went years hardly being able to engage a woman in conversation. No, if they were over...

He smiled. "A connect is a connect," and then he repeated, "I may be able to get some info." He scrolled through his past calls and dialed his friend Jon Jon in Vegas.

"Hey, man, I'm back in Seattle. Man, if you can help me out real quick, I'm in a hurry, and I was hoping I could have Erika Corwin's phone number?"

Tylowe looked up at Psalms and Psalms handed him a pen. "Hey, thanks, Jon Jon. It was good seeing you guys. I'll call you in a day or two. Later."

Psalms poured straight shots of Evan Williams Black Label Bourbon. Tylowe dialed. "Erika, this is Tylowe. Yeah, I know you didn't think you'd hear from me, and I'll keep it straight from the gate. I need your help."

"Can we talk about that maybe later? I need for you to find out all you can about a woman who was found dead in Vegas. Maybe you can take a Homeland Security angle and help me out for old time's sake. I can reassure you, nothing you tell me will come back on you in any form. I just need to know more.

"I'll gladly fill you in when it's a better time for us to talk. Erika, thanks. Can you have something for me in a couple of hours? Great." Tylowe talked to Erika for a bit longer, giving her some information that Psalms had on paper and had put in front of him.

He finished talking to Erika, and Tylowe told Psalms and Suzy Q about seeing Erika, Jon Jon and Rufus. Psalms remembered them from college, had a good laugh, and gave praise to Tylowe for not going rolling in the old swamp waters with Erika.

"Hell, man. Married or not married, I wouldn't go there with her now. Oh, hell no!" Tylowe shook his head. "I don't know about either one of you, but some of the sex I had twenty to thirty years ago, I need a special sanitary memory wipe for. What in the hell was I thinking? I wish I could pull back all the sweat I excreted while having sex with her and others like her from back in the day. I wish I could delete a few moments in time. Now that would be a sweet device someone needs to invent. I know experience is the best teacher, but damn. Not everyone we slept with deserved our time. Sometimes when we run in to someone we have exchanged anything physical with, it feels like scars on parts of our bodies, like when we fell down as kids, and we picked at the scab, and left a characteristic indicator reminding us of the stupid shit we did."

"Damn, dude, lighten up; it was thirty years ago."

"Yeah, maybe I should."

"Eh, are you ex-whores finished going down memory lane? 'Cause if you are done, we have people's lives in our hands, and some lives out of our hands, and in the ground. I certainly don't want to have a pity party for ye-old peckers, my dear mates, eh."

Suzy Q sat, tired and bothered. She wasn't the kid-friendly type after a few hours. "Hey, I had to ride and drive back from Vegas to Seattle playing nursemaid. I like you guys, but can we keep it moving?"

"Sure, boss," Psalms responded sarcastically. He was the last word in the room as to what was going to happen in their plan, but sometimes called her the boss. "Not that it matters much now after we have the children here, but do you think those are Elliot's children?"

Tylowe nodded and then said, "I'm pretty sure the girl, Celia, is Elliot's. She looks so much like Mia and even walks like her."

"The tone in her voice sounds like a younger Mia," Suzy Q said.

"The boy, Cleophus, he is smallish and don't look like Elliot, and when I ask the great-aunt, she says she not sure. The only thing she knows is that her niece birthed them, and we have to treat them as one for all."

Tylowe's phone vibrated. He looked at the screen, answered, and walked out onto the balcony.

Psalms and Suzy Q went over all that they knew and made notes. They also had other affairs needing attention. A concert security project and the situation with Darcelle and her ex-husband needed a solution, and there was a new matter of importance to Psalms: Where was Evita?

"Q, I need you to take the lead on this for me. I'll just get angry and lose my objectivity. I know you don't care for her, and I don't understand why, but it is what it is. Track her down and I'll take it from there. You're better at that than I am. You're the boss lady when it comes to tracking people down."

"I'll get it done. I want Zelda to help, so free her up from baby-sitting by tomorrow. She's sharp and analyzes well. She's ready for something deeper. Then, I want something else. I want you to stop letting Evita put you in such bum moods. You have the beautiful Gabrielle, and you have yourself, mate, eh?

"I'm trying to stay in my lane and mind my own business, but you know us Brits. We drive on the wrong side of the road in some of our colonies."

"You ain't British, you're Canadian, and the Brits about lost all their colonies, which is why we have weird-ass civil wars in Africa, but I digress."

"Yes, mate, you do digress, but hear me out. I know you consider Evita to be some kind of soul mate. I have to ask, how did you come to this conclusion? Evita has had drama following her since the day of her birth. A serial killer would love to borrow her résumé of troubles." Suzy Q stared at Psalms knowing much more about the woman that Psalms would protect to the death.

Suzy Q knew things from the underground world that she crawled in and out of when she wanted her type of loving. Suzy Q knew that Evita was deceiving. The thing that Psalms praised Suzy Q for was her extraordinary ability to track a person down. In the past, she had tracked down Evita without Psalms' knowledge, and it had led to finding out about Evita being a hermaphrodite.

The reason Suzy Q disliked Evita is she had been deceiving the man who loved her. She had been hoodwinking him for decades. She thought Evita had gained a strange trust in him that made Psalms weak and blind. To her, Evita used his trust much like in the story of Samson and Delilah, with Evita playing the part of Delilah, subduing Psalms' strength and his vision as if fires had burned his eyes out.

"PB, someone else's path cannot be for you unless they are for you. I think one of the ways you can know this is when times are not so sweet and hot, and how are you are loved and cared about. PB, you have had way too many ugly moments in life because of her. Those cannot be the reason she is your soul mate."

Suzy Q wasn't the touchy-feely type, but she took her middle finger and forced his balled-up fist to open, then pushed her finger into the center of his hand and tapped it softly.

"So, you're telling me I can only know how someone feels about me when life is ugly? Give me a minute to think about that. I have to pee." He left the room, but Suzy knew she had touched a nerve in the hardest man she knew. Suzy Q had watched men all her life take their act-macho-man attitude to the extreme when it came to her. As a lesbian, she noticed men would try to be tougher for strange reasons, as if they would convert her to being sexually attracted to a man. She laughed almost too loud when she recalled several incidents in her life. She broke the nose of a male detective while she was a Royal Canadian Mounted Policewoman. The male detective stepped one time too many times over the line in the overzealous macho-man act.

Tylowe was still on the deck talking on his phone, and Psalms walked back in the room and headed to the stereo and hit "play." Lalah Hathaway started singing "When Your Life Was Low."

He sat down next to Suzy Q on the couch, and turned toward her and nodded, signaling her to resume the conversation.

Suzy Q continued. "How does a person treat you when the money is short, or work depletes your energy, or you lose someone like family or a friend? You have to get to a low point in life to see how that person supports you. You have, for the most part, never been in a low spot, except when your grandfather died. And Evita was nowhere to be found. She wasn't there for you at a time that, maybe, was the first time she should have been there for you.

"Psalms, your grandfather killed a man to protect her, and then years later you did the same thing. That is twelve feet worth of dirt thrown over dead men for her sake, and every time she pulls another one of her disappearing acts. It's like shovels full of more insulting dirt thrown in your face.

"If Evita is your soul mate...her behavior and ill-responsive nature is soul-wrenching to me, eh.

"What's love got to do with it? Love can come about without someone being your soul mate. Is it possible for someone to develop in to a soul mate, without being born to be? I say yes, but this is not the case here, and you know it, but deny it...Samson."

Tylowe walked back in from the deck, and saw a look on Psalms' face as if someone had taken his ball from him on the playground. He had never seen that before.

"Hey, guys, I had to talk to my wife a bit. I have not clued her in on any of this, and I'm feeling that I need to when I get home."

"Yes, you should tell your soul mate what's going on in your life," Suzy Q said, and then poured a double shot of bourbon for her, and one for Psalms. She lifted her glass up, and slowly Psalms lifted his, and they clinked glasses.

"Touché," he said.

Tylowe sat down. He didn't pour a shot and he refused one. "Erika called back. The dead woman was unmercifully tortured. It's her. Her name was Queen…Queen Ivanov, and her maiden name is Frêche. She's the daughter of the former President of Martinique. Fingerprints identified her. They have been withholding the information as a precaution because of the connections to a dead Russian mob boss and her being the daughter of a head of state. It appears that whomever tortured her—and we know who that is—the Russians never found out where she was staying. The FBI and Homeland Security found the house down the block and one street over from where the kids and the great-aunt were staying. The house was tidy and well kept, and there are pictures of two kids, a boy and girl, found there. An oddity though—apparently Queen had a heroin addiction. Needle marks and toxicity tests confirmed it. A clean house and druggie don't jibe in my book."

"Not in mine either," Psalms interjected. "They shot her up when they found her and must have held her a long time trying to get information out of her."

Both men had knowledge of addiction. Psalms had witnessed a lot through the kids who had come through the foundation that Evita and he administered. Tylowe and his wife had run a drug rehab center in Vancouver, B.C. for the past twelve years.

"Authorities found a fake passport, and a work visa. The name on both was…Elnah Runway." Tylowe said the name slowly, as if he were spelling it.

Suzy Q knew the name from her first encounter with Tylowe, and helping him through a tough situation. Elliot's last name, Piste, means "runway" in French. It's the same last name Meeah, Tylowe's wife, used as her last name because she didn't want to be associated with Elliot while they were separated. Tylowe explained this to Psalms.

"It's *Color Purple*, Shug Avery time. God is trying to tell us something. The more we know, the more we don't know," Psalms said.

He got up, went to his elaborate stereo, and turned a knob. Nothing happened for two seconds, but then a wall behind the stereo lifted and rolled up like a garage door. He went into the room, and came out with two small guns and holsters. He turned the knob, and the wall came down again.

Psalms walked over and placed the guns on the table. "You keep your permit on you at all times and keep a gun low on your ankle, and one in your back waist," he said to Tylowe.

A voice floated from the back of the three-thousand-square-foot condo. "Psalms?"

"What's up, Faelynn?"

"Gabrielle wants you to call as soon as you can."

"Tell her in about twenty minutes."

"Okay."

Psalms, Suzy Q, and Tylowe discussed the conflicts and knowledge of what they did know. The problems presented—what they did know, what they didn't know, and how to find out—dominated the conversation. Twenty minutes later, Tylowe headed home to his wife.

Suzy Q left to get a few hours' sleep, and then to track down Evita.

CHAPTER 25

The Sweet and Hard Core

Tylowe walked through the door of his home and disarmed himself, securing the guns in a safe place.

He walked down into the sunken living room. He stared out at the lake and the last of the daylight. Anchored in the middle of the lake, two boats bobbed in the water from the slow waves caused by a gentle breeze. Tylowe felt like his feet were standing on solid ground for the first time in a long time.

From behind, he felt an aggressive tug and hug on his back. He heard her walking his way, but didn't turn. He felt Meeah, clamping onto his back, as if he were air to breathe for survival.

She jumped up and wrapped her legs around him. Tylowe put his hands on her smooth calves and squeezed the beauty in his hands. He knew wherever he touched her, he could find loveliness. Her heart was on his back, and he thought he could feel her heart beating; for sure he felt her breathing on his neck. Maybe he thought he could read her mind, because he sure wanted her to know his thoughts. He wanted her to understand that the world might be breaking apart, but no matter what, he knew in his heart and mind, she was his one safe place to lay his burdens down.

She relaxed her body as if she was a child riding on her father's back and had fallen asleep. With her arms draped over his shoulders, he walked them toward their bedroom and straight into their bathroom.

He laughed to himself. She was no longer the feather-weight woman he had married, but she felt more adorable with her filled-out body close to his. He backed up to the bathroom sink vanity and let Meeah sit. Facing her, he laid his head on her shoulder, and she cupped the back of his head. She was trembling, and his heart raced. He was happy to be home and close to his wife.

The bedroom stereo played in low volume, but the two of them heard Robert Glasper and Lalah Hathaway doing an abstract version of Sade's "Cherish the Day."

Tylowe lifted his head to see that his wife was in her bra and panties only. A part of him wanted to be near her so badly that he almost became blind to what she had on at the moment. She could have been cloaked in diamond and pearls, or as she was now in her flawless skin—the color of a golden fall leaf, soft as silk, and as rich tasting as cocoa.

Meeah reached and unbuttoned his shirt. Her natural nails made trail lines over his heart, as if she were writing her name in multiple languages. She stroked his chest and up and down his stomach.

He no longer had the six-pack muscles of his youth, but he was still solid. She held his sides and leaned in and whispered. "I need a little to hang on to; I love it. It lets me know I'm feeding you... at least sometimes." Then she slid her tongue into his ear and let her tongue slow dance to Will Downing and Rachelle Ferrell singing "Nothing Has Ever Felt Like This."

They rolled their foreheads together and came face to face; they smiled and began gently biting each other's lips. Their noses pulled in each other's breath, and their mouths were getting hot from tangling.

Tylowe stood up straight, and Meeah ran her fingers down to his belt buckle and unbuckled it slowly, pulling the belt to the point that it hung and swung. From there he unbuttoned his own jeans and stepped out of his shoes. With a little extra effort, he had to facilitate his jeans over his ass. Meeah smiled and bit her wet bottom lip. Quickly, she reached and grabbed his belt and slapped his ass hard with it. He didn't flinch as she had always done that, but he took notice that he hadn't realized that she still love tapped him. Tylowe stepped out of his jeans and pulled off his socks.

He was wearing the cream-colored sports thong she'd bought for him. She'd purchased twenty different colors for him to wear. She loved seeing her man walking around in a manly styled thong with his long, bronze legs. The pouch of the thong was silky smooth, and Tylowe filled the pouch well. The wide waistband had one-inch straps attached, coming from under his ball sac, curving over his ass, and connecting to the waistband. Meeah often requested he wear them and nothing else while walking around the house. At that moment, he thought about it.

Meeah twirled her finger, signaling she wanted him to turn around and put his back to her. She lightly dragged her natural nails down his back; she knew that he loved the feel of her scratching his back. To him it was like an intoxicating drink. He relaxed and laid his head back, and she kissed his baldness. The tip of her tongue traveled along his bald head, as if she were writing Egyptian hieroglyphics.

He slowly pulled away and walked over to the shower sliding doors. He turned on the shower that was larger than some houses' full bathrooms. The marbled walls had seating that allowed two to lie down comfortably. The eight showerheads pulsated with a hot mist pouring down on their completely prone bodies. The lake-front home had a specially designed hot water system that provided as much hot water as anyone could use for hours.

Tylowe walked back over to Meeah and forced his hands under her ass. He picked her up, and put her down standing on the floor. She had already removed her bra. Her breasts were average in size, but huge with feelings from the simplest touch. Her nipples were gumdrop thick and perfect for his lips to suck on as he stooped down, and he did so. He made as if he was pulling her nipples with a sucking motion to make them longer. She loved that feeling, and he kept that up for some time as the bathroom filled with steam. Under her panties, a sweltering, sticky humidity needed to escape.

Tylowe stood as erect as his dick, which had pushed out of the side of his thong and exposed his protruding hard-on. He moved in behind Meeah and let her feel his hardness rubbing on her ass as he walked her forward into the shower. His arms held her tight as he bit and sucked lightly along her neckline and collarbone. He kept walking her in to the hot, spraying water that covered their bodies from eight different directions.

He exited the shower temporarily, letting Meeah feel the wetness and warmness, but he came back shortly with the music playing louder, and with bottled waters in hand.

They had only said a few words. At the moment, words would only get in the way of what was coming from their souls. In their time and space, silence was like vows of forever. Nothing could make being home simply better, and together they made nothing else matter. They were loving in the now; they were loving for tomorrow; they were loving for the times over the years they had not loved, or had forgotten. It was beyond yearning, or wanting to feel a bodily connection; it was beyond forgiveness—of what didn't matter. It was as if God had sent them to be with each other.

"Hurricane" by Eric Benét ended, and faded in to Earth Wind

and Fire's "Would You Mind." Meeah had removed her panties, and he had removed his thong. He got down on his knees and kissed over her belly as did the raining shower. She ran her hands over his head, as if it was his dick head, stroking the moisture. His mind was orgasmic from her touch.

He cupped her ass and pulled the roundness of her belly to his lips, and he licked her navel. He let his tongue catch the raining shower at the point of her navel and swallowed. He loved the roundness of her belly. He told her often in the past, "Your belly is perfect; you may not have birthed both our children, but nevertheless your belly brought beauty in to this world, so I adore the sight of it. Each time he told her this, tears rolled down her cheeks. Still down on his knees, Tylowe's tongue danced up and down her leg. She looked down to see the water misting off his back and funneling down the crease of his ass. He got down on all fours, and his head parted her thighs. He placed his nose on her pussy lip and sniffed her scent. His dick thickened as it hung down. Looking up in to her face, the shower blurred his vision. He tapped her on her ass, and she knew to sit down.

On his knees like a dog, he moved back between her thighs. The shower was full of steam; heat surrounded them, and it was coming from them.

Meeah spread her legs, placing her feet up on the platform she sat on. The water felt like walking in warm rain, naked, along a warm beach at night. The bathroom lights had dimmed when they stayed in one place. The only lights were in the floor of the shower, illuminating their bodies in reds, greens, and white. With her legs apart, Tylowe licked her pussy in long, slow-dragging laps and took in her sweet wetness. She was slippery and sweet; it had him eating her like tomorrow wouldn't come so he had to take all she had now. He licked her up and down, near and far. His tongue started in between her two openings. She was ready for his tongue to slide in her ass, but he opened his mouth wide covering her whole pussy. The showerhead sprayed shots of hot water right onto her clit, and over his nose. She groaned each time the spray hit her clit. She angled her body to increase the direct contact. Meeah almost squirted herself as she was losing control. She grabbed her breasts hard, as if she was trying to save them. She squeezed her nipples as sounds wheezed from deep within her lungs. Her feet stirred, and toes curled. She slapped the back of his head almost too hard. Her body was out of control as she fought back from cumming. He curled his tongue, and she placed her hands behind his head and helped his tongue to make deep thrusts, inside and out. She kept pushing his head into her pussy. As she called his name aloud, he honed in on her clit. She'd felt the shower raining down hot water a moment before on her clit; now his tongue was bathing her, circling while varying the pressure.

Unconsciously, she slapped his back again. He slipped two fingers inside her pulsating pussy, and massaged the inner, upper ridge inside her. His tongue flicked on her clit, and he never missed a beat. He stayed at it knowing it was just a matter of time before her body would go in to an upheaval of motions. She would be loud, so damn loud, and it started. Tylowe fought to keep his tongue in place, and she damn near pushed him away. Meeah screamed, and he fought to keep licking her. Finally, she was able to persuade him to pull away with a smile on his face.

He knew she had not had an orgasm like that in a long while. He wondered if he had not been spiritually loving her as she deserved as his woman. Maybe he had been having sex with her all too often, and not making love to her. Both had fallen in to the idea that sex was good and plentiful, and sometimes that's all you had. But making love—it had to happen more often.

He joined her as she lay on the sitting area. It was enough room to allow them to lie next to each other and spoon while feeling the warm rain. The eight showerheads had changed five times, once every five minutes. The steam and hot water misted over their bodies; it felt like a water blanket of warmth.

Years ago, they used to make the annual hike down behind the Snoqualmie Falls. The 268-foot-high waterfall in the Cascade Mountains was forty minutes from Seattle, and then a half-mile hike. Meeah and Tylowe had been able to pull off having quickie sex behind the hard, cold mist of the falls. It was dangerous, romantic, exciting, and cold. Now, behind the eight-foot-long glass shower windows and door, love rained down. The mist was hot and pulsating softly on their bodies.

Meeah sat up and then eased her body to a standing position. Tylowe sat up and looked up at her. Movement in the huge shower triggered the lights to brighten a bit. As he looked up at his wife, he saw himself; she was him, and he was her. Maybe their growth as one had slowed, but they wanted more love to keep growing to wherever it could go, as long as it went—far, wide, and high.

Meeah leaned down and kissed his forehead, then his nose, and then rushed her tongue into his mouth. She kissed him hard and wet as the hot shower poured over their faces. The spray pattern changed to quick bursts of spray, almost too hard, from all of the showerheads.

Their mouths opened wide and their tongues intertwined, seemingly trying to take each other's last breath.

Her hand reached down and cupped his balls as he spread his legs. She loved feeling his balls stirring in her hand and his shaft thicken and harden. She leaned down and put her lips over the underside of his dick, then licked and sucked on the thick vein. Her mouth went up and down, sucking hard on the shaft of his dick. He grunted as he pulled her head tighter to him. She kept sucking the shaft as she moved one hand up to his wide, flawlessly shaped mushroom dick head. Meeah squeezed and stroked his dick head as if she was trying to make it squirt to the ceiling. She relaxed her grip.

"I want you inside me."

She anticipated the feel of his dick, knowing it plunged deep, and how the wide ridge of the head stroked her G-spot going in and coming out. He leaned back, and she closed his legs a bit and straddled him.

With her hands on his shoulder for support, she rotated her hips, making her pussy lips kiss his hardness. Hot water poured off her breasts and onto his face, and he drank the water for her to see. She centered her opening, and slowly pushed down on his dick, grunting loudly as he glided in an inch. She stopped her descending human waterfall and held still. Her mouth opened wide, and her eyes rolled up for a moment, but then she stared down in to his eyes. Tylowe rushed his tongue into her mouth, and kissed hard as if he wanted his tongue to go down her throat. She felt it through her thick pussy lips. Her wetness, like slippery virgin olive oil, increased and impelled her to receive his hardness and width with ease. She wrapped her arms around his head, almost smothering him. He heard and felt her high-pitched release of air as she eased down on his longing hardness. She rested her ass on his thighs to adjust.

With her arms around his head, she pulled him to her breasts. Meeah spoke loud and clear, "I love you, Tylowe. There is nothing I want more than to be with you. You treat me like a queen, but if you ever wanted me to be your slave, I wouldn't hesitate for one moment. I know you would still treat me like a queen."

Tylowe squeezed her body with his strong arm as the shower-head changed pattern to a sweltering rainforest mist. As Meeah lifted her head and leaned back, Tylowe could not tell if tears were rolling down her face or if the shower was fooling his eyes. He leaned in and kissed her cheek. He tasted salty tears.

He looked up in to her wet eyes, and said, "I have many things to tell you, and none of what I have to say is about us being apart. But, there is a lot going on. Maybe because we haven't had troubles like so many others, we lost our way, but you know trouble brought us together. Maybe some struggle will remind us of what we mean to each other."

Her tongue slid in his ear and she said, "Could we talk in the morning? Right now, I want to ride this hardness, and feel you get off inside me. I want your dick to go to war inside and make me give you my last breath. Then, my dear, I want to sleep in your arms like I haven't in a long time."

He didn't have to answer as her hips started going up and down on his dick. She rode him in a funky-sexy-rhythm, prompted by the band Incognito with Maysa Leak singing "Beneath the Surface." The song's intensity picked up as did Meeah, while riding her husband's hardness. The showerheads changed pattern again to short, powerful squirts. Tylowe made Meeah stand up, and turn around. She braced herself against the shower wall. With his hands holding her hips firmly, he looked down on her spread, round ass; he was rubbing his dick on the crease of her ass, watching his dick head pop through. When he stopped, a clear stream of pre-cum was attached, like a string connecting his head to her ass in the mist of the steam beading on her ass.

Tylowe moved her over to a specific spot. He reached over and hit a button, and eight more showerheads started spraying up from the floor and sides. He angled his dick, and she felt a driving force shocking her. When Tylowe pulled out of her pussy and off her ass, just a little with each hump, several shower heads jetted long streams of hot water up and under the shaft of his dick, and on her asshole and her clit. He humped harder, trying to cum inside her. Both of them were loud, swallowing panting breaths.

He leaned his chest on her back and wrapped his arms around her stomach. He arched his feet up to his toes and humped like a wild dog, yet it was not long, deep penetration. The head of Tylowe's dick was just past her opening, rubbing on her G-spot. Meeah humped back with short, rapid thrusts. She was working on a mini orgasm when finally Tylowe held still. He let out one long grunt as his cum shot hard into Meeah. She felt a vigorous force of warm fluid inside her. The hard gush felt as if it could have shot across the room. His body followed with short, erratic, animalistic lunges.

He rested on her back; his thighs were camping a bit. She held him up as she felt his hot shot inside her flooding around his dick, and oozing out as he lost his firmness.

As the showerheads changed their spray pattern again, they finally showered.

CHAPTER 26

Revelations, Terminations, and Culminations

C ome morning, the rain was washing the windows with a deluge as Tylowe and Meeah sat up in bed. Gold-toned, heavy-thread-count sheets covered their legs. Her breasts and his chest were bared to the world—they were comfortable and at home. The mirrored ceiling over their bed reflected the two leaning on each other. The rain made the lake look blurry, and the cloudy sky seemed to be at eye level as the wind blew. A powerful wind caused whistling sounds that died down and returned in sweeping bursts. The early morning gray sky went grayer in their eyes, as if smudged with a paint brush. The night before, a beautiful sunset had met them in the living room, and had set in motion the love they had made in the shower as the last of its light disappeared.

Many events in their life had set the stage for a conversation long overdue. It was time. With so much on his mind, he hoped all he had to say to his wife would not turn into a storm all by itself.

When…just when, do you tell the person closest to you difficult things?

Missing pieces of knowledge call out for understanding, if you don't know who knows what and when. He had information to share. He had questions of his wife that included their past. Tylowe told his wife about Elliot reaching out from prison, and how he and Psalms had visited him. He recounted the part about slugging Elliot finally, as he had wanted to many years ago. Elliot had hurt Meeah, and his own daughter, treating them badly with his perverted life-style and criminal activities.

In a previous life, Elliot and Meeah married because her father pressured her, for reasons she wished he would burn down in hell. In her life with Elliot, he treated her like a marble. He rolled her in and out of games, all for his own personal gain. The man drained her soul, and twisted her family. He mixed with the Russian mob, leading a criminal enterprise.

The stress of feeling trapped caused her to lose her emotional balance and disconnect her from reality for a short time. The mental breakdown allowed Elliot to take Meeah's daughter away.

Meeah regained her balance, but then she was forced to live apart from her daughter. Elliot manipulated Meeah's agony. Forced to remain married to him for the right to have some interaction with her daughter, she did what any mother would do. She bowed down to his ugliness and evil deeds to be in her daughter's life.

How did it all go bad? Elliot conned her father, an influential Caribbean artist with a sizable fortune from his art galleries and an enormous art school in Vancouver, B.C. In a well-planned blitz, Elliot gained full control of all his holdings after Meeah married Elliot and her father died.

Prior to Elliot ripping her life apart, Meeah was a model working runways all throughout the Caribbean, Canada, and Europe. She had art skills, too; she'd inherited her mom's and dad's artistic abilities, and Meeah's talent was receiving recognition.

Meeah loved her father to no end, but he was a playboy, with art groupies sucking his human ink. Her parents worked together as a team, but not as a loving couple. Her mom loved her dad, but Dad painted many women down on vertical canvases with brush strokes of sex.

After her father passed away, Meeah met her father's other women and her other grown half-brothers and half-sisters. They emerged from all over the Caribbean, contacting her or Meeah's mom. Some came with a hand out; others just let their truth come forward.

Meeah and Elliot had a baby together, Mia. Thinking Elliot would be different from her father, Meeah eventually opened her eyes. Elliot also had other children around the world. As Elliot became increasingly verbally sadistic, she was determined not to be a fool like her mother.

Her saying no to Elliot's behavior and trying to walk away with their daughter became a nightmare. Tylowe just so happened to have walked in to her life, and woke her up the moment they met.

Before Meeah made the break from Elliot, he planted one of the ugliest seeds a man could plant in a woman's mind and between her legs. He told her he had other women because she was a bore in bed, and he'd rather make love to a dead virgin.

When Meeah met Tylowe, and she thought that he wanted to make love to her, she told him she might not be able to satisfy him. Meeah was strong, but damaged, when Tylowe met her. Tylowe, the man he was, took the time needed to listen to her. He understood for his own sake that she was the woman who could heal him. He had been living with his own version of a fractured spirit. Tylowe stepped up and took on the challenge of loving Meeah. In doing so, he found loving her and accepting her love was easy. Tylowe found her love for him to be perfect.

The challenge was the fact that Elliot and Tylowe used to be best friends. When he met Meeah for the first time, Tylowe did not know that Elliot was her husband. It was a distressing case of déjà vu, but the tables were turned.

Tylowe and Elliot had a nasty history, like having a mouth full of vinegar and not being able to spit it out. Elliot had been one of the major factors that caused Tylowe's breakup with his fiancée over twenty years earlier. Because of that breakup, Tylowe didn't know that he had a daughter for ten years. Elliot only agreed to give up certain information to reduce his prison sentence.

Tylowe and Meeah married after all the dust settled. They raised their two girls together. Tyreene Pearlene, was Tylowe's daughter by his ex-fiancée. The ex-fiancée had passed away before he found out about his daughter. Other people were raising her, but they had hoped one day Tylowe would find out and come for her.

The girls were grown now, living healthy, productive lives, leaving Tylowe and Meeah alone with each other, but maybe missing the responsibilities that helped to bring them together.

As Tylowe told Meeah of Elliot's other children, she cried. Hearing his name more than in passing made her sick. Hurt and angry, she understood it fit the life of a man who had once made her life hell. She had heard there could be other kids, but she never connected with them or knew where they were. She had assumed most of the kids he'd fathered had no knowledge of who he was.

Tylowe had much to tell her, and even told of his meeting an ex-girlfriend. She got up out of the bed, and got his belt. She playfully threatened him, and told him he'd better not give her good thing to an oldie-and-no-goodie-anymore hoochie mama.

"Well, babe, if I'm willing to tell you, I am more assured than you. There is no woman I know whom I could tell. I feel proud of you, myself, and our relationship that I can come home, and not have to carry any guilt. It's foolish for either one of us to act as if other people aren't attracted to us."

Meeah kissed his forehead. "Oh, babe, I see women still looking at you. In a strange way, I get turned on when I know I have you, and another woman is checking you out." Meeah leaned against him again and squeezed his hand.

He told her about finding the kids and the trouble they encountered, though he didn't give her the details of all Suzy Q's deeds. Meeah knew better than to ask.

"Honey…Tylowe, let me get us some coffee. I always pray in front of you, all the time, with no problem, we both do, but I'm going in the kitchen and have a little talk with God. You could have been hurt. Maybe even worse could have happened while you were in Vegas messing around with dangerous people. This stuff bothers me! I'm disturbed. I thank God for delivering you back to me, but dammit, Tylowe." Her face was tight, and her brown skin lost the battle to crimson tones. His eyes opened wide, turned to circles, and lit up like new silver dollars.

"Honey…" She took a deep breath. "You are the man who excites me and you've stepped up and been the man I needed. There is no doubt you can take care of yourself." She took an even deeper breath, and then took a long pause before she continued. "I'm trying to be careful how I say what's on my mind. I'm saying this because in no way do I want to belittle you. You know that's not me. I never talk crazy to you. I learned a long time ago to trust you, and let you lead because I have faith in you as my man. So forgive me if what I say comes out wrong, but I will mean what I say. You are not Psalms Black. You are a hell of a man to me, but Psalms Black is some kind of warrior that you are not. I don't want you to be anything like him. I'm not putting him down. He is your friend; I respect him, and I respect your friendship with him. I do like him. He has been your friend since you two were in grade school, yet there is a dark side of Psalms that I fear. I fear you will try to emulate what he is capable of if pushed to the wrong corner. I'm not scared that he will put you into something bad, but I wonder will you, in an effort to prove yourself, do something that you… are…not…made…for!

"How he would handle a dangerous situation, as opposed to you, is like a runaway freight train running into a Benz sitting on the railroad tracks. He does things I don't know about, and don't want to know, but I do know they are different from how you approach things. With that said, I don't want you in any type of situations he's apt to be involved in at that level.

"You won't react like him, and that might have me receiving a call telling me you will not be coming…home. I believe Psalms will kill to protect us, and that could be a blessing. Men like him see justice through a different scope. He and Suzy Q live by another code and Q is my sister in many ways, so I know how she thinks just from being near her all these years.

"Psalms is like The Black Avenger. Hell, he protected the president; I wish he was protecting the black president now with all these crazies. He protected Gabrielle abroad. When I see him, I think he comes right out of a superhero comic book, and it's for him no joke.

"I know you know, Tylowe. He's been your friend forever. I know he don't don a cape and fly, but he can cause destruction on his way to saving people. And…most likely, sleep well, believing he's done the job needed.

"It got around about what happened on the boat about the husband who was beating on his wife and now he is soon to be an ex-husband. The woman says she doesn't know what happened to her husband in that room, but he damn near delivered his whole paycheck to Darcelle's office when she told him to only give twenty-five percent."

Tylowe smiled, as she did, too. "It does sound funny, but if a man gives up that percentage enthusiastically, no questions asked, he smelled his own hurt close by."

"Yeah, babe, you're right about that."

"Gabrielle loves Psalms something fierce. If his underwear is funky, she'd love the smell of them, so I know he's a man that knows how to love, and must have positive qualities of a softer side, I'm sure.

"Gabrielle, she understands things I don't. She worked in a world where she could justify which country got aid for sick kids and no aid for other poor kids in another country. For her to have a man like Psalms, it works on whatever level it is.

"Baby…honey, please be my kind of stud, my kind of man, and my kind of lover as you have always been. Be my blessing at the start of the day and before I close my eyes at night, but please don't try to be a mercenary-type warrior against people who don't have a heart like you. Be my kind of protector and please keep being the man I have loved, but please don't be a headstone I go visit once a year."

"Meeah—"

She softly she placed her finger over his lips. "Shhh," she cut him off. "I know you have to do what you have to do concerning this situation; I'm just asking you to be careful. I love you. Now I'm going to get some more coffee, and pray some more, giving more thanks. When I come back, tell me more about these children, my daughter's half-brother and sister."

"Okay, baby, I'm glad I'm back here with you. Tell God thank you for me. But there is one thing, though, I need to know right now."

Meeah turned her head to the side, and she saw a puzzled look on Tylowe's face. "What, baby? What's wrong?"

"Don't you love me enough to smell my funky underwear?"

She slowly walked away while saying, "Baby, since the first time you left your funky drawers on the floor, I've been smelling them. That's why all this works." She ran her hand over her ass and made sure he saw her switching as she left the room.

The rain was letting up and the wind was dying down. The skies were now light gray as Tylowe and Meeah drank another morning cup of coffee. Tylowe told the rest of the story about the kids, their great-aunt and their mother. He told her how the mother had been using the name Elnah Runway.

"Her real name is Queen Frêche. She's my sister. She is an older half-sister," Meeah said.

Tylowe's head whipped to the point he felt a sharp pain. "Baby, I've met some of your half-sisters and brothers years ago. We have pretty reliable information that she's the daughter of a former president of Martinique."

"Yes, you know my father had other children. I met many of them after he passed. Well, Queen was one of them. I saw her on and off during my childhood. I was told she was my second cousin by my mother and father. I always thought it odd that my father had this girl with him sometimes while we vacationed in different parts of the Caribbean. The truth is my father had an affair with her mother, who was married to President Frêche, and he raised her as his own to avoid embarrassment. Maybe he didn't care, and just loved her, period.

"My father and the president are cousins. When my father passed, Queen was at the funeral in Cuba. You know we Canadians often go to Cuba, and that's where my father wanted his ashes to be thrown in the sea. Queen told me she thought she was my sister. The president could not have children. The man who raised her had suspicions that her father was the one who provided the seed."

"Meeah, my head is spinning." Tylowe saw the sweeping view from his bedroom go back to darker gray.

"My heart is ripping, Tylowe. You said this woman—my half-sister—was viciously murdered. She has a child whom you say the girl at least looks and sounds like Mia."

"This is confusing, dear. Do you know why she would use the name Elnah Runway, since you used the same last name?" Tylowe asked.

"Simple. She, too, was married to Elliot. I told you when we met, and after you found out that Elliot was my husband, that he had done a lot of dirt. I heard rumors he had another wife before me. When I asked him he said no, but others whispered in my ear. I'm assuming it was my half-sister, Queen. It makes sense now."

"Why?"

"When she and I met as adults in Cuba at my father's funeral, she was going by the last name Runway. As a child, the few times I was around her, she went by the name Elnah because she hated the name Queen for some reason. I could be wrong and there could be another connection, but I don't see how."

Tylowe stared blindly out of the windows as his mind strained to comprehend. Nothing made sense, but in other ways it did. Men creating children, not knowing they had created lives they should care for. Women having children and not knowing by whom, and potentially by someone they wished it wasn't. It tore at Tylowe. He had gone ten years with a child on this earth, not knowing his sperm had created her.

"I'll be back with more coffee," Meeah said. She went back into the kitchen and sat at the breakfast nook, praying again while she wept.

She came back into the bedroom. From across the room she saw Tylowe sitting in a chair by the windows. He had on a blue silk smoking jacket and black silk pajama bottoms. She viewed her husband as black royalty, but right now he looked so sad. She walked over to him and handed him his coffee.

"Tylowe, I want the kids to come here. I want to do this along with you and raise them and protect them." She dwelled on what she wanted and along with him, watched the clouds over the lake move like something was pulling them. Bits of sun peeked through. "Those kids didn't ask for any of this, and they stand a good chance to be left along the wayside with no one to love them. We have a lot to share. And we need to do this for them, and Tylowe, we need to do it for us.

"We have two grown girls, and they should be a part of this, especially Mia." Meeah sat in the chair across from him. She placed her long brown legs in his lap. He rubbed the bottom of her feet.

"Are you sure? Every day you could be reminded of the hurtful times you had with their biological father."

"He's a nonfactor to me. I have you. I have the kind of man who has run away the storms that evil man poured on me. No matter how many kids he fathered, I believe all kids should have a chance, no matter what country they come from or what human provided the seed."

"Meeah, if that's what you think we should do, I'm all for it. I will say this, though. We need to know everyone you are related to, and I hope are not."

"What, you don't want to be my cousin?" They laughed, but it was subdued.

"Meeah, we have to think beyond just giving the kids a home. It appears that someone wants these kids dead. Money sitting in foreign bank accounts to the tune of millions is slated to go to the kids when they reach a certain age. We are dealing with Elliot, we are dealing with the Russians, and we have been there before. It wasn't easy. You know it took the Canadian government and lots of lawyers to untangle us from all that many years ago."

"The question is, is it the right thing to do?"

Tylowe stood up and lifted Meeah's hand and she stood with him. He kissed her forehead. "Yes, it's the right thing to do, and the only thing to do."

The rest of the morning they talked about the lives coming their way, and all the things that would have to be done. There was still a great danger in all that was going on. Precautions were necessary and changes had to be made.

After the morning filtered in to the afternoon, Tylowe called Psalms and let him know a new day brought forth new revelations, terminations, and culminations.

The man screamed as the injection went in his back, but the sound was muffled by a rag stuffed in his mouth. Mommy Dearest would have screamed, but her vocals played defiant and she was gagged. Her face showed her true feeling—fear.

Dillard and his mother, Lilly, had terrorized Darcelle Day's future and her daughter's well-being. Now Psalms and Mintfurd were doing the same to them. The ex-husband of Darcelle had picked a fight that he would leave from with more than a black eye.

The ex-husband's mother also played her revolting part in creating the hell that had Darcelle living in confusion about her and her daughter's safety.

Anyone who had an evil thought about a child declared war with Psalms Black. This was his war now. Psalms served his righteousness as if he were a white hot poker straight out of hell, and he accepted no pleas for leniency.

Often Psalms' vengeance involved someone harming or threatening children. In thinking about a child, he'd quickly think about the hell Evita had lived in her father's house of horror.

Most people were talkers. Psalms Black was not a talker. He was a man of action. Knowing most would act as if they saw nothing if faced with civic duty, hearing people say things such as, "If someone does this, I'll cap their ass, or I'll kick someone's ass" would draw his anger.

Darcelle's ex-husband lay prone, tied down right next to his mother. As a matter of fact, Dillard and his mother, Lilly, were tied together face to face, hip to hip. Naked. Strange. The foulness of their own incest for the first time felt ugly.

"Maybe this is some old English monarchy shit, but you endanger your own daughter with this uncouthness and I'm gonna make you deal with a lifetime of pain." Psalms' words crawled up to their ears like a rattlesnake. He paced around them as if he was about to strike with deadly force.

"So you two fuck each other...dear mommy and her birthed child, and then want to add the foulness of your sickness as a threat to a child? You threaten to blackmail the mother of your child by exposing your own sickness. And you do this for more money so you can keep living in this beautiful condo?"

Psalms looked over and nodded to Mintfurd who had another electronic device in his hand. Mintfurd, with his pretty, handsome face that never changed expression, tapped several positions on a touch pad. The ex-husband's body jerked as if he were in an electric chair, and he gurgled a sound not known to humans.

They were on the top floor of an extremely nice, but older, condo on the Southwest side of Queen Anne Hill. From the unit, there was a spectacular night view of the Puget Sound waters and downtown Seattle. It was the opposite view that Psalms had from his condos on the Northwest side of Alki Beach.

A cruise ship was coming in from Alaska; several tugboats assisted it into port. The new Ferris wheel on the pier shone blue and bright against the night sky. The top of the Space Needle glowed orange to symbolize the coming orange full moon.

Psalms walked around the place in a white lab coat, holding his white latex-gloved hands behind his back. He looked like a bodybuilder playing a surgeon. Mintfurd was dressed the same way, but with his size, he looked like a whole church choir dressed in white.

"I want this place," Psalms said.

Mintfurd nodded.

Darcelle's ex-husband was still screaming, but it was faint to the ear. The injection he was receiving with a needle made for a horse felt like a spinal tap with no pain killer as it went into his back. Mommy Dearest couldn't comfort her mother-fucking son. She vomited in her son's face as she finally lost control of her defiance.

She reminded Psalms of a man he and his Navy SEAL team had captured to extract some information. She had the same look of defiance despite taking the same ass-whooping that would stay with that man the rest of his life.

At midnight, Psalms had exited a black SUV, carrying what looked like a bottle of wine in a pretty red silk bag. He wore a slightly oversized fedora with a wide brim tilted downward along with round glasses. He looked to be a gentleman caller for a late-night rendezvous. It was not an altogether rare sight in Seattle, a black man coming into a nice building at night. Mintfurd had already made it possible to enter through the electronic door. He had already bypassed the security system and camera digital recording through the Internet. He downloaded footage from other nights, showing people going in the building, but now it would be time stamped at the same time Psalms entered. Mintfurd killed the feed of the back entrance and dubbed in other footage, so he could come in when Psalms opened the back door.

It wasn't super spy science; it was simple matter for today's electronic engineers. Traveling up the service elevator and down the hall safe and sound, Mintfurd pushed a button on a control key fob and electronic magnets unlocked the door. With a dart gun in hand that could have been a hundred years old in design, Psalms entered the condo.

The TV was on a Sirius XM radio station. The Beatles' "Sergeant Pepper's Lonely Hearts Club" played throughout the condo.

Psalms walked up to the man sleeping in a lounge chair on the deck. The deck was glass-enclosed, so it was warm enough to sleep with the Seattle night skyline as the last thing to see as one fell asleep. Psalms walked around him and put the gun in front of the man's face.

Something in humans alerts the subconscious and makes most aware danger in front of them. He opened his eyes and he saw death coming if he yelled. Psalms signaled to get up and come inside. Inside on the living room floor, Mintfurd had Mommy Dearest already naked and gagged, lying on a plastic painter's tarp. The Beatles music changed to the song, "Come Together."

Twenty minutes later, Psalms had a rather long and wide hypodermic needle inserted in the man's back and Mommy Dearest had just vomited in her son's face. She couldn't take the look of pain on his face anymore, and she cried like a mooing cow. Her turn with pain was still to come.

"Here's what's going on folks. You will leave Darcelle alone. You're not even allowed to have a bad dream about her. From this moment on, you don't have a daughter and you were never married to Darcelle. You will sell this condo. My people will be in contact. All the money will go in to a trust fund for Darcelle's daughter because, as I said, you don't have a daughter anymore. You and

Mommy are filthy pieces of shit, and I'm not allowing you to smell her sweetness, and I sure as hell don't want her to think you're worthy of her child's love.

"What is happening to you, what you're feeling, in your back, is me inserting a small electronic capsule in the muscle near your spine. Now, don't worry; it's not close enough to cripple you... yet. But what do you have to worry about?" Psalms did something unusual when he was putting in work. Work was life and death. He chuckled with a sinister growl.

Mintfurd narrowed his eyes.

"What you have to worry about is that if I push a button and the pain you feel from the capsule goes into you, you will have a little explosion inside your body.

"Your life is in that capsule. If you make one false step, I will release the meningitis in your body. If you don't know, it's an infection of viruses and bacteria, or other bugs, in proximity of your spinal cord leading to your brain.

"All you have to do is fuck up and come near Darcelle and her daughter in this lifetime in any form whatsoever. Be prepared for how the end will come. It starts with headaches and stiffness, fever, confusion or, vomiting, and an inability to tolerate light and lots of rashes. Now if you survive the meningitis, the long-term consequences, deafness and epilepsy, will crawl through you. You'll want your life to end.

"All I have to do is signal the little electronic capsule inside, and your hell will be in full play. If you think a drug or doctor can save you, that's not going to happen. The capsule is close enough to your spine that it will kick your ass just like that pain you feel now, but much worse.

"If you think, maybe, you can get far enough away, remember

I'm also tracking you, and you will feel an irregular painful jolt. That will be me checking in on you. I'll just be reminding you I can get to you." He chuckled again once again with a sinister growl.

Another Beatles song, "Eleanor Rigby," played. Psalms nodded his head to the song beat and mouthed the words,

"All the lonely people
Where do they all come from?"

He and Mintfurd finished with the man and then went to work on the mother. She was tougher than her son, but the fear made it clear to the immoral mother and son that their blackmailing game was over.

A Rolling Stones song, "You Can't Always Get What You Want," came on.

"But if you try sometimes you just might find
You get what you need

When justice was finished, and the cleanup done, Mintfurd left first, and Psalms did a walk-through, not that he worried about leaving evidence of a crime. These two were so scared they wouldn't shit for a week, maybe two. A couple of huge black men had come into their place, as smoothly as a whale rises out of the water and blows, and did things to them only heard of in Cold War times.

Psalms knew the incest these two shared would never happen again, not that he cared. He didn't think the man would ever put another diaper on and ask a woman to have sex with him. The two would never get meningitis, either. Psalms didn't mind inserting diabolical thoughts, but fear was the actual sentence he had injected into them. The electronic devices inserted into both of them would send harsh periodic pain through their bodies as a reminder to be fearful.

Ms. Melfae said, "No, I'm not going, and I'm not selling. I don't owe anybody for my house, and I have taken care of it. It's not falling down, and no one is going to knock it down!"

Despite the new world around her, she refused to cave in by selling her house to developers. They built condos and other commercial-use structures next to and across from her. The city hall gangsters sent "progress" after her to eventually drive her out of her home. It came in the form of taxes due. The tax bill was no longer for residential housing, but rather set to an unbending commercial land ownership tax. The bill put Ms. Melfae in a flux making it hard to keep her home. She got too old for a city she had lived in most of her life and loved. Ms. Melfae was trying to live the American dream, but progress tried to tell her that her American dream was dead.

Psalms became aware of her struggle when zoning laws became a problem for him as he wanted to build his condos. Ms. Melfae used to be one of Psalms' grandfather's lady friends. To what level that meant, he didn't know. He assumed she was close enough since she was there in the house when he woke up a few times as a child. The story of Ms. Melfae not wanting to sell her house hit the local airwaves. The progressive liberals got their signals crossed and acted like conservatives by not stepping up, and putting their convictions aside to do the right thing and support her. They were too busy thinking about all they had to do was think green.

Their idea of doing the right thing was to put Obama stickers on their Priuses, and cruise their little electric cars at 50 mph on overly congested freeways. They acted numb to the old lady's pleas. But, Psalms laid out the real green and paid her taxes, then financed the conversion of three floors of her house into a unique restaurant.

Ms. Melfae lived at the top on the fourth floor, so it worked

An eye for an eye! Psalms could not justify killing the man and the mother, when they had not physically caused pain to Darcelle and her daughter. Death was only for those who caused death or tried to cause loss of life. Psalms often reflected on his and his grandfather's Bible study on the weekends they'd spent on Orcas Island in the little house.

Psalms walked around, admiring the new condo he was about to own. He watched the two nasty humans lying on the floor, out cold. "They will wake up lying in their own piss and shit and wish it was a bad dream, but fear will have them stir-crazy."

Before he walked out the door, the band Heart was jamming "Magic Man," then another song from the Northwest rock-funk band, "Barracuda."

He laughed. "Yep, a barracuda will leave your ass in pain, or dead."

He closed the door.

CHAPTER 28

Them Changes

Mintfurd turned into the parking lot of Ms. Melfae's BF. The neon sign on a tall pole read:

Ms. Melfae's BF
Baked or Fried
24 Hours Always Open

The four-story house converted into a restaurant stood as lonely as an outcast. Other similar turn-of-the-century homes, with small pillars and tall steps leading up to their doors, had gone by the wayside of inner-city progress. The old house quartered between the Central Area and Capitol Hill of Seattle, where many blacks once resided close to downtown. The modern-day city crept up like a military coup and ran the people away, defeating the culture of its old hood, and leaving the house in arrested development.

Eddie Cotton, the famous 1960s Seattle boxer, had a great diner in the area that closed down, and then the church on the corner sold. Next, other black businesses—cleaners, pool halls, bookstores and houses, one and two at a time, sold off.

First-floor retail buildings replaced homes, adding on high-end apartments that now soared above an inner-city strip mall. All the houses disappeared or deteriorated from neglect, except for the owner of one house.

perfectly for meeting retail and housing zoning codes just like the other brand-new buildings squeezed around her. Ms. Melfae was very well known for cooking for every person she met, and with Psalms' help, she now had a twenty-four-hour restaurant, which stayed busy with many of the customers from liberal Yuppieville.

Mintfurd turned the ignition key hard and quick to turn the engine off. The stereo kept playing Jimi Hendrix's "Machine Gun."

He and Psalms listened to Jimi burning hell up with his guitar spraying ice from his cold- ass soloing. After the song, Mintfurd's voice had more bass than a teenager with a car trunk full of speakers. Psalms waited for Mintfurd to say what he had to say.

"PB, we do business and business only; it's never personal, and never should be. Our job is to remove danger, and help those who don't have options."

Mintfurd looked at Psalms the same way he had when they were college wrestlers about to face off; they gained respect for each other. Enemy competitors back then, but loyal friends and business partners now, they were punishers of wrongdoers.

They were Black Muslims—less the Muslim part—ridding the block of those who would bring harm to regular citizens. Their thuggish prosecutions brought justice to individuals who did thug deeds. They were a chastising force: the law itself, dovetailed into judge, jury and sentence givers. Men on fire.

Sitting in the SUV, these two had enough testosterone, courage, and warrior skills for eleven football players to win in any game. The stereo changed to Jimi Hendrix and Buddy Miles jamming live, "Them Changes."

The song had ended many minutes later before Psalms responded.

"I'm wrong! I'm all the way wrong. I slipped up by letting my attitude have a piece of this job. I deserve your wrath pinning me down on my actions. I displayed anger. I made it personal. I know how this works."

Psalms and Mintfurd, for all the right reasons, still were criminals in the sense of man's legal laws. To keep their business of avenging, one's ego could not overrun the other partner. Crime partners had to love each other's freedom; if not, like most crime partnerships, they would fail.

Psalms and Mintfurd never set out to be avengers, but as one case kept leading to others, more complicated justice had to be served. The two never looked back, always looking forward to righting wrongs.

"Man, I apologize. A couple of things have me swaying in the wind and off my A game. Let's talk inside; I'm hungry. I know your big ass is hungry."

Ms. Melfae's spacious restaurant had almost no inner walls dividing the rooms. Each floor had a kitchen at the rear, with a stairwell connecting each kitchen and food elevators to deliver food to the right floor. At the front, large glass windows overlooked the busy street. On the third floor, one could view downtown Seattle as if on a big-screen TV. With her living quarters above the restaurant, Ms. Melfae had a picture-perfect view. Psalms and Mintfurd walked up to the third floor. An elevator could take patrons up to each level. In the basement, a 1950s Harlem-style speakeasy had jazz on the weekends.

The corner table was always reserved for Psalms and his friends. The restaurant light was almost shadowy, but each table had a lighted gold-toned table lamp that gave an ambiance of private dining. Ms. Melfae's daughter, Akilah, approached the table with two bootleg dark beers. She managed the graveyard shift, and had a singing voice and sent her orders to the kitchen by song.

"Uncle Psalms and Uncle Mintfurd, what would you like?"

"Send us the last of and the most of what is in the kitchen. No need to make anything; just give us what's in the pots that is already made."

Natalie Cole's "Just Can't Stay Away" was playing low, and Akilah sung over the top to the melody. "For table number one, two plates of the last of what's in the kitchen; fill them up to the top, and bless them." She walked away, and people clapped lightly.

"Velvet tells me you're almost a virgin again. Don't trip, you know she was going to tell me, and you would have told me if I had asked," Psalms said.

"I thought you had an issue you wanted to tell me about, because me not paying for pussy is not an issue."

"Nah, man, that's not an issue, but what I have to say is related."

"How is that?" Mintfurd's lip moved toward the side of his face, a facial expression he made often when he asked a question.

Psalms' eyes ventured to the black art on the wall. Jean-Michel Basquiat, Jacob Lawrence, and more contemporary artists like Kehinde Wiley, Nina Chanel Abney, Xaviera Simmons, and Jayne Alexander adorned the walls. Small fused spotlights put the art in perfect light to view from many angles. He had admired the original prints many times, and had helped curate the striking display.

Psalms' mind traveled a road he thought he had already mapped out on what he wanted to say to Mintfurd. His eyes diverted while searching for the right words. Finally, he just let it flow. "Tonight that revolting man and his vile mama threatened the well-being of a woman I met. That brought us to this job. What has my skin crawling, and my mind squeezing hate, is that this woman wants to do beneficial actions for others. She's been naïve in her choice of men, and it has cost her time in life, disrupting her journey. The woman is extremely beautiful, although not my type because she is small. But she is old-school foxy.

"The lady doesn't seem to know how to protect herself. She's been in the mode of letting love go away and just dealing, before moving into the mode of hating, gunning, knifing, boiling and throwing hot grits. So many people say they love, but do the bare minimum to preserve it, instead of pouring their complete soul in to it. When that happens, folks just start dealing before hating."

Mintfurd's lips moved to the other side and adjusted his body in his chair. In most places, when he sat down, the chair almost disappeared. His shoulders were nearly the width of the table, but because that was their revered table, one of the chairs had his name on it, and was super-sized. An average person sitting in his seat looked like a baby in a high-chair.

"What's all that have to do with me?" Mintfurd's lips pushed back to the other side for a moment, and his handsome face relaxed.

"Man, shit, I…damn, man, I'm trying to make sense, and it's not making sense, but I'll get there. Some women love harder than any man can conceive. Men often receive love they can't feel, or don't know what to do with it when they feel it. A woman's heart is unlike a man's heart when it comes to the depth of compassion. A woman's love can go deep. Certain things don't compute, or convert into a language men will ever understand. A man often loves through the fantasy of what he wants his woman to be, and pretends that she is his fantasy for a length of time, but you know sadly that relationship will have problems. A woman loves what's in front of her. She tends to adapt, and love the ground her man walks on, and the air he breathes. She can't help it.

"Women are born to love and nurture, and nest. We men benefit from that nurturing, because a woman leads us to understand it's in a man's best interest. Men may rule this earth, but women hold it together when we tear it apart.

"Men want their sons to be soldiers, race car drivers, and professional athletes and so on. A woman only wants to be proud of her son and wants him to find a suitable woman to be one with, honoring God, and blessing the world with children. Some of those things she may not have herself."

Mintfurd nodded his head. "Yeah, that is something I know about, but never really give it much thought. My mom, after all these years, still expects me to come home with a wife, and make babies. She still wants me to have a wife so they can go to Women's Day programs at church."

There was a strange look on Psalms' face as he was contemplating. What would his mother think, or say, about him bringing home a bride?

He passed through those thoughts as fast as he could. He had already let emotions get in the way tonight. "You and me, and most men, want our daughters to be pretty, successful, and to find husbands so they can run off and have pretty kids. All so we can say, 'Look at my daughter.' A woman never wants her daughter going through the hardships she had to, and may still be going through.

"A woman wants her daughter to believe in herself and never base her worth on what a man thinks. Ask a man does he believe in that and he'll say yes, but only when brought to his attention.

"In a man, a woman may want more, but she bends and fits in to a man's way of thinking more than we as men rethink and bend. As men, we don't flow as easy in to reshaping or changing for the love of a woman. Many women, all they know is how to love, and not how to defend their souls. And they shouldn't have to. But as the world turns, men want to control everything even when it makes no sense."

Mintfurd honed in. "Man wants to control even the mongoose, even though the mongoose kills the snake that would kill a man."

"Yeah, that's about right, and women are always in a fight to be what God intended them to be—lovers of men's souls, despite a man's shortcomings.

"You've heard women say, 'I wish a man would love me as I'd love him.' Even when a woman doesn't give as much as she thinks she has, it's still that's all that matters."

Psalms got up from the table and went over to a 1960s Magnavox stereo floor cabinet. He lifted the top and inside was a mix of old and new electronics. He pushed a button, and "Days Like This" by Kenny Lattimore played.

A woman across the room popped her finger and bopped her head and pointed toward Psalms. Seeing his old high school classmate, he walked over to the table and had a short conversation with her. Officer CC is what most called her. Her perfect black skin, tall statuesque figure, and sensual, sauntering walk snapped many heads out of place. She was a black policewoman who rolled in her own squad car before many policewomen did. She could handle most men with just a stare that said, "Try me." She had the Pam Grier tough and fine appearance cloned to perfection.

She and Psalms shared street information. Although she did not fully know what Psalms did, she had an idea. He had dropped off or led her to a few hand-delivered busts, and she in return, had provided information when he'd asked, with no questions. They shared some intel before he went back to his table.

Mintfurd had a question he wanted to ask before Psalms left the table and asked when he returned. "You said even when a woman doesn't or hasn't given as much as she thinks she has, nevertheless it doesn't matter. How is that okay?" His lips went to one side.

Psalms almost finished his beer, and swirled the bottom around before he responded. "No matter what, we men don't understand what their heads and hearts believe. We have to support them without tearing apart their hearts just to prove we are right. The same God made us; He just made us different from, not less than, each other. Yeah, for sure, there are some damaged women. No matter what any man will do, there is no man who can satisfy their soul.

"This is where often the dishonest side of relationships crop up and destroy hope of having a good relationship. Now think about this before you respond. Most often, women lie for survival, and men lie for gain. So, depending on how bad one wants to survive or how bad one wants to gain, you'll find out who's the best liar. When women lie for gain, I have to say they can be rather obvious, almost like they want us to know, but men try to act as if they don't. When men lie for survival, they often get caught up in their lies, because women expect men to lie and already know the truth before a man opens his mouth." Psalms took the last swig of his beer, and laughed.

Mintfurd took in a deep breath that several others could have used. "Man, this is a lot to take in concerning getting into and being a relationship. I'm kinda scared for many reasons, and I've heard a lot of people have mental issues, and the ugly side of their mental problems show up after you like or love the person."

"Yeah, you're right. Some folks have mental bruising, and it affects their perception and nothing is normal for them or level in their lives."

Psalms thought about Evita and her struggles in life, brought on by a father who abused her. She was missing now, giving him pause to think what it could be again. His friend, Ayman, the basketball coach at East Seattle City College, and University of New Mexico college alum, had a relationship with a woman with mental issues. Suzy Q had to step in because it caused him troubles.

"Let any person who has psychological injuries, twisted sensitivities, and medicated or unmedicated issues, and put into the mix a broken heart, and castles made of sand will wash their heart out to sea. Sometimes people don't realize they are not giving as much as they think they are. Shit, even so-called normal folks come up short, and refuse to let anyone help them understand the harm they cause others.

"Now, take the woman who is deep into giving her soul to a man, well, that's one of the reasons I was pissed tonight. The woman we did some work for tonight is a good woman. Even though I should have control of my emotions when we are doing business, this woman's situation pissed me off. "

"Okay, I'm cool with you dropping some knowledge about women on me. Did you come to this all on your own?" Mintfurd laughed.

"Most of what I know came from the many conversations with my grandfather. He loved my grandmother who was blind. After she died, he had other women like Ms. Melfae and others. He was always honest with them, and gave them the choice to be in his life as he was. If they didn't want to, he still loved them and kept them in his life as friends.

"Later, when I traveled the world on assignment, I saw love in every language, and despite cultural differences, it was as my grandfather told me. Men are either honest or they're not, and women are lovers of the soul despite the good or evil in men.

"I observed and had a world view while working in Washington,

D.C. It was not all, but a lot of folks there are looking for a mate or an escort or booty-fling in that town. I did see some strong relationships endure the onslaught of dog eat dog, and the other side of the moon weirdness. The political hoopla of playboys and girls in that town—it reeks of fakeness and lies, so much so that people accept someone lying to their face."

"That's a lot, man—that's a lot to think about for someone like me."

The two men dropped their conversation as Phyllis Hyman's voice flowed in the room. She was singing "Hurry Up This Way Again."

"Oh how it hurts loving someone who has someone else
So many nights I spend here all alone by myself."

The song faded in to the instrumental version. Psalms responded to Mintfurd's last thought. "Man, it's a lot to think about no matter who you are, or where you are in life. There will always be more single people in the world, many of them telling that lie they want to be single. They lie, saying it's not worth the effort, yet let the right person smile just long enough, and they rethink their position."

"Yeah, Velvet said that to me."

Psalms laughed. "She kind of said the same thing to me just recently. Of course, I'm sure she said it to you much nicer than she told me, but many can't overcome some kind of hang-up. Hell, so many simply have the hardest time with the thought of being intimate with someone, so they become bitter and tear in to everybody else's less than happy home to make it worse. Single people are often like functional drunks. They go through life twisted, but seem normal. Those same people toss and turn in the bed feeling lonely whether they are twenty-eight or eighty-eight."

"So what are you saying? Should a person be with someone just so they're not lonely?"

"Nah, dude, a person can be lonely even with a person humping them right at that moment. What I am saying is, if you're lonely, be honest. Miserable people get in the middle of other people's love affairs, and hate on everyone else's relationships. Single people should shut the hell up talking about somebody else's relationship. So many souls are depleted of a balanced insight concerning relationships, because they've ingested so much pain that they feel the need to vomit sadness upon others, so not to be alone in their lonely sickness."

Mintfurd shook his head. "Yeah, that's scary when I hear that mess. We haven't talked about this in years, but I told you way back when that I didn't know about being in love, and having someone love me. Shit, my last girlfriend was in junior high. We're talking about almost forty years, a lifetime ago."

Mintfurd looked out on downtown Seattle. He understood for every light flicking there was a woman nearby, but wondered where was the light that flickered for him? A man his size, six feet six inches and 400 pounds and not obese, but toned and simply immense—he was a novelty to most women. A man with a golden voice and poetic thoughts was single and lonely. He had been all his life. When he was younger and smaller, women did come his way, but he was so shy and reserved. While in college, he was introduced to paying for a woman's physical love. Mintfurd's mind and body overtook his heart's need.

Akilah brought two huge platters of food and two more beers. Three ladies came in and sat nearby. The ladies of the evening were done selling sex for the night, or perhaps they were on break and still had work to do until the break of dawn. They wanted some attention other than from men in the streets wanting to buy them and use them. The three ladies interrupted the guys with silly jokes about how big they were, and how powerful they must be. Their attempt at flirting wasn't cute.

Akilah quickly did her hosting job and redirected the working girls to turn their attention away from Psalms and Mintfurd. Mintfurd wished more places provided that same professional care of their patrons.

Mintfurd did feel for the ladies, because even though he paid for his sexual needs with high-end expensive women, he felt the women sitting in the restaurant were no less women than those he paid a thousand a night to sleep with him. The only differences were more makeup, Macy's vs. Kmart attire, cute heels vs. old, run-down heels, and sexual mileage. He realized he was the common commodity in the equation, adding to the destruction of women who were high class, and mostly ended up low class, like the girls sitting not far away, because he paid for physical love.

Mintfurd made a change in life a nearly a year ago, and the only person he had told was Velvet. He was conflicted—the man needed the touch of a woman, but a year without having a nipple in his mouth made his dick get hard from the slightest thought of women.

Mintfurd's sexual urge raged when he woke in the morning, and when he went to bed. After a year of being without physical love, his dick would get thick and heavy in his hand even when he pulled it out to take a pee most times. His mind ventured to past sexual experiences, and the last time flashed though his cerebral streams like lightning.

The good thing about paying for sex and going through a professional service was he could order what he wanted, and needed. What he needed was a woman who was not uncomfortable with his size. Not simply speaking of his bodily size, but his penis girth. Long, yes, but also round. Some women had a problem putting their mouth around it and sucking it for very long. That meant few women could handle his hardness going into their pussy. She had to be wet. She had to be relaxed. Her pussy had to be receptive. Many times, women jacked him off with two hands instead, but even then, it was hard work.

He told Velvet this was a problem, and she had to know for herself if it was true. Curiosity sent her legs twitching and striding to the workshop one day. "Let me see it," she had demanded.

He had laughed, and dropped his pants. The sight of his massive thighs was a sight for science, the look in her eyes had said. Then he had dropped his boxers that could hold three men, and there it was.

"I would touch it, but that would mess up our friendship 'cause I would try to take it by hand back to the elephant you stole it from." They'd shared an intimate laugh. When he decided to forgo having sex with call girls, Velvet would ask whether he had "fed the elephant" to check if he had fallen off the call-girl wagon. It was a little joke between them.

"PB, I've heard it said with a woman, you share and learn to grow in love with a woman, but only another man can teach you to love women. It sounds like your grandfather shared a lot about learning to love a woman. I'm gonna share something with you.

"The last time I had sex with a woman, she rode my hardness in reverse cowboy. She had her ass facing me, and I could see my dick spread her pussy as it went deep in her. Her hands were on my thighs and her ass was trembling from taking me inside her expanding pussy. She had to go so slow descending down on my thickness. Her pussy juices ran down faster than her pussy could take my dick. When she finally took as much as she could, she leaned forward and pressed her breasts on my thighs, resting as if she had run from wild dogs. I could see my dick surrounded by her creamy pussy lips and I could see her asshole puckering and twitching. I tried to slide a finger in her ass, but my fingers are..."

"With those big-ass fingers, oh hell no. Man, you can't be a doctor and doing rectal examinations, dude. I see the size of your fingers, and I think surgery." Psalms laughed hard, and Mintfurd chuckled.

"Yeah, yeah, heard it all before. Anyway, once this woman adjusted to my size, her ass rose and came down working up in speed. Man, the visual from the last time keeps me horny as all get-out and lusting, wanting the bare skin of a woman curled into my body. She rode me for a long time, but suddenly she stopped and dismounted my hardness. The woman stood on the floor, and I sat up.

"She said, 'You're a nice guy, really sweet, and I love that we talk for hours...after we have sex.' Her eyes filled with tears for a while, and then she said, 'You pay me well, but...I'm getting out of doing this. I found a man to marry me.' She ran into the bathroom and came out a few minutes later and left.

"Man, I sat there for hours, asking one question. Was I supposed to ask her to marry me? Was I?" Mintfurd leaned back in his chair and took in the city lights flickering.

Psalms went to the Magnavox stereo, pulled an LP from the side-bin, and put it on the record player. A Marvin Gaye LP dropped, and "Trouble Man" played. He came back to the table as Akilah brought two more beers, and removed their empty food platters.

Psalms jumped in with what he had wanted to get to from the start. "Ms. Darcelle Day is that woman. She is going to do whatever she can to please a man even if it inflicts heartbreaking pain. I want you to meet her. I'm going to give you her number, and you call her and ask her out.

"This is a smart, intelligent, nonjudgmental woman. I think you'll find you'll have a lot in common. I know for a fact she is digging on you. Mintfurd, I think you can experience reality with her. She's gonna give you every opportunity to be the man you are and not change how you are, I have to believe. One of the blessings is she wants a man who won't lie and play games, and, well, you know that's not who you are.

"Dude, I know you're a humble man. And she's going to put energy in to having you be happy and pay attention to your relationship, first and foremost. I think you'll see rather quickly neither of you is going to want to stay away from enjoying each other.

"I can't speak on whether she is going to be able to handle you in bed, but her experiences with the men she's been with…well, she has an open desire to please.

"I think you should put that out there from the get-go, about who you are, and what you want, so you don't waste each other's time. Let her know, you ain't a little boy inside and out. As far as that goes, there is nothing that you shouldn't share. If you're not sharing everything, you could end up sleeping with an enemy. Some people are sleeping with strangers. Be each other's best friend. Why, of course, that's if you like her."

Another LP dropped, and a few pop and click sounds entered the room. People left and more came into the twenty-four-hour restaurant. "Strawberry Letter 23" by The Brothers Johnson made Psalms' foot tap, as his hand played a little air guitar.

"Oh, man, you playing a jam from way back. Look, check this out. PB, I know you ain't a matchmaker, so I'll give it a try. I'll call her and ask her out. This may sound strange, but I have never asked a woman out on a date. I've asked women to hang out, but they were in the friend camp all the way.

"I may not know much, but I do know how I would love to be touched, and how I would love a woman to talk to me. I may not know how I'll be heard and understood. I don't know what it feels like to be adored, and how would I inspire a woman to adore me, yet I know I need to find all that out."

The two men sat back in the chairs. Psalms went back to looking at the art on the walls. Mintfurd noticed a couple.

A man and woman sat across from each other with the table lights setting them aglow. He saw what he thought look liked love on their faces as their lips pursed. They leaned in toward each other while they held hands under the table. Smiles adorned their faces, and their lips never parted to speak words. He saw a lot being said in their time and space, in them staring at each other. Mintfurd pushed his lips to the side. He sensed that the woman loved the man in front of her, and he assumed the guy was in love because he had a silly little boy look on his face. Mintfurd chuckled, thinking he might be jealous at heart. At least he was hopeful for a change.

CHAPTER 29

Difficult Conditions

The room filled with a scream so loud it may have buckled the floor boards. Evita screamed with her body now tied at the ankles and the bed posts. Two leather straps held her wrists tied to the other bed posts. Naked. Oiled. Front and back.

A female with a strap-on dildo entered into Evita. Evita could not see because of the black hood, but she felt the woman's breasts on hers. She smelled the scent of a woman. The rubber dildo felt like a cold penis. Her vaginal walls and depth were not fully developed to take on an average-size penis, much less an artificially large one. Her own penis actually developed to a healthier size, relatively, but she was a female, physically and psychologically.

She had sensitivity in both of her genitals, but her female insides were less developed and made sexual intercourse difficult. She would set the conditions for a man and make sure he understood how deep he could go inside her.

She preferred sex with a woman, but she longed to be touched by man whom she could dominate. It became a skill of knowing and finding men with small penises. Part of her skill was in finding men with the right kind of freakdom to want to be with a hermaphrodite. She enjoyed being with a woman but had no desire to be with a woman wearing a strap-on, much less a big one.

The room filled with a scream again.

"Shut her up," The Voice said. Evita felt the sting of a needle, and it took only seconds after the needle prick to feel relaxed and tranquil.

This was the second day in a row of horrible violation. Yesterday she'd felt a man humping her and jacking off on her pretty feet. It had happened twice, two different men at different times. Each time they'd jacked off on her feet, and then each time she could feel a woman's touch and mouth on her feet, licking and fondling. She could tell it was two different men. One had a tight small ball sac, and the other one had heavy balls that hung down.

Each time she'd lain there and made no sound. She'd barely moved.

The pain of having a body humping between her legs with a strap-on going too deep inside made her lose her control. She screamed. Now, shot with drugs, she felt her body slow down. Her heart had pumped hard before, but now it slowed as she felt warmth encasing her small penis, as if someone was sucking on her. Her body went to sleep, and her mind followed.

Madam Secretary Brandywine

Gabrielle

"Speaking for the Washington, D.C. Royal Chamber Society, we want to thank the former Secretary of State, Madam Brandywine, for coming to the John F. Kennedy Center, here in Georgetown.

"Madam Secretary, I found an excerpt from your speech quite noteworthy. If I may quote, 'We as people have become consumed by pop culture, instead of having a culture that's lasting and positive.' On that note, that concludes the program for the evening. I thank everyone for coming out."

Damn. Forty minutes later and I'm still shaking hands. I want to get out of here. Damn Bob is over there on the phone. He has seen me waving my hand repeatedly, signaling him. "Hello, Bob, hey, Bob, I'm sorry to disturb you, but I need to be moving along."

"I'm sorry, Madam Secretary; I was on the phone with GB. He wanted to know how your speech went tonight, and whether we are planning any other events for you while you're back here in D.C."

"You say GB? You are referring to our former president, whom I served under." I knew the answer, but it caught me off-guard. He may think I'll say something about me not wanting to support that mess down there in Texas. I know he's upset with me, because

I will not come out publicly and support giving federal funds to some mess he created by letting that company operate with no oversight. GB had better tread lightly with me. I don't work for him anymore. I'm a private citizen and I may start expressing my own personal views on his horrible domestic policies and the after-effects…I'll do it professionally if I do—"

"Madam Secretary Brandywine, did I say something funny?"

"No, Bob. Life has a funny way of telling you factors you already knew, but failed to recognize the importance."

"Well, I'm sorry you had to endure the long line of well-wishers; we just love you. Your town car is in the back, and I'll escort you out."

"Thank you, Bob, but I'll need to go to the restroom first. Please have my car meet me in the front. Always come in the back for security, and leave out of the front, even though a black person coming in through the back has a sad historical significance."

"Oh, I'm sorry, but now that we have a man of color in the oval office, things are equal for all—that's the greatness of America, don't you think? Even though you and I don't agree with his policies."

I can't wait to fly out tomorrow morning. I don't miss D.C. and the phony over-the-top plastic people. You have to talk different languages here; the language of the real, and the language of the unrealistic. I just want to sit in this limo for a while and decompress, and fix me a drink.

"Driver, I need to make some phone calls, and I don't want to drop any of them, so stay parked here. I'll let you know when we can go."

"Yes, Madam. Should I let the security in the front and behind us know we'll be sitting here for a while?"

"Yes, please. Tell them it won't be long."

My security team has been hired as independent contractors. A service provided to me after serving in an administration. It's on the taxpayer's dime for life when I have to come to D.C., and certain other public appearances.

I love this town for the sights. I'm sitting across from the Potomac River, and even at night, the cherry blossom trees are beautiful. The eats are the best in the world, and there are some places to go hang out, but you're going to run in to plastic people.

I assume some people ask, what is my problem? I'm sure they look and think of me as a black woman with an elitist attitude, when I'm not that way. I wish I had the ground under me to walk and talk as I please. Many times, I'm that plastic person smiling at assholes trying to keep them from sniffing up my ass trying to get a favor.

I'm in a bad mood. Gin and cranberry juice over the rocks is my choice tonight.

This has been somewhat of an upsetting trip. I shared some news with Psalms before I flew out here. I thought he might like the news, but he didn't take it too kindly. I couldn't wait to talk to him about it, so I called, and I guess he has other things going on, but I had to tell him. When I told him, he became cold and distant.

He wasn't upset with me, and I do understand what I told him could be troubling, but he needs to look forward in a more positive way.

My sister, my dear baby sister—she loves Psalms with all her heart. She was there when I finally talked to him. Oh, no worries about Psalms and my little sister. She's devoted to me and loves me, and Psalms—he has only misled me once, and I think it was an omission. He didn't tell me Evita was going to be at a social function. I don't like their relationship, but I've put up with it. It's coming to an end. It has to; it can't go on as it has. I've come to that conclusion.

My sister Faelynn has several problems that leave me shaking my head. She's an airhead with looks. My little sister is a pretty girl. Men lick the bottom of her feet just to be close to her. But, she's clueless about having to function in the real world. I've bailed her out of trouble, and I babysit her, and yes, I do love my sister. She is giving, and she is loyal to me, but her problems in life are often brought on by her being just not that bright.

Our dad spoiled her because she was an accidental baby—Mom and Dad thought they couldn't have any more. In some ways I raised her, so I laugh at myself that I was part of the problem.

She's irresponsible with money; she blows cash like a person with a weak bladder flushes—all too often. She is the mother of my niece and nephew. Two almost perfect kids. We know kids are hell, but Faelynn birthed two beautiful children. Now the children's father, it brings me tears and fears. He is an ass, and in my sister he found a naïve girl he could run over, and he did. The man worked her mind, and had the kids with him when he traveled, or when he went to their other house. He left Faelynn at the main house. She thought he was a good father. Clueless as she is, she didn't realize the dutiful dad was a shiftless husband who didn't want her.

Pretty or not, some men have more than their fair share of cute bimbos. Now he has the kids eighty percent of time, and he takes them around the world and around his whores. Unacceptable.

I'm in a bad mood. I didn't put enough gin in this drink. Sweet is nice, but I'm not in a nice disposition to sugarcoat anything.

Faelynn is in Seattle, hanging out to help relieve the stress she gets when she has to take her kids back to their father. This last time she had the kids, she received disturbing news about their last trip with their father. Supposedly the kids heard their dad having sex. In the Spanish villa where they stayed, there were no doors. Designed to look like a Moorish castle, the villa had no private enclosed rooms. Now I understand the father well enough that he didn't make his kid watch or promote them watching, but he needed to be more careful. Kids are going to hear moms and dads going at it, but they should not hear different women getting a piece from dad. He has different women coming and going, and that's not a good look around my niece and nephew. Something has to be done.

I'm in a bad mood. I'm biting on the ice from my drink. I had to slow down on the alcohol since I have another meeting tonight.

Psalms—what's going on lately with his jobs? He seems to be more involved than just setting up security. I've procured things for him that are not the norm. Then when I call lately, he's busy, and I get the "I'll get back to you." I'm a submissive woman to him. There is no other man on this earth before him. For the most part, I enjoy being that woman for him, but I'm a woman, and sometimes I need to be first when I call. In the past week, something is different.

I don't hunt him down when he is busy. I give him all the space he wants, yet there are a few times I want his attention right then and there, and I should get it, since it's not often I demand.

What I wanted to share with him was to his benefit.

"Driver, take me to 1401 Pennsylvania, the Willard Hotel, and to the back entrance. Let my security detail know."

I look out of the windows of the limo and see structures of architectural and design beauty, but this town is ugly and racist. Lawmakers, with their lobbyists thriving on the cow shit from a hundred cows, all lodged on the senate floor.

After I gave my speech this evening and shook hands with people, many of whom don't wash their hands, the first place I wanted to go was to the VIP bathroom. Often for a high-profile person where there could be a security issue, they would go to a private bathroom and a back staging room. I was in the bathroom and the wife of a philandering former senator of a redneck state came into the VIP bathroom—and not to use the bathroom.

"Why, Gabrielle." She spoke to me as if she knew me, and she didn't. One should not call me by my first name, and in Washington D.C., and most other places, I'm afforded my title whether it's former or present. I let it slide. "My dear, your speech was terrific, although bordering on the liberal side of things, but you were lovely and, my-oh-my, you're absolutely gorgeous.

"As tall as you are, you could have been a good player on one of our state college sports teams. And your heels—everybody speaks of your heels. I must say they are nice, if not rather large, but then again you people have such great bones. Why, of course, gorgeous. That dress is just wonderful. You are well-trained in what to wear and what not. Your skin is so perfectly brown. When I was a young girl, our maid had skin like you, but your hair is straighter, and prettier.

"My husband thinks your face is so pretty I almost get jealous, but he thinks you should run for office, maybe a Senate seat."

The war paint on her face didn't hide the evil in her mind, and the bile that spewed from her mouth.

"Well, that's lovely of him to say, but I have too much of an in-dependent mind to follow blindly with straight party lines. I would vote for laws to move the country forward, and not ass backward to the days when you had a maid with hair you didn't think was as pretty.

"I know so many people like you want a pretty black face, but with a closed white mind. I will run, all right. I will run as far away from people like you, and your young intern-chasing, drunkard husband." Her war paint about chipped off. "As if you didn't know? You knew, but the nice house on the old plantation and the pure-bred dogs that you don't train just to take pictures with make you happy. You look the other way while your husband pressures young interns to screw him like Thomas Jefferson screwed his slave girl because she had no options, either.

"A lot of meetings in the White House had nothing to do with public policy; it was about men like your husband, and who they were screwing, and whether it could come back on the administration. By the way, I assume you don't sleep with the old dirt bag of a husband because I'm sure he would need plenty of pills to get it up when he looks at you. I would guess he didn't have any problem getting it up to screw those young intern…boys. You have to give it to him though, he had a perfect voting record against any and all gay rights.

"Now, if you don't mind, the smell of the gas you just passed from your bubbling stomach is tearing you a new asshole. You and your husband are exposed like dead meat in the desert, and vultures are picking at boney-ass meat."

Backroom deals can be sinister, and backroom conversations can bite with a deadly scorpion sting.

I'm in a bad mood. I need another drink, but I'll get another once I'm inside. I'm gonna need it, when I give the okay on what I should have done a long time ago. It will give me the peace of mind; it will rid me of this distraction.

Before I go inside this lounge, let me call Psalms again…and damn, he's not answering again. It's Evita, it has to be, she…fuck it!

I'm trying to talk to Psalms about…his birth mother wants to meet with him. It is one of the saddest pieces of history and he has refused to deal with the pain. With his mother, the rich meet the almost poor—well, with his mother and their family's money, being rich makes anyone poor. With his mother, white met black and created the most unique man I know. With his mother, shame meets hurt, and their story will never end.

Shortly after Psalms and I became a couple, if that's the right label, he let me know he had little knowledge of his birth mother. His grandfather shared almost everything known to man except the knowledge of his birth mother and father. Psalms had some basic information on his father, a rebellious child and man, and the devil is in the details of his father. He hardly knew much about his mother.

It turns out she's about as famous in history as any one woman can be. She would be well-known in certain circles of life, despite what became one of the most newsworthy situations in history.

As Psalms and I became more than just lovers, and he became my confidant, I realized that his mysterious past troubled him. Throughout his career, he felt commanders and superiors whisper knowledge about him. To be confirmed in to a high-security position, a complete background on every person is done through research and even spying in to a person's past with unlimited resources. When it comes to clandestine service officers such as Navy SEALs, Secret Service agents, FBI, and CIA operatives, it is imperative that the government know everything about them, even down to where their tiniest birthmarks and pimples, are located. They need to know what they last ate, even if it requires a stool examination. Who your parents are, and where they are—and they will find out, trust me.

Routine assessments are the order of the day and week and month. No one can do anything that is dubious or potentially compromising to national security. Even lie detector tests could be a routine part of personal inquests of truth. Too funny though, that Psalms passed his lie detector test, even when asked whether he had any lovers or love interests while he and I were sleeping in beds around the world. I used to joke that he didn't really love me. I know he does…I have to believe.

In my capacity as the Secretary of State, I had access to confidential files. I had, and still have, connections make the right call to get information if not accessible in a confidential file. I put information in Psalms' hands. When he received the information, what happened was good and bad, but mostly sad.

The story of Psalms father, DaDa Q Black, was that of a bad guy turned to an armed robber to domestic terrorist. He went from an angry black kid to a bank robber, kidnapper, and killer and he ultimately died from a brutal shootout with the police.

Psalms' mother, Picia Darling, is a magazine millionaire heiress, a socialite, and an alleged kidnap victim of DaDa Q Black. She finished her part in a crime wave as a convicted bank robber. Many believe she faked having Stockholm Syndrome, an emotional experience in which captives show positive feelings toward their captors, sometimes joining forces with them to do crime as in Picia Darling's case.

It was one of media history's biggest news frenzies. The case is often studied to this day. The rich little white girl and the black thug domestic terrorist were lovers long before any of the kidnapping and bank robbing with the urban guerillas called the Black Star Emancipation Army.

Picia Darling and DaDa Q Black were teenage lovers. The billionaire Darling family of old American money owned several estates, a famous one in southern California and another smaller, but still large, estate on Orcas Island.

Psalms' grandfather, the landscape engineer, worked on the estate spending the weekends with his wife, and his son, DaDa Q. DaDa Q and Picia played as children all over the grounds, but as kids do, they come of age. DaDa Q at the age of sixteen and Picia at fourteen made the backwoods into a young lovers' bed.

A scared young girl, she had missed three periods before she told her mother and father she was pregnant. All the money they had made no difference: it was too late for an illegal abortion. Money did make a difference in persuading Psalms' grandfather and grandmother to raise the baby. They signed an agreement promising to hide the truth, and Psalms' grandfather made it clear to his grandson a man must keep his promises: it's biblical.

DaDa Q ran away from home, angry, because he and Picia were not allowed to see each other. Years later Picia, ran away with him—or he kidnapped her. It appears she joined in willingly and joined the criminal activities. DaDa Q died in a police shootout, and she was captured. Picia served a short sentence only because the courts believed she was a sweet, little white girl that the big, bad black man made do terrible things. That's what the history books tell us.

Her family's money and political clout, and cluelessness had misled the public, and unlocked her jail cell. America loves little lost white girls and a president granted her a complete pardon a decade later.

Fast forward to decades later. I secured the truth of his hidden past, and arranged a meeting for Psalms to meet his mother. We thought she was anticipating meeting her half-black, grown, successful, noncriminal son. We thought she'd be happy to have a son who was protecting the president of the United States, and other high-profile people like me.

My limo is driving past the meeting place right now. When he'd walked into the office, it was full of lawyers, and there was a contract on the table offering millions upon millions. All he had to do was keep the same agreement his grandfather had made. Keep hush-hush; tell no one, and there was a green dollar heaven that was the culmination of the reunion.

Rich and poor. Psalms became both.

I sent her a long letter while I was the Secretary of State, with ways to contact me if she ever needed to. I had the letter stamped from the president of the United States, so I know she got it. This past week, Picia Darling contacted me. I'm hoping Psalms' pride will lead him to meet with his mother. She's married, and he has a brother and sisters in their mid-twenties.

Psalms' grandfather showed to be a man of morality. In his will, he set Psalms up to receive another inheritance upon his retirement. Psalms retired from the Secret Service after he received millions from the Darling family to continue keeping the family secret. Then his grandfather's inheritance kicked in. Unknown to Psalms, all his life he had millions in holding from when his grandparents received a payoff at his birth. They never spent a dime; they made sure he was to be taken care of after he had worked hard in life and was ready to rest. Psalms works just as hard now as always, doing for others. It's just who he is as a man. Now, if I can only make this other problem disappear.

"Driver, take me to the back entrance of the Willard Hotel. I have your number. I will text when I'm ready to leave. Alert my security."

I have certain access to people who are loyal to me. If I have a problem, I can have it handled. I've got a problem that Psalms won't handle, so I've made up my mind, enough is enough.

I love this bar. It's private enough. People know to mind their business, or they could find trouble and regret. I spent many evenings here talking shop, making deals. Before Psalms, before I was the Secretary of State, I had a man-friend; an older man who went from playing in the NBA, to the Hall of Fame, and to front office management. We met here often before going upstairs to a room.

Unfortunately for him, I had my connections do surveillance on him. I didn't mind sharing him with his wife, but sharing him with the other women, that was a bit too much for me.

I'm sitting and waiting for my connection. The bartender makes the best My Fair Lady martini. 1 part gin, 1 part lemon juice, 1 part orange juice, 1 part strawberry syrup, 1 dash of egg white, shake with ice and strain into a cocktail glass.

"Madam Secretary, may I have a seat?"

"EL'vis. Please have a seat. As I remember you don't drink; that's orange juice in front of you."

"Thank you, Madam Secretary."

"Now that you're out of the Treasury, are you getting enough work to keep you busy, and fed?"

"I'm doing well, but honored to serve you."

"Thank you, EL'vis."

"May I ask how my former commander is doing? Captain Psalms?"

"He is well." I'm looking into eyes that are cold, but not deceiving. He's all about doing his assignment, no questions asked. He wants to be Psalms. He wants my admiration. Psalms knows I have EL'vis do certain kinds of work.

Psalms is my man, not a spy or doer of deeds for me that could come back on either of us. I need to know things sometimes. I need to know who is doing what sometimes. I need people to do what I need them to do.

"EL'vis, I need this to happen. I need to rid myself of the problem as I expressed to you the other day. You'll find your compensation deposited in the off-shore account I set up from the last time."

I'm careful of what I say if it's not meant to be heard by anyone else other than the person I am speaking to. I have a piece of equipment on in the form of a bracelet that scrambles any electronic listening device. Otherwise, people in my situation would be forever tricked and trapped. I trust EL'vis, but one never knows who else might be trying to eavesdrop.

"Madam Secretary, with all due respect, I must ask: Are you sure?"

I nod my head.

"I'll handle it as you requested," EL'vis says, and leaves my table taking his cold eyes with him. My decision makes me cold, but my life, and some others, will be better in the long run.

I text my driver to have the car in front in twenty minutes; I want to have one more martini. I'll have a light one. I'm feeling that I've almost had enough; I'll sleep well tonight.

CHAPTER 31

One Too Many Martinis

Gabrielle felt the gin working a wobble into her stride. Her bladder requested a pit stop to the ladies' room. Trips back to Washington, D.C. always made her fall in to an old habit of one too many drinks at the end of the day. The stress of making, or being a part of, world-changing decisions affected her ability to relax, so drinking became an unhealthy habit. Tonight she had followed through on a life-changing decision. The new stress helped maneuver her hand to lift too many gin-filled martinis.

Strolling out of the ladies' room and heading out to the town car, people recognized her—as they should have—some of whom she knew and had associated with. She nodded and gave purposeful waves goodbye, as she didn't want anyone to stop her. She knew she'd had too much to drink. A conversation with someone would be embarrassing. She was done for the day.

Her security man met her at the door. The hotel door man opened the door. The night air gave her a surge of alertness like a caffeine shot. She stopped to wave to one of the few black female congresswomen and her Chief of Staff grandson as they were going in another door.

The other security person was not at the door of her car. The security escort in front of her looked around and opened the door himself, and moved to let Gabrielle get in the car.

Boom! Boom! Boom!

Three gunshots.

Screams loud enough to shatter glass filled the air. Shattered glass surrounded Gabrielle's body lying on the ground in a pool of blood.

About ten minute minutes later, a little more than a mile down the road—

Pish...another gunshot.

And about two minutes later, *Pish*...

CHAPTER 32

Unclear and Present Danger

USA Today, May 14, 2014

FORMER SECRETARY OF STATE GABRIELLE BRANDY-WINE WOUNDED BY GUNMAN

Psalms read the online news on his Kindle tablet, passing a newspaper stand as he walked through a small private airport terminal outside of Washington, D.C. He and Suzy Q had flown in on a private jet, since tools were not allowed on commercial airlines. Although it was fifty shades of blackness outside, they both wore their trademark sunglasses in and out of the terminal.

UNCLEAR AND PRESENT DANGER

That was the subtitle written for the online article. It spoke of the dangers many former public officials go through in places they could imagine. Are they safe, if ever? The story told of others who'd had close calls. The story told of private security and its cost, and how some former public officials couldn't afford the A-Team. Often, others felt their lives were less at risk as the years had gone by. The story went on to note that opposing factions might hold lifelong grudges, whether inside America or from a foreign source. Maybe some would lie in wait, almost like a sleeper cell.

Every news channel made soft and hard claims as to who might be the gunman or gunmen. Information was sketchy; no statement from the FBI had come forth. One cable news channel made claims that some dark-skinned men were the assailants. Another station, known for its racial attacks and extreme conservative views, suggested that it might be a militant, revolutionary black man, who hated the former Secretary of State Gabrielle Brandywine because she wasn't black enough.

The President and the First Lady had come out to the front lawn of the White House to ask for prayers and healing for all of America. The former president whom she served under made a plea for justice, and sent his best wishes for a speedy recovery to his friend.

Before flying from Seattle, Mintfurd warned Psalms to be about business. "Keep it straight from the gate, and not about emotions so you can control the justice sought—and for the future protection of your lady." Outside the terminal, a dark-blue SUV awaited Psalms and Suzy Q.

After they had put their bags in the back, Suzy Q got in the front and Psalms in the backseat.

"Commander Psalms Black, I'd like to say it's good to see you, but under the circumstances, I'm sorry that you are here."

EL'vis Dean was at the wheel. He looked in his rearview mirror and saw Psalms' gold-colored, steely eyes, burning bronze with focused control. "EL'vis, although I appreciate your respect, I'm not your commander. Call me PB. "

"Yes, sir—I mean PB."

"EL'vis, this is Q. If you have something to say to me, you can say it to her, and I advise you to do just that. She is everything we are, and don't doubt her." Suzy Q's face looked mummified; she didn't appear to be breathing. "Where are you taking us?"

"Sir, I have a bunker in the Maryland suburbs. I can assume Madam Brandywine is safe from any other possible attacks. Phil Armstrong is assigned to her protection. You can call him at any time."

"Dial him, please."

"Your Bluetooth connect code, sir?"

"Pusher man 2014."

EL'vis tapped the steering wheel in the middle and spoke the code. "Bridge-Water Overpass-Air-Span 4 to 4…search Bluetooth Pusher man 2014."

"Sir, your phone should be ringing into Phil Armstrong's phone in thirty seconds."

"Phil, this is Psalms Black. Thank you."

Phil connected Psalms and Gabrielle after five minutes. They talked for ten minutes mostly in coded words in case. She let him know she was grazed across both breasts by a bullet. Her moving at the right time and the position of her body helped to keep the bullets from going directly into her heart. She would have two nasty scars.

A doctor was ready to perform cosmetic surgery to minimize the scarring, but Gabrielle declined. She wanted tattoos over the scars, which made Psalms flinch.

Psalms' mind took quick turns. Evita might be missing, but most likely she was just being Evita, he assumed. He contemplated how, like Evita, Gabrielle wanted tattoos over her breasts' scars. A non-sexual image entered his mind of four breasts painted with tattoos. He knew if ever Gabrielle did get tattoos, they would be small compared to the ones that adorned Evita's breasts.

Gabrielle's head hurt from hitting the ground pretty hard when her bodyguard shoved her down. Considering her life had been only breast fat away from being over, her spirits were reasonable. In all her years of going to dangerous places as the American liaison, her sense of fear had disappeared, and a conscious courage had supplanted that fear.

The bodyguard had not been so lucky. He had sworn to take a bullet for the person he was assigned to protect, and that he did, with a courageous display. He was in critical condition. He had taken a second bullet across his vocal cords. That bullet barely missed vital structures in his neck, and could have killed him. Fortunately, it passed through at the right place and the right angle and missed the spinal cord, esophagus, and jugular veins. He would never talk right, if ever again, and would have serious complications with his vocal cords and damaged trachea. But, it was better than death.

The third bullet had hit the car roof.

Gabrielle expressed to Psalms that she had to do something for the young bodyguard, and Psalms replied that it would be done. She wanted to talk more, but he reminded her about security. She was under the protection of others beyond his control. He trusted Phil Armstrong, who served under him, but others might be listening. He had to shut it down for now.

After driving forty miles, the SUV pulled into a long, dirt driveway in Greenbelt. At the end, there was a small house. Two barns, one larger than the house, sat on one side; on the other side sat a barn more the size of large one-car garage.

EL'vis headed to the smaller one, and pushed a button on the steering wheel. The garage bay door rolled up. They drove in, and ten seconds later as the door rolled down, the whole floor lowered seven feet. EL'vis drove forward and down a ramp to an even lower floor as the garage floor rose back up in place.

They parked and exited. In clear view, there were two wounded men strapped to tables by metal wrist and ankle clamps.

Psalms always had EL'vis, an ex-Special Forces soldier turned Secret Service agent, shadow Gabrielle in D.C. and other East Coast cities for extra protection. EL'vis worked for both of them on separate jobs. He understood his worth, and allowed Psalms to mentor him. He was a good-looking, six feet two inches of chiseled, lean body.

After a man had insulted his family in Puerto Rico by revealing a family secret that caused EL'vis father to have a heart attack, EL'vis avenged his family honor with no regard for his current position. His decision came back on him, and he was dismissed from the Secret Service. Nevertheless, Psalms added him to his tight-knit security team with no reservations.

A pale-skinned man, EL'vis could pass for two different races. He spoke Spanish and French fluently, and his English had no trace of an accent. He affirmed Puerto Rican nationality and culture on the same level as American. When he left the Secret Service, Psalms met him moments after he turned in his badge. EL'vis called them his *familia*.

After EL'vis met with Gabrielle in the Willard Hotel lounge, he was outside next to his vehicle forty feet away, and positioned to see everything. He saw the second security officer leave his post and walk away quickly, but before he did, he saw the man looking up at a building. EL'vis scanned the building and noticed an open window with a small mirror reflection, most likely a rifle scope. The gunman fired three shots.

EL'vis watched Gabrielle, and the security officer go down. People ran to help them quickly at that scene. He went after the security man who had left his post. He jumped into his vehicle, U-turned, and drove in the other direction. He drove assuming the man would get in a vehicle, or head into Chinatown. He hoped it wasn't the latter; he would lose him there.

Three blocks down, he spotted the man entering the driver's side of a car. EL'vis drove by without slowing down; he hoped the man wouldn't drive away and head to pick up his accomplice, and wait there instead. EL'vis turned the corner, and hit another U-turn before he parked on the corner. He had a clear view of the car, and it didn't move, as sirens were filling the air.

He guessed the man had to be waiting for him, and doubted he would come from the same direction. EL'vis opened his center console and took out a small case, then exited his vehicle. He looked behind him, and sure enough, a man was walking his direction. He was wearing a long coat and walked abnormally. The man was looking around. Out of sight, EL'vis hid.

He pulled his gun out with its silencer attached. The man acted nervous and concerned about who might be behind him. EL'vis waited until the man was within twenty meters. He aimed for the man's hip bone and fired.

Pish...

The man went down, and like lightning striking the ground, EL'vis was on top of him, disarming him of the rifle he had strapped to his leg. EL'vis pulled out an injection needle and shoved it in the man's ass. His squirming stopped within seconds. He picked the man up, and threw his arm on his shoulder, imitating two drunk men walking down the street to a car.

Next, EL'vis removed the man's coat and hat, put them on, and approached the car parked around the corner. He put his back against the passenger door, as if he were looking around for danger. Blue lights flashed, and sirens sang in the late-night air. EL'vis used his natural instincts and the things he had learned in dialogues with Psalms. He utilized his critical thinking skills like the Navy SEALs that captured and killed Osama bin Laden.

He angled his body so the man sitting in the driver's seat couldn't see it was the wrong person. A slight pull of the door handle indicated the door was unlocked, and he pulled it open quickly and caught the man off-guard. He shot him in the hip bone, too, inflicting so much pain on the man that he was easy to disarm. EL'vis rendered him silent and unconscious with an injection.

Without being discovered, he was able to get both men in his vehicle and to his bunker. He contacted Psalms.

Suzy Q, Psalms, and EL'vis unloaded the tools from the SUV, and then stood near the captured men. The men had death in their eyes. Their own death. They knew torture would come first, not for payback but for information, then death would be a blessing. The same thing could come from the FBI or CIA if captured out of sight of the public. Obviously, both men were connected enough to commit a crime of conspiracy to assassinate a public political servant.

Psalms and the other two knew the men would have limited access to the chain of command in their mission, but he could still seize building blocks of information. At some point, two plus two would make the four corners of a castle that must fall, along with those who lived in it.

Four hours later, the two men, nor any trace of their existence, were to be seen ever again. A local, closed-down crematory burned their asses to ash. Suzy Q kept one thing that identified one of the men.

It is said there are so few times the perfect crime has happened. A successful crime depends on other people or other things, and both can fail.

The two men took orders for a job, and that was to assassinate the former Secretary of State. They were hired guns who had killed corporate CEOs, dirty cops who had gotten scared and were about to turn state's evidence, and other like assassinations.

The assassins had received payment through a foreign bank account, and they had a code name for the assassination. The building blocks leading to the castle were close by, but the castle was too far and high to touch without a master plan that Psalms and his team did not yet have. All he had was a couple of words.

"Black Goose."

EL'vis had heard the term when he was on assignment protecting the former president of the United States. He heard the term used when Secretary of State Brandywine was going to meet with the president. There, they would drink Grey Goose vodka. Once, Secretary of State Brandywine had bought a case of Black Zephyr Premium Reserve Gin, and given it to the president, who had joked about her trying to get him to switch to gin instead of vodka. In response, the president had asked her, "Well, can't we call my Grey Goose, Black Goose?" After that, whenever outside of her hearing range, he referred to her as Black Goose, with a slightly racist connotation.

The former president was not exceptionally bright in many areas, and when it came to memory of details, he was almost childish. While protecting him, Psalms had overheard his code number, 43-33-23-13-3-C, during a conversation between the former president and The Duck, the short, squat man with the nasal voice who was behind the scenes of many political evil deeds.

Psalms and EL'vis knew nothing came directly down from the former president, but The Duck had his hands in everything as a political maker or breaker: no holds barred.

Outside of the little house, Psalms and EL'vis spoke, and Suzy Q listened.

"I need to go visit with Gabrielle before we plan to do anything. They have taken a shot at her. I think they have tried to put a scare into her, but I have to evaluate this situation more."

"I agree, sir. We can head into the city and let Phil know we are coming."

"Let Phil know Q and I will have tools on us, and we will need to come through with them and not be checked."

"Got it. Sir, I have debated whether I could share some information, but with what has taken place, I feel I must. Last night, less than an hour before the attack, Madam Brandywine gave me an assignment. No relationship to the attack, but—"

Psalms cut EL'vis off. "Was it a Level Six?"

"Yes, sir."

"I'll think on it. She has her life, and I have mine."

"To hell mate, if you do!" Suzy Q froze the soft ground with her cracking icicle tone. "Yer lady friend set up a kill, and she is then the victim of a long-range bullet across her baby feeders. Have you lost touch with what we do, eh? We need to search every centimeter for worms that might be crawling out of the ground." Suzy Q's eyes sliced a Zorro slash across Psalms' face.

"Big Boy said keep your fucking heart out of it. I'll sit my little bony ass inside a jail cell on a cold metal toilet for the rest of my life for you, but you better give me a running chance to avoid that crap. I don't give a fuck about yer love life and about trying to protect her privacy!"

At that moment, Psalms regretted telling EL'vis that he could, and should, say everything he would say to him in front of Suzy Q. Despite it being the right thing.

When Suzy Q pulled her weapon out, whether it be her gun or her tongue to give you a lashing, you were going to get both barrels. "If yer woman let some red ants get loose, just stomp them little buggers to death and kiss and make up with her ass at a later date. That's of course what yer supposed to, eh?" Suzy Q removed her sunglasses, cocked her head, and eyeballed the giant of man in front of her. She could hug him or shoot him dead either way, and would still love him.

Suzy Q could claw or beat most men to death. Over the past days, she had to beat down his heart twice, and keep it from ruling his mind. Psalms was being hard-headed about his one weakness. First Evita, and now Gabrielle, the two women he loved. Suzy Q took her thumb and forefinger and made the gun pointing to the head gesture as if to say, "What will it take before you wake up, or die?"

Psalms removed his sunglasses. His golden eyes locked on Suzy Q's blue ones. He loved that anyone would stand up to him. It was so rare, and she was right to leave no stone unturned. He kept staring, and thought of what his grandfather said about King David, the man who killed Goliath. David sinned against Bathsheba and her husband Uriah when he was supposed to be at war taking care of his nation, instead of his tending to his personal desires. King David let his emotions control him, and instead his actions led to ruin by not being able to finish what he started.

There's a time for love, and there's a time a man must take control and complete a task. It doesn't matter he hurts as long as his heart is pure. Grandfather had told him, a pure of heart is the deepest love of all. Love is about completion, your best effort, the culmination of brains and brawn, of thoughts and actions, words and behaviors. Love is not about victory. Love is being pure of heart when all is all done. Why put new doors in an old house when the house is falling down? Crooks and critters will find other ways to come in and keep hurting your presence and your future. Put your house in order.

Psalms nodded and Suzy Q nodded back.

They headed back into Washington, D.C., and Psalms had EL'vis tell him what Gabrielle wanted. It hurt. It angered his soul. On top of that, EL'vis said he was hesitant because each time he had spoken about the assignment with Gabrielle, he could tell she was under the influence of strong drink. EL'vis peeked at the rearview mirror, and saw Psalms' face changing color to match his wine-stain birthmark. He was turning purple black.

CHAPTER 33

Read Between the Lines

On their way back into Washington, D.C., Psalms got a call from Gabrielle. She told him her wounds were not enough to force her to stay in the hospital. Psalms had flown Faelynn in on a separate flight. Her sister was nursing her at the hospital, then Gabrielle decided to leave. She arranged a private flight back to the other coast.

Psalm instructed her to fly into Boeing Airfield in Seattle where he would have her picked up by his security management team. Before he got off the phone, though, he told her they needed to talk. His tone gave off the same fear as that of an airline pilot coming on the intercom to say the landing gear was stuck and that the passengers needed to get ready for a rough landing.

Psalms understood his thinking might be clouded, so he let Suzy Q take the lead and realized it was about the team: as EL'vis would say, *la familia*. Suzy Q hatched her plan. Psalms and EL'vis listened and agreed. A quick response would send a message that Gabrielle and the people behind her had just as much power and knowledge as the assassins, and more.

First they needed to find The Duck. The attack on the former president would be a suicide mission in the effort to get even. The former president most likely had sent the order down, but The Duck had to be the driver and planner. Back in Seattle, Mintfurd and Velvet worked the Internet and intel lines, compiling a profile of information.

Why did they go after Gabrielle? It was always to shut someone up: it's always to get rid of opposing ideas. No one even asked the question aloud.

The team would fly back to Seattle in the morning. Psalms, EL'vis, and Suzy Q left their hotel rooms that evening for fresh air and a change of scenery. They headed to 14th and U Streets to eat at Busboys and Poets. The team had time on their hands while they waited for Gabrielle to land and get to Psalms' condo safely.

People were walking the streets talking about the shooting, and the state of affairs of the world. Comments like "no one is safe" filled the streets like out-of-town tourists.

All three drank either coffee or tea as they sat in the corner. They had some privacy, and Psalms had his tablet out, communicating with Mintfurd back in Seattle.

On stage, the renowned poet Alexandria Cornet had the audience captivated with socially conscious spoken word:

Limited Access
If you talk to me or listen to me with a constricted mind
You'll get your mind blown.
Caution, I don't play well in small intellectual places.
Been known to break out of tight spaces
And I don't subscribe to your actions of "holier than thou"
I remember dates, years, hours and minutes
Yeah I'm that bookworm dude.
Who…what…and where is etched in my mind and depending on others
actions, it may be etched in my heart
Been places and done some things that I should write,

"1000 Shades of My Black Ass" that would drop your jaw and make you choke yourself

Don't expose your lack of IQ by challenging facts put in front of you, with no fact to support your disbelief

Saying, "Well, that's just how I feel" as a counter belief in the face of well-known facts that are unknown to you, is simply ignorant.

Radio Raheem in Do The Right Thing *said, "D, Mutha Fuuuker"… meaning did you hear me correctly?*

I say IQ…did you hear me correctly?

Smart is asking, "Where did you get those facts from?" Then you come back and say, "I found these facts." Now we can educate one another, and expand our collective knowledge

I've been around I have slept around on the shores of places you have only seen while thumbing through magazines you only pick up when in the checkout line next to the magazine with the 400-pound baby found on Mars

I've read: Claude Brown, Maya Angelou, Alex Haley, Alice Walker, Toni Morrison, Langston Hughes, Richard Wright, J.A Rogers, W.E B Du Bois, Octavia Butler and James Baldwin. I've read: Ralph Ellison, and Zora, and Gwendolyn Brooks, Nikki Giovanni, and for my faith, I read the Bible, and Brother Sterling A. Brown, a poet, a literary critic, a professor, a poet laureate of the District of Columbia.

I studied the art of war, the physical fight and the mental battles though the minds of Sun Tzu, Bruce Lee, Julius Caesar, Hannibal, and the Native American Chief, Shooting Star, and the Apaches who perfected guerilla warfare, and Ali, Joe Louis and Jack Johnson.

I listened and heard Jimi Hendrix, Beethoven, Mozart, Miles and Coltrane, and Sly Stone, Billie Holiday, Muddy Waters, Mahalia Jackson, and Aretha, Sam Cooke, and Prince.

I can stand in any room with anyone and bring knowledge or a well-thought-out opinion

And yes, be careful, I do eat my spinach and broccoli, and I move my ass off the couch, and away from reality TV, so I can whoop your ass physically and mentally.

I watch movies with artistic realistic dialogue from many countries and cultures, and don't give a damn what the stars name is, and what they wear to awards shows, and who they have a baby with or by, and make no assumption about their lives from images and tabloid gossip.

Don't expose your lack of IQ by challenging facts put in front of you, with no fact to support your disbelief.

No need to look around to see if I see your pants are down, and your head is twisted out of joint.

That's you

Mr. and Ms. Fake Stories

I see you

Wide open

Trying to judge me

Knowing what's best for me…really.

How is that when your ass is stuck in a narrow mind?

Oh, but here you go again with your actions of, "holier than thou"

I just called you out.

You looking for me to let you slide.

Yeah, you're greasy.

Yep, you straight with no sharp corners?

But, if you don't know nothing, from nothing, leaves nothing…your shit is limited.

You can't see anything but, your narrow thinking ass…as being right, and you play like…I'm wrong because your trick bag is busted?

So, now you come looking to see what's what.

Well, just like Tupac said, I ain't hard to find.

But…

If you talk to me, or listen to me, with a constricted mind
You'll get your mind blown
Caution, I don't play well in small, intellectual places.
Signed, Four-eyes, aka Bookworm, aka Fearless Fly, with a Black Belt
in words-upside- your-head-if-you-can't-hear-I'll-drop-kick-you in to
a new reality
And ah, P.S....read between the lines, you find some facts, and the
fact is I don't care about how you feel if you don't know the facts!

People stood and waved their arms, as if they were trying to cool him off. He left the stage and other talented poets graced the stage.

Finally, Psalms was able to connect with Gabrielle on his electronically cloaked tablet that blocked anyone from reading or listening. Mintfurd created software that made the computer change its IP address every five seconds. Psalms typed questions to Gabrielle about what possible problems may have brought on the attempted assassination. He told her the attack came from close to home, from someone in her former administration. He heard her agitated response through his Bluetooth. She told of the recent explosion in Texas, and how GB had asked her to come out and speak up for federal funds for the company that had supported him. She told Psalms she had refused, and that GB was furious, as if she was still under his thumb. She heard rumblings that her speeches as of late were leaning more liberal. Conservative party leaders had asked her to stay the path of what had been. The Duck had asked her personally. Gabrielle let him and others know, she was now a private citizen and could take positions on policy that were different from theirs, and she did not have to stay on a scripted narrative anymore.

He told her to stay awake if she could because he would be calling back soon.

The three traded thoughts and ideas, but Suzy Q had a plan ready to go; she just needed the target and location. Finally, her plan to flush out the target came together, and Psalms called Gabrielle back.

He typed:

Tell The Duck you have had a change of heart and now want to support the federal dollars going to that company. Tell him to call a press conference next week. He's gonna assume the assassination attempt scared you in to changing your mind, which will give him satisfaction. He'll relax. That's what we need.

Gabrielle responded: *Okay. Psalms, did EL'vis tell you what I wanted done? I—*

He typed:

Stop! I will talk to you…when I decide to talk to you about this. I will say this: no one will change my life or your life in the way you planned by taking someone else's, And, oh, Gabrielle, get your ass into rehab. Not a place just to dry out from drinking, but a place to change the culture of why.

He disconnected.

Psalms told EL'vis he should leave in the morning with him and Suzy Q. It was time to head to Seattle for now. EL'vis had never been to Seattle. Suzy Q was at the bar talking to a smooth-featured black woman with a spiked red mohawk and shaved sides. Her leather tank top had red rhinestone art all throughout and matched her leather hot pants.

Psalms walked over to the two and whispered in Suzy Q's ear about the plan to leave in the morning. He also said her plan was a go—in about a week.

She told him she would be at the plane in the morning, but tonight she needed to blow off some steam. She was going to a place called Phase 1, over on Eighth Street. She invited Psalms to come and enjoy a drag king show, and to listen to some queer indie/punk music. She said it was Jell-O wrestling night, and thought she might enter and win, or just shoot pool.

Psalms understood Suzy Q was not taunting him by inviting him. He had hung out in many different settings around the world. His mind was far from being closed to how big and different the world was. It did not raise a hair on his body to be in places where others felt uncomfortable or acted like childish voyeurs. He needed to shake off some tension, and maybe a total change of scenery might be beneficial to get all that had been going on off his mind, at least for a while.

Psalms went back to the table to let EL'vis know he was heading out with Suzy Q, and that he was welcome to come along. EL'vis joined in, since he had done a lot of securing and avenging, and a little party time might help ease his mind.

CHAPTER 34

Hypothetically, Literally, and Figuratively

"Hello?"

"May I speak to Darcelle?"

"Speaking."

"Hello, Darcelle. My name is Mintfurd."

Darcelle knew it was Mintfurd from the words "May I." It was a voice of the man who recited sweet passionate poetry on a band stage on the ferry that night. "May I?" she heard, and her inner vision took over; she could see the immense man standing and commanding her attention. He was on the stage in clothes tailored to his body. His clothes fit perfectly, as if he was a male runway model. His sheer size was what made his presence. His black wool slacks had perfectly tailored pleats, creases, and cuffs. Although he was an enormous man, he had no belly fat extending his body out and hanging over his belt. He was no Santa baby or a sloppy-looking man. He was straight up and down muscle. His physique looked strong enough to pick up twenty of her.

Darcelle had been waiting to hear Mintfurd call her name, and when she heard, "May I speak to Darcelle?" her heart raced.

"Darcelle, I'm ah... well, our friend Velvet thought it would be beneficial for me to give you a call. She gave me your phone number, and I hope that is okay?"

"Yes, it is. It's good to hear from you. Actually, I encouraged her

to have you call me, so I guess I should be asking is that okay?"
They both chuckled.

Darcelle envisioned Mintfurd's pretty, but manly, face smiling.
His brown skin was the brown a banana turns when it is still firm,
but best to peel and devour right away before it goes soft. She
pictured the phone in his hand, remembering that day when he
put his hands on the microphone and recited to her soul. She saw
his fingers long and wide, but not chubby. She wanted his hands
around her waist. Darcelle wanted his fingers to brush against her
breasts. She wanted to feel controlled by his powerful hands. She
wanted those hands cupping her ass, massaging her feet, and
picking her body up and doing whatever he wanted.

"Hey," he said. "Is this a good time or is there a better time?"
Why did his voice feel like it was under her bare feet on her hardwood floors? Why did it feel hot in the room when it didn't just
moments ago, and the windows were open? Why did her inner
thighs twitch? Why was she squirming when a moment ago she
was simply relaxing?

"No, I'm sitting here unwinding and reading a book. I can have
a pretty hectic life at times. I'm ah...a lawyer, and, ah...I'm a single
parent, and I finally found some down time to relax."

"Oh, okay. What are you reading?"

"A collection of poems by Alexandria Cornet."

"Yeah, he's a great poet and he's all over the place nowadays. A
friend said he saw him just last night in D.C."

"Oh wow. I've seen him here, in a coffee shop years ago."

Both felt nervous, wanting to explode and ask a million questions.
It was tempting. Two people wanting and needing one safe place,
dreaming of holding hands, not tumbling. Neither soul could stand
any more Russian roulette dating games.

Darcelle had grown timid of men. She had not felt the loving touch of a man in six years. She'd had a sad affair with a married judge. She knew he was married, and that it was dangerous, but sometimes a dangerous place looks like the most safe. Perilous and distressing situations are often made to feel normal; sometimes dysfunction is a haven, a refuge—even when that's all one knows.

The sex with the judge wasn't dangerous or exciting. The sex was dull, nothing to look forward to each time they met. It was an odd, new experience to be in a bed with a man who did not have funky stuff going on. He had no freak in him at all. Darcelle's idea of normal sex most of her life was perplexing, bizarre. Not with him. The judge didn't even eat pussy, and he didn't want much more than face-to-face sex, and it was over in ten minutes or less. During her affair, Darcelle often asked herself why he was even cheating on his wife. But he didn't talk, either.

"Mintfurd, I hear music. Who are you listening to?"

"I'm on a Leela James groove as of late. She did a remake of Bootsy's Rubber Band's "I'd Rather Be With You." She puts a little funk and blues in to her sound instead of this bump-bump stuff. I need real music made from real instruments. Darcelle, I hear your music in the background, and I know who that is. It's Raúl Midón. I can listen to his artistry daily."

Mintfurd was standing when he first called, and now had taken a seat. He relaxed with a beer in hand. He put his arm over the back of the couch. The conversation eased his soul, and Darcelle's love of quality music made the conversation pleasing. The musical choices of the woman on the other end of the phone showed she had taste. He was more than interested in her.

"Oh, you have heard of him? So few are into creative, new music. So many of the pop stars—or what they call stars—they all sound alike, and the backing tracks are not pleasing to my ear. So yes, I have something playing that has good lyrics, and it's soulful and romantic; it goes well with a good glass of wine and an enjoyable book.

"Mintfurd, you sure won't hear me listening to the music that these kids think is brilliant. It's downright disappointing when I go around adults who grew up listening to Al Green, Luther Vandross, Stephanie Mills, Teena Marie, and Prince, and now they settle for a computer correcting the notes for some flavor-of-the-week pop star."

"Could you tell me how you really feel?" Mintfurd was already laughing before Darcelle finished. He loved her attitude. "I feel the same annoyance with mature adults who gave up listening to pleasurable music. I'm a live music junky. I don't care for hip-hop spinning the same monotonous, repetitive beat in the club or in my car or home."

"Well, we have that in common. I didn't grow up in a home hearing only black music, but all types of music filtered through my ears, so I have a wide range of listening pleasures."

"Darcelle..." Mintfurd called her name softly.

"Yes?" Every time Mintfurd said her name, she felt moisture loosen her womanhood. She clamped her thighs tight as if his voice vibrated through her thighs.

"Darcelle, you're making this easy for me. Thank you."

"Making what easy?"

"I'm not a phone guy, and I haven't called a woman in a real long time, so thank you for helping me through this."

"Hey, I'm harmless, and your call is welcomed. I saw you on stage on the ferry, and your poetry and the ease in how you delivered some pretty romantic and erotic flow had me wanting to know about you. I hope that doesn't sound too forward, but that's me. I'm a lawyer, so I say what's on my mind."

"Is that hypothetically, literally, and figuratively? Because all of that can be dangerous in the wrong hands and mind."

"It can be quite pleasing to someone on the receiving end, from the right hands and mind."

"Touché! A lawyer, huh? Can you defend me and get me off? Oh, oh I didn't mean that as it sounded…really." Mintfurd didn't mean it, but Darcelle was cracking up.

"It's all right, Big Boy. It's okay. I know what you were saying. You're innocent until proven guilty, but I can get you off."

"Oh, so you got jokes?"

"Yes, I do…I do."

"Okay, Ms. Taking-Advantage-of-My-Slip-Up. They do call me Big Boy. That is my nickname I've had since I was a baby, as anyone might tell you."

"I might have thought you'd had a nickname like that for a while."

"I'm a big man, as you have seen. That wasn't a problem in your eyes?"

"No, not at all. You are a handsome man, and you've made me laugh, and that makes you fine in my eyes. Now, do you know I'm a short woman?"

"I have no clue what you look like, and as of now, I honestly don't care. You're funny and insightful. From the short time we have been talking on the phone, this feels good. Ah, but hold up; you don't look like a female version of Li'l Wayne, do you?"

"My twin."

"Oh, hell nah."

"Big Boy, I think you'll be pleased to meet me in person."

"Don't have me running a marathon to get away."

"Keep it up, and I'll have you running after me."

"Maybe you're worth it."

Two hours later, Mintfurd and Darcelle had talked about Seattle, her daughter who was at Darcelle's mother's for a few days, and politics, teasing each other and laughing.

"Mintfurd, I should get off this phone and get ready for another day. I have to say, after our conversation, it makes you wonder whatever happened to a good old-fashioned telephone calls where we could feel smiles and hear laughter. It's gratifying to have engaging, meaningful conversation."

"Darcelle, you are so right. People have dumbed down with the overuse or misuse of texts, IMs and other forms of digital communications. The intimate human interaction of voice to voice is a lost art."

"Mintfurd, you're right. You hit it in the heart of what is going on. We have lowered our capable minds to use social media and tweets, to convey thoughts of what we used to keep to ourselves. In return, we expose our lack of communication skills, laced with insecurity and other issues."

"Yes, Ms. Lady, sadly, you are so right. It seems no one wants to talk, because of lost, or never-learned, effective one-on-one communication. As a man, I don't mind talking on the phone, but I need to have an intelligent conversation coming back at me in order for me to open up and engage. Talking with you—as I said, you made it easy for me, thank you."

"You're welcome, and thank you, Mintfurd. We all have fallen in to the trap of lazy communication, some more easily, and some more reluctantly. Some of us try to limit the smartphone and its multiple choices of dumbing down, but talking face to face or on the phone is a pleasure and treasure we're losing."

"Darcelle, if I could find a telephone booth, could I call you? Would you answer and speak from your heart, or would you let me go straight to voicemail? Would you text me back, or would you replace a face-to-face opportunity with an email, block me, or simply ignore me?"

"I can tell you I'll be waiting to hear from you again real soon, how about that? They say actions speak louder than words."

"The song says, 'I'd rather hear you breathe than to hear nothing at all,' so I'll call you soon—like in about five minutes." They laughed.

"Rather hear me breathe than nothing at all, huh?" Darcelle thought a minute. "Mintfurd, would you recite a poem for me before you go?"

"Like what kind of poem?"

"Something sexy."

"Are you grown enough?"

"Big Boy, quit playing and recite me a sexy, adult poem, please."

"Okay, check this:

"Good Love
My body and soul wants to lie in your warmness
As I feel your hands on me seemingly reaching inside parts of my soul
I feel you twirling and mixing us
Blending with your inner body, we let our juices intoxicate
...We are high, and we are hot, as we lay face to face, eyes aligned and
aimed
We kiss, our tongues invade
With my hands lifting your legs, you brace for my fall from the sky
My landing pad...an oasis, soft and wet

Pressure of inches wide, you're melting, inches down, you smile, and more inches I'm melting, into the birth place of mankind

...and it feels like I'm tearing out the screen of the back door

About then, fingernails cut trails from my shoulder blades and down to my thick muscles in my ass

Ah baby, it's about more than just inches and pain

It's the rock and roll of my hips, and you don't have to call my name, your groan has told me all I need to know

You are my Eve

I am your rising sun

Good Love

Rising and heating, a place deep within

Like the moon, earth, and sun...you rotate

On all fours, you expose multiple sights, as I place my hands on your hips

I pull that hair to keep you near

As I cruise slow, then drag race to the no finish line

Take a break, and lick the bowl clean

Slight rest

We dream, and turn fantasies into what we do

I'm mesmerized by your velvet skin, and how you feel against my chocolate peel

I do, as you say, and I place my teeth lightly, but tightly around your breasts, where normally my head would rest after you have drained me

You're holding me tight

We love being perfect at what we do

Your love, my love

You and I, there is no greater love, when we make love

Good love."

"Okay, Mintfurd, let me go get a gallon of water. I've sweated that much, I'm sure. Goodnight, Big Boy."

"Goodnight, Darcelle."

Hearing Mintfurd call her name once more, Darcelle felt more wetness. His voice seemly vibrated deep between her thighs, but now he had recited intense erotic words and each line vibrated on her clit. She hung the phone up and pulled off her panties; all she had on was a T-shirt. She closed her eyes and played a movie of Mintfurd's face sliding in and spreading her legs wide apart. She let her fingers be his tongue for an encore.

CHAPTER 35

Explicitness of Foul Folks

Two more people left the room after they had sexed all over Evita. She learned that screaming produced more harm than good in her situation. An injection of some kind of drug had put her in La-La Land. It took hours to recover from the drugs injected in her, and she had lost count of time. All her earlier calculations of distance, doors and the window were rendered useless.

Several times a day, they used Evita's body for nastiness. Men and women came and used her body. Some used forceful sexual intercourse, and some performed softer, but just as destructive, abusive molestations. Evita realized she was a pawn in a sex game. Freaks paid to come do her any way they wanted. The only saving grace was that at least the men wore condoms. She believed she was getting injections of pain-killers near her genitals and anus to most likely keep her calm.

Her tattoos were an attraction for the freaks; many of them licked and sucked all over them. She was a fantasy for those who wanted to commit rape, but didn't have the means or balls. She was a toy, a human dildo.

Evita knew of such things. She had participated in human toy shops while living on the wretched side of her past life. She had pimped and whored a couple of decades ago. The human sex toy business was for buyers who had money to waste, and had a lot to lose if caught, so they paid only the best organizations to provide their kink and to not get caught or outed.

The illicit organizations often kept some kind of proof to make deals with if they didn't get caught. The rich and ignorant users of the game never seemed to understand they were recorded, photographed, or both. All of the foul records of the foulness were a setup to protect the head of Humpty-Dumpty's mini-mafia. The masterminds behind them needed one safe place to protect themselves from spending time in prison.

Who used these illicit organizations and paid crazy money? Cops, politicians, CEO, wealthy business owners, and their housewives and husbands who couldn't get freaky, dick-hardening sex at home.

In the days when Evita had her hands dirty in the human toy business, kidnapping had not been a part of it, nor did holding anyone against their will. At least Evita didn't run her game like that. She had a history of abuse and that wasn't the game she wanted forced on someone else. She knew a few of the kids in her program had a taste of the new rules in the game now. The new players in this game beat, killed, discarded, and acquired the newer human toys.

Evita understood she was a human toy worth a bit more than the average. She was an adult with a young person's body, with scars and tattoos, and a black woman. Most human toys were young and many were underage, and often Eastern European or from South of the Border. To some eyes, Evita's deeply tanned flesh with her rare and beautiful tattoos, and no silicone implants, made her highly marketable. She knew her feet were a selling point for foot fetish freaks. They were perfect, with lovely arches, straight toes, and no imperfections. Since she'd been captured, many users had licked and sucked every inch of her feet, both men and women. Several men had ejaculated on her feet.

Her rare and beautiful tattoos had the freaks grunting, almost chanting, in religious tongues. Her body was a work of art that lined her scars. Like mapping out a travel plan, men rubbed their dicks along Evita's tattoos. A tattoo of a painted face covered her ass, with the tongue seemingly coming out her asshole. It was perfect in design and color, and the customers licked along every inch, going in and out of her body, using fingers, tongues, toys, and dicks. Several women tried to force their nipples into her pussy or rubbed them on Evita's male-female genitals.

Three to four times a day, these people touched Evita's body revoltingly. She knew her captors were trying to keep their customers separated by hours. She noticed the two who were watching her at first were no longer there. Another pair guarded her now, and took her to use the bathroom and to shower. The hood came off when she was not being used as a sex slave. Being allowed to see handlers' faces, she knew, meant that one day she was going to die. Evita assumed other sex slaves were in different parts of the house. She alone could not produce enough money for The Voice, assuming he was the head pimp.

She knew The Voice now; she was aware who Pretty Boy was. It took a while, but she remembered that accent, and that he loved to take a belt to a woman's ass. It was a former client from her days of running in human sex toy joints. He would never let his face be seen. He came in with a leather face mask, as did others who thought it made them weirder.

The word in her friendly circles that came to her joints was that he was a minority owner of the Seattle Supersonics before he and others sold the team. When she first met The Voice, he was the owner of a moving company that had gone national, but later, he was shut down for ripping people off. He kept his hands in many small, lucrative ventures, and amassed money, but once again, he had participated in unscrupulous business deals and lost it all.

Evita serviced him and his friends with bondage, S&M, and other kinkiness. With Evita being a rare hermaphrodite, she was a valued prize in the human sex toy business.

From time to time, she heard foghorns from big ships outside. She had to be on the western side of the Puget Sound on one of the islands, across from Seattle. Maybe she was in a house near a bluff of Vashon Island, or Bremerton, or Whidbey Island. She had to be up high, because she couldn't hear any wakes—waves made by big ships and tankers—against the shore. The people holding Evita never opened any windows, and the blinds were kept closed. But, she thought she detected ocean water smells.

Bathroom and shower time—to pee, shit, and wash off the explicitness of foul folks—was the best part of her day.

That was when they changed the sheets, too.

CHAPTER 36

Kinship

Psalms

The plane tips its wings. I see a ferry crossing the Sound and it reminds me of my grandfather. The blue ocean waters of Puget Sound look calm, and the islands still have more trees than man-made structures. There are still more lakes and more parcels of land from when only Native Americans owned and ruled the land.

My grandfather often found hidden burial grounds, where small native villages were surrounded by old growth trees. Whenever the land's new owners wanted something built over them, my grandfather often told them it wasn't possible and couldn't be done. He knew they wouldn't give a damn about the sacrificed dead souls. He would tell them the ground had problems, and whatever they built there would not be safe and sound. He would smile, and say ghosts would come and swallow up the house, and suggest they build houses a hundred feet away from this spot.

When my grandfather found the Native American grounds, the new owners wanted to put a garden or golf course in that parcel of land. He said the water table was too high, that it would change the land in time, and destroy anything as it reshaped it. Although my grandfather had no Northwest Native blood living in him, he had Southwest Navajo kinship flowing through his heart, and he respected life differently from the people he worked for who now resided on the land.

The plane tips its wings again, and I see a little house next to a big one. It feels strange in my soul like fiery, melting silver pouring through my veins.

Looking out of the plane window, I see the sunset's red streaks in the blue water. I see the islands in the Sound between Seattle and Tacoma, Vashon Island and Whidbey Island. I see a reflection of the past. Her face. Her face...staring through the window overtakes my vision. A little white girl, not much older than me: she used to stare in the windows of the little house on Orcas Island. She came from the big house, the little castle. Grandfather and I might be eating, and she would peek in one of the windows. Sometimes, as Grandfather was doing his Bible study, she would appear in another window.

When my grandfather would read to me by the fire at four years of age, the little white girl would be there, staring in the window. She would have such a sad face. There were times when she would raise her hand in almost a wave, and I think I remember smiling, but I never waved back. In some ways, she might have frightened me.

I know now that the little white girl was my mother. That is the message she passed down through Gabrielle. I wanted to meet her years ago, but lawyers met me instead, offering money, and a shut-the-hell-up clause. I signed legal documents that told me to keep my mouth closed. Not even a wave, not even a hello, not even a face to face.

What world has she been in? Did she have nightmares of her black son born out of wedlock, the shame of her perfect, white world? Maybe. Has time been cruel in her dreams? What kind of world has she lived in that made her refuse me when I reached out? Is her nightmare that the world will find out she once had a child with a man who didn't kidnap her over forty years ago? Is it a horror of reality that she and he blew up other peoples' worlds?

Now she wants to meet me…does she want to blow mine up, to hurt me, too?

As this plane is about to land, I can't help but sit here and think I might be a man who has problems with women as it stands right now:

My Mama Dearest, Gabrielle, and Evita.

I have trusted Gabrielle wholeheartedly, and now that trust is gone after her decision to alter my, and her life, with her death decree. How dare she make a ruling about people close to me out of pure shrewdness, as if making a decision to send a smart bomb in to kill a terrorist?

I reflect on my relationship with her. Maybe she and I were irrational to cross the line as we did when we became lovers. If we had been exposed, the government could have been sidetracked in all that it was doing for the American people, right and wrong. Think of the headline:

SECRETARY OF STATE IN A RELATIONSHIP WITH HER SECRECT SERVICE AGENT.

That would have overshadowed deliberations about whether we should have gone to war to stop a man from killing his own people.

She and I, as black people, would have been burned in a modern-day burning at the stake. In some circles, the conversation would have been all about how we hurt other black people. We would have hurt many people no matter who they were. I say all this, but when I'm in her presence, I'm the happiest. I'm confused right now about what is right and wrong, and I need to be clear. If it is true that we were irrational, then anything we have done is wrong— but it can't be, can it? We did nothing wrong other than fall in love while on the job. Now she's done with that job and they want her dead. The irony of it all.

Evita has caused me a lifetime of hero shit, as well as having my grandfather put a notch on his belt that he didn't need when he took a man's life to protect her. Then I do the same thing years later, saving her ass. I have tricked my heart and mind in to a form of love…is that irrational, too?

We do care about each other, but she is never going to be my woman in the classic sense. Shit, I have known it since the beginning, but I enslaved my head into some ass-backward thinking.

I look over to Suzy Q and she is asleep, holding a trophy: the reigning Jell-O wrestling champ. Her crazy ass has told me the truth about Evita. I need to stop thinking she is my soul mate. I care about every breath Evita takes, but with this latest little act of floating away as if it has no effect on others, I'm pissed and concerned all in one.

Now my birth mother says she wants to talk to me. How can I not have a warped way of thinking when it comes to what good this is going to do for me now?

I understand why my father wasn't in my life. I'm sure I'm feeling like a lot of grown-up children, wondering where the other parent went or where they were. Like a lot of hurt children, I'm going to have to find out what she wants…now that she has pulled her head out of her ass some four decades later.

CHAPTER 37

In One Safe Place

I t was 4 a.m. when Psalms finished sitting down first with Mint-furd, Suzy Q and Velvet, and then with Tylowe and Meeah. So much was going on. Things were starting to mix together where they shouldn't, but it seemed it couldn't be helped.

Temporarily, Tylowe and Meeah would move into the condo with the kids. The crazy shakeup of their world needed to be slowed. At first Tylowe and Meeah thought to take them home, but Meeah's motherly sense made them reconsider. Having just moved them to Seattle, moving again would be too much stress for them. The main thing was to keep their kids from living in fear.

All calls from the condo, both cell and landline, were recorded in the computer system Mintfurd had set up. Other than to pay her bills, the great-aunt had made no calls from either. What to do with her to maintain her safety was still up in the air. For the Russian, Sasha Ivanov, to kill an old lady would be like flicking a bug into a fire. If she pursued her intention to secure the kids' money, she would circle back repeatedly until she got what she wanted. It was a matter of security. Safety for the kids and the great-aunt had to be maintained, and the condo was the place to be until…

After handling ten different women in a Jell-O wrestling contest, Suzy Q needed a day's rest. Some of those women had been men, who had been allowed to fight as women in their bras and panties. She had a shiner that looked more purple than black. She mocked Psalms that she had a wine-stain birthmark under her eye resembling his, so they were now twins. He told her she must have been getting weak because it wasn't a she-male that had given her the black eye; it had been another woman.

"Yeah, but they carried her out of the Jell-O right, eh?"

"That they did, after you almost choked her out. Damn, Q, it was supposed to be a fun contest, not an MMA cage match. That's the stuff Zelda does."

Suzy Q and Psalms had decided to avoid a conversation about Evita and her disappearance until they'd come back from the East Coast. Now Suzy Q would return to tracking Evita down. Before going to Washington, D.C., she'd had no luck. Zelda had found Evita's car sitting in a parking garage at a high-end lounge for several days before it had been towed. According to a woman Evita worked with, she had last seen her there when they'd met for drinks. When she'd left Evita, she said all seem to be fine. When Evita didn't come to work the following Monday, she thought it strange. Evita didn't leave a message, but that had happened before, so the woman let it be. Zelda had said she would go back and talk to that woman again.

Suzy Q turned to Psalms. "Our journeys in life have had wrecks and flats, eh? Sometimes, mate, we run out of gas. Those times are our fault for not paying attention. Other times we trusted the wrong people to give us a ride. That's our fault, too, for not paying attention. When they crash, it still rearranges one's life, eh?"

Mintfurd and Psalms had a conversation about their security projects all around the world. What was going on in Seattle right now was not the center of their business. They had security teams around the world and team leaders to communicate with to stay in front of potential problems. People paid Psalms to keep them safe, but not all of them were straight. Customers sometimes went in the devil's direction and started using their security business as a cover to do drug dealing, sex slave trading, or oppressing people. Psalms would kill that contract, and perhaps "redistribute" some of the profits to the oppressed.

Along with the help of a select few, Psalms and Mintfurd helped bring justice to an unjust world. It was a small slice of the pie, but some people slept better at night because others tried to make life fairer. The registered name of Psalms' business on the letterhead said it all:

ONE SAFE PLACE
Security and Protection

Mintfurd spoke of his engaging conversation with Darcelle. He said they first talked for about two hours, then he'd called back at midnight and they talked until birds started chirping. They would be going out this weekend if all was clear.

Psalms thought about Gabrielle upstairs in his bed, and knew she was waiting. He doubted she was asleep unless the pain-killers took her down, but even then he was aware she didn't sleep well. Part of what he and Mintfurd had talked about was Suzy Q's plan to go after the man—possibly men—who set had Gabrielle up for assassination. Gabrielle was a part of a plan to send a message to back off.

The part of the night that gave some levity to his troubled mind was when they arrived at the office. Velvet saw and met EL'vis. Her reaction to seeing a hot-looking man walk through the door was almost comical. Velvet lost her cool and sassy veneer when EL'vis took her hand and spoke to her in French. The two had spoken on the phone before and knew of each other, but never met. Her astute perception could tell he had a different blood in him. She opened a dialogue with EL'vis in French, and switched back and forth between French and Spanish. That conversation lasted for an hour. Psalms took his bags upstairs and went to check on Gabrielle.

Velvet let her imagination roll with the fact that EL'vis worked with Psalms when they were both Secret Service agents. Velvet automatically thought the man who called her "velours de Madam" was Superman, by his looks and work and panache. Her eyes saw EL'vis in a Superman suit with a chest made of steel, arms made of iron, and legs chiseled out of oak. EL'vis' face had a square jaw, but with soft corners, and Negroid lips that fit as if the best plastic surgeon designed them. His brown eyes seemed to stare away, but he had Velvet's eyes pinned on him.

One could tell EL'vis was used to women putting the move on him. He stayed kind and charming, but didn't lead or let Velvet become unprofessional. It caught Psalms off-guard and amused him. When Psalms came back down to the office, Velvet was escorting EL'vis to an apartment in the condo. He laughed at how many times he had asked her to do that with other guests, and she would respond that she was not a bell-hop or check-in clerk.

Psalms needed sleep. He walked into his bedroom and touched Faelynn's arm. She lifted up from lying next to her injured sister. Faelynn didn't say a word. She left the room, closing the door behind her and went to her room down the hall.

Psalms had taken a quick shower earlier—eight hours earlier—and felt he needed another one. He was about to lie down next to

Gabrielle, and even though she was hurt, it had been too many days since he had touched her. Between them, sparks normally flew like electricity. When they came near each other, they wanted to connect in the most primal way possible.

Anger and illness are often not enough to stop the body from wanting when it wants. Men and women play down what the body wants, as a way of acting pure, yet within minutes, most people know if they want a certain person to touch them or not. If not that person, then someone else of their choosing.

To go without sex is not so simple. High stress and a sexual release is the only way to ease a troubled mind…for a while. If you're going without, the body still hungers to be touched. It desires to insert or to be penetrated. The body seeks out scents that only the human body can emit. The mind wants to hear certain sounds of flesh, lungs, and mouths, even a bed squeaking from the pleasure of being out of control rather in than in control. The eyes send begging and pleading signals of desire to see another body moving, lying, turning and spreading in its vision. The heart races and sweat glands moisten. The lips and tongue fill with blood, as well as the genital area of male and females, and get excited by often just a thought of sex. In short, the body is horny! The body craves; it thirsts and hates rejection, delays, and complications that impinge on what the body wants.

Psalms wouldn't think of trying to have sex with his lover, whether he was upset with her or not. A bullet had grazed her; having been shot at, her mental state had to be fragile.

Hot water shot on Psalms' body from four showerheads pounding on his hard body from each direction. Stress from days of intense situations needed a physical release. For sure, he thought, before he lay down next to Gabrielle, he didn't want her to feel an instant hard-on. He needed sleep. Little sleep would come with a throbbing hard dick the whole time he was next to her round, ample ass.

He smiled, holding his hard dick as he massaged a little oil on the head. He laughed. "Her breasts are hurt, not her ass."

In the bathroom, only nightlights in a star pattern on the ceiling emitted enough light to see. The lights brightened a bit as the sensor detected an entrance.

"PB..."

Psalms heard a faint voice through the thick shower glass. The glass prevented outside sounds from being clear and in the shower, the waterproof speakers were playing low. "In The Morning" by Ledisi flowed with the steam swirling.

Psalms opened the frosted-glass shower door and saw Gabrielle sitting on the toilet. She was leaning forward on her toes. Her head was down and her long mane of hair appeared to be thrown over the top of her head, covering her face. It all blended with her thick, milk-chocolate body with curves and made his dick jump. Her full breasts had a patch on each one.

Through her hair, he heard a plea. "PB, I need to be near you. I need to know something is normal in my life right now. Please. Can I come in the shower with you? My patches are waterproof; the doctor said I can shower with them.

"PB, you have every right to be upset with me, and we can talk about it when you want to. But please, right now, let me touch you, let me please you. I have to feel there is some part of my life that is normal."

He watched her wipe, stand and flush. He thought about the firmness of her round ass that could almost hold his weight with its density. As she stood at the shower door with her head down, he lifted her head and pulled her hair back. She had a small butterfly Band-Aid high on her temple near the hairline. He looked into her wet eyes. He opened the shower door wider, leaned out toward her thick lips, and he kissed her. He tasted tears; the salt was still sweet. He pulled her into the shower with his hands lightly on her waist.

"Don't treat me like a baby. Take me. I need that, and I know you may not understand, but I need your body; I need your hard dick in me. I need to make sure I'm alive. I need to know."

He understood her plea.

"Ah baby, just don't grab my breasts." She smiled and kissed his chest. The steam was almost overpowering once he closed the door to the sealed floor-to-ceiling shower.

"What Kind of Man Would I Be" by Mint Condition inspired her. She placed her back against his chest, and he carefully wrapped his arms below her breasts. They slow-danced without moving a foot. She cried, and he let her bleed her pain down the shower drain.

Her tears slowed down as she started to relax and enjoy being close to the man she loved. She was in his protection, and never wanted to escape the air he breathed.

The events of the last days gave her a sobering examination of what she wanted for herself, and what she wanted to be to others. Life was a bullet, inches away from making her a Level Six. She pushed her back firmly into the man who made her think and connect into one-on-one sensitivities, the feelings which she had always wanted. She had almost lost that connection, and hoped he would forgive her for lacking trust. She wanted to forgive herself, too, for not considering the effect her decision would have on him and others.

Right now she needed an injection of the man she loved to feel alive. What Psalms feared had happened: his horniness was in a fiery rage, and that's what Gabrielle wanted. As her ass was grinding into his hardness, he had to move his dick to lodge in the long crease of her ass. He started to hump her ass, pushing his dick deep between her firm ass cheeks. He was grunting and getting louder than the music.

She was glad the waterproof patches covering her wounds on her breasts had time-released pain-killers, to lessen the discomfort of moving around. She placed her hands on her knees to give him full view of her ass. She gyrated her ass, and it excited Psalms. He became assertive. That's what she wanted.

He squatted lower and lifted the cheeks of her ass up at the same time and worked his dick into her ready wetness. She wasn't as wet as she normally was. She was also tighter than usual. It might have been that her mind and soul wanted more than her body. He pressed into her; she groaned. Psalms was always a tight fit at first. She loved the force of his girth going into her and after two long strokes in and out, her wetness came, but she stayed tight.

"You okay?" Psalms asked.

"Yeah, yeah, baby, yeah, come on. Let me feel you cum inside me. Fill me up, don't hold back." Her voice was faint, but encouraging, to keep going. He put his hand on her hips and began to stroke her to the rhythm of the song, "If It's Love" by Kem. Gabrielle's tightness and his thickness matched the repeated stroking in and out, and the steam-filled shower helped him cum hard and powerfully inside Gabrielle. She felt alive in her one safe place.

CHAPTER 38

Unattended Misrepresentations

A ferry horn blew in the fog, and both Gabrielle and Psalms opened their eyes to each other. She placed her hands to her breasts and a tear rolled off her cheek and onto the pillow. Psalms slid his leg over hers and placed his arm across her, below her breasts. Her hand reached and gripped his forearm. She fought with more tears, dampening her pillow.

Her voice went to the ceiling. "I have scheduled a local counselor from the Betty Ford Clinic to come here today. I hope that is okay?"

Gabrielle lost control and covered her face. At one time she was the most powerful woman in the world. Now she was lying there, with her breasts wounded and her soul bombed out. She had at one time the power to starve a country, but now her own soul was feeling impoverished. She felt no different from a woman squatting outside of a Third World hut. Gabrielle felt poor and mentally destitute. Her drinking was undermining her, destroying her footing, disrupting her life and the things she wanted most: family, love and the strength to be herself, not what the world wanted her to be. It all teetered on the out-of-balance axis of symmetry in her life. Her loss of equilibrium had her falling down.

Psalms moved to hover over her face. His gold eyes connected with her brown ones. "Gabrielle, you're not weak, you're wounded, and not just behind those bandages. You're wounded behind your beautiful eyes. We all handle life our own way, even as you and I love each other; we have our own way of coming to decisions that might affect each other. I live with things I've done, and at times I'm conflicted. Those things I've done—I ask myself was it for me or was it for the greater good? I struggle sometimes, just as you did when you were a part of world decisions.

"For me, my hurts stem from my mother thing. Her adult misrepresentations of why she handed me a purse full of money, but not her soul, made me turn and face God and ask him for guidance, and learn to forgive myself for the ugliness that comes into mind. Then I have to forgive myself because of those troubling thoughts, and constricted parts of my mind. We can think some cruel things.

"With your help, I think I can meet my Mama Dearest, and be ready for any hurt that might come of it. I'm sorry if I hurt you by not listening to you about something so crucial, but I have a lifetime of hurt.

"We hide our souls from the world because it will chew on us like a dog chews on a bone. Knowing this, sometimes we chew on that same bone, but we must evolve.

"We must keep decisions from being personal when it comes to others close to us. We must keep outside influences such as your drinking from having any part of the decisions we make. So, yes, Gabrielle, have a counselor from the Betty Ford Clinic come here today. If it's the right place for you, your sister and I will be there for you. Be humbled by God's light shining on you, not man's dim view. Don't worry about what the world will say. You don't answer to the world."

Psalms had Gabrielle go out onto the deck to get some fresh air. He had her lie on a lounge chair with blankets. Outdoor deck heaters warmed the area. He went in and changed her sheets, cleaned up his bathroom, and got dressed. When he went back on the deck, he saw she was asleep. Psalms admired her sleeping beauty. The sun kissed her while playing hide-and-seek through fast-moving clouds. He had Faelynn go out to the deck to check on Gabrielle as he left.

EL'vis was across the street on the beach working out as Psalms often did. When Psalms walked into the office, Velvet's son was doing schoolwork in the quiet room. Velvet was standing at the window watching EL'vis.

"Don't," Psalms said.

"Don't?" Velvet's voice gave her away; she knew what Psalms meant. Psalms didn't say anything else, he simply stared at her. He didn't look at her like he was mad or ordering her.

"PB, I'm not getting any younger. I want a man in my bed that can still bring some joy and some funk to my hot ass. Seeing it in front of my face is something hard to pass up. Don't worry, I haven't touched the goods yet, or told him. But, I will if given a chance."

"Yet given the chance you will drop your bloomers in a heart-beat, right? Just let him be. He's seen it all, and heard it all. What he has, his worldwide intellect and charm, he uses all of that to do his work. It's not him I'm trying to protect."

"Oh, so you're saying you're trying to protect me? Well, I'm grown, thank you. Or…maybe you're trying to tell me I'm not his type and he's just polite because what…he doesn't want to hurt my feelings? I'm not his type because I'm a single mother?"

Psalms gave her a blank stare response.

"Is it because I'm not cute enough for a fine-ass man who looks like him? What is it? Is my butt too big? Why can't you see him with me? What…am I not sexy enough for him? He only wants a woman on his level of hotness? What…I'm not hot? What? What… you don't think I can swing from a roof, or the back of a boat? Is the thought of me loving him a joke? What, what, what? I can't hump him in the cold dark water at midnight? What is it?"

Enraged red eyes and red cheeks fired across the room at Psalms. Velvet snapped the pencil in her hand. She grabbed her expensive coffee; the top popped off, and some spilled on the floor. She threw the whole cup in the recycling bin instead of the garbage. She turned away from Psalms, and looked at EL'vis across the street, kicking high in the air and spinning quickly in some form of capoeira.

Psalms said calmly, "EL'vis is gay."

A long moment of silence etched on the walls as Velvet slowly sat in her chair.

"He fooled the FBI lie detector test too; don't feel bad."

"PB, I, I—"

"Don't," he said. "Don't apologize." He walked over to her and forced her to turn her chair his direction. He squatted down, and kissed her forehead. He pulled a chair up next to her. "Velvet, all you said speaks to the fact that you're harboring negative thoughts about yourself. Thinking that nobody else is having a first or second thought when it comes to you.

"If ever someone had undesirable thoughts of you, why would you want them anyway? Why want someone who doesn't want you? I know you know better than this. You can't treat life like a Face-book status. You can't post some positivity you don't practice in real life. You're displacing some inner hurts and negative thoughts about yourself. How quickly were you ready to demonize me, or anyone, because of your own disheartening thoughts about yourself?

"Velvet, you are a superstar to me. I see you, and I'm amazed at all that you can do. Yes, you're not the size your friend Darcelle is, but your ass is round and moves as if you can give it and take it. I'm sure that's not your problem. But mentally you seem to be beating yourself up, so maybe a little activity is in order. Not because you need to lose weight, but to feel better about yourself. You dress classy and sexy. You do turn heads. You don't overcompensate with the fake gaudy nails and makeup, and your voice is sweeter than that coffee you just threw in the recycling bin.

"You raise your child with manners, and he is well-behaved. A man is not going to run from that—maybe the other way around if he's bad. No worthy man is going to run away from you because you are a single mother."

Psalms and Velvet sat in silence. His mind was trying to wrap his head around what was going on in hers. It was unbelievable that such a pretty woman seemed to have no self-confidence. He thought about the many times he had heard Velvet put herself down, and he felt bad he had never stepped in and pointed out her beauty.

"Velvet, please tell me about your life. Please tell me all that I don't know. Not that I can fix anything or have the magic to make it all better. I want to know your story. Like, why do some of your friends call you Skillet, and why you could own your own company, but you work for me. You had money before working for me. You told me your son's father hit the Lotto, but I'm confused about you.

"I had choices of great people to hire, but you were that superstar that said loyalty first. I had chosen to not delve deep into your past, because from the day we met, I know I could trust you, and I've been right. My company is better because of you, but now today, after hearing you go off, and about what set you off...Please tell me about Skillet, the woman that so few know."

"I'll need coffee first, and I'm sorry for going off, but get me a coffee, and I'll tell ya what I can tell ya about little ol' me with the big butt, and big mouth."

Psalms leaned in and kissed her forehead, and left to go get Velvet an expensive coffee. When he came back, her hair was back to perfect as well as her makeup. Her son was out with EL'vis. He came in and got some car keys, and went out touring the city with her son as his tour guide.

Velvet told Psalms her story. Lois Mae tagged her with the nickname, Skillet. She'd had an affair with Lois Mae's husband at that time. She knew he was married, but he'd brought the sex better than any man she'd known. Velvet's mind did the classic trick when she was seeing a married man. He'd leave her for me, she'd thought, but of course that didn't happen. Velvet had run in to Lois Mae in public and greeted her with a fake, "Hey, let's get together some time. I'd like to get to know you." Lois Mae had thought it odd, but she was an outgoing person, and she'd agreed. All the while Velvet said nothing like "I'm sleeping with your husband." They had gotten together, and while Lois Mae was cooking, Velvet had spilled the beans thinking she was helping the both of them. She had told Lois Mae she had been sleeping with her husband. Lois Mae almost had hit Velvet upside the head with a skillet. The name Skillet stuck after that.

Velvet told Psalms she'd grown up with men always all over her for her looks and tight round ass back in her youth, and she'd acted out of control at times. She'd taken advantage of how she'd caught men with her looks. At some point, she'd realized she was used for her allure. Men had fawned over her exceptional looks, but she'd selected unprincipled men due to her drinking.

"I drank like I was filling bottles of wine from a faucet. That's why I can tell your girl Gabrielle has a problem."

Psalms had never seen Velvet drink and it had never crossed his mind. Now he realized he knew two women with high IQs that could both run the world, and drink it under the table.

Velvet finished her story about meeting Lois Mae. Both women realized they were victims made to behave like enemy combatants. They understood how the same man regulated them and made them helpless.

They became friends although their lifestyles were different. Lois Mae remarried, to a good man named Sterlin.

In the last few years, Velvet mixed and matched with younger men. She thought it made her feel young and desirable. Then after childbirth, the last of her self-esteem was cut off like an umbilical cord.

"Velvet, it's easy for anyone to find reasons to quit trying for love or at least trying for a decent relationship. You picked a reason that many people fall in to: it must be my looks. People assume they don't have someone because of their looks. Yet, you know how many perfect, pretty people don't have anyone, either? Just as money can't buy you happiness, neither can someone else's idea of perfect beauty bring you love. Good looks can bring you dick, but not necessarily love.

"It's still up to you if you want love, but dear, you're only hurting yourself with these young boys. You're raising a son, and you could have a son who could be thirty or so.

"That's not to say one can't have someone younger, but if that is your driving force up front, thinking 'Let me find a younger man to feel desirable'—that's foolish."

"Older men do it," said Velvet. "They go find some young thing."

"Yeah, we see that, but chasing young girls and having one you want to be with are two, for real, different things. The older men who get a young woman pay for it with pain-in-the-ass misery. A pretty showpiece on the arm is not the same kind of pretty behind closed doors.

"If I was to get with a young chick, and I was going to keep her happy, I would have to do things I thought I was done doing. Young girls think they have the power of pussy to play games. They want to hang with other young people, and they might want you there—or not. Either way, it's a pain in the ass to be somewhere you indubitably don't want to be. There is a lot to think about when you step out of your age range when it comes to day-in and day-out living.

"Those older men have to deal with are they paying for it with their wallets. Yeah sure, there is the rare couple in love for better or worse and he's sixty and she's twenty-five, but that shit ain't real to most of us."

"Yeah, I guess you are right on that account. I was a pain for older men's asses when I was young. Hell, I wouldn't want to live with myself back then." Velvet chuckled.

"Velvet, you are not too old, but you have old hurts. Finding the person with a hurt you can deal with is trying times. You are a powerful woman because you have a higher IQ than most men, and you are a woman with a woman's emotions as I heard earlier."

"Yes, I am woman…hear me roar."

"My grandfather often told me you will never, ever make a woman entirely happy because she keeps moving the line in the sand. She can't help it because her rational, psychological, conceptual, and often her spiritual levels are always evolving and progressing to a new attitude, and changing viewpoints on uncountable subjects.

"As men, we change slower. That don't mean better, but it's just slower. You know, men are mocked, and rightfully so, when they act as if all they want is sex and food, but sadly it shows very little depth of a man who has stooped so low in life to not seek a more complete being. Sad commentary.

"But, like I said, you are a powerful woman, and you need to act upon it by being where other powerful men are. Men will come at you hard for a touch of your power. Some men will come to get some of your power, and some for bragging rights, and some to get over on you. Some men show their asses because they want others to see who they can get, and some men don't give a damn.

"At the end of the day, they will all be the same—the good, the bad, and the ugly. You set the standard for how they go about caring for you in the long or short run."

Velvet smiled and then let out a loud laugh. "Okay, but a woman needs a little bit every now and then, no matter what the end game is. I don't want to have to train a man on how I want to be treated."

"I hear ya, yet I know you've met men who are slobs in suits, and some men who are so anal that you'll never be good enough for them. Some men will want to change you, and some won't stand up to you when they should."

"I do need a man with some balls because I will run over him if he won't stand up and be a man, and tell me sometimes to sit down and chill...just as long as he's nice about it, and then let me—"

"Velvet."

"Okay, I am actually listening to you, I needed to hear this. I come into this office with my son and act as if I'm okay, but I'm not. Losing my head earlier has shown me that, and I think PB—well, I know—I give you a hard time. I hate to say it, but it's true, that many days you are my one safe place where I can just be me, and not have to worry about you walking out on me, and not coming back like most men have done in my life."

"I'm here, and I'm not going nowhere. As the song says, 'You belong to me, you're my family.' You know I don't have much family, so we're stuck with each other.

"No matter how young or old, whether at church or a business social, some men will have whores waiting for them on the other side of the country. Some men can't escape mama drama. Some will bore you, and some men will excite you for a while. Now, how do you find the diamond over in that sand across the street?

"Stop harboring negative thoughts about yourself. Don't displace inner hurts, and place them on other things, and other people. That drains you and keeps you from seeing who might want you. You always have to be ready for that chance. I think that was your line, right?"

"Yeah, that's my line and I'm gonna have to work on that. Damn, EL'vis is gay, huh?"

"Yep. Velvet, how long have you been sober?"

"PB, ever since I found out that my son was growing inside me."

"Eight years. I see I was right; you are a powerful woman."

CHAPTER 39

A Plan, Planning, and Planned

A month later, the effort to pin down The Duck, the right-hand man to the former president, had hit all dead-ends. The team figured, the man directly connected to Gabrielle almost losing her life from an assassin's bullet was lying low to avoid any possible retaliation.

Gabrielle and The Duck and his conservative party had had a few run-ins and disagreements. He had treated her as if she were a token, and that didn't go over well with her. Gabrielle was not a die-hard, through-and-through-conservative on all issues, and that had brought friction to the Oval Office. When Psalms had directed Gabrielle to send a message to The Duck that she wanted to support fully all causes in an attempt to learn more about the attempt on her life, he'd responded that he appreciated hearing that and would get back to her soon. Psalms and the crew believed he had to know his boys were either dead or on the run, and that, at minimum, somebody was tracking them since they had not collected their money.

The plans had to be put on hold, but not forgotten. Psalms, EL'vis, and Suzy Q had grown cautious about sending a message to never attempt to come after Gabrielle.

Gabrielle's wounds were healing, and for the last two weeks, she'd participated in an outpatient treatment program in Seattle to help with her drinking. It was a one-on-one setting, and Velvet supported her. Both women went to a meeting with the new psychiatrist.

Velvet did some soul searching, and in an effort to feel better about herself, she had joined Lois Mae in the gym. Getting Velvet to go to the gym was something Lois Mae had tried for years to do and until now, she had failed. Velvet's primary goal wasn't to lose weight; she wanted to feel more confident in her overall health, mentally and physically. She worked hard at putting a stop to the self-deprecating humor.

Watching her son work out daily with Psalms or Mintfurd, and over the last weeks with EL'vis, made her think she should be an example for him, and one day possibly be around to see his children. Last week, Velvet, Gabrielle, and Lois Mae worked out together in the gym on the second floor of the condo.

Gabrielle was a bit limited with her breast wounds. Her psychiatrist had suggested physical activity would help with her overall recovery. While sweating out the bad, she could start to feel better about what she put in her body.

A month later, under tight security, the two kids went to Tylowe and Meeah's house on Lake Washington and spent the weekend. The responsibility of caring for the kids gave Meeah and Tylowe joy that they had lacked in the last few years.

It also made them proud to see their grown girls living successful lives. Tylowe's daughter, Tyreene Pearlene Dandridge, was in the WNBA and married to Larentzo Sir John, who played in the NBA. The two had become the poster couple of professional sports in the media.

Meeah's daughter, Mia, had become a freelance photographer working with some of the best magazines in the world. Tylowe and Meeah gave both their girls a stable, maturing environment for them to flourish, and that was their joy when they came together.

Now with their girls gone, it took away a vital part of their lives that helped complete them, and affected them more than they understood. The empty house started to tear them apart. How quickly a sense of need could change people's perspective.

Even with security placed near Tylowe and Meeah's house, clearly the kids were still in danger. The problem was hard to figure out. In some ways, the solution was dangerous: let the enemy show its head before a coordinated response could be brought forward.

Psalms' efforts to find Evita seemed to be lost in the cracks of Seattle's sidewalks—but which crack? Her expensive car had been found and towed. Her coworker had said they had drinks, but that she was okay when she'd left. No phone calls. No signal Mintfurd could track. The last time a signal had pinged off a tower was in downtown Seattle on the Friday she was last seen. No credit card charges. No airline flights. Suzy Q flew into Atlanta to check her sometimes lover girlfriend out: she had not seen or heard from her.

Psalms tried to act as though he wasn't panicking, but he was constantly worried. Evita had disappeared before, sure, and for long periods in her life. Psalms was away living his life during some of these times, so he didn't know the reasons why or how. He had been around at times when she withdrew from daily life for weeks, but it had been years since she had done that. The search moved in to panic mode, but dead-ends were in every crack, above ground and below.

Mintfurd and Darcelle had spent time together twenty-four days out of thirty-one. The day before yesterday, Mintfurd had met Darcelle's daughter by accident—actually a setup. Mintfurd and Darcelle had agreed to meet at the mall, simply to see each other and to stop and talk. Darcelle wanted to see how her daughter would react to seeing her mother having a long conversation with a man. In some ways, it was also a test to see how her daughter would respond to seeing such a huge man talking to her mother. Mintfurd did tower over her, enough to block out the sun.

In a computer store in the mall, Darcelle and her daughter contemplated purchasing new laptops or tablets.

Darcelle asked a hulking man, who so happened to be walking by, what would be his opinion.

"Hello, I'm sorry to bother you, but my daughter and I are shopping for either new laptops or tablets. Although I'm sure we'll be happy with either, what would you purchase?"

Darcelle's beautiful daughter, Diedra, craned her neck to look up at Mintfurd. Darcelle's anxiety that her daughter would have fear of such a huge man was mistaken: her daughter's reaction was the opposite.

"Hello, mister. Could you help us?" He smiled, and Darcelle's nervous shoulder tension relaxed. Mintfurd helped them pick out a laptop tablet combo to cover their computer needs, and they walked to the food court and had a terrific time. Unlike Psalms, Mintfurd was a natural with kids. At his size, he developed an approach of facial expressions and body posture early in life to disarm children.

Born and raised in Barstow, California, Mintfurd had eight brothers and sisters, and he was the baby. The largest, the smartest, the most athletic, and the one to leave what many called "the ghetto in the desert."

Before he'd left to go to college, drug dealers had abducted a little Hispanic girl whose father owed money. The drug dealers had bragged and made no secret that they had the girl. They were trying to send a message to the townspeople that they controlled the area.

Despite, or maybe because of his size, Mintfurd was a chess player in thought and action. Through an elaborate plan one night, the drug dealers watching the house had ended up bound and gagged and asleep. Beepers and call message centers were the trend at the time. Mintfurd had deciphered their codes, and because he spoke perfect Spanish, including the street vernacular, he had sent messages to confuse the other drug dealers that were away from the house, sending them into police traps. Mintfurd had hacked the old DOS police computer. He had sent information to the FBI and police on where the drugs and the bad guys were. Finding their hideout, Mintfurd had piped sleeping gas into the house. With the drug dealers down and out cold, Mintfurd had found the little girl, sleepy but alive. She thought he was a giant coming to hurt her, but he took his time to relax the little girl, and to help her understand he was there to take her home. Mintfurd had taken all the money the drug dealers had on them, and the ten thousand dollars they'd had in the house. With the drug money, Mintfurd had helped the family move to northern California, and had put the fear of God in the dad to stay away from drug dealers and their ugly friends. The next day in the local news the headline was:

LOCAL AUTHORITIES AND THE FBI ROUND UP DRUG DEALERS AND MAKE SUBSTANTIAL DRUG BUSTS

The news account failed to mention that the six men were found bound and gagged and sleeping.

CHAPTER 40

Nature on the Rise

Since the meeting at the mall, Darcelle and her daughter had eaten dinner twice at Mintfurd's home. The not-quite-yet couple cooked in the kitchen together, and the three of them sat at the dinner table. Darcelle and her daughter had never sat down at the dinner table with a man. It had her daughter asking if Mintfurd could come over to help her mommy cook again, and sit at the dinner table altogether, and say grace. That had never happened. Mintfurd took time to teach Diedra to say grace.

Today, Mintfurd and Darcelle were taking advantage of some alone time. They walked the Seward Park loop, after having dinner at Tylowe and Meeah's. It was constant amazement for Darcelle to see how well Mintfurd moved. He moved better than many average-sized men. A power walker herself and sometime 5K runner, Darcelle challenged Mintfurd to keep up with her going around the loop. It was now their second lap around the three-mile loop, and he was almost carrying her at the pace he set.

Seward Park in Seattle is the one place black couples will go out for a stroll and other park activities. Mintfurd and Darcelle passed and waved to people and enjoyed the beautiful water that surrounded the walking loop. He asked her to cut through the woods with its gradual trail incline to add to their workout.

He started to jog up the hill, and she couldn't keep up with him.

He made it to the crest of the incline and waited for her. When she finally arrived, she fell against his huge body, and he wrapped his arm around her. Her head height rested on his firm stomach. Her arms barely made it from side to side of him. He was warm, and despite the fact they had been moving for an hour, his scent was full of sweet, musky, male pheromones.

Her intake ignited certain senses in her body that felt like a high and glowed with warmth. Her body was responding to want. It had been such a long time. She pulled back and stared up at Mintfurd. Nervousness overtook her. They had not kissed other than pecks on the cheeks and a few brushes of lips. After twenty-four dates and days in each other's presence, not one hard, deep, lip-locking kiss. A month of long nightly phone conversations, and many daily mini phone chats, and the only bodily contact they shared were light hugs when they came together, or when they parted from each other.

Mintfurd reached for her hand and guided her forward. Her head was down; her body language expressed shyness, and a need for help, but she was not alone in her feelings.

"This is new for me, too, Darcelle. How to be romantic, and in the moment, I'm a rookie; help me," he said teasingly.

"Pick me up, please," she said.

"Love to." He reached under her ass and lifted her as if she were a bushel of flowers. She worked her legs around him and locked her arms around his neck. She kissed his cheek and kept her face to the side of his. What she needed to say was that she couldn't look him in his eyes yet.

"Mintfurd, I have shared a lot with you. You know my family was different from most black people and I've been married twice. But I have only told you the surface about why I'm not with either one."

"Shhh, hold up, Darcelle. We all have stories. I have one of my own. Because of my size, I chose to accommodate my life with certain pleasures and I—"

"No, let me go first." Darcelle kissed his cheek again.

Tall trees and a small forest surrounded them. Trails led up and down with hidden lookouts over the water. Mintfurd carried Darcelle with her arms wrapped around his neck. He walked a little over sixty feet off the trail and into a small clearing. It overlooked an old closed fish hatchery that used to release salmon and trout into Lake Washington. There was a tree stump and he sat down with her now sitting on his lap.

He reached for what looked like a car key fob and pressed on the keypad. He set a heat sensor that would give warning beeps if a human or large animal came closer than fifty feet to his location. As he finished, he wrapped his arms around Darcelle and held her tight as she nestled her chin on his shoulder.

She told him her story of Husband One who had chased every tail, or let every tail chase him, because he had sports celebrity status. She told of his sexual practices with her and how he had deprived her of a child, even though he was making babies elsewhere. Although it was difficult, she told him about Husband Two and his abnormal sexual practices. She left out the recent events that involved her asking Psalms for help. She had no idea that Mintfurd was a part of the fix.

"Mintfurd, I'm telling you all this, so you know I'm gullible and naïve. On the other side of this, I've been told my level of sexual acceptance, of free to be me, is on another level from most women. I'm not going around sleeping with a bunch of men. It has been six years. But, I'm busting at the seams for some sex. I'm busting at the seams for someone to be good to me and not take advantage of my needs no matter how strange they may be.

"I'm in need of love, and maybe you can't love me because I'm too weird for your taste, but could you, would you, please come get in my bed or let me get in yours? I feel we can be good to each other. Where it leads from there—" She kissed the side of his face.

The sun had crested over Seward Park onto the other side, and they were now in the cool shade of tall trees. The lake turned bluer and calmer. While sitting-straddling Mintfurd, Darcelle noticed the arousal from his crotch area when she shared her past sexual situations. It sent stimulating excitement between her legs. She felt dampness and a tingling inside her panties, and her skin felt hot despite being in the shade.

"Darcelle, I'm sure women have all kinds of reasons why I couldn't be a viable lover for them, and because of that, I don't know the love of a woman. I have never been in love or given love, yet. My physical release has been with professional women I have paid to be with me. I have, for most of my adult life, paid for sex. I have ordered women like anyone would order a cheeseburger to be cooked without the secret sauce. I have placed orders most of the time for six women over six feet tall, with a lot of ass, and who are strong and flexible."

Darcelle's inner vision pictured this, and she felt more dampness and tingling.

"A little over a year ago, a woman who serviced me…she told me she couldn't do it anymore because she found someone to marry her. It messed me up, and I have gone without ever since, but you feel me under you. All I have known since is porn, Vaseline and my hand." He laughed, and she did, too. Mintfurd took his hand and rubbed and squeezed her ass several times. She groaned for the squirrels and the birds to know her feelings at that moment.

"I-I-I have a rather sensitive ass, and it don't take much of a touch to get me off."

Mintfurd laughed, and she felt the vibration his body gave off. Darcelle was on fire with the possibility she would feel a man soon.

"I'm glad you have a sensitive ass. Besides me staring at it all the time I could, I would... Okay, let's finish talking about us. Whew.

"Does my size give you pause, because as I said, I've only been with the kind of women that could handle me the best."

"I'm flexible, and yes, I may be a small woman, but you see I have breasts, I am top-heavy, and you see all this booty. Don't let the small waist and my shortness fool ya, Big Boy. You don't scare me."

"Then yes, I want to get in your bed, and for you to lie in mine. But I must add, my dear, I want love from you. If you can find a way to love me, that's what I need."

Darcelle placed her eyes inches away from his pretty handsome face. They both stared almost through each other's eyes as if searching. Her lips rested on his, and they froze as blood rushed to their lips and warm breaths intoxicated their passions. She felt his hard-on pushing and stirring under her. She moved her hips in a circling motion as if his hardness was inside her. Their lips parted and she slid her tongue into his mouth, and he sucked her tongue and her air. They kissed hard and liquid escaped from the corners of their mouths as their lips were all over each other's. Darcelle dry-humped his raging-wanting-to-escape hardness. She stopped and lifted off his lap quickly.

"Stand up," she ordered him, but he acted as if he didn't understand. "Stand up, Mintfurd." He did, and she squatted easily down and she rubbed the side of her face on the length of his long dick. She felt his girth and the twinge she felt between her pussy lips almost made her feel she had to pee.

She pulled at his sports pants waistband. She had to stand to work them over his hardness. Her eyes blinked. His dick was pretty like his pretty, handsome face. Mintfurd's dick head looked molded for an art display of perfection, and he dripped a thick stream of clear life from the opening. The clear, syrupy, pre-cum slowly but surely ran down the thick vein under his dick and over his balls. He appeared to be a slow-running faucet. She watched the stream come to the end of his tight ball sac, and she caught the thick drip in her hand.

In the middle of nature, his dick seemed to be as thick as the fir trees around them, and it pointed straight up to his belly button and maybe above it. Squatting down and looking up at a man, she saw his head was in the sky.

Darcelle wanted to get her mouth on his dick. With it being the size it was, she could sense she could suck as hard as she wanted; it was going to feel wonderful in her mouth, but first she wanted to make his face lose its composure. She took the slipperiness in her hand and wrapped her forefinger and thumb tightly around his powerful dick head, and she squeezed and stroked. This time he was the one who groaned, and the forest absorbed his guttural animalistic moan. She stroked his hardness as more clearness came forth as if someone needed to turn off a valve. Mintfurd was getting off, and was humping the air, and she masturbated his hardness, and then he felt her mouth on his dick. She was sucking hard on the shaft near his balls as she stroked him.

Her head was angled, and she could see his unrestricted facial expressions. It made her reach under her sports bra and squeeze her breasts. She pulled on her nipples and then slipped her hand down and into her wet opening. Her pussy throbbed.

She thought about sitting him back down on the stump and climbing on his dick, and riding him right there in the middle of the forest. She was fantasizing while having a real fantasy. She could see her naked ass squatting on his dick, as she was bouncing up and down on his hardness with her arms wrapped around his neck. She imagined she could look out over the water as the sun was falling to sleep, and feel him rising inside her lonely internals. She wanted to feel her skin rubbing on him wholly and unconditionally, but she fought off the thought of riding the dick that was in her hand and against her lips. She stood up.

"I want you to stroke that dick for me. I want you to cum on my ass." They both heard others walking the trail laughing, and singing, in the distance. They were far enough away, yet she placed her fingers to her lips to tell him to keep the noise down, but she wanted to hear him get off. She quickly licked her fingers for him to see. He was so high on the whole ordeal. Mintfurd didn't know if that was his wetness on her fingers that her tongue devoured, or her own wetness she tasted. It didn't matter; he was getting high watching her.

He groaned almost too loud. She missed hearing that sound, and she missed making a man lose control. She had always been skilled at doing just that—never mind that it had been a long while.

She turned around and slipped her top off, pulled her sweatpants down and stepped one leg out along with her soaking panties. She wouldn't be putting them back on. Darcelle was short, but her womanly features were on par with any curvy woman. Her ass was art in how it curved and was slightly larger than one would think. Her body was athletic, but short.

She placed her hands above her knees and started working her ass for Mintfurd to enjoy, and he was feeling his hardness throb in his hand. The huge man had his pants down at his ankles, and his massively sized hands were stroking his hardness with potent strokes. She worked her ass in a nasty, gyrating motion.

Darcelle spoke in a hushed voice. "Let it go, baby, I need for you to get off. Look at my ass; it wants you. Here, look at this." She leaned over more and reached back and pulled her ass cheeks apart, and it didn't matter that she was so much shorter than he was. He could see her plump pussy lips, and a tight puckering asshole. He moved in behind her and squatted down so that his balls and the shaft of his dick touched her ass.

That was it; that was the touch that made him want to shoot his warm release of cum hard and he did as he backed up. As he stroked his dick head, he shot on her ass and his thick cum swam down the crease. He groaned and threw his head back and then down. His breath was heavy and his chest expanded. His warm release of cum slipped down and off her pussy and onto the ground. She turned to hug him, but he was still hard.

"Come on, Big Boy, let's go before the cops come knocking on a tree and arrest us for doing what they would like to do." She squatted down, lifted his pants and marveled at his powerful-looking thighs. She wanted to feel his power, and it was coming soon.

CHAPTER 41

Don't Touch

Psalms Black, Suzy Q, and EL'vis, who had flown back to the East Coast, all met in Killeen, Texas. Psalms flew into Houston, Suzy Q into San Antonio, and EL'vis into Dallas. Each drove into Killeen and they stayed in three separate places. A plan was in place. They came to get even for the wrong done to Gabrielle, and to send a message.

The Duck would be in Killeen to meet with business leaders. He had been clueless about what had happened to his assassins, and so he had kept a low profile until now. But, it was time for him to come out of his hole. The government provided tax dollars to The Duck, just like Gabrielle, for expensive security, but they were not the Secret Service. A highly trained, highly qualified, private security company protected him.

Psalms tracked the team protecting The Duck. Psalms knew the head man from his days as an agent. The man had served under five other presidents, and now was an independent security contractor. Tracking him would set their plan in motion.

The week before, Suzy Q had stalked the man into a stylish restaurant, where he sat with a couple of his agents, having dinner. She had tracked him with an electronic device from Mintfurd, and she had captured all his phone calls using the cell tower switching stations.

The success of the plan depended on total coordination. They didn't use cell phones, but old-fashioned walkie-talkies to transmit in code instead. Psalms understood The Duck's security had their own high-tech abilities. Morse code and walkie-talkies were a limited, low-band type of communication that would pass below their radar.

The Duck walked out of the meeting, escorted by his security team, to a convoy. The convoy was heading back to Dallas, a two-and-a-half-hour drive on I-35 N. They would never get to the freeway. In three blocks, life would change for America.

Once out of office, presidential staff and ex-senators didn't have motorcades that would draw city or state police to help provide security during travel. Security became much more of a low-profile patrol of protection.

Stationed in a closed-down business looking out through blinds, Psalms observed. The convoy turned left and drove down a rarely traveled street, on their way to the freeway. As he waited he laughed, but without humor. The former president and his administration had brought on this recession that had closed down hundreds of businesses. Psalms thought about the pain of politics. Politicians did not weigh the honest effects of the suffering of real people. Many cities had streets of business that used to thrive and had survived decades of down years, but the last recession had made many streets into little ghost towns. Super-mega stores of cheap goods from sweatshops in foreign lands sent Americans to the unemployment line or worse. Big banks with no regulations over-invested in bogus investments due to the former president and his administration giving tax breaks to their rich friends. Psalms shook his head and smirked at the claim that giving corporations tax breaks would generate jobs; it never worked. This time it crip-pled the last of the mom-and-pop small businesses.

Psalms chuckled again. He was in a boarded-up store, a byproduct of the administration that Gabrielle was a part of, and they targeted her to die for not supporting this part of the grand scheme. The little abandoned store would help bring some justice. Psalms did something way out of character; he drew a smiley face in the dust on the floor with his gloved finger.

Psalms pushed a button. The engines died shortly after that. The three SUVs all stopped. The second one collided into the first one, sending the third truck crashing into the middle one. Psalms pushed another button and the door of the middle SUV unlocked.

EL'vis had tanned his skin to take on a different look, to confuse someone who might try to identify him. He was dressed as a gun-slinging Mexican cartel drug dealer, with fake tattoos on his fore-arms that Popeye would envy. Likewise, Suzy Q had disguised herself in a hoodie and a spray tan, and they rushed the middle SUV and pulled out the sleeping Duck. They had their man. They dragged him to the building where Psalms waited. The few people who saw their big guns stayed way back, almost frozen.

Mintfurd was the mastermind. The former Olympic and world wrestling champion was also a double science major with a double Ph.D. in electronics and biochemistry. Over the years, Mintfurd perfected his sleeping gas, how to use it and how to apply or deliver.

How did Mintfurd and Psalms come to understand that each had an avenging way of life? The two of them had witnessed each losing on points a few times at national wrestling tournaments over their four years of college. Despite the fact that one day they might have to wrestle each other, they spoke often when at wrestling events. In talking, they put one and one together and discovered that the same referees had scored their losing matches when both of them knew they had not lost. Individually, they thought maybe they were victims of some unlucky calls. The lightbulbs went off when they spoke about their losses. An examination of those referees proved they sided against all black wrestlers. No one had ever said anything. Mintfurd and Psalms conspired to put the fear of God in those referees. They retired when illicit pictures of each of them with black prostitutes had made their way to all the coaches. Mintfurd and Psalms had forged a partnership of righting wrongs with brains and brawn.

By tracking The Duck's lead security officer, they'd found the parking garage with the company's security vehicles. Psalms evaded the security system, broke in, and without knowing which vehicles they would use, installed the sleeping gas in every one. Electronic signals controlled the delivery. Psalms hit the switch the moment the SUVs moved away after The Duck's meeting. This was no game: if by chance the gas didn't work, each vehicle had a bomb installed inside. Gabrielle had permanent scars from an assassin's bullets—it was eye-for-an-eye time.

Bound and gagged, they threw The Duck in the trunk of a car sitting in the alley behind the building. Three cars left the alley and kept space from each other to signal trouble. They drove twenty minutes to a house on a private road outside of Dana Peak Park. Suzy Q took the lead. The Duck knew EL'vis and Psalms, as each had crossed paths in the Secret Service world. Suzy Q was the ace in the hole. She could hide her face, but wasn't going to. She was going to take The Duck to a psychological river and baptize him with the fear of his death.

When he awoke from his gas-induced slumber, the fear almost killed him. Suzy Q had a souvenir for him. A tooth with the engraved initials, *T.D.*, made his eyes bug out. It was a tooth from the assassin that had shot at Gabrielle. The Duck's response told her, along with Psalms and EL'vis who watched on a camera in another room, that he recognized the tooth.

For the last twenty minutes, Psalms had monitored the news and police radio. The networks had asked if it was a terrorist network that was targeting the personnel of the former president. Over a month ago, the former Secretary of State narrowly had escaped an assassin's bullet. Now the former chief of staff had been ambushed and abducted, possibly by terrorist Mexican drug cartel warlords who might be angry at the United States.

Psalms and his crew had to be done and out in thirty minutes. Suzy Q was fast. She yanked a tooth from The Duck's mouth—the same tooth pulled from this hired assassin—and super-glued it in his hand. She made it clear if he or any of his people came after Gabrielle, they would get to him, his family, and friends. She also didn't take her time as Psalms and Mintfurd did whenever they injected a pain bullet. She was heartless as she injected a pain shocker near The Duck's spine. His muffled scream could still peel paint off a wall.

Another shot of sleeping gas and The Duck dozed, but would wake up in terrible mouth pain, and pain near his spine where a bomb of non-reversible deadly toxins had been planted. The message: no one is untouchable.

The Duck woke up naked and in extreme pain that night in the Rio Grande, five hours away from where he was originally abducted. He had a note pinned to his skin:

DON'T TOUCH OUR PEOPLE.

Of course the news, and mostly the FBI, thought the note was from a terrorist or Mexican drug cartel warlords.

Psalms and the crew had pulled off a masterful plan. Even the CIA was most likely applauding the skill and the precision. Not one single trace of evidence was found. Psalms, Suzy Q, EL'vis, and Mintfurd all believed there would be no more problems coming from the real terrorist.

CHAPTER 42

I'm Every Woman, Well, I Want to Be

Gabrielle

I've been pinned up for weeks under tight security. One saving grace is that the workout room here in Psalms' condo helps me to relax and burn off some tension. The tinted glass allows me to see outside, but people can't see inside. I see ferry boats crossing with cars and people walking carefree along the beach; I wish I could be that free. I see the shuttle that carries people going up and down to the Space Needle, even if it is a tourist trap rip-off. I wish I was free to do the same without a team of security.

I'm working out with the ladies. Lois Mae is on the treadmill. Damn, she's always on that treadmill, working it out. As short as Darcelle is, that girl can lift some weights. When you look at her in her tight body suit, you see a brick house. Velvet, bless her soul, is not really into the gym thing. She is talking a lot of mess as she works out with me. I think she's working out the need of a man working her out. Well, she talks about it often enough. Meeah is here and a young girl is with her. She is the half-sister of Meeah's grown daughter. Vanessa, Coach Sparks' wife, has joined us. I love her style. She drove up in a pretty 1967 Mercedes-Benz convertible. Her husband rebuilt the Benz for her, and she is one happy woman: you can tell by how she carries herself. Yes, I am envious. There are a few other women here whom I met on the ferry that night of entertainment. We are doing Zumba with Coach Toni who's doing a private session with us.

The music is '70s and '80s dance music. She and the music are damn near killing us, except the young girl, who is putting us to shame. I'm up here trying to kick my leg up to Chaka Khan's "I'm Every Woman," and I'm hurting, but it feels good at the same time.

Most people thing I'm living the life. Flying here and there on someone else's dime, sleeping in expensive hotels with fine wine. Most would ask, why am I complaining?

It's hard to explain to the average person that when your name is well-known, you live your life in a bubble. Depending on what your name is known for, that bubble can be life or death. I knew that before, but until you feel the pain in your soul and on your body, you cannot walk in my shoes.

I have a better understanding of the soldiers who wake up on the battlefield and pray they see the end of the day. The man who was protecting me on the day I was shot—his life is forever changed.

I have a better understanding of what I want in life, knowing now that tomorrow is not promised.

"Damn, Toni, how am I supposed to keep up?" I ask. "This song is too long."

She switched the music to Graham Central Station's "The Jam."

"Thanks a lot, Toni, for another long-ass song."

"You can do it; breathe and work it, gurl."

Psalms has me under strict security, and as I watch the news I see why. I am watching a report on The Duck and what has happened to him. Some suspected terrorists or the Mexican drug cartel ambushed his convoy. They kidnapped The Duck and tortured his ass.

The Duck tortured, that's funny, and me shot by a sniper's bullet, leaving imprints on my breasts…not funny. That's all that's been on the TV for the last month. The news stations and newspapers have sold millions in commercial time. My story was just now starting to die down and here's The Duck, kidnapped and tortured; this will start a new news cycle: same story, different name. If there was an earthquake somewhere in America, it would be the last news story of the day. I know The Duck put those marks on my breasts; that bullet was inches away from taking my life. I have no proof that Psalms and his people are behind what is on every news station, but I believe he went at The Duck to get even.

None dead...I can't help but laugh. The whole security team would be dead if a Mexican drug cartel had done this. The Duck would be on video, damn near beaten to death, begging for mercy.

I doubt the CIA has a team that can do any better than Psalms and his crew with their training, intelligence, and cleverness. I know this. Psalms will never tell me this is his work I'm seeing on TV. I will never ask.

I'm breathing eeeeasier. I'm breathing with renewed understanding of my life, and of my life's purpose.

But I'm not physically breathing easier right now. Coach Toni doesn't know how to give a sistah a break, and my breasts still hurt a bit. Now she's jammin' The Blackbyrds' "Rock Creek Park." I need some water; I step out for a minute, and Coach Toni gives me a playful evil eye. I hold my finger up as if I'm excusing myself during church like back in the day.

I pray that this ordeal is over. I have personal apprehensions about what is next in life for me. Not drinking has been easier physically than I thought, but as time goes on, I will find out how I react to stress. I wonder what I will do. Will I want a drink and give in? How do I find ways of dealing with stress, and how do I learn to relax without pouring a gin and tonic? I've come to understand that I was just looking for an excuse to drink, and the stress on me manufactured one in my mind.

I've amplified some issues. I've turned up the volume in my head and I've tried to drink the noise down—you know, a "making a mountain out of a molehill" kind of thing. In life, we can be our own worst drama and call it someone else's. My therapist has helped me trace back to when I started down the road of negative responses. My reaction to what I have been a part of when it comes to politics, the loss of my father, my mother's current mental state…I have reacted by pouring a drink…drinks. I have reacted poorly to my sister's issues and have treated her as less than an adult, when in actuality, I made adult decisions while inebriated.

On the day I was shot, just twenty minutes earlier, I gave EL'vis permission to eliminate my sister's ex-husband. Kill him! I made a calculated decision to take a life to promote a personal agenda, and I was under the influence of too many wrong things and thinking. I was wrong. Maybe having someone aim for my heart and almost losing my life is, in part, why I understand how wrong I was.

My nephew and niece would have had their whole lives torn apart. Was I thinking my love for them could replace someone they love? Yes, the man ripped my sister's heart apart. But, broken hearts and broken families can and do survive. As an individual, like many people, I have appointed myself as the judge and jury for other's lives, thinking I know best. I was wrong, and I am sorry. I can never say I am sorry to my sister about what I was about to have done, but I owe her and my nephew and niece.

I join back in Zumba, mainly because the music has slowed down. The Stylistics' "You Make Me Feel Brand New" soothes my soul and body. Coach Toni has us stretching in slow motion.

I have to realize that being smart, and doing smarter things with people I want close to me is more valuable than what happens around the world. If I'm indeed a smart person, I have to find ways to make the lives of those I care about better, and not by taking someone's life. What a fool I was. Every time I swallow the thought of what could have happened, my breasts hurt where the bullets seared my skin. It has to be my mind playing tricks on me, but the pain feels real.

Psalms has lost trust in me. I believe he has forgiven me, but he has reason to fear the decisions I make out of his sight. I pray I have a lifetime to find ways to rebuild that trust in him as well in myself.

He, too, is one of my problems when it comes to my future. I have told him so. He seems to understand, but we have a journey. My therapist is helping to bring clarity to many parts of my life without telling me what to do. She is not painting one thing as wrong, and one thing as better. She is doing as a therapist should do.

I'm becoming aware that as a woman, I need to know where I stand in a man's life. I need to know as any woman would want to know, where I fit in when it comes to the long term. I need to know where he and I go as man and woman, as lovers, and when sooner or later we'll go our separate ways. Will I always be a secret? Will I be hidden in the clouds as in the deeds he does for the welfare of others?

I am clear though, I cannot demand, command, beg, or give ultimatums to Psalms or any personal relationship. I must develop an open dialogue that is not threatening. Why would I want to force my wants on someone if they are not ready? I must learn to communicate without treating it as if it is debate, contract, or a negotiation. I know that's the world I once worked in, but my personal life must be kept separate.

One great thing about being around my people of color is we listen to music so few hear or understand. Coach Toni finished kicking our butts, and the cool-down music is Bootsy's "Hollywood Squares."

Maybe the shooting, in a strange way, confirms to me as a private citizen that anyone can be a victim of violence. I can live or die like anyone else. Have I believed that it is worth it to keep my private life secret because of what people will say? Before I die, I want whole and complete companionship. I have the man I love, and I have my joy of being in love. I have to find another way to live with that love, and I have asked Psalms to work on what that shall be.

To my surprise, he has had no problem with the subject; it all came down to how I approached it. I'm learning now that my mind is getting clearer and recovering brain cells that wine and gin were killing.

One cannot compare oneself to others in anything we do. That thought brings a smile to my face as I look at the young girl whose world is ahead of her. I have to be an example, not only in achievement, but also in living.

Ooooh...The Spinners' "We Belong Together."

"Thanks, Toni, and see you next week, if you have not hurt anything else over here on my body."

I want what other women have. Lois Mae found and married Coach Sterlin, and she said it was no cake walk getting there, but he loves her as if she saved his life.

I want to drive home through maybe maddening traffic, and have that unique somebody there to greet me with a long, loving hug. I want that single, long kiss on my forehead. I dream of that special somebody taking me by the hand to the bedroom, requesting I remove my clothes as he watches. I want the special somebody to touch me and take my pain away, even if just for a few minutes. I want to lie next to him and be offered the crook of his arm and chest to lie upon and listen to his heart beating a love song to me, telling me I'm his baby.

Right now, as it stands, I don't have that soul waiting to make me feel valued when I get home. I have to fly in week after week, and month after month. Is it going to be this way in years to come?

I need a social life. I need to start doing things with people that are not connected to politics as a part of my normal life. I've invited all the ladies up for a healthy brunch that I'm having catered. I'm making changes.

CHAPTER 43

Flow Chart

Psalms had always kept his previous work friendships intact, and they came in handy when he needed to know a few things. He could call friends he made as a Navy SEAL and Secret Service agent with questions like, "Hey, what's going down? What's with all the craziness; are we doing anything? Are we moving in on someone?" He made calls to feel out what, if anything, someone knew. People with secrets like to tell secrets. A best friend has a best friend, who has a best friend.

It appeared nothing was happening, only pure amazement at the precision of The Duck's abduction. The FBI was puzzled, not believing that a Mexican drug cartel did the job, and The Duck didn't reveal any helpful information.

Psalms listened intently to all the people he spoke to. He listened with a different kind of ear. Liars have lies in their voice, whether they are in front of your face or not. He was exceedingly adept at keeping a straight face when someone was lying to him. He was as proficient when listening over a phone line.

He had learned from Gabrielle when she was on the world stage, and staring down world leaders. She was skilled at dealing with liars. Most liars, she said, simply want to one up you or outdo you in a lie. She told him her best approach was acting as if she was interested in a world leader's lie, and then giving them misleading information to see how they would react.

Psalms felt comfortable with the information that came in; he considered it solid. He slept like a baby back in his bed, feeling Gabrielle's body curled in his. In the middle of the night, he turned his back to her, and she curled into his body as tightly as she could with her breasts still being tender. She held him, sensing he needed baby love.

At 7 a.m., Suzy Q called and told him to meet her in the office. No rest for the weary. She lived off four hours of sleep or less.

When he arrived, he found Suzie Q and Zelda at the conference table. Zelda, the security agent apprentice, was working. Velvet was not in yet. Spread out on the table was a large flow chart full of notations, information, and questions.

"What do we have?" Psalms' voice bounced off the wall while he stretched against it. He looked as if he were pushing the wall over to the next building. Then, he grabbed his leg and lifted it above his head. Being strong and limber were tools of his trade. Since he had hurried down from his bed, he was doing his daily ritual now while meeting with Suzy Q and Zelda.

Suzy Q walked over and faced him, and suddenly threw fast, powerful punches at Psalms that would hit most anyone else, but he blocked each one.

"I guess you're awake, mate, eh?"

"What's on the table?" He looked down at the flow chart.

Suzy Q nodded to Zelda.

"This is all the info I have gathered about Evita's disappearance." Zelda had a singer's smoky voice as if she was trying to sell herself on a corner. She came to Psalms' company by way of Officer CC, the Seattle policewoman who traded work favors with Psalms. Zelda had played lone wolf, and avenged herself on the job where something went wrong. Instead of arresting her for murder, Officer CC brought Zelda to Psalms. Officer CC knew Zelda had done the right thing, but because of her troubled past, she could be found guilty. Suzy Q helped to clean up her mess, and Zelda became a part of the team.

While Suzy Q and Psalms worked on Gabrielle's problem with The Duck, she let Zelda hone her skills to track down and trace Evita. Zelda followed up on the leads Suzy Q gave her, and came up with a few on her own. She went underground, and put money in the right hands to find things out. She used the computers. Velvet helped her learn how to comb through crime and news reports, and to find sources of info on the computer.

Zelda stood tall over the table. Clearly her body was built for speed. With long legs placing her slightly over five feet ten inches, she was the best female track runner in the state of Texas years ago. But life had been rough on her. Her hair had been through too many wrong turns of worthless advice, but as of late, it was growing out. Her flawless, dark skin and narrow almond eyes made her appear suspicious, and dangerous, yet ultra-pretty at the same time. Men and women kept their distance from her.

She had never lost a fight, but had gained a few chipped teeth in them, and her broken nose twisted her attitude. She treated herself as ugly when she was actually an extremely pretty woman. Suzy Q, Mintfurd, and Velvet had guided her with her health inside and out. Her teeth were now perfect, and she had received surgery to fix her nose. As of late, Lois Mae was guiding her in her education, and in a year she'd graduate from college.

Zelda pointed to a position on the flow chart. "We can trace her movements from the last day anyone saw her. Two people for sure came in contact with Evita: her coworker, Jamie, from the True Essence Humanity Foundation, and the parking lot attendant at the lounge where her car was towed. We can clear the coworker, but after asking her several times, she did admit that Evita had assaulted a man who groped her butt. Another man did sit at her table, but Evita had told her, he was showing off buying drinks for everyone in the bar.

"The coworker, Jamie, was hesitant to say anything because she knows you, Mr. Black, and did not know how cool it was for her to say that Evita was in contact with other men."

Zelda pointed to another spot on the chart. "The other person to come in contact with Evita was the parking lot valet. This is where we find a direct problem, other than the man who sat at Evita's table and bought drinks. I do have some question about that, but first this.

"The valet's name is Phoenix. She is a cross-dresser and known to be inappropriate in her behavior. Evita had evicted Phoenix from the program several times, and Phoenix has had a few stints in prison. Phoenix, a naturalized citizen from Canada, has been on both sides of pimps and pimping, and drugs. She targeted other kids in the program for sexual conquests. It looked as if this Phoenix cleaned up her act and Evita helped her out by finding a job as valet."

Psalms stood, and craned his head side to side and rotated his shoulders. He was tight and tense from all the airplane rides of late, and the work he and the crew had done. He sat down and stared at the flow chart. He wanted to let Zelda know she had done an impressive job, but he could see there was much more.

Zelda continued. "We know the keys to the Audi R8 that Evita was driving were still in the valet station when the car was towed. Being that the car is high-end, they didn't have it towed away as fast as other cars. The lounge is connected to a marina of million-dollar yachts, and so all assumed maybe a yacht owner was out on his boat, and had overstayed his parking time.

"Another part of this is that on Friday, Evita was there when Phoenix asked for days off to go to Canada. She never came back to work a week later."

Zelda pointed to another position on the chart. "Three weeks ago the body of Phoenix Royce washed up in Puget Sound near downtown. The police believe the body drifted over from one of the islands or maybe the middle of somewhere. Her body had a bullet hole at the base of her skull."

Psalms sat up straight and looked at the printed Internet news article that Zelda handed him. He walked around the table reading, and stopped and poured some coffee.

"A day later, the harbor police found a man's body a little farther down, and he, too, had a bullet hole at the base of his skull. When I checked both their histories, I found out the man worked security at a youth prison that Phoenix spent time in a few years ago."

"Yer did good, mate, yer really doing good," Suzy Q said to Zelda.

"I couldn't find out any more through news accounts, so I did a people search on both dead folks, and all I could trace was the next of kin for Phoenix and the man. She has someone who appears to be her aunt or maybe an older sister in Vancouver, Canada using the last name of Royce. The man appears to be related to an ex-husband of this aunt or sister."

Psalms closed his eyes slowly and concentrated on a visual. A name tag came into his mind's eye. It was the name tag of the female guard at the prison where he and Tylowe had visited Elliot. She was the one who'd come over and flirted with him and Tylowe when they'd knocked Elliot out. Her name, Sergeant Royce, came into full view in his mind. He remembered her unattractiveness, and how he thought someone had told her she was cute when she was not.

What made Psalms proficient at protecting is remembering when and where, and when something felt odd. Something was definitely odd about how Sergeant Royce wanted attention and a connection that he and Tylowe would never give her.

His eyes were open now, and outside, the morning sky reflected in his golden eyes. But, his vision circled back on that visit to a man he detested. He and Tylowe had been set up. Psalms filled the two ladies in on what he knew, filling in more missing information.

"That lily-livered fucker is still in play, eh?" Suzy Q cleared her throat and turned away and spat in the trash. She put a small, white tipped cigar in the corner of her mouth, although she never smoked. "What is going on has all been in play for a long time, mate."

Psalms opened the door to let in some fresh Puget Sound air. He motioned to Velvet to come in, but she still was still getting out of her car carrying her morning drink. She no longer bought expensive coffees. She bought expensive, no-sugar-added fruit smoothies.

He turned back to the ladies. "Yeah, you are so right. We need to put our heads deep into the hot house and focus on how we counter, how we hide our cards, and what is the end game for Elliot. We also need to know who else is connected."

"Mr. Black," Zelda said.

"Zelda, you have worked for me for a year now, and I'm your employer, but I'm your friend first. Call me Psalms. You do excellent work. More responsibility is coming your way. You are valuable to this company, and with that, do you think you still need to do ultimate fighting? I know you're the best on the West Coast, but we need you healthy. Plus, those teeth and that nose job cost us a pretty penny."

"Thank you, sir. I'll keep my mouth and nose protected. Besides, it's the other women that need to keep their faces clear of my fists and feet. Anyway, I have some information on the man who sat at Evita's table. I wish I could get more, but he has money, and a trace has been hard. The man did buy a round of drinks for the whole place to the tune of a thousand-plus dollars. He also tipped the staff two hundred dollars.

"Evita's coworker, Jamie, had said Evita mockingly called him 'Pretty Boy.' I'll need Mintfurd's help to override and send in a tracking worm to that lounge's computer system to allow me to get more information on the credit card he used. The waitress does remember a good-looking, highly manicured man who used his phone and a barcode that they scanned to pay for the drinks."

Suzy Q sat quiet as she knew things about Evita that she kept to herself. Evita loved pretty boys to have her sexual fun.

"I need to call Tylowe. He and I need to make a trip to Vancouver, to let Elliot know we have the kids, and to get a read of what he might know. He wants to play poker. We can do that. Gotta make him feel he is winning, and if we don't go up there, he will know we are on to his ass.

"Q, it now makes a little more sense what that Russian told you in Vegas about serving a black and white Russian."

CHAPTER 44

Full Meal Deal

O ut of the corner of his eye, Mintfurd saw that his phone started blinking; it was a message of urgency. His head was propped up high on several pillows. He was on his back, and Darcelle's pussy was parked right at his nose. Her thighs were spread as she had pulled her knees toward her upper body, much like how a baby sleeps arched with their butt in the air.

He took deep breaths of her scent with his nose. Her pubic hair at the bottom of her pussy and between her asshole touched his lips. His tongue slid out and in as he licked the moist lips of her pussy. They had come back from taking an invigorating shower after sheets-ripping-off-the-bed sex late in to the night. She had stepped out of the shower before him and had put fresh sheets on the bed. She had a cup of hot water with honey. She told him to hold the hot water in his mouth and lick her. She knew the warmness, and the honey would make her pussy feel good, and the sweetness in his mouth mixed with her taste would make him eat with sweet pleasure.

Darcelle wanted something she had never felt before, a man who loved to eat her, and he had skills with his tongue and lips and fingers. Mintfurd was skilled, and loved what he did with his tongue. And he had no limits.

She took all of his thick, throbbing dick, but damn, he had made her sore inside. She couldn't take any more dick. She smiled while looking at it lying on his belly, as the head drooled into his belly button. She meditated on the sight, and loved all she was feeling. She reached for the dickhead, held it mildly, and slowly stroked him. He groaned, and she felt his body vibrate through his vast chest as she hunched over his body. His dick went up like a flag on the pole. She wanted some sexual healing. She wanted…she wanted…wanted her kitty licked. And he licked. He reached under her arms and almost lifted her with his massive strength. She loved that he could make a rag doll out of her. He sat her up straight, and she felt his hot muscled tongue curl, and slide up into her ass, in and out and out and in. She placed her hands on his chest and humped his face until she couldn't take it anymore. She hunched her body back over his chest again and backed up until she felt his tongue on her clit. His tongue felt like a flexible dickhead, and a flicking human vibrator. It felt so good her fist pounded on his thigh. Her hips circled on his face.

Late last night, it was the other way around. He had her on the bed and had hovered over her with his dick in her mouth. She had held his dick with two hands, and sucked hard as he went in and out of her mouth. She had made sucking sounds as his dick sometimes came all the way out of her mouth. He had exhaled loud breaths with each stroke of his dick as he humped her mouth.

He had stood up off his tall bed. She almost had to hop up to get in his bed it was so tall. Mintfurd had moved to the edge of the bed. Darcelle had moved her head to the edge, almost letting her head hang off, and he had squatted down for her to lick his balls as he stroked his dick. He loved that he didn't have to tell her to do anything. It was as if she knew to put herself in the action right away, no matter what he did. Most women he encountered loved a good fuck, and in return let him do what he wanted to do. It was something entirely different when a woman was just as active and wanting to give.

He had picked her up and put her legs in a wide V, hanging over his back. His hands pushed her ass up and toward his face. He had driven his tongue into her pussy, as if he were in a pie-eating contest. He had tongue fucked her pussy, driving deep into her sensitive tunnel. She wished she could have reached his dick somehow with her mouth or been able to stroke him in her hands.

He had put her down, and she had turned over on all fours. With the bed's height, she had backed her ass up to the edge, and her pussy and his dick lined up. He only had to squat a little, and that was because she had spread her legs so far apart as she angled her ass up. He had taken his hardness in his hand and massaged it in a circular motion, right at the opening of her pussy lips. He softly had worked inside a little at a time. She hadn't felt pain, but she'd felt pressure, and let out a deep vulgar grunt; it had made his dick throb. His girth and length had gotten to every internal limit she had. She had felt discomfort for a quick moment, but she was so ready and wanted him, she had found herself quickly pushing back in to his dick and riding it. She could take it deep, but his girth made her breathe erratically.

Mintfurd didn't have to move. She rode his dick, hard, as she moved her ass back and forth. She was almost taking his dick to the edge of her opening, and all the way back inside her. She was pumping hard as she was fucking him and blowing his mind as she kept her ass humping for a long while. He had barked and grunted and slapped her ass every once in a while. She loved the feel of his dick when she adjusted to it all. It allowed her to show off her sexual, athletic prowess. Her power walking and 5K running conditioning gave her strength and endurance. All he had to do was stand there and feel her tight, wet, hot pussy stroke his dick. She reached under herself and rubbed her clit at the same pace she was riding his hardness.

Darcelle got louder, and a puddle of wetness dripped on the bed. She squirted as she had several orgasms before she slowed down.

When she did, Mintfurd put his hands on her hips, and curled his massive body over Darcelle, and he started humping her as if he were a wild dog. His hand squeezed her waist tight, and his toes curled on the hardwood floor. His cheeks bellowed, and he held still as his flow of hot cum filled her.

She knew to hold still and let him relax. She could feel his hardness pump and throb as he slowly lost his hardness. He pulled out and lay across his bed. She crawled on top of his back. They both fell asleep soon, but Darcelle woke quickly, feeling his flow draining out of her and onto his back and ass. She got up and went to the bathroom and came back with warm, soapy, wet towels. She took her time and washed his whole body.

Now come morning, and Mintfurd kept seeing his phone beep. It only beeped when it was hot zone time—a call to duty was calling. Darcelle's sweet taste was on his tongue as he licked her pussy, and her scent was making him horny all again. They had been at it every other day since the time in the woods.

He was trying to make her cum before he got up out of the bed, and said, "Come on, baby. Come for me before I go; come on, let it come."

Darcelle placed her hands on his thighs, and she lifted her body up just enough so she could crane her head and look down between her breasts, and see his tongue extended out of his mouth and licking her clit. She rotated and moved so he could keep licking her and she could watch his tongue and feel it at the same time

Her scent and taste made him lick harder, and she watched and felt. It sent her mind and body reeling and ready to explode. Her nose flared, her lips grew fuller, her eyes widened as she sucked a breath and her stomach caved inward as her back arched. He saw and felt her body jerk as she released sweet wetness onto his face. Her upper body let go and she fell onto his body, and her arms flew to each side of the bed, and she grabbed the sheets. She screamed as if hollering in the wilderness, hoping to be found or happy to be found.

A moment later, Mintfurd checked his message, and then called the office. He let Zelda know he would be in soon. Darcelle was already in his kitchen before he was off the phone. By the time he was out of the shower and dressed, a full meal was waiting for Mintfurd on the table—grits, toast, and eggs.

CHAPTER 45

Poker Plays vs. Chess Moves

It took a couple of days of research and planning before Psalms and Tylowe headed to Vancouver. They were going to drive their motorcycles, but the weather in the Northwest was playing psycho.

Instead, they drove in Psalms' classic 1962 Pontiac station wagon. Along the way, they had to take a detour because a bridge on the interstate had fallen into a river. Psalms teased Gabrielle that her government was ineffective. She reminded him he once worked for that same government and still paid taxes.

Tylowe told Psalms that having the kids around Meeah and him was bringing something significant to their marriage.

"I'm not sure if it's just having the kids, or because we have taken the time to sit down and talk more often, instead of just being nice to each other while passing by."

"So, the famous question: Would you do it all over?"

"Only with Meeah. I'm not blind. I see so many people struggling with their mates, boyfriends, girlfriends, husbands, and wives. Everyone looks for a profile instead of true passion. Meeah and I have a passion that goes beyond being simply horny and needing a mate.

"The worst influence on people trying to find a mate is the 'crabs in a barrel' influence of friends and family. They get in to people's affairs, and judge with ugly thoughts. I will never understand how people who don't have anybody, and rarely if ever have had a successful relationship—how in the hell do they get in other people's? I think she and I have made it work after all these years for us to endure these recent trying times...Team Meeah and Tylowe Dandridge, we get the job done."

"So, you are saying, if there was only one woman ever you could have this team with, that is Meeah, despite that we are going to check this MF up here in Canada?"

"Psalms, I have my reasons that I can't always put into words, and maybe that validates in some ways that I am with the right person. Yes, dealing with Elliot in the backdrop has hurt, but Meeah and I have never let him affect how we treat each other."

Tylowe's head turned from looking at another casino site along the highway and looked at the side of Psalms' face. "Man, tell me why Elliot nauseates you so much, as it is obvious he does. Anyone can tell. I have my reasons, but is it because he has messed with my life that you hate his ass as you do? I appreciate your help in all this. Don't think I don't. It does sound like Elliot has set his BS to affect many people if he has a connection with Evita's disappearance. But you didn't even like him before all this."

"I'm going to pull over before we cross the border and get some coffee, and I have a story to tell. I, too, have a history with Elliot that goes back to college." Psalms drove a little longer. The stereo blasted Curtis Mayfield's "Kung Fu" as he pulled up to a coffee shop. He let the song finish before going in.

Just after they crossed the border, Psalms took the time to tell his story. "Back in college, I heard about Elliot, and that he slept with a few of the girls our friends had gone out with, or had dated. You weren't the only person to confront him about it. I know Malik Coop did, and Mayland Howard told him it was a punk move, but we were also boys and didn't put a lot weight in to what other people did.

"You were running track and playing football. Mayland and Coop were on the basketball court. I was in the weight room working out, or I was on the wrestling mat. We all thought if he had a thing for sleeping with women we had slept with, he was just a twisted freak. Maybe in a strange way, it served us right to be going through girls like jelly beans. We all had egos out of control.

"I was seeing a Hispanic girl who lived off campus near Old Town Albuquerque. I was in to her. I liked her. I believe…no, I know I loved her, so I kept her away from the college scene because as you said, crabs in the barrel. If people see others happy, they want to pull you down if they don't have a good thing. I spent a lot time at her home with her family.

"One day, she was in a sad mood, all emotional. I was holding her and trying to make her feel better about whatever was bothering her. We were at a park at night in my car and it went from sadness to being all over each other. We made a mistake there. We got too hot, and we didn't have condoms. We always had plenty, and just like some teenage idiots, we had sex without a condom, and she came up pregnant."

"Dude, I remember seeing a Hispanic girl you were dating, or at least I thought you were dating. She was always at your wrestling matches, and she always came over, and hugged you. Folks knew or thought she was someone significant."

Psalms and Tylowe talked on and off along the trip to the prison. Tylowe sensed Psalms was troubled and didn't press him. They made it to the prison and parked.

"Mina was her name. She committed suicide." Psalms turned the stereo volume up for a while, listening to the Latin soul of the band War's song, "The World is a Ghetto."

Psalms stared at the wall of the prison, burning a vision all the way to Elliot's cell. "She left a note, and she wrote that Elliot had raped her, and she was not sure who the father of the baby was. She took her…she took my baby's life. It had to be my child—my child. My child came from love. That had to dominate over an evil seed, right?"

Tylowe knew Psalms was not asking.

"Elliot acted as though I didn't know, and maybe he didn't realize that I knew that he raped my girl. This went on for a week with him smiling in my face. I don't know if he knew Mina had taken her life. I doubt if he even knows right now. He did pay a small price, but not the price he should have paid. I knew where he practiced his motorcycle riding, on a back road, out in back of the mountain area near the Tram. I shot him with a BB gun while he was riding. He hit the ground like a sack of rocks."

Tylowe looked at him weird.

"Hey, I didn't have guns back in college. Anyway, he came off his motorcycle at about 45 miles per hour. Elliot was hurt, not serious enough, but he was dazed. He didn't see me as I beat him to within inches of his life. The only thing that stopped me was my grandfather had killed a man before and that it involved Evita. I wasn't ready for blood on my hands…yet."

Tylowe stared at the prison gate, and then out of the corner of his eye at Psalms, knowing that, in Psalms' life, he had taken a life or lives. The man was a trained Navy SEAL, and Tylowe knew that Suzy Q had, and would again if need be, as she'd helped a man take his own life a few years ago.

"I do remember Elliot being in the hospital from a motorcycle accident. He left school after that, and went back to France. He made a name as a celebrated Grand Prix motorcycle racer, as we all know. We all thought that was where he made his money. Later, I found out he was trafficking drugs with the Russians and using the motorcycle dealerships as front, using Meeah and her family."

"Yeah, that's our boy, and he's still at it after all this time." Psalms sounded tired; he was living with a memory he had shared rarely, if at all.

"So, do you think after all this time Elliot has not known all that you know? Your girl Mina becomes pregnant, and she committed suicide, and then you beat Elliot's ass. I have to think he knows something. I know you're a mastermind, and you can handle most situations, but if you are wrong, it can hurt more than you and me. Why is he targeting you? I know why he's messing with my life, and he may want his kids, but most likely he only wants their money. He may have enemies, but we seem to be his prime targets for revenge.

"Psalms, I know you don't like anyone to stand up to you, so I have to ask, are you letting your emotions or your ego cloud your thinking?"

"If my thinking is clouded, so is his, and trust me, a man with an ego like his, he may plot, but he doesn't know when to stop. I'm clearer than he is as of right now. I beat his ass silly before, and now…well, you don't want to know what I will do, and it won't be because he's running on stupid. This is not about whose dick is bigger, and this is not about which man can lift his leg up higher, and win a pissing contest. This is life and death."

"I hear all that, man, but keep in mind we have people back in Seattle. I have a wife and two grown daughters out there, and now two more children. You have Gabrielle, who has been through hell herself as of late; you need to find Evita, and you have all your other friends. They are counting on you and me. We can't bring harm to them just because we seek revenge against this dude. He may have the same idea."

"Tylowe, trust me, I have everybody in mind." Psalms handed Tylowe a piece of paper. "Don't read this until after we come back outside and get into the car."

Tylowe looked at Psalms with a blank look. They exited the car and went inside.

At the sign-in desk, Psalms showed his high-level U.S. government papers and ID. Tylowe also had Canadian ID because he and Meeah owned property there, and his motorcycle dealership franchise was still in Vancouver, although it had been downsized.

A guard entered their information in a computer, and said, "I see you visited an Elliot Piste last time you were here." The guard's eyebrows arched.

"Yes, we'd like to see him again," said Tylowe.

"That won't be possible; he is no longer an inmate here." The guard looked up from the computer with a look that said, *You should know that if you came all this way.*

Tylowe's head jerked toward Psalms with his eyes wide open. Psalms acted indifferent and unfazed. He asked the guard a question.

"We met a very helpful guard last time we were here. A Sergeant Royce."

"Oh yeah, she's been on vacation since last week," the guard said while handing back their paperwork.

"Thank you for your time," Psalms said.

The two Americans had not said a word as they walked back to their car. In the car, Tylowe opened the piece of paper. The information on the paper read that Inmate Elliot Piste, a French citizen, filed a grievance with the French Consulate that he had received cruel and unusual punishment. His jaw was slightly fractured, and a few teeth were knocked out. He had received wounds that brought about minor internal bleeding from an attack from visitors in the visitors' room.

The French and Canadian governments had an agreement to protect each other's citizens in war, or convicted criminals imprisoned on each other's soil. A settlement was agreed upon due to the grievance. The prisoner was due for parole in two years, so they had given him an immediate release as of one week ago.

"So why are we here?" Tylowe asked.

"Because he might be watching us or has people watching us. If we didn't come, he'd be a step ahead of us in knowing we know what we know. Yep, he played us from the start. Chess. I got caught off-guard because he was in prison and he'd been out of circulation, but I can assure you he's been working his ass off from the day you put him in prison. Give that MF credit though; he played us.

"When we came up here the first time at his request, he had to know you and I hang together. At least he had to be hoping I'd be a part of helping you. Once we were in front of him, he gave us more attitude than all of the forks full of nasty food he has eaten inside those walls. He would have called your mother every name in the book for you to hit him. You popped him in the mouth, and I took another beat-down swing at him some thirty years later, after the last one I gave him."

"Damn, that asshole was a good chess player. So, since I see you know more than I could have imagined, what's next?"

"I can play chess, too, and don't like to lose. I had Velvet rent two motorcycles from your dealership up here, and they delivered them to the Hilton parking garage on Robinson Street. We'll check in, and leave the station wagon. We have somewhere to go on the bikes."

They drove back from North Vancouver crossing the Lion's Gate Bridge. The beautiful city of Vancouver could be a pageant contestant. The city had more high-rise condos and apartments than New York City, and a city park much larger than Central Park.

In the city of Vancouver, every nationality on the earth seemed to converge and blend as one people. A half-hour away from America, and the color line of ignorance almost disappeared.

Checked in and back out on their motorcycles, Psalms and Tylowe headed to Harrison Hot Springs. Tylowe knew the Vancouver area well, and chose a lot of winding, twisting roads to make the motorcycle ride enjoyable. Once they were close, Psalms set the address by GPS, which took them to a duplex. They drove by and parked at a coffee shop and walked to the duplex. They slipped into the backyard by way of an alley.

Tylowe asked no questions, even when they drove into the parking garage in the station wagon, and even after Psalms turned the old radio dial to 99.45, the radio face flipped down, and a tray slid out. On the tray sat two nine-millimeter pistols. Psalms took one and gave the other one to Tylowe.

Psalms and Tylowe kept low and peeked in windows; they saw nothing. Psalms sniffed the air and checked to see which way the wind was blowing, and shook his head while pressing his lips tight. The neighboring fence stood tall enough to conceal their presence. They went down some steps to a daylight basement door. With Psalms' broad shoulders, he leaned firmly against the door until it gave in. The door opened as the door frame cracked, but made little noise. Psalms headed up to the first floor, but told Tylowe to stay. Twenty seconds later, Psalms called for Tylowe.

On the floor, Sergeant Royce, Phoenix Royce's aunt, lay dead. Psalms evaluated quickly, and determined someone had snapped her neck. His military training had taught him she had most likely been dead almost a week. Psalms searched the house and the computer. Tylowe went outside and walked back to the motorcycles. The smell of death was too much to stomach.

Five hours later, Psalms, Mintfurd, Suzy Q, El'vis, and Zelda were all meeting in the condo office.

CHAPTER 46

My Own Worst Enemy

Evita

I've been able to sit in this room with the hood off when no one is here to use my body. It's on now, though. I hear The Voice, my kidnapper, Pretty Boy. He is talking with a woman and man. They are talking openly about me, and I hear of my possible end or continued torture.

The other voices in the room are a woman with an Eastern European accent. The other voice sounds black. That black voice is different from the average black male voice. His voice has a tad Caribbean, maybe French, accent. It's almost like Pretty Boy's, but blacker and rougher.

"We need to keep her alive as a safety net. They'll be getting our little request later today," the black male's voice says.

"Are you sure we need her? I don't want any trace of us tied to anything that could hold us back, or cause me problems later. All I want is my money. What you do is not my concern—unless you bring me unwanted attention." The female's Eastern European accent sounds like she is the master of the other two.

The Voice pierces me with his valued opinion of my worth. "Well, she's brought in a lot of money for me. My customers love her boy-girl appeal. Shit, we had an ex-Fox Network commentator come in here, and lick and suck on everything she had. Come to find out he's originally from Mt. Vernon, Washington where that interstate bridge fell in the river. So I'm not so interested in getting rid of her yet.

"I had to rid myself of the two who guarded her. They played with her when they were warned to keep their hands off. I have a video camera in the light above the bed. I've taped everyone who has touched her. It will give us a poker chip if we need to get out of a jam. We have a police chief and a judge, a pastor of a megachurch, and the Republican party boss and more, all on video."

"Please don't kill me," I cry out.

"Shut it," the Voice that kidnapped me yells, but I can't help but weep aloud. This hood is so wet around my neck.

"Well, I have not had the pleasure of something strange since I've been in prison. I need you to turn that camera off so I can play with her, but that hood gonna have to come off, if I'm gonna get off. Plus, her boyfriend, I owe him one!"

The black man sounds foul and gruff, like a pain. *Is he speaking of Psalms? Does he know Psalms? What is he talking about he owes my boyfriend?* I hope he don't touch me.

The female screams. "Let me be clear, your black ass can go back and rot in a Canadian jail, and your partner here with his puny little French ass, he can go pimp horse shit. I want my money soon. I financed this so-called perfect plan. It looked good at first, but now the man I sent to Las Vegas is missing, and I assume he's dead. The kids have not been found. Where the hell are they? Before my man came up missing, he told me he found that bitch, Queen. Why would my old-ass father be so in love with her, despite the fact she was fucking you, I'll never know. I want those kids found, and I want them dead! I want my money! Get my money!"

She's the boss for sure, and she doesn't give a damn about my life.

"Sah—"

"Shut the fuck up, you stupid, black no-account good-for-nothing! Don't say my name around her. I want her dead now!"

"Whatever you want to call me, we can't kill her yet. Be patient. And don't think you own me?" the black male says, with some push-back in his voice.

I've been my own worst enemy. I put myself under this hood. I got myself tied to this bed. I put myself in this hell. My need for attention has made me cry wolf one too many times. With the madness that I have lived, I assume Psalms has had enough of me. He would have found me by now. He would have found me. He would have.

But I set myself up. I asked to be kidnapped. I asked for help from someone from my past life on the streets when I was pimping human toys myself. I asked her to help me set up my own kidnapping, and not know when exactly it would take place.

We set it up to happen within a two-month period, and I wouldn't be harmed. I was supposed to have water and food and be left in a room. A fake ransom note would make it to Psalms. Because he is who he is, he'd find me easily.

I wanted Psalms to come rescue me, as he had done before again and again. As the years have come and gone, I have felt Psalms getting closer to Gabrielle. She's a good woman. I don't have anything against her. It's me. It's me knowing I can't be the woman. I understand, but I need to stay relevant in his soul.

The last night he spent the night with me, I twisted like a wet dish rag thinking I needed to call off the kidnapping. I thought I had time to call it off. I guess it played right in to me being here. The woman from my past life must have made a little money selling my ass to these people. She only wants money.

Psalms always told me about hiring the right person for a job. Never hire someone who needs the money; always hire someone who makes money. The person in need will bring you drama; the one who makes money will do the job right.

Who are these kids they are looking for, and who is this woman, and the black man? Please don't let him touch me. I've had nasty people all over me for weeks, but he sounds horrendous.

Something awful has ripped into my soul. To have made the decision that I did to get attention…a part of my soul has died and will never come back. My life has known hell since my birth. Born with a woman's soul, but with a part of a man between my legs. I know I have gone through and fought demons. I can identify with not always being myself, but being what, I don't know.

If I live, if I live on, I'll get right. I'll make it all right. I have to learn to love myself. The hardest part is finding my way. I'll have to learn to trust God, after He has done His work with me here.

Am I thinking like a child who prays they don't get a whooping declaring, *Dear God, if you don't let me get a whooping this time, I'll never be bad again.* Is that me now? Is that what I'm doing? *Dear God, look into my heart.*

I need some mental and emotional growth. I need to find out what being a woman is really about, because I do have love to give. *Please God, set me free from this pain in my heart and soul; I've spent enough time in a mental jail of all the sins of man, and all my immoralities.*

I treated some people real bad, very bad, being two different people at times, living in self-indulgence, doing what I wanted regardless of how it would affect others. Now my egotistical self wants to live. The bad person in me has me crying under a black hood tied to a bed, and the bad in me has my body being used as a human sexual toy. I do not want to let the good person in me die with the bad seed my father polluted me with.

Will I live? I don't know.

Psalms' grandfather had told me a story, one to help me get through a tough time when he'd shot my father who raped me. I didn't know if I could go on and live. I felt I would suffer every waking day.

He'd told me of a man who was dying of cancer. The doctors had told him he was going to live maybe a year when they found the cancers. The man said he was going to live as long as God said he would, and if he had to suffer, it was also God's will.

The man decided he would live the best life he could until his time was up. He flew to Africa to go on a safari to hunt lions. He and another man got lost from the rest. The two men were found eaten by lions; only their bones remained. Two men died, one simply out for the hunt, and the one with cancer. The question was, did God save the man with cancer from long-term suffering? Did the devil take the life of the other hunter? It is not for us to question God's way. I haven't followed God too much, but...

The door slams. I hope they have left... *Oh shit, that hurts.*

"Hey, turn that fucking camera off." It's his voice. The one I don't want to touch me.

"Now for you. Yeah, let's get that hood off you, little freak, and if you try to hit me or bite or kick, I'll knock your teeth out. We are going to have some fun, girl."

He's untying me. *Oh no, he has horrible teeth. They're broken off. He's staring at me like a cannibal. His body is bloated. I want to put the hood back on.*

CHAPTER 47

Going Down

Elliot opened the bedroom door to exit with a shit-eating grin. He had just done horrible things to Evita, and hurt her deeply. He forgot his belt and turned back to fetch it.

Boom...boom...boom...boom! The house shook, like a California earthquake. Elliot awkwardly fell backward and hit his head hard on the bed post, breaking it. Stunned, his sight went black, and his mind went blank. Gunshots went off, and screams echoed in the halls.

On the first floor in a bedroom, Suzy Q fired her long-barrel .45 pistol. Four well-placed bombs exploded at different locations in and around the house built on a bluff over the water. Sasha Ivanov had her gun up and ready to fire, but the smoke was too thick for her to see. Suzy Q, wearing a gas mask that covered her eyes and nose, aimed at Sasha Ivanov. A red beam of light put a target on Sasha Ivanov's forehead and in that spilt-second, Suzy Q shot Sasha Ivanov point-blank in the middle of her forehead.

On the floor above, EL'vis shot through a door at a man who was shooting wildly at him. The man then ran into a room and slammed the door behind him. EL'vis yelled at whoever was in that room to come out, or he was coming in with his gun firing.

Two more smoke bombs went off. EL'vis also had on a gas mask that covered his eyes and nose as he kicked the door, but the door had a weight against it. He kicked the door again, and the weight moved. It was dead weight. The Voice that had kidnapped Evita, Pretty Boy, took his last breath when EL'vis pushed him over. Two bullet holes pierced his chest. In that room, video recording equipment lights blinked. EL'vis pulled out bags, and gathered hard drives and DVDs from the equipment.

Outside Zelda checked on the four men with zip ties around their wrists and ankles. All were sleeping and gagged. The men had been stationed outside the house when Psalms and his crew ambushed them. All Russians, all armed, and not nearly bad enough. None of the men could get their guns out in time when Psalms and his crew surprised them. Hand-to-hand combat lasted less than twenty seconds. One man got off a single punch that hit Zelda in the mouth, loosening a tooth. Zelda knocked him out with one punch, then she lit his ass up with ten punches to the head and body before he hit the ground, wailing on him much longer than she had to. On to her next task, she released some kidnapped young women and a couple of teenage boys from different wings of the house, and helped them into cars and SUVs captured from the henchmen.

Mintfurd's sleeping gas was not feasible to use in the house. The house had four floors and separate wings, with no central air to load the gas into to let it flow through the house. The bombs on the outside were meant to rock the house, and to throw things into chaos.

Evita was on the fourth floor. Psalms moved quickly up the stairs. Psalms encountered a Russian on the third floor as fearsome-looking as he was. The man was shaken from the explosions, but was ready for battle and surprised Psalms. He lunged down the stairs bringing all his weight down on Psalms' shoulder. His shoulder dislocated, and the pain ripped through his upper body as his head hit the wall hard enough to put a hole in it. His head exploded in pain. He shook it off, but the pain in his shoulder was like a hot poker branding his flesh. Psalms went in to warrior mode, spinning hard and quickly bringing his other elbow around against the man's jaw. The power of the connection slammed the man's face in to a horrid position against a rail as it snapped his neck. Psalms lifted the large man up, injured shoulder and all, and threw him down the stairs.

In the room, Evita was getting some revenge. She had bitten her nails over the weeks to remain sharp and pointed. She sliced the face of Elliot as an eagle's claws tear the skin off a fish. Though he was bloody, she kept slicing his face as if her fingers were eagle claws. She had lost her mind and control. She could have escaped from being anywhere near Elliot, but she was in a daze. His bleeding face looked like a *Rocky Horror Picture Show* prop.

She went for his eyes, and self-preservation alerted Elliot to fight back. He stood up to fight against her slicing nails. He grabbed blindly for her and charged her.

Psalms ran through the door with a gun aimed and ready to shoot. Elliot and Evita were tussling as if she were a salmon evading a bear's teeth.

"Stop!" Psalms yelled.

Elliot stopped, but Evita kept squirming. Elliot held Evita's hair, forcing her forehead to his chest, but kept her teeth away from him. He twisted her tight enough to let her know he could snap her in two. Her naked, tattooed ass faced Psalms. Elliot held her tight by her hair and around her waist in front of him. He squeezed her violently and smiled at Psalms with his broken teeth.

"You whooped my ass that time you knocked me off my motorcycle. I have never forgotten that, and I'll be damned if I let you put a bullet in me."

"Do you know why?" Psalms asked.

"What, did I screw one of your girls? Was that the reason you tried to kill me? It was just pussy."

Psalms moved closer, keeping the gun trained on Elliot's face. Evita held still as fear laced her face, and Elliot used her as a shield.

"Well, here we are for a little reunion. I just took this one's little pussy and played with her little dick and had fun."

Psalms' face twisted, not understanding.

"What, dude, you don't know that your woman is a freak of nature?" Elliot laughed at the same time he tried to turn Evita around.

"Nooooo," she screamed. Evita thrust forward toward Elliot's body, as if launching her body like a sprinter out of the blocks. It threw Elliot off his feet forcing him to go backward. He was against a patio door window. Because he was holding her tight, they both fell through and Evita kept charging as if she were Superwoman trying to take off and fly. The two of them hit a wood rail and broke through. Both Evita and Elliot sailed off the deck jetting down to the water. Psalms rushed forward, but he was unable to grab Evita.

The sounds that Evita had heard and that told her where she might be were of freighters and their fog horns passing through the Puget Sound. She knew the house was on one of the islands across from Seattle, and near a bluff. Psalms saw nothing but dark water and waves crashing against the shore as Evita and Elliot fell. He heard Elliot yelling, but the volume faded, and then there was no sound other than a splash.

Psalms ran down the stairs and out of the house, down the flights of stairs that led to the water, leaping six and seven stairs at a time. Once at the water, he already had most of his clothes off. He jumped in and swam in the cold ocean water. He was going to find Evita.

He found her body in the shallows near big rocks. She was dead. Her body was broken, as she had landed on the rocks. He had to swim around the rocks to bring her back to shore; it was a struggle. He swam past a dead floating Elliot. He walked out of the water with Evita in his arms. His shoulder burned from the dislocation. His muscles were seizing from being in the cold water for over ten minutes. He felt another pain overshadowing his physical pain. EL'vis and Suzy Q made it down to the water. Psalms continued to carry Evita's body in his arms. He could see her whole pelvic area was mutilated from landing on the rocks. Psalms would never know the center of Evita's troubles. His body was trembling with chill, and his soul was numb with feeling some guilt from not being able to save her. He saw Suzy Q and El'vis, but walked away with her body as if he didn't.

"Go. We'll take care of all this," Suzy Q said to Psalms' back. He walked up the long flights of stairs, and away in to the night.

CHAPTER 48

Healing

Psalms Black

I t has been two weeks. I still have to sleep on the other side of my bed. I'm trying not to turn on my injured shoulder, because if by chance I do fall asleep, hopefully, I won't wake myself in pain. I haven't slept.

Pinned to my back is Gabrielle. I feel her glued to me since I came in that night. I think she's becoming one with my skin, and her breasts at my back are trying to connect to my heart. Every night and day since, she hasn't let me go pee without her holding my dick in her hand to assist me. I know she is worrying about me.

She saw my tears. I have only shed tears once; when my grandfather passed. Okay…I shed tears when I walked out of a room after my birth mother's lawyers handed me documents of deposits after I signed papers to leave her alone and to never try to see her again. Crying in front of Gabrielle hurt me to the core, because I had been hard about the things I didn't have to be, when you love someone.

I told Gabrielle everything that had been going on with Evita, the complete story about the kids, and the Russians, and Elliot. I told her everything current, except about any death I may have been a part of causing, but I didn't lie to her. She asked to be left out of the loop on anything like that. Although I know about her misguided endeavors, which could have brought about a loss of life, we respect certain things as off-limits to protect each other.

Gabrielle has told me Evita will be with me with every breath I take for the rest of my life, and she is perfectly okay with that. She found a picture of Evita and me on a beach in Spain, and Gabrielle had it blown up, and framed. The picture hangs on a wall in my place.

I could not imagine a woman being so sure of herself, and not threatened, but Gabrielle is cool about it. It says something about what I didn't know about love. It says a lot about how I don't know about women period, or at least as much as I thought I knew. She is rare.

Even though my grandfather told me many things, until you have experienced life and love stories for yourself, they don't matter. I know now that until you have practical involvement living in love and applying all that is associated with love, you don't know anything, and each encounter will leave you with more questions. I have treated love like an educated fool, but surely I have acted uneducated in how I have responded. My grandfather said, "It's not about what you do know about a woman. It's about what you don't know that should drive a man to love her hard enough to know what she truly needs, what you need, and how to give and appreciate receiving."

Gabrielle smiles and looks at me in a way I now admit makes me weak. I'm in love, and I didn't know that, but I do now.

I loved Evita, and I knew that, but in love…no. I loved her, but I cared for her well-being more than the thought of being in love with her. In life, I wonder how many of us get it confused? How many think jealousy, or appearances, and maybe someone's attributes of gaining and controlling equates to loving them? I was to be Evita's one safe place where she could have one faithful friend.

Being in love with Gabrielle is my one safe place.

I see Gabrielle's drive to improve herself, and her becoming aware of her gifts, no longer influenced by what used to go inside her mind and body. She is making a new life of awareness, not only for me, but for her. She sees herself being happy with or without me. If I was her emotional pacifier, it is over now. She used to think she needed me, but she has grown to understand she wants me, and she only needs herself to be whole.

In some ways, maybe Gabrielle and I both relied on each other in passionate ways to free our minds so our asses would follow. In some ways, maybe we both relied on each other's intellectual challenges of wanting to solve the problems of the world as one. There is nothing wrong with all that. Yet our personal world is the most important world. Our world should be about loving those who love us. Our world should strip away how smart we are, and strip away refinements so we can be primal and spiritual with each other. In our world, we should treat ourselves to things as if we didn't have a dime.

I have learned a lot about myself. Number one, I have no control, no power to change others. Learning how Evita putting herself in to a rat trap of evil, made me so angry with her. At the same time, I miss her. I loved her in a special way, but I could not change her. I couldn't.

Evita apparently wanted to be kidnapped, for reasons only she would know. It had to be that she wanted more attention, but she got more than she bargained for and a raw deal. The woman Evita thought would help set up the abduction sold her straight up to a slave ring to support a drug habit. As if anyone with a long-term drug habit can be trusted.

Mintfurd was able to trace the credit card of the former Supersonics basketball team minority owner who kidnapped Evita. The information led to people he dealt with, and most were criminals. Elliot and the former Seattle Sonics minority owner did business before and it all connected. The sex-slave ring just happened to feed back to Elliot by way of the female guard and her niece who were in to the sex-slave circuit.

We traced money transfers that happened through the former owner's cell phone while he was on Bainbridge Island across from Seattle. From there it wasn't hard to GPS to locate the house. Surveillance of the house for only a half-day and we knew we had the right place. Why would a local judge and his wife, and other wealthy business associates, catch a ferry to come to an isolated mansion that had security thugs watching the house? The local police were turning their heads for sure. A nice payoff was being placed in the right hands.

When we went in, we had no idea what we would find, but we figured Evita was there, or already dead. We used heat sensors to know that too many people were in isolated places that were not coming out.

It was not just about rescuing Evita. We have to be about doing the right thing for people who cannot fend for themselves. Street intel told us young women and teenage boys were disappearing, and being used up as human sex toys, and then returned to the street hooked on drugs.

I'm lying on the shoulder I don't usually sleep on due to my shoulder dislocation, but pain is worth the freedom for those who seek it, and people should not have their freedom taken from them. Most of us, in our comings and goings, believe the police are protecting us from the boogeymen.

While we hear about an ugly world, most of us get to drive by and watch it from a distance on a TV. Let the boogeyman step on your porch, and then you'll know who has your back. The police and their backers don't care about you, and your problems. People like Darcelle suffer through threats and intimidation. A civil court, a police department, or a lawyer cannot help many people when an ugly world slimes them. I've been able to help people who couldn't drive by and get out of the way of a bully, who got hit front and center, and I will continue to help when I can. I said it before; I believe in justice, I just don't believe in a justice system set by laws put in place by unjust men. Add to that, any justice that comes from the hands of someone who receives money or favors will sooner or later deliver an excess of deceitfulness laced with prejudices fulfilling an unjust self-righteousness.

I try to save lives. I do the best I can. I honestly do. I love my crew. They are smart, and they are about doing the right thing.

Suzy Q may take some pleasure out of hurting people, but never from the sheer fact that she's out to hurt someone. It's always because it's the only thing that can be done. Suzy Q does what she does well. She grouses about being good at her job. My team—Velvet, Mintfurd, Suzy Q, EL'vis and my newest, Zelda—they let me lead, but will step up and get in my face or have me rethink or think deeper with less emotion when I slip up.

I love my best friend, Tylowe; he keeps me grounded and helps me to be a regular guy. He loves his family, and he laid it on the line to protect them. To protect these kids could have caused his own demise. I often sensed that Tylowe might have struggled with the warrior thing that happens in life for some of us, but for most, hardly ever. My man Tylowe was an athletic stud growing up, but life can mellow you out after you get off the playing field of chasing women, and the playing fields of athletics. Tylowe did his man thing quite well. I'm proud of him.

He and his wife, Meeah, are now raising kids again. They are giving instead of taking away as many do. We could have, but we didn't, do DNA tests to see who the children's father is. In the end, it doesn't matter, because they are in a safe place away from strife and greed.

We looked at the great-aunt frontward, backward and sideways, and it was as she said: the mother, Queen, had placed the kids in her care. She was caring for them very well. Tylowe and Meeah have a small cottage house on their lakefront property, and they are fixing up so the great-aunt can live there for as long as she likes. Tylowe is shipping all her things to Seattle. It also helps to have a live-in sitter for when you want to go and live a little, and spend some time lovin' your spouse.

What did we do with the rescued victims from that night raid on the sex-slave house? We are helping those who were slaves with school, drug rehab, and jobs. Through Evita's foundation, True Essence Humanity, we are helping the hurt and lost to get on a path of recovery, and stay the course.

The security thugs were all illegal Russians living in America. Coming into America is—well, as we know, it is a lot easier if one appears less stereotypically threatening. Just look at the two brothers who did a horrible thing at the Boston Marathon, blowing up innocent Americans. We made sure Homeland Security found the illegal Russians.

I'd rather not say what happened to the bodies of the former Seattle Supersonics owner who kidnapped Evita, the man who dislocated my shoulder, and Sasha Ivanov. It wasn't pretty. Elliot's body floated up near downtown Seattle, the same as the other two earlier bodies.

Evita. I buried her with her mother in the same cemetery plot.

I bypassed the legalities, but she has a final resting place with someone who loved her the best she could. I went with Evita a few times over the years to put flowers on her mother's grave, so I hope her spirit will finally be at peace. I know Evita struggled with many awful evils, some self-inflicted, some done to her. I wonder whether she knew there was a cliff below that window. She had to. I think she wasn't pushing Elliot through, but was throwing herself to end her pain. Evita died on March 26th, 2013. Rest in peace, Evita. Rest in peace.

I'm meeting my birth mother next week. She is coming to Seattle, and she has asked me to come to the place I was born, the old castle on Orcas Island. I was brought into this world by a doctor and private nurse in the old castle. She has told me I was misled by other family members about her not wanting to meet me. They told her I only came for money, and they paid me off. She only asked the lawyers to check me, not to bribe me to stay away because she didn't want to meet me. When I see her face to face, hopefully, I'll know for sure if she is being honest. Gabrielle and Velvet have both told me that whether or not she is being entirely truthful, my birth mother wants to know her child. They told me to be the more human, and give the woman what she needs. In return, I feel better about myself and discover it is time to release some of this anger.

My birth mother—I say birth mother even though there has been no other mother to raise me. I say birth mother because she has never been a mother to me, so as of now, she is just my birth mother. Anyway, she and I had a two-hour Skype conversation. She revealed to me that being an heiress, a socialite, and an actress over the years, has been a joy in many ways, but she has had to live with what people think, one way or the other, about whether she was a real kidnap victim and bank robber alongside my father. She has lived with what others think: was she a victim of Stockholm Syndrome? She said when we meet, she will tell me the truth. She did say that, as a teenager, she and my teenaged father loved each other, and there is no doubt in that fact. She said he was many terrible things to most people, but he never mistreated her or used her. From that, she said, I can start to come to some conclusion about the truth of what happened.

I met my brother and sisters via the Internet, and will meet them in person soon. No matter the outcome of my relationship with my birth mother, I have a blood half-brother and half-sisters and I want to know them. I have a nephew and nieces. I'm looking forward to being a part of their life.

Gabrielle has released her breasts from my back and goes and opens the curtains. It is a pretty day on the water; a lot of sailboats are out. I'm going to go out for a walk. I need some movement. I've been relaxing and healing, but I need some exercise to get my blood flowing.

Gabrielle stands at the foot of the bed naked. She holds her breasts that are pretty much healed, and I'm sure they have left an imprint on my back. She gazes at me with her sleepy, seductive eyes and with her lips slightly parted. She pulls the covers off me, and she leans down and starts to slide her tongue up from my feet and over my legs. Her legs spread over my thigh. I turn onto my back. It hurts my shoulder, but her lips are making the pain bearable as she kisses my face. Well, my blood is circulating, and I'm going to let her get her exercise. I'm just going to lie here and heal.

CHAPTER 49

Until Then I'll Be Dreaming of Loving U

One year later, on a warm summer's night, the ferry moved in a wide, slow circle. At the top of each hour, the ferry had only made one full turn. The Seattle sky was blue and clear. Enough lighted sky gave the Lake Washington water a blue beauty.

In the distance, the I-90 floating bridge was a mile of white and red light streaks. Dressed up in after-five attire and gowns, the women shined bright and alluring. The men, in suits, ties and perfectly-polished Stacy Adams shoes, socialized under the Seattle night sky, aided by lights from the house ashore. Soul music from the '70s, '80s, and '90s played as bartenders made drinks and served water and coffee.

Coach Ayman Sparks and his wife, Vanessa, along with Sterlin and Lois Mae, were jamming on the crowded dance floor. People danced freely and openly, having a marvelous time. All the people aboard were colorful in headwear. Everyone wore hats: most of the women wore the enormous Sunday best hats from the South, and the men wore derbies, fedoras, or cowboy hats, among other types.

Psalms and Gabrielle walked around the boat, stopping to greet and chitchat with everyone. Gabrielle hung onto Psalms' arm. For some time now, both had shown a small amount of public affection. It wasn't a put-on. They truly felt it, and had relaxed into its naturalness. They headed to the dance floor to do a light, two-step cha-cha. Their eyes blocked out the sight of everyone else.

"Excuse me, may I cut in?" Playfully, Velvet nudged Gabrielle to move.

"I want him back." Gabrielle laughed. She started to walk away, but stopped and added, "I need him back, so he and I can go swimming a little later."

"Don't let me turn on the TV tomorrow and hear about one or both of you in a freaky situation."

"Skillet, be quiet." Psalms shook his head.

"Ain't nobody gave you permission to call me Skillet, and listen to me. I have someone I want you to meet that I have been seeing for a while."

Psalms noticed that the last couple of months, Velvet dressed even nicer than the past, and that was hard to do. She would tell Psalms, "When you have hips, you better cover them to shine as something that you want to see."

A man slightly taller than Psalms approached, with his hand out to shake. The man removed a baby-blue Kangol he had on, revealing perfectly flowing white hair. Dressed in a white suit that was for sure tailored, the handsome older man resembled George Clooney with a deeper tan. He could pass for EL'vis' twin, but older.

"Hello, Señor Black, my name is Renaldo Dean. EL'vis is my nephew. He speaks so highly of you, and this incredible, absolutely beautiful woman also speaks volumes of prodigious pronouncements of you."

Psalms shook the man's hand. "I pay them to say pleasant things. It is good to meet you. Are you here visiting?"

"Yes I am, but I do have a home in Houston, Texas, and I still have my family home in Puerto Rico, so I travel between all of them. Maybe I should look into a home here in Seattle." Renaldo Dean gazed down in to Velvet's glowing face.

"Sir Renaldo Dean, please have a terrific time on the boat and come by the office sometime. If Velvet is trying to keep you in one place, like right before her eyes, I will take you out and about."

"Señor Black, I look forward to it. If you don't mind, may I cut in, and dance with this queen?"

Psalms nodded and left to go find his own queen. He smiled, and had an itch to scratch. As soon as he could get Velvet alone, he'd tease her about the things she must say about him.

Psalms also went looking for Mintfurd. It was almost time to perform. The help crew was starting to set up the dance floor with tables around the outer edge and leaving a little dancing area. The boat was at maximum capacity.

A set of stage spotlights in different colors highlighted all the hats below as people took their seats. The show started with local comedians. Darcelle Day came to the stage to run the fundraising raffle. She also had a "Vote for Me" button pinned to her shoulder. Her dress highlighted her perfect curves, yet she looked professional. The raffle was to raise funds for the True Essence Humanity. Darcelle announced that Evita River had passed away while on vacation in Spain.

Psalms swallowed hard, but Gabrielle whispered in his ear, "She will be with you with every breath you take for the rest of your life." He looked at Gabrielle, knowing he was in love with her, and adored her for the support that made him grow as a man.

After the raffle, Darcelle took a seat next to Gabrielle. The two had become close, and Gabrielle was helping behind the scenes as Darcelle's campaign manager and strategist. They had even double-dated. Gabrielle wanted simple freedoms just like that, too, just to be able to double-date. It helped her feel like the average person she wanted to be.

After some vocal performances and poets, Psalms went to the stage. He picked a stand-up bass and played a solo performance. Mintfurd Big Boy joined him on stage afterward. Mintfurd stepped to the microphone.

Mintfurd started to recite, and Psalms played the bass line to Marvin Gaye's "I Want You." Mintfurd's pretty, handsome face flowed erotic romantic words of soul. The women in the crowd closed their eyes and took a mental journey with him, their hearts losing beats.

"*Her pheromones floated through the door before I saw any trace of her*
I sensed she was here even though I had no idea who she was
But I got distracted by being the greatest dancer
Stealing eyes as I danced by myself
Some wondered
Is he available?
Can he move with me just like that?
Others stepped to me
They moved well, but they didn't move me
I let my moves speak for themselves
Flowing my freeness
I don't have restrictions on how I move
Once again I sensed a one-of-a-kind sensual misting of secretions floating in the air
She saw me before I saw her
But like I said, her pheromones floated through the door before I saw any trace of her

Oh, but when she did appear before my eyes…
Her ass sauntered
Her pretty face glowed
I caught her stare, and I threw one back
Her eyes turned shyly away
She strolled by the dance floor
Her walk was a fine dance
She got sexier the closer she came
I kept my eyes on her, and my dance steps began to tango in her eyes
Her presence, others took notice stealing their hope
I started dancing as if I was holding her
End of a song and others left the dance floor
I stood alone
As Marvin Gaye's voice foreplayed
'I Want You'
She came forward
I met her in the center
If there were others nearby, we didn't see them
I gazed in to her sultry eyes
She started to move her body in an enticing fashion
She was a fashion statement of class
I danced around her admiring her knowing she wore a soul-a-thong
Before I came face to face with her again, she slapped me on my ass
Then she licked the palm of her hand
I took that hand brought it to my lips
I licked as if her hand tasted minty
I licked between her fingers in slow drag
She watched intently as my tongue danced nastily between her fingers
Her body shook
Then I spun her

Bent her backward in my arms
Took her down low to the ground
She was confident in how I held her
I wasn't letting go
We didn't dance around the dance floor
We moved the dance floor around us
We were dancing in the stars
Other dancers were just stardust
We were the only two stars
The greatest dancers
As Marvin Gaye's voice foreplayed
'I Want You'"

Mintfurd stepped back from the microphone, and Psalms put the bass down. The audience, in all their colorful hats, roared to the night sky in appreciation of the performance. As the two men walked off the stage, Tylowe and Meeah stepped in front of the microphone.

Mintfurd and Psalms walked together as if they were body guarding someone behind them. They stopped in front of Gabrielle and Darcelle and kneeled. They bowed their heads. At first Gabrielle didn't understand, but Darcelle did right away, and then Gabrielle covered her mouth in shock.

With Meeah standing by his side, Tylowe read a poem.

A Vow To U
I come to my knees
To ask you can I claim U
As mine?
In my heart

In my life forever
I love U
Every day
Mere words
No
Much more
Because
I think of U and love is perfect
I see U in my dreams and I'm not perfect enough
I wish I could be
Every day

Our days are getting shorter
I pray
God's will
I'll be loving U and you'll be in love
With me
Making our days
Happy

As I kiss U
You're in my arms
I'm loving your
Skin
Eyes
Lips
Curves
Hands and feet
Walk
and

Whispers
and
How you listen to me

I want you in my life forever
Sweet dreams
Watching U sleep
Next to me
I kneel, to give thanks
To admire
Your mind, body & soul
and
Loving U while overlooking the best views in the world
Holding your hand and walking with U
Stop and tell you
I love you
To death do us part
I love U
and
One day
This earth will lay us to rest
Until then
I'll be dreaming
Of loving U
In heaven
While you are my heaven right here on earth.

CHAPTER 50

Everyone Wants and Needs One Safe Place

"Good morning, America. With us today, is the former Secretary of State, Gabrielle Brandywine Black. Madam Secretary, it is thrilling to have you on with us. All of America wants to know how you are doing, and what's going on in your life?"

"Well, thank you for having me on. Life is good. I've been out of politics for nearly eight years. I've taught college, and I'm a part of a foundation to help older children. Many are younger adults trying to adjust to life after maybe things got off to a bad start, and I've done some traveling as a regular citizen."

"Well, Madam Secretary, about a year and half ago, you had the scare of a lifetime. But you're doing okay?"

"Oh yes, I'm doing well, I'm fully recovered physically, and I'm better for it mentally. I made many changes in my life. I became aware that life is too short, and I wanted to be able to do my best in all I do. 'Girls just wanna have fun,' as they say. I've been given what many may call a second chance."

"That is wonderful for America to hear. I guess in many ways, you are still showing us leadership."

"I'm happy if young ladies and young men can see that one can recover, and move forward, no matter the challenge."

"Well, Madam Secretary, speaking of 'girls just wanna have fun,' clue us all in on that pretty ring on the ring finger."

"A month ago, I married a wonderful guy. I married the perfect man for me. He's my best friend, and he is my protector. I married my soul mate."

"Oh...wow. Do you hear that, America?"

Meanwhile, deep in the heart of Texas, a conversation is taking place...

"She married an ex-Secret Service agent; the black man with that wine-stain birthmark under his eye. Let that birthmark be the bull's-eye target we aim for."

"Sir, with all due respect, I don't think we want to go after him, or anyone associated with her."

"Don't you want to get even for the little dunk in the river they gave you? The Black Goose—that woman—had to be behind you being kidnapped."

A sharp pain, imagined or real, shot down the spine of a cowardly, squat-looking man who resembled a duck. Pain pricked his ass-hole and his head, sending a reminder to his evil soul.

"Like I said, sir, with all due respect, I don't want to go after her or him, or anyone associated with them."

"Okay, we'll leave the both of them alone."

Meanwhile, in the meeting room of One Safe Place, Security and Protection...

Psalms, Suzy Q, Mintfurd, EL'vis, and Zelda were in the midst of a meeting evaluating their latest mission. Two years before in Florida, a young black male was walking home from a store. He had candy, a can of pop, and a cell phone on him. A cop-wannabe saw the teenager, and profiled the kid as trouble because he wore a hoodie, even though it was raining.

The cop-wannabe had a history of trouble. He initiated an encounter with the young black male by getting out of his vehicle and following the young man, after he had been told by the police he should not. The young man was talking on his cell phone to a friend when the cop-wannabe decided to confront him. Moments later, the defenseless teen was gunned down.

The following year, the cop-wannabe was brought to trial and was acquitted of all charges. Undoubtedly, the man was guilty. Many in the nation hurt, shouted, and marched as they had so many times before, and then things died down until the next injustice.

Many of the people who were involved in helping to rob justice for the family of the dead teen thought their life could move on without retribution.

Many lost hope and faith, and feared for their children's safety. Children and parents lived in more fear than another time since the days of lynching black men. People with cold hearts, such as ultra-conservative gun-toting nutsos, politicians, and TV pundits mocked the teen's death. Some people in power tried to pass even more laws that would encourage more offenses.

Recently, Velvet was out power-walking with her son near sundown, and a car of white teens drove by and yelled, "Hey, where's your Skittles and hoodie? You're gonna need them, black boy."

Psalms and the crew rarely did a job without being requested, but this time they decided to see if they could change the national conversation and attitude through fear. They wanted to send a clear message: You can't hide from real justice.

In the media, it became prominent news that the cop-wannabe disappeared, and an untraceable electronic message of information was released.

The information stated:

We found him, and we got him, and anyone can be found sooner or later if you play any part in the harming of a child, or taking an innocent life. If unfair laws are used to protect killers, wrongdoers will be found.

There was a juror who went on national TV in anonymity, and used racist-coded words that assured the murderer was going to get off no matter what. That juror lost their house in a fire bomb, and all assets electronically disappeared.

Another electronic message was released following that incident, that read:

We can find you sooner or later if you play any part in the harming of a child, take an innocent life, or profit from the loss of that life.

Others were dealt with in different forms. A few racist radio and TV loudmouths and overtly racist politicians, had petrifying fear injected into their…spines. More related information was sent to the media. The national conversation did change, and many who lacked scruples in making just laws have started committing to speaking of change. The crew did not set out to prevent people from having a difference of opinion, or to take away people's rights to have conservative or liberal trains of thought. It was about bringing more honesty, with decreasing the immoral, hidden agendas and racist actions of people with power to influence or cause harm. It was a big undertaking, but the One Safe Place crew put the work in.

Psalms and the crew believed in justice, but not in a justice system set forth by laws put in place by so-called impartial men. Judges, lawyers, and the police had a motive different from what the people often needed. The One Safe Place crew understood that sometimes justice was to prevent avenging.

Then there were those other times…when one safe place may not have been found.

For Discussion

The themes of *One Safe Place:*

1 To those who attempt to rewrite history to attempt to profit and control the narrative of open dialog.
   To those who attempt to rewrite history cannot hide the ugly truth behind their vanity and ego.

   Your thoughts on that statement after reading *One Safe Place?*

2 A Cause must stand alone as a value.
   You cannot be larger than the Cause.
   Or the Cause will die…when you are no longer a value.

   Your thoughts on that poetic statement after reading *One Safe Place?*

3 WE need less talk and more action, and less gossip and offer more sincerity.

   WE need less doubt in each other, and more solidarity for good causes in honest support.

   WE need less negative verbal responses to differences of opinions.
   Let me say that again…

WE need less negative verbal responses to differences of opinions, and let the church say "Amen."

WE need a whole lot less seeking weak people to do our biddings.

WE need less conning or using folks to get the hook-up or getting over on others at their expense

We need less backroom arrangement, back-door deliveries, and behind-your-back transactions WE all lose in the end if we cheat honest dealings.
Let the church of *One Safe Place*, say, "Amen."

Your thoughts on that poetic statement after reading *One Safe Place*?

4 We have dummied-down our ability to communicate. Because either, we take each other for granted, or we never had it, or lost our way when it comes to communication. In generations before, as a child, you were kept out of adult conversations until you were old enough to comprehend all that was said.

Households decades ago, as a whole you were allowed to mentally and physically mature to understand before you opened your mouth.

Now it may seem men and women, we speak less from the heart out of fear that the other person can spread our life out in the open in social media. Often when we do speak our minds in social media, we are meanly ridiculed, called names, bullied and or mocked in kind-a-like the small-town mentality of everyone knows your business, and you're humiliated.

Have we become surface-level people making it harder to get to know others and trust asking questions or telling our stories. We want so much to open up and feel we have a safe place to let what is inside us out and not be judged for the thoughts we can have without borders. So we suppress and don't share and we pass each other like strangers in the night while chit-chatting on our cell phones and social-media outlets to strangers.

Your thoughts on that statement after reading *One Safe Place?*

Praise for Alvin L.A. Horn:

"Lusty, heady, action-packed; is there a safe place to hide when mystery collides with betrayal, wealth and deception? Beautifully resurrected from Alvin Horn's novel, *Perfect Circle*, Psalms Black and Tylowe Dandridge are enmeshed in adventure and scandal all in *'One Safe Place.'*"

—L'Nora, *author*

"A true storyteller that knows how to arouse your deepest emotions. Alvin L.A. Horn's words are captivating, alluring, and heartfelt. His poetic flow is one that is undeniable."

—Niyah Moore, *Literary Artist/Author*

"Simply put, Alvin L.A. Horn is of the elite of storytelling. He captures a vivid narrative of incredible surreal intense reality in novel writing that in my opinion, positions him amongst the best now and in the future."

—Flava Coffee News Book Reviews

About the Author

Novelist Alvin L.A. Horn is also a poet, a spoken word artist and musician. His talent has shined through. Alvin was an award winner at the 2012 Spoken Word *Billboard* Awards.

He states:

I credit my mother for sending me to the library when she placed me on restriction, often for daydreaming in school. Pages of autobiographies and biographies of other people's lives became daydreams and made my imagination run wild. Upon hearing and reading the work of Nikki Giovanni, I knew I wanted to be a writer of love poems and stories. "Some of my erotic writing imagination came from my dad leaving men's magazines in a not-so-secret place. My friends peeked at the pictures, but I read the stories, most of the time…" I laugh.

Born in 1957 and growing up in the "Liberal on the surface" Seattle lifestyle, the Northwest flavors flow through my writing as I have lived on a houseboat with perfect views for writing inspiration for most of my current writing life.

I'm inspired to write and recite the heartfelt honest emotions that I have felt or someone may have shared with me at some time in my life. I try to speak for those who would write or say how they feel. I want to remind people of lost thoughts, hidden feelings and create new contemplations and desires whether it be about love, money, social issues, family issues, passions and sex. I want people to feel worthy, beautiful, sexy, and informed. I want to write and speak in ways, as Miles Davis said, "It's not how many notes you play; it's when you play them." I feel I bring a different perspective to my writing in that I have lived and traveled the world for over a half a century and seen fads, fashions, music and politics change and how we communicate.

Contact the author:
www.alvinhorn.com
www.facebook.com/alvinhorn
Twitter @alvinlahorn
www.goodreads.com/author/show/5778091.Alvin_L_A_Horn
http://en.wikipedia.org/wiki/User:Alvinlahorn

IF YOU LIKED "ONE SAFE PLACE," BE SURE TO CHECK OUT

Perfect CIRCLE

BY ALVIN L.A. HORN

AVAILABLE FROM STREBOR BOOKS

1

Playing the Blues

"Coach Sparks," one of the trainers called out, "you have a phone call in your office."

Ayman Sparks walked through the locker room, his top lip curled up in front of his nose. The funk and noise in the locker room was thick and loud. Locker doors slammed and reverberated. The young men were all talking loud, and cracking jokes. Someone called out, "Your mama smells like doo-doo."

"Knock it off! I've told you guys that I won't have that kind of shit on this team!" Ayman stood still, piercing his glare at any eyes that dared to look his way. "Look at what you guys just made me say."

The young men laughed. They understood that the coach's sternness came with humor.

"Coach, the phone is for you," said a large, dumpy white male with a whiny voice.

"Okay, Meredith, do some extra footwork drills. Silly fouls are cutting into your playing time. I'll be checking your weight. Do you hear me?"

"I understand, Coach. I'll work harder."

Coach Sparks did not understand why anybody would recruit Meredith; he didn't. The former coach had made a commitment that Ayman had to keep.

Ayman headed to his office and kept thinking. *Two hundred and eighty pounds of no defense and can't guard his own shadow. No wonder Bucket was a loser.* Ayman chuckled to himself.

Coach Sparks made his way through the weight room while giving instructions to some and praise to others. His attention bounced between evaluating practice and replaying the nasty attitude his wife had displayed earlier that morning. *What's her trip? Last night she was a freak in bed, then this morning she's the queen of the ice-asses.* He reached his office and punched the flashing line on the phone.

"Coach Sparks here."

"Ayman." He heard Vanessa's voice come through with sub-zero coldness. He knew right then he would stay at the gym and watch more game film.

"What?" His voice let her know he was annoyed.

"I'm going to the bank, and I'm going to take all the money out of the second account!"

"What?" Ayman's voice slowly slid through his teeth. He repeated, "What?"

"I'm moving back to Oakland. The second account is mostly mine anyway!"

"Why, and how many times have you threatened to leave? As much as I love you, I really hate…" Ayman took a big breath.

Ayman Sparks and his wife, Vanessa, had been acting out a deteriorating marriage for years. Threatening each other was almost foreplay. Sometimes, it was foreplay.

Ayman felt the anger heating his bald head. He turned the air conditioner on in his office. "I'm really tired of this," he said.

"You're tired?" Vanessa screamed through the phone. "You don't have time for me, and you know it! We've had this black cloud hanging over our heads, and you don't even know it."

"Black cloud? What the f—"

Vanessa quickly cut him off. "Don't dare curse at me! I'm not one of them referees."

"Then tell me what you're talking about. Stop talking in code. If you have something to say, say it! Maybe we can work out whatever your problem is."

"My problem, huh?" Vanessa made a sound that let him know she was disgusted.

Ayman spoke as if his nose was inches from hers. "Whatever it takes for you to stop all your trippin' over yourself; you need to reevaluate what you're doing."

Sarcastic laughter filtered back through the phone. "You feel better now? That was like a halftime speech when you're losing, right?"

Ayman grimaced. He was always out for the win. He didn't know how to respond now. Vanessa had him off balance. "It sounds like the problem is money. Now, we both know I make plenty, but I have to work for it. If it's about time, my coaching career is about being successful. That means I have to put in the long hours. That's what a coach does. You'd rather I work in a straitjacket job. You know what? Most likely, I would come home and still hear you bitch.

"I never hear you bitching about the nice house you live in. I don't hear you complaining about the gardener or the woman who cleans your house twice a week. Oh, you fly home to Oakland and everywhere else you want. You're right, maybe it's time for you to step. If you're talking about my job and the money it puts into the bank for you to take out, I—"

"You egotistical son-of-a-bitch! Why do you think it's all about you and your money? I carried your ass when you went back to school to be a teacher. I've moved around the world for your dreams." She cursed. Ayman's eyes blinked. The F-word was something she'd only said during sex. "You never spend any time with me." Her voice lost strength.

Ayman was sitting on the edge of his desk, twisting and turning in one spot.

"We don't spend time alone unless it's alone in the bed, and I need more—more than sex."

Ayman's jaw clamped tight, as if something with long fangs had bit into his flesh. The pain of what she'd said dripped like venom, killing his ego. Silence over the phone let the emotional poison churn his stomach; he reached in his desk for some Tums.

"I'm sorry if it hurt, Ayman. Look, I need it as bad as you do, but having sex every night as our only connection has become hard on my soul. You got things going on that I didn't sign up for, and now that I know you about—"

"About what? You think there's another woman? Whatever. I'm not jumping off the Aurora Bridge for your insecurities." His tone had no humor in it, but he snickered.

"Laugh, go ahead. You might be one of these fools here in Seattle who would jump if—" A minute-long silence ensued. "Ayman," her voice cracked. He heard weeping. "Maybe you've forgotten all that I've done and been through with you."

Ayman's defense was loud. "No! You can't let me forget it, not even for a week. You know, I don't need this shit today! I'm on my job!" he shouted. "The same job that keeps your ass in Nordstrom and Macy's."

Ayman turned the air up higher. "Enough is enough! File for divorce. I'll sign anything to stop the madness. I'm getting ready for the season, and I don't need your bullsh—"

Ayman's assistant coach and best friend, Sterlin, walked into the office. "Ayman!" Sterlin called out in a hushed voice, trying to stop Ayman from raising his voice any louder. "Man, chill!" Sterlin put his hand up to signal for him to calm down.

A long wavering note of a saxophone solo flowed into Ayman's ears just as Sterlin reached across a table and tapped him. It was two years later. A lounge full of people came into view. They were not in a locker room and not in his office. Ayman had been daydreaming/nightmaring about the last episode of the breakup of his marriage.

The two coaches were in a jazz club in Lexington, Kentucky. They were drinking a little and listening to live entertainment. A sax player's solo had charmed him into his past.

It was Wednesday night. The players from East Seattle City University were back at the hotel, on lockdown, resting for tomorrow's game. The two coaches were taking a break trying to relax. Ayman needed to unwind before the game tomorrow against the University of Kentucky.

A vocalist started singing Stevie Wonder's "Superwoman."

Through the bitter winds love could not be found
Where were you when I needed you, last winter, my love?

The groove of the music was climbing up Ayman's past and present mental walls. The club was alive with people swaying, and fingers popping. Tall, red brick walls lined with staircases led to different levels for seating. There was no room for dancing other than standing at your table. A few ladies were standing and grooving in place. The two coaches were on the main floor. Two tables away stood a caramel-colored, shapely sister. Her red-apple lips and close-set eyes had helped to put Ayman into his hypnotic state. Her long, raven-black hair to the flowing tightness of her black silk dress and her feet, clad in thin leather-strapped heels, locked him into tunnel vision. Ayman was lost in her display of sexiness.

The red stage lights silhouetted her groove. She was joyriding his attention; she knew he was watching. She reminded him of a body he used to know, and her image helped burn a hole into his past. He rode a bumpy ride into a sad rhythmic pulse. Angry noises from days gone by had drowned out the jazz blowing in his ears.

There were other noises going on in his life. As the head coach at East Seattle City University, he was facing losing a third consecutive game. The team was having pre-season difficulties. They had played two games against Top Ten teams and lost both. Their wins had not been impressive. Uneasiness grew like mold when people started asking questions of why, and how come, and when.

ESPN-TV had done a segment on East Seattle City University and its slow start. ESPN wondered if Coach Sparks' last three Sweet Sixteen finishes in the NCAA tournament would be over-stating. "Coach Sparks, a preacher of defense, might have lost the attention of his congregation. The players might not be buying into his intense coaching style anymore." In response, Coach Sparks told a local newspaper that he thought the article hinted of racism.

"How many white coaches are compared to preachers? In America, we seem to associate the Black men in different forms of leadership as some type of preacher. As a coach, unless I am a preacher, there should be no comparison. I am a man who believes in God, but there is no connection to me being a preacher.

Coach Sparks was quoted in the local newspaper: "Dean Smith, who coaches North Carolina, is a deeply religious man. Was he ever compared to or called a preacher? Why am I? We know the Bobby Knight types and other white coaches, are intense coaches, and no one calls them preachers. Could it be white men are just called leaders? Can Black men of leadership only be related to being some type of minister? This is the subtle type of racism that Black Americans are tired of."

Ayman felt strong about what he'd stated, and he would not back down. He told friends, colleagues, and other news media, "If I don't speak up, I'm part of the problem."

Shortly after arriving at the team hotel, he got a call from Coach Nolan Richardson, the former basketball coach at the University of Arkansas.

"Coach, you're a winner in my book for telling it like it is. The work you're doing is thankless," Richardson commented.

"Thanks, Coach Richardson."

"Call me Nolan. You know critics are snakes. They will build you up and tear you down. You must stand your ground as the man; let their crap roll off your back. Stay Black. You said what I wish others would say." Coach Richardson continued, "Coach, at one time the white media hated Muhammad Ali and everything he stood for. Now they honor him for fighting against them. Life is a circle. Stay the course, my brother."

"You're right. Float like a butterfly, sting like a bee!" Both men laughed.

"I had a lot of success at Arkansas, but I knew sooner or later they'd come after me." Coach Richardson laughed. "Now you're playing the U. of Kentucky, and they aren't going to let you come in there and get a win on their home floor. Remember you're coach, first and last. Stay focused on your team and the game."

Ayman reflected on the conversation while the crowd's conversation mingled with cocktail glasses clinging. Sterlin was perplexed that Ayman was so despondent.

"What is going on with you? Wake your dead ass up."

"The boys practiced as if they know they're going to lose."

"Oh yeah, right, as if that's what's going on with you. Look, we have the toughest schedule in the nation, but the schedule will pay off at conference time. You said so yourself before the pre-season started. You got another bug up your butt. What is it?"

Sterlin, tall and wide at the shoulders with a big baby face, was not looking at Ayman as he spoke. He was flirting with every woman in the club that he could engage with glances and grins. His physical stature and good looks received plenty of submissive expressions. Changing colored lights reflected the whiteness from Sterlin's smile.

Ayman leaned forward so he could be heard. "I'm all right, man. It's just that sister standing over there reminds me of Vanessa. I was just thinking—"

Sterlin cut Ayman off, "Don't even go there again! You've been divorced for two years. You should be over it, man."

Ayman jerked his head back.

"You need to move on. What's it going to take? Everywhere we go, you got honeys checking your ass out, but you act blind. You may be known for 'preaching defense,' but damn!" Sterlin smiled at his mocking statement, and Ayman chuckled a bit as his friend continued to talk. "Nigga, you need to go on the offense in the women's department."

Ayman's stare became hard; he was upset. He leaned forward so the flickering candles highlighted the tightness of the lines on his forehead. "First of all, Negro, you need to quit saying 'nigga' before you let it slip at the wrong time. These kids all ready think it's okay. I had to correct a white kid from saying 'wigger' and 'poor white trash,' even though their mommas and daddies got MO-money, MO-money."

"You're right. It's an old habit."

"Well, it's an old habit that sometimes I think of Vanessa."

"Cool, but don't bite my head off. I'm not the one you were married to. How about you freezing all that past misery. You need to be over there talking to that fine female; she's dancing to get your attention. That's what you need—a woman. If I was you, I'd be all over her."

Ayman laughed. "Excuse me, but unless my eyes are going bad, that is a Black woman over there, and you don't do sisters…right?" Ayman knew Sterlin's lifestyle when it came to the type of women he pursued.

"Man, hold up! It's not that I don't do sisters. I like all women, and I mean all women, of every color and nationality." Sterlin's voice was full of ego.He looked around the club, his eyes stopped, and he nodded at a not-so-thin, blonde woman. Ayman rolled his eyes in non-amazement.

A comedian had taken the stage and cracked a joke that had everyone laughing, but Ayman and Sterlin didn't pay attention.

Ayman leaned forward and said, "Just like I said, you don't do sisters. All the women I see you with seem to have blonde, brunette, or red hair. I find that a little strange, but whatever right now, watch your ass, man. We are down South."

"Please! I ain't worried about nobody's South. Don't they call it the New South?" Sterlin smiled.

"Okay, Mr. New South, I'm sure the club is a safe zone, but I bet you still can't walk the back streets with a big booty Blonde Peach."

"Yeah, well, toast to the booty, my man! At least, I pick the ones with a sista booty. You ever watch a blondie with a big booty dance? That's some sweet funky stuff. Ahhhh, I like that shit."

"You freak! Is it all about the tail end?"

"I like me some thighs and booty."

"Okay, Dr. Booty Freak, you're a trip!"

Sterlin's next comment stopped Ayman dead in his tracks from laughing. "It's all about the booty, so I don't end up like you—sad, blue, and alone!" Sterlin tilted his head to the side and lifted his eyebrows up.